SIR WALTER SCOTT
NOVELS

GUY
MANNERING

VOLUME II

Distributed by
HERON BOOKS

LIST OF ILLUSTRATIONS

CHAPTER XXX

I renounce your defiance ; if you parley so roughly I'll barricado my gates against you—Do you see yon bay window ? Storm,—I care not, serving the good Duke of Norfolk.

MERRY DEVIL OF EDMONTON.

JULIA MANNERING TO MATILDA MARCHMONT

'I RISE from a sick-bed, my dearest Matilda, to communicate the strange and frightful scenes which have just passed. Alas! how little we ought to jest with futurity! I closed my letter to you in high spirits, with some flippant remarks on your taste for the romantic and extraordinary in fictitious narrative. How little I expected to have had such events to record in the course of a few days! And to witness scenes of terror, or to contemplate them in description, is as different, my dearest Matilda, as to bend over the brink of a precipice holding by the frail tenure of a half-rooted shrub, or to admire the same precipice as represented in the landscape of Salvator. But I will not anticipate my narrative.

'The first part of my story is frightful enough,

1

though it had nothing to interest my feelings. You must know that this country is particularly favourable to the commerce of a set of desperate men from the Isle of Man, which is nearly opposite. These smugglers are numerous, resolute, and formidable, and have at different times become the dread of the neighbourhood when any one has interfered with their contraband trade. The local magistrates, from timidity or worse motives, have become shy of acting against them, and impunity has rendered them equally daring and desperate. With all this, my father, a stranger in the land, and invested with no official authority, had, one would think, nothing to do. But it must be owned, that, as he himself expresses it, he was born when Mars was lord of his ascendant, and that strife and bloodshed find him out in circumstances and situations the most retired and pacific.

' About eleven o'clock on last Tuesday morning, while Hazlewood and my father were proposing to walk to a little lake about three miles' distance, for the purpose of shooting wild ducks, and while Lucy and I were busied with arranging our plan of work and study for the day, we were alarmed by the sound of horses' feet, advancing very fast up the avenue. The ground was hardened by a severe frost, which made the clatter of the hoofs sound yet louder and sharper. In a moment, two or three men, armed, mounted, and each leading a spare horse loaded with packages, appeared on the lawn, and, without keeping upon the road, which makes a small sweep, pushed right across for the door of the house. Their appearance was in the utmost degree hurried and disordered, and they frequently looked back like men who apprehended a close and deadly pursuit. My father and Hazlewood hurried to the front door to demand who they were, and what was their business. They were revenue officers, they stated, who had seized these horses, loaded with contraband articles, at a place about three miles off. But the smugglers had been reinforced, and were now pursuing them with the avowed purpose of recovering the goods, and putting to death the officers who had presumed to do their duty. The men said, that their horses being loaded, and the pursuers gaining ground upon them, they had fled to Woodbourne, conceiving, that as my father had served the king, he would not refuse to protect the servants of government, when threatened to be murdered in the discharge of their duty.

'My father, to whom, in his enthusiastic feelings of military loyalty, even a dog would be of importance if he came in the king's name, gave prompt orders for securing the goods in the hall, arming the servants, and defending the house in case it should be necessary. Hazlewood seconded him with great spirit, and even the strange animal they call Sampson stalked out of his den, and seized upon a fowling-piece, which my father had laid aside, to take what they call a rifle-gun, with which they shoot tigers, etc., in the East. The piece went off in the awkward hands of the poor parson, and very nearly shot one of the excisemen. At this unexpected and involuntary explosion of his weapon, the Dominie (such is his nickname) exclaimed, "Prodigious!" which is his usual ejaculation when astonished. But no power could force the man to part with his discharged piece, so they were content to let him retain it, with the precaution of trusting him with no ammunition. This (excepting the alarm occasioned by the report) escaped my notice at the time, you may easily believe; but in talking over the scene afterwards, Hazlewood made us very merry with the Dominie's ignorant but zealous valour.

'When my father had got every thing into proper order for defence, and his people stationed at the windows with their fire-arms, he wanted to order us out of danger—into the cellar, I believe —but we could not be prevailed upon to stir. Though terrified to death, I have so much of his own spirit, that I would look upon the peril which threatens us rather than hear it rage around me without knowing its nature or its progress. Lucy, looking as pale as a marble statue, and keeping her eyes fixed on Hazlewood, seemed not even to hear the prayers with which he conjured her to leave the front of the house. But, in truth, unless the hall-door should be forced, we were in little danger; the windows being almost blocked up with cushions and pillows, and, what the Dominie most lamented, with folio volumes, brought hastily from the library, leaving only spaces through which the defenders might fire upon the assailants.

'My father had now made his dispositions, and we sat in breathless expectation in the darkened apartment, the men remaining all silent upon their posts, in anxious contemplation, probably of the approaching danger. My father, who was quite at home in such a scene, walked from one to another, and reiterated his orders, that no one should presume to fire until he gave the word. Hazlewood, who seemed to catch courage from his eye, acted as his aide-de-camp, and displayed the utmost alertness in bearing his directions from one place to another, and seeing them properly carried into execution. Our force, with the strangers included, might amount to about twelve men.

'At length the silence of this awful period of expectation was broken by a sound, which, at a distance, was like the rushing of a stream of water, but, as it approached, we distinguished the thick-beating clang of a number of horses advancing very fast. I had arranged a loop-hole for myself, from which I could see the approach of the enemy. The noise increased and came nearer, and at length thirty horsemen and more rushed at once upon the lawn. You never saw such horrid wretches! Notwithstanding the severity of the season, they were most of them stripped to their shirts and trowsers, with silk handkerchiefs knotted about their heads, and all well armed with carbines, pistols, and cutlasses. I, who am a soldier's daughter, and accustomed to see war 'from my infancy, was never so terrified in my life as by the savage appearance of these ruffians, their horses reeking with the speed at which they had ridden, and their furious exclamations of rage and disappointment, when they saw themselves baulked of their prey. They paused, however, when they saw the preparations made to receive them, and appeared to hold a moment's consultation among themselves. At length, one of the party, his face blackened with gunpowder by way of disguise, came forward with a white handkerchief on the end of his carbine, and asked to speak with Colonel Mannering. My father, to my infinite terror, threw open a window near which he was posted, and demanded what he wanted. "We want our goods, which we have been robbed of by these sharks," said the fellow; "and our lieutenant bids me say, that if they are delivered, we'll go off for this bout without clearing scores with the rascals who took them; but if not, we'll burn the house, and have the heart's blood of every one in it":—a threat which he repeated more than once, graced by a fresh variety of imprecations, and the most horrid denunciations that cruelty could suggest.

'"And which is your lieutenant?" said my father in reply.

'"That gentleman on the grey horse," said the miscreant, "with the red handkerchief bound about his brow."

"Then be pleased to tell that gentleman, that if he, and the scoundrels who are with him, do not ride off the lawn this instant, I will fire upon them without ceremony." So saying, my father shut the window, and broke short the conference.

'The fellow no sooner regained his troop, than, with a loud hurra, or rather a savage yell, they

fired a volley against our garrison. The glass of the
windows was shattered in every direction, but the
precautions already noticed saved the party within
from suffering. Three such volleys were fired without a shot being returned from within. My father
then observed them getting hatchets and crows,
probably to assail the hall door, and called aloud,
" Let none fire but Hazlewood and me—Hazlewood,
mark the ambassador." He himself aimed at the
man on the grey horse, who fell on receiving his
shot. Hazlewood was equally successful. He shot
the spokesman, who had dismounted, and was
advancing with an axe in his hand. Their fall discouraged the rest, who began to turn round their
horses; and a few shots fired at them soon sent
them off, bearing along with them their slain or
wounded companions. We could not observe that
they suffered any farther loss. Shortly after their
retreat a party of soldiers made their appearance, to
my infinite relief. These men were quartered at a
village some miles distant, and had marched on
the first rumour of the skirmish. A part of them
escorted the terrified revenue officers and their
seizure to a neighbouring seaport as a place of
safety, and at my earnest request two or three files
remained with us for that and the following day,
for the security of the house from the vengeance of
these banditti.

' Such, dearest Matilda, was my first alarm. I
must not forget to add, that the ruffians left, at a
cottage on the road-side, the man whose face was
blackened with powder, apparently because he was

unable to bear transportation. He died in about half an hour after. On examining the corpse, it proved to be that of a profligate boor in the neighbourhood, a person notorious as a poacher and smuggler. We received many messages of congratulation from the neighbouring families, and it was generally allowed that a few such instances of spirited resistance would greatly check the presumption of these lawless men. My father distributed rewards among his servants, and praised Hazlewood's courage and coolness to the skies. Lucy and I came in for a share of his applause, because we had stood fire with firmness, and had not disturbed him with screams or expostulations. As for the Dominie, my father took an opportunity of begging to exchange snuff-boxes with him. The honest gentleman was much flattered with the proposal, and extolled the beauty of his new snuff-box excessively. " It looked," he said, " as well as if it were real gold from Ophir "—Indeed it would be odd if it should not, being formed in fact of that very metal; but, to do this honest creature justice, I believe the knowledge of its real value would not enhance his sense of my father's kindness, supposing it, as he does, to be pinchbeck gilded. He has had a hard task replacing the folios which were used in the barricade, smoothing out the creases and dogs-ears, and repairing the other disasters they have sustained during their service in the fortification. He brought us some pieces of lead and bullets which these ponderous tomes had intercepted during the action, and which he had extracted with great care ;

and, were I in spirits, I could give you a comic account of his astonishment at the apathy with which we heard of the wounds and mutilation suffered by Thomas Aquinas, or the venerable Chrysostom. But I am not in spirits, and I have yet another and a more interesting incident to communicate. I feel, however, so much fatigued with my present exertion, that I cannot resume the pen till to-morrow. I will detain this letter notwithstanding, that you may not feel any anxiety upon account of your own

' JULIA MANNERING.'

CHAPTER XXXI

Here's a good world !
——Knew you of this fair work ?

KING JOHN.

JULIA MANNERING TO MATILDA MARCHMONT

' I MUST take up the thread of my story, my dearest Matilda, where I broke off yesterday.

' For two or three days we talked of nothing but our siege and its probable consequences, and dinned into my father's unwilling ears a proposal to go to Edinburgh, or at least to Dumfries, where there is remarkably good society, until the resentment of these outlaws should blow over. He answered with great composure, that he had no mind to have his landlord's house and his own property at Wood-bourne destroyed; that, with our good leave, he had usually been esteemed competent to taking measures for the safety or protection of his family; that if he remained quiet at home, he conceived the welcome the villains had received was not of a nature to invite a second visit, but should he show any signs of alarm, it would be the sure way to incur the very risk which we were afraid of. Heart-ened by his arguments, and by the extreme indiffer-ence with which he treated the supposed danger, we began to grow a little bolder, and to walk about

10

as usual. Only the gentlemen were sometimes invited to take their guns when they attended us, and I observed that my father for several nights paid particular attention to having the house properly secured, and required his domestics to keep their arms in readiness in case of necessity.

' But three days ago chanced an occurrence, of a nature which alarmed me more by far than the attack of the smugglers.

' I told you there was a small lake at some distance from Woodbourne, where the gentlemen sometimes go to shoot wild-fowl. I happened at breakfast to say I should like to see this place in its present frozen state, occupied by skaters and curlers, as they call those who play a particular sort of game upon the ice. There is snow on the ground, but frozen so hard that I thought Lucy and I might venture to that distance, as the footpath leading there was well beaten by the repair of those who frequented it for pastime. Hazlewood instantly offered to attend us, and we stipulated that he should take his fowling-piece. He laughed a good deal at the idea of going a-shooting in the snow; but, to relieve our tremors, desired that a groom, who acts as gamekeeper occasionally, should follow us with his gun. As for Colonel Mannering, he does not like crowds or sights of any kind where human figures make up the show, unless indeed it were a military review—so he declined the party.

' We set out unusually early, on a fine frosty, exhilarating morning, and we felt our minds, as well as our nerves, braced by the elasticity of the pure

air. Our walk to the lake was delightful, or at
least the difficulties were only such as diverted us,
a slippery descent for instance, or a frozen ditch to
cross, which made Hazlewood's assistance absolutely
necessary. I don't think Lucy liked her walk the
less for these occasional embarrassments.

' The scene upon the lake was beautiful. One
side of it is bordered by a steep crag, from which
hung a thousand enormous icicles all glittering in
the sun; on the other side was a little wood, now
exhibiting that fantastic appearance which the pine-
trees present when their branches are loaded with
snow. On the frozen bosom of the lake itself were
a multitude of moving figures, some flitting along
with the velocity of swallows, some sweeping in the
most graceful circles, and others deeply interested
in a less active pastime, crowding round the spot
where the inhabitants of two rival parishes contended
for the prize at curling,—an honour of no small
importance, if we were to judge from the anxiety
expressed both by the players and bystanders. We
walked round the little lake, supported by Hazlewood, who lent us each an arm. He spoke, poor
fellow, with great kindness, to old and young, and
seemed deservedly popular among the assembled
crowd. At length we thought of retiring.

' Why do I mention these trivial occurrences ?—
not, Heaven knows, from the interest I can now
attach to them—but because, like a drowning man
who catches at a brittle twig, I seize every apology
for delaying the subsequent and dreadful part of
my narrative. But it must be communicated—I

must have the sympathy of at least one friend under this heart-rending calamity.

'We were returning home by a footpath, which led through a plantation of firs. Lucy had quitted Hazlewood's arm—it is only the plea of absolute necessity which reconciles her to accept his assistance. I still leaned upon his other arm. Lucy followed us close, and the servant was two or three paces behind us. Such was our position, when at once, and as if he had started out of the earth, Brown stood before us at a short turn of the road! He was very plainly, I might say coarsely, dressed, and his whole appearance had in it something wild and agitated. I screamed between surprise and terror—Hazlewood mistook the nature of my alarm, and, when Brown advanced towards me as if to speak, commanded him haughtily to stand back, and not to alarm the lady. Brown replied, with equal asperity, he had no occasion to take lessons from him how to behave to that or any other lady. I rather believe that Hazlewood, impressed with the idea that he belonged to the band of smugglers, and had some bad purpose in view, heard and understood him imperfectly. He snatched the gun from the servant, who had come up on a line with us, and, pointing the muzzle at Brown, commanded him to stand off at his peril. My screams, for my terror prevented my finding articulate language, only hastened the catastrophe. Brown, thus menaced, sprung upon Hazlewood, grappled with him, and had nearly succeeded in wrenching the fowling-piece from his grasp, when the gun went off in the struggle, and the contents were lodged in Hazle-wood's shoulder, who instantly fell. I saw no more, for the whole scene reeled before my eyes, and I fainted away; but, by Lucy's report, the unhappy perpetrator of this action gazed a moment on the scene before him, until her screams began to alarm the people upon the lake, several of whom now came in sight. He then bounded over a hedge, which divided the footpath from the plantation, and has not since been heard of. The servant made no attempt to stop or secure him, and the report he made of the matter to those who came up to us, induced them rather to exercise their humanity in recalling me to life, than show their courage by pursuing a desperado, described by the groom as a man of tremendous personal strength, and completely armed.

'Hazlewood was conveyed home, that is, to Woodbourne, in safety — I trust his wound will prove in no respect dangerous, though he suffers much. But to Brown the consequences must be most disastrous. He is already the object of my father's resentment, and he has now incurred danger from the law of the country, as well as from the clamorous vengeance of the father of Hazlewood, who threatens to move heaven and earth against the author of his son's wound. How will he be able to shroud himself from the vindictive activity of the pursuit? how to defend himself, if taken, against the severity of laws which I am told may even affect his life? and how can I find means to warn him of his danger? Then poor Lucy's ill-concealed grief, occasioned by her lover's wound, is another source of distress to me, and every thing round me appears to bear witness against that indiscretion which has occasioned this calamity.

' For two days I was very ill indeed. The news that Hazlewood was recovering, and that the person who had shot him was nowhere to be traced, only that for certain he was one of the leaders of the gang of smugglers, gave me some comfort. The suspicion and pursuit being directed towards those people, must naturally facilitate Brown's escape, and, I trust, has, ere this, ensured it. But patrols of horse and foot traverse the country in all directions, and I am tortured by a thousand confused and unauthenticated rumours of arrests and discoveries.

' Meanwhile, my greatest source of comfort is the generous candour of Hazlewood, who persists in declaring, that with whatever intentions the person by whom he was wounded approached our party, he is convinced the gun went off in the struggle by accident, and that the injury he received was undesigned. The groom, on the other hand, maintains that the piece was wrenched out of Hazlewood's hands, and deliberately pointed at his body, and Lucy inclines to the same opinion—I do not suspect them of wilful exaggeration, yet such is the fallacy of human testimony, for the unhappy shot was most unquestionably discharged unintentionally. Perhaps it would be the best way to confide the whole secret to Hazlewood—but he is very young, and I feel the utmost repugnance to

15

communicate to him my folly. I once thought of disclosing the mystery to Lucy, and began by asking what she recollected of the person and features of the man whom we had so unfortunately met—but she ran out into such a horrid description of a hedge-ruffian, that I was deprived of all courage and disposition to own my attachment to one of such appearance as she attributed to him. I must say Miss Bertram is strangely biassed by her prepossessions, for there are few handsomer men than poor Brown. I had not seen him for a long time, and even in his strange and sudden apparition on this unhappy occasion, and under every disadvantage, his form seems to me, on reflection, improved in grace, and his features in expressive dignity.—Shall we ever meet again? Who can answer that question?—Write to me kindly, my dearest Matilda—but when did you otherwise?—yet, again, write to me soon, and write to me kindly. I am not in a situation to profit by advice or reproof, nor have I my usual spirits to parry them by raillery. I feel the terrors of a child, who has, in heedless sport, put in motion some powerful piece of machinery; and, while he beholds wheels revolving, chains clashing, cylinders rolling around him, is equally astonished at the tremendous powers which his weak agency has called into action, and terrified for the consequences which he is compelled to await, without the possibility of averting them.

' I must not omit to say that my father is very kind and affectionate. The alarm which I have received forms a sufficient apology for my nervous complaints. My hopes are, that Brown has made his escape into the sister kingdom of England, or perhaps to Ireland, or the Isle of Man. In either case he may wait the issue of Hazlewood's wound with safety and with patience, for the communication of these countries with Scotland, for the purpose of justice, is not (thank Heaven) of an intimate nature. The consequences of his being apprehended would be terrible at this moment. I endeavour to strengthen my mind by arguing against the possibility of such a calamity. Alas! how soon have sorrows and fears, real as well as severe, followed the uniform and tranquil state of existence at which so lately I was disposed to repine! But I will not oppress you any longer with my complaints. Adieu, my dearest Matilda!

'JULIA MANNERING.'

CHAPTER XXXII

A man may see how this world goes with no eyes.—Look with thine ears : See how yon justice rails upon yon simple thief. Hark in thine ear—Change places ; and, handy-dandy, which is the justice, which is the thief ?

KING LEAR.

AMONG those who took the most lively interest in endeavouring to discover the person by whom young Charles Hazlewood had been waylaid and wounded, was Gilbert Glossin, Esquire, late writer in ——, now Laird of Ellangowan, and one of the worshipful commission of justices of the peace for the county of ——. His motives for exertion on this occasion were manifold; but we presume that our readers, from what they already know of this gentleman, will acquit him of being actuated by any zealous or intemperate love of abstract justice.

The truth was, that this respectable personage felt himself less at ease than he had expected, after his machinations put him in possession of his benefactor's estate. His reflections within doors, where so much occurred to remind him of former times, were not always the self-congratulations of successful stratagem. And when he looked abroad, he could not but be sensible that he was excluded from the society of the gentry of the county, to whose rank he conceived he had raised himself. He was

18

not admitted to their clubs, and at meetings of a
public nature, from which he could not be altogether
excluded, he found himself thwarted and looked
upon with coldness and contempt. Both principle
and prejudice co-operated in creating this dislike;
for the gentlemen of the county despised him for
the lowness of his birth, while they hated him for
the means by which he had raised his fortune.
With the common people his reputation stood still
worse. They would neither yield him the territorial
appellation of Ellangowan, nor the usual compliment
of *Mr.* Glossin;—with them he was bare Glossin,
and so incredibly was his vanity interested by this
trifling circumstance, that he was known to give
half-a-crown to a beggar, because he had thrice
called him Ellangowan, in beseeching him for a
penny. He therefore felt acutely the general want
of respect, and particularly when he contrasted his
own character and reception in society with those
of Mr. Mac-Morlan, who, in far inferior worldly
circumstances, was beloved and respected both by
rich and poor, and was slowly but securely laying
the foundation of a moderate fortune, with the
general good-will and esteem of all who knew him.

Glossin, while he repined internally at what he
would fain have called the prejudices and prepossessions of the country, was too wise to make any
open complaint. He was sensible his elevation was
too recent to be immediately forgotten, and the
means by which he had attained it too odious to
be soon forgiven. But time, thought he, dimi-
nishes wonder and palliates misconduct. With the

dexterity, therefore, of one who made his fortune by studying the weak points of human nature, he determined to lie by for opportunities to make himself useful even to those who most disliked him; trusting that his own abilities, the disposition of country gentlemen to get into quarrels, when a lawyer's advice becomes precious, and a thousand other contingencies, of which, with patience and address, he doubted not to be able to avail himself, would soon place him in a more important and respectable light to his neighbours, and perhaps raise him to the eminence sometimes attained by a shrewd, worldly, bustling man of business, when, settled among a generation of country gentlemen, he becomes, in Burns's language,

'The tongue of the trump to them a'.' *

The attack on Colonel Mannering's house, followed by the accident of Hazlewood's wound, appeared to Glossin a proper opportunity to impress upon the country at large the service which could be rendered by an active magistrate, (for he had been in the commission for some time,) well acquainted with the law, and no less so with the haunts and habits of the illicit traders. He had acquired the latter kind of experience by a former close alliance with some of the most desperate smugglers, in consequence of which he had occasionally acted, sometimes as partner, sometimes as legal adviser, with

---

* The *tongue of the trump* is the wire of the Jew's harp, that which gives sound to the whole instrument.

these persons. But the connexion had been dropped many years ; nor, considering how short the race of eminent characters of this description, and the frequent circumstances which occur to make them retire from particular scenes of action, had he the least reason to think that his present researches could possibly compromise any old friend who might possess means of retaliation. The having been concerned in these practices abstractedly, was a circumstance which, according to his opinion, ought in no respect to interfere with his now using his experience in behalf of the public, or rather to further his own private views. To acquire the good opinion and countenance of Colonel Mannering would be no small object to a gentleman who was much disposed to escape from Coventry ; and to gain the favour of old Hazlewood, who was a leading man in the county, was of more importance still. Lastly, if he should succeed in discovering, apprehending, and convicting the culprits, he would have the satisfaction of mortifying, and in some degree disparaging, Mac - Morlan, to whom, as Sheriff-substitute of the county, this sort of investigation properly belonged, and who would certainly suffer in public opinion, should the voluntary exertions of Glossin be more successful than his own.

Actuated by motives so stimulating, and well acquainted with the lower retainers of the law, Glossin set every spring in motion to detect and apprehend, if possible, some of the gang who had attacked Woodbourne, and more particularly the individual who had wounded Charles Hazlewood.

He promised high rewards, he suggested various schemes, and used his personal interest among his old acquaintances who favoured the trade, urging that they had better make sacrifice of an under-strapper or two than incur the odium of having favoured such atrocious proceedings. But for some time all these exertions were in vain. The common people of the country either favoured or feared the smugglers too much to afford any evidence against them. At length, this busy magistrate obtained information, that a man, having the dress and appearance of the person who had wounded Hazlewood, had lodged on the evening before the rencontre at the Gordon Arms in Kippletringan. Thither Mr. Glossin immediately went, for the purpose of interrogating our old acquaintance, Mrs. Mac-Candlish.

The reader may remember that Mr. Glossin did not, according to this good woman's phrase, stand high in her books. She therefore attended his summons to the parlour slowly and reluctantly, and, on entering the room, paid her respects in the coldest possible manner. The dialogue then proceeded as follows:

' A fine frosty morning, Mrs. Mac-Candlish.'

' Ay, sir; the morning's weel eneugh,' answered the landlady, drily.

' Mrs. Mac-Candlish, I wish to know if the justices are to dine here as usual after the business of the court on Tuesday?'

' I believe—I fancy sae, sir—as usual'—(about to leave the room).

'Stay a moment, Mrs. Mac-Candlish—why, you are in a prodigious hurry, my good friend!—I have been thinking a club dining here once a month would be a very pleasant thing.'

'Certainly, sir; a club of *respectable* gentlemen.'

'True, true,' said Glossin, 'I mean landed proprietors and gentlemen of weight in the county; and I should like to set such a thing a-going.'

The short dry cough with which Mrs. Mac-Candlish received this proposal, by no means indicated any dislike to the overture abstractedly considered, but inferred much doubt how far it would succeed under the auspices of the gentleman by whom it was proposed. It was not a cough negative, but a cough dubious, and as such Glossin felt it; but it was not his cue to take offence.

'Have there been brisk doings on the road, Mrs. Mac-Candlish? plenty of company, I suppose?'

'Pretty weel, sir,—but I believe I am wanted at the bar.'

'No, no,—stop one moment, cannot you, to oblige an old customer?—Pray, do you remember a remarkably tall young man, who lodged one night in your house last week?'

'Troth, sir, I canna weel say—I never take heed whether my company be lang or short, if they make a lang bill.'

'And if they do not, you can do that for them, eh, Mrs. Mac-Candlish?—ha, ha, ha!—But this young man that I inquire after was upwards of six feet high, had a dark frock, with metal buttons, light-brown hair unpowdered, blue eyes, and a straight nose, travelled on foot, had no servant or baggage — you surely can remember having seen such a traveller?'

'Indeed, sir,' answered Mrs. Mac-Candlish, bent on baffling his inquiries, 'I canna charge my memory about the matter—there's mair to do in a house like this, I trow, than to look after passengers' hair, or their een, or noses either.'

'Then, Mrs. Mac-Candlish, I must tell you in plain terms, that this person is suspected of having been guilty of a crime; and it is in consequence of these suspicions that I, as a magistrate, require this information from you,—and if you refuse to answer my questions, I must put you upon your oath.'

'Troth, sir, I am no free to swear*—we aye gaed to the Antiburgher meeting — it's very true, in Bailie Mac-Candlish's time (honest man,) we keepit the kirk, whilk was most seemly in his station, as having office—but after his being called to a better place than Kippletringan, I hae gaen back to worthy Maister Mac-Grainer. And so ye see, sir, I am no clear to swear without speaking to the minister— especially against ony sackless puir young thing that's gaun through the country, stranger and freendless like.'

'I shall relieve your scruples, perhaps, without troubling Mr. Mac-Grainer, when I tell you that this fellow whom I inquire after is the man who shot your young friend Charles Hazlewood.'

'Gudeness! wha could hae thought the like o'

---

* Some of the strict dissenters decline taking an oath before a civil magistrate.

that o' him?—na, if it had been for debt, or e'en for a bit tuilzie wi' the gauger, the deil o' Nelly Mac - Candlish's tongue should ever hae wranged him.   But if he really shot young Hazlewood— But I canna think it, Mr. Glossin; this will be some o' your skits* now—I canna think it o' sae douce a lad;—na, na, this is just some o' your auld skits. —Ye'll be for having a horning or a caption after him.'

'I see you have no confidence in me, Mrs. Mac-Candlish; but look at these declarations, signed by the persons who saw the crime committed, and judge yourself if the description of the ruffian be not that of your guest.'

He put the papers into her hand, which she perused very carefully, often taking off her spectacles to cast her eyes up to Heaven, or perhaps to wipe a tear from them, for young Hazlewood was an especial favourite with the good dame. 'Aweel, aweel,' she said, when she had concluded her examination, 'since it's e'en sae, I gie him up, the villain—But O, we are erring mortals!—I never saw a face I liked better, or a lad that was mair douce and canny — I thought he had been some gentleman under trouble.—But I gie him up, the villain!—to shoot Charles Hazlewood—and before the young ladies,—poor innocent things!—I gie him up.'

'So you admit, then, that such a person lodged here the night before this vile business?'

---

* Tricks.

'Troth did he, sir, and a' the house were taen wi' him, he was sic a frank, pleasant young man. It wasna for his spending, I'm sure, for he just had a mutton-chop, and a mug of ale, and maybe a glass or twa o' wine—and I asked him to drink tea wi' mysell, and didna put that into the bill; and he took nae supper, for he said he was defeat wi' travel a' the night afore—I dare say now it had been on some hellicat errand or other.'

'Did you by any chance learn his name?'

'I wot weel did I,' said the landlady, now as eager to communicate her evidence as formerly desirous to suppress it. 'He tell'd me his name was Brown, and he said it was likely that an auld woman like a gipsy wife might be asking for him— Ay, ay! tell me your company, and I'll tell you wha ye are! O the villain!—Aweel, sir, when he gaed away in the morning, he paid his bill very honestly, and gae something to the chamber-maid, nae doubt, for Grizy has naething frae me, by twa pair o' new shoon ilka year, and maybe a bit compliment at Hansel Monanday'—— Here Glossin found it necessary to interfere, and bring the good woman back to the point.

'Ou than, he just said, if there comes such a person to inquire after Mr. Brown, you will say I am gone to look at the skaters on Loch Creeran, as you call it, and I will be back here to dinner— But he never came back—though I expected him sae faithfully, that I gae a look to making the friar's chicken mysell, and to the crappit-heads too, and that's what I dinna do for ordinary, Mr. Glossin—

But little did I think what skating wark he was gaun about — to shoot Mr. Charles, the innocent lamb!'

Mr. Glossin, having, like a prudent examinator, suffered his witness to give vent to all her surprise and indignation, now began to inquire whether the suspected person had left any property or papers about the inn.

'Troth, he put a parcel—a sma' parcel, under my charge, and he gave me some siller, and desired me to get him half-a-dozen ruffled sarks, and Peg Pasley's in hands wi' them e'en now—they may serve him to gang up the Lawn-market* in, the scoundrel!' Mr. Glossin then demanded to see the packet, but here mine hostess demurred.

'She didna ken — she wad not say but justice should take its course — but when a thing was trusted to ane in her way, doubtless they were responsible—but she suld cry in Deacon Bearcliff, and if Mr. Glossin liked to tak an inventar o' the property, and gie her a receipt before the Deacon —or, what she wad like muckle better, an it could be sealed up and left in Deacon Bearcliff's hands, it wad make her mind easy—She was for naething but justice on a' sides.'

Mrs. Mac-Candlish's natural sagacity and acquired suspicion being inflexible, Glossin sent for Deacon

* The procession of the criminals to the gallows of old took that direction, moving, as the school-boy rhyme had it,

Up the Lawn-market,
Down the West Bow,
Up the lang ladder,
And down the little tow.

Bearcliff, to speak 'anent the villain that had shot
Mr. Charles Hazlewood.' The Deacon accordingly
made his appearance, with his wig awry, owing to
the hurry with which, at this summons of the
Justice, he had exchanged it for the Kilmarnock-
cap in which he usually attended his customers.
Mrs. Mac-Candlish then produced the parcel deposited with her by Brown, in which was found
the gipsy's purse. On perceiving the value of the
miscellaneous contents, Mrs. Mac-Candlish internally congratulated herself upon the precautions
she had taken before delivering them up to Glossin, while he, with an appearance of disinterested
candour, was the first to propose they should be
properly inventoried, and deposited with Deacon
Bearcliff, until they should be sent to the Crown-
office. 'He did not,' he observed, 'like to be
personally responsible for articles which seemed of
considerable value, and had doubtless been acquired
by the most nefarious practices.'

He then examined the paper in which the purse
had been wrapt up. It was the back of a letter
addressed to V. Brown, Esquire, but the rest of
the address was torn away. The landlady,—now
as eager to throw light upon the criminal's escape
as she had formerly been desirous of withholding
it, for the miscellaneous contents of the purse
argued strongly to her mind that all was not right,
—Mrs. Mac-Candlish, I say, now gave Glossin to
understand, that her postilion and hostler had both
seen the stranger upon the ice that day when young
Hazlewood was wounded.

Our readers' old acquaintance, Jock Jabos, was first summoned, and admitted frankly, that he had seen and conversed upon the ice that morning with a stranger, who, he understood, had lodged at the Gordon Arms the night before.

'What turn did your conversation take?' said Glossin.

'Turn?—ou, we turned nae gate at a', but just keepit straight forward upon the ice like.'

'Well, but what did ye speak about?'

'Ou, he just asked questions like ony ither stranger,' answered the postilion, possessed, as it seemed, with the refractory and uncommunicative spirit which had left his mistress.

'But about what?' said Glossin.

'Ou, just about the folk that was playing at the curling, and about auld Jock Stevenson that was at the cock, and about the leddies, and sic like.'

'What ladies? and what did he ask about them, Jock?' said the interrogator.

'What leddies? ou, it was Miss Jowlia Mannering and Miss Lucy Bertram, that ye ken fu' weel yoursell, Mr. Glossin—they were walking wi' the young Laird of Hazlewood upon the ice.'

'And what did you tell him about them?' demanded Glossin.

'Tut, we just said that was Miss Lucy Bertram of Ellangowan, that should ance have had a great estate in the country—and that was Miss Jowlia Mannering, that was to be married to young Hazlewood—See as she was hinging on his arm—we just

spoke about our country clashes like—he was a very
frank man.'

'Well, and what did he say in answer?'

'Ou, he just stared at the young leddies very
keen like, and asked if it was for certain that the
marriage was to be between Miss Mannering and
young Hazlewood—and I answered him that it was
for positive and absolute certain, as I had an un-
doubted right to say sae—for my third cousin Jean
Clavers, (she's a relation o' your ain, Mr. Glossin,
ye wad ken Jean lang syne?) she's sib to the housekeeper at Woodbourne, and she's tell'd me mair
than ance that there was naething could be mair
likely.'

'And what did the stranger say when you told
him all this?' said Glossin.

'Say?' echoed the postilion, 'he said naething
at a'—he just stared at them as they walked
round the loch upon the ice, as if he could have
eaten them, and he never took his ee aff them, or
said another word, or gave another glance at the
Bonspiel, though there was the finest fun amang
the curlers ever was seen—and he turned round
and gaed aff the loch by the kirk-stile through
Woodbourne fir-plantings, and we saw nae mair
o' him.'

'Only think,' said Mrs. Mac-Candlish, 'what a
hard heart he maun hae had, to think o' hurting
the poor young gentleman in the very presence of
the leddy he was to be married to!'

'O, Mrs. Mac-Candlish,' said Glossin, 'there's
been many cases such as that on the record—doubt-

less he was seeking revenge where it would be deepest and sweetest.'

'God pity us!' said Deacon Bearcliff, 'we're puir frail creatures when left to oursells!—ay, he forgot wha said, "Vengeance is mine, and I will repay it."'

'Weel, aweel, sirs,' said Jabos, whose hard-headed and uncultivated shrewdness seemed sometimes to start the game when others beat the bush—'Weel, weel, ye may be a' mista'en yet—I'll never believe that a man would lay a plan to shoot another wi' his ain gun. Lord help ye, I was the keeper's assistant down at the Isle mysell, and I'll uphaud it, the biggest man in Scotland shouldna take a gun frae me or I had weized the slugs through him, though I'm but sic a little feckless body, fit for naething but the outside o' a saddle and the fore-end o' a poschay—na, na, nae living man wad venture on that. I'll wad my best buckskins, and they were new coft at Kirkcudbright fair, it's been a chance job after a'. But if ye hae naething mair to say to me, I am thinking I maun gang and see my beasts fed'—— and he departed accordingly.

The hostler, who had accompanied him, gave evidence to the same purpose. He and Mrs. Mac-Candlish were then re-interrogated, whether Brown had no arms with him on that unhappy morning. 'None,' they said, 'but an ordinary bit cutlass or hanger by his side.'

'Now,' said the Deacon, taking Glossin by the button, (for, in considering this intricate subject, he had forgot Glossin's new accession of rank)—

'this is but doubtfu' after a', Maister Gilbert—for it was not sae dooms likely that he would go down into battle wi' sic sma' means.'

Glossin extricated himself from the Deacon's grasp, and from the discussion, though not with rudeness; for it was his present interest to buy golden opinions from all sorts of people. He inquired the price of tea and sugar, and spoke of providing himself for the year; he gave Mrs. Mac-Candlish directions to have a handsome entertainment in readiness for a party of five friends, whom he intended to invite to dine with him at the Gordon Arms next Saturday week; and, lastly, he gave a half-crown to Jock Jabos, whom the hostler had deputed to hold his steed.

'Weel,' said the Deacon to Mrs. Mac-Candlish, as he accepted her offer of a glass of bitters at the bar, 'the deil's no sae ill as he's ca'd. It's pleasant to see a gentleman pay the regard to the business o' the county that Mr. Glossin does.'

'Ay, 'deed is't, Deacon,' answered the landlady; 'and yet I wonder our gentry leave their ain wark to the like o' him.—But as lang as siller's current, Deacon, folk maunna look ower nicely at what king's head's on't.'

'I doubt Glossin will prove but *shand** after a', mistress,' said Jabos, as he passed through the little lobby beside the bar; 'but this is a gude half-crown ony way.'

---

* Cant expression for base coin.

CHAPTER XXXIII

*A man that apprehends death to be no more dreadful but as a drunken
sleep; careless, reckless, and fearless of what's past, present, or to
come; insensible of mortality, and desperately mortal.*

MEASURE FOR MEASURE.

GLOSSIN had made careful minutes of the information derived from these examinations. They threw
little light upon the story, so far as he understood
its purport; but the better informed reader has
received, through means of this investigation, an account of Brown's proceedings, between the moment
when we left him upon his walk to Kippletringan,
and the time when, stung by jealousy, he so rashly
and unhappily presented himself before Julia Mannering, and wellnigh brought to a fatal termination
the quarrel which his appearance occasioned.

Glossin rode slowly back to Ellangowan, pondering on what he had heard, and more and more
convinced that the active and successful prose-
cution of this mysterious business was an opportunity of ingratiating himself with Hazlewood and
Mannering, to be on no account neglected. Perhaps, also, he felt his professional acuteness interested in bringing it to a successful close. It was,
therefore, with great pleasure that on his return
to his house from Kippletringan, he heard his

servants announce hastily, 'that Mac-Guffog, the thief-taker, and twa or three concurrents, had a man in hands in the kitchen waiting for his honour.'

He instantly jumped from horseback, and hastened into the house. 'Send my clerk here directly; ye'll find him copying the survey of the estate in the little green parlour. Set things to rights in my study, and wheel the great leathern chair up to the writing-table—set a stool for Mr. Scrow.—Scrow, (to the clerk, as he entered the presence-chamber,) hand down Sir George Mackenzie on Crimes; open it at the section *Vis Publica et Privata*, and fold down a leaf at the passage "anent the bearing of unlawful weapons." Now lend me a hand off with my muckle-coat, and hang it up in the lobby, and bid them bring up the prisoner—I trow I'll sort him—but stay, first send up Mac-Guffog.—Now, Mac-Guffog, where did ye find this chield?'

Mac-Guffog, a stout bandy-legged fellow, with a neck like a bull, a face like a firebrand, and a most portentous squint of the left eye, began, after various contortions by way of courtesy to the Justice, to tell his story, eking it out by sundry sly nods and knowing winks, which appeared to bespeak an intimate correspondence of ideas between the narrator and his principal auditor. 'Your honour sees I went down to yon place that your honour spoke o', that's kept by her that your honour kens o', by the sea-side.—So says she, what are you wanting here? ye'll be come wi' a broom in your pocket frae Ellangowan?—So, says I, deil a broom will come frae there awa, for ye ken, says I, his honour Ellangowan himsell in former times——'

'Well, well,' said Glossin, 'no occasion to be particular, tell the essentials.'

'Weel, so we sat niffering about some brandy that I said I wanted, till he came in.'

'Who?'

'He!' pointing with his thumb inverted to the kitchen, where the prisoner was in custody. 'So he had his griego wrapped close around him, and I judged he was not dry-handed*—so I thought it was best to speak proper, and so he believed I was a Manks man, and I kept aye between him and her, for fear she had whistled.† And then we began to drink about, and then I betted he would not drink out a quartern of Hollands without drawing breath—and then he tried it—and just then Slounging Jock and Dick Spur'em came in, and we clinked the darbies‡ on him, took him as quiet as a lamb—and now he's had his bit sleep out, and is as fresh as a May gowan, to answer what your honour likes to speir.' This narrative, delivered with a wonderful quantity of gesture and grimace, received at the conclusion the thanks and praises which the narrator expected.

'Had he no arms?' asked the Justice.

'Ay, ay, they are never without barkers and slashers.'

---

* Unarmed. † Given information to the party concerned.
‡ Hand-cuffs.

'Any papers?'

'This bundle,' delivering a dirty pocket-book.

'Go down stairs, then, Mac-Guffog, and be in waiting.' The officer left the room.

The clink of irons was immediately afterwards heard upon the stair, and in two or three minutes a man was introduced, hand-cuffed and fettered. He was thick, brawny, and muscular, and although his shagged and grizzled hair marked an age somewhat advanced, and his stature was rather low, he appeared, nevertheless, a person whom few would have chosen to cope with in personal conflict. His coarse and savage features were still flushed, and his eye still reeled under the influence of the strong potation which had proved the immediate cause of his seizure. But the sleep, though short, which Mac-Guffog had allowed him, and still more a sense of the peril of his situation, had restored to him the full use of his faculties. The worthy judge, and the no less estimable captive, looked at each other steadily for a long time without speaking. Glossin apparently recognised his prisoner, but seemed at a loss how to proceed with his investigation. At length he broke silence. 'Soh, Captain, this is you?—you have been a stranger on this coast for some years.'

'Stranger?' replied the other; 'strange enough, I think—for hold me der deyvil, if I been ever here before.'

'That won't pass, Mr. Captain.'

'That *must* pass, Mr. Justice—sapperment!'

'And who will you be pleased to call yourself,

then, for the present,' said Glossin, 'just until I shall bring some other folks to refresh your memory, concerning who you are, or at least who you have been?'

'What bin I?—donner and blitzen! I bin Jans Janson, from Cuxhaven—what sall Ich bin?'

Glossin took from a case which was in the apartment a pair of small pocket pistols, which he loaded with ostentatious care. 'You may retire,' said he to his clerk, 'and carry the people with you, Scrow —but wait in the lobby within call.'

The clerk would have offered some remonstrances to his patron on the danger of remaining alone with such a desperate character, although ironed beyond the possibility of active exertion, but Glossin waved him off impatiently. When he had left the room, the Justice took two short turns through the apartment, then drew his chair opposite to the prisoner, so as to confront him fully, placed the pistols before him in readiness, and said in a steady voice, 'You are Dirk Hatteraick of Flushing, are you not?'

The prisoner turned his eye instinctively to the door, as if he apprehended some one was listening. Glossin rose, opened the door, so that from the chair in which his prisoner sate he might satisfy himself there was no eavesdropper within hearing, then shut it, resumed his seat, and repeated his question, 'You are Dirk Hatteraick, formerly of the Yungfrauw Haagenslaapen, are you not?'

'Tousand deyvils!—and if you know that, why ask me?' said the prisoner.

'Because I am surprised to see you in the very last place where you ought to be, if you regard your safety,' observed Glossin coolly.

'Der deyvil!—no man regards his own safety that speaks so to me!'

'What? unarmed, and in irons!—well said, Captain!' replied Glossin ironically. 'But, Captain, bullying won't do—you'll hardly get out of this country without accounting for a little accident that happened at Warroch Point a few years ago.'

Hatteraick's looks grew black as midnight.

'For my part,' continued Glossin, 'I have no particular wish to be hard upon an old acquaintance —but I must do my duty—I shall send you off to Edinburgh in a post-chaise and four this very day.'

'Poz donner! you would not do that?' said Hatteraick, in a lower and more humbled tone; 'why you had the matter of half a cargo in bills on Vanbeest and Vanbruggen.'

'It is so long since, Captain Hatteraick,' answered Glossin superciliously, 'that I really forget how I was recompensed for my trouble.'

'Your trouble? your silence, you mean.'

'It was an affair in the course of business,' said Glossin, 'and I have retired from business for some time.'

'Ay, but I have a notion that I could make you go steady about, and try the old course again,' answered Dirk Hatteraick. 'Why, man, hold me der deyvil, but I meant to visit you, and tell you something that concerns you.'

'Of the boy?' said Glossin eagerly.

' Yaw, Mynheer,' replied the Captain coolly.

' He does not live, does he ? '

' As lifelich as you or I,' said Hatteraick.

' Good God !—But in India ? ' exclaimed Glossin.

' No, tousand deyvils, here ! on this dirty coast of yours,' rejoined the prisoner.

' But, Hatteraick, this,—that is, if it be true, which I do not believe,—this will ruin us both, for he cannot but remember your neat job ; and for me —it will be productive of the worst consequences ! It will ruin us both, I tell you.'

' I tell you,' said the seaman, ' it will ruin none but you—for I am done up already, and if I must strap for it, all shall out.'

' Zounds,' said the Justice impatiently, ' what brought you back to this coast like a madman ? '

' Why, all the gelt was gone, and the house was shaking, and I thought the job was clayed over and forgotten,' answered the worthy skipper.

' Stay—what can be done?' said Glossin anxiously. ' I dare not discharge you—but might you not be rescued in the way—ay sure—a word to Lieutenant Brown,—and I would send the people with you by the coast-road.'

' No, no ! that won't do—Brown 's dead—shot— laid in the locker, man—the devil has the picking of him.'

' Dead ? — shot ? — at Woodbourne, I suppose ? ' replied Glossin.

' Yaw, Mynheer.'

Glossin paused—the sweat broke upon his brow with the agony of his feelings, while the hard-featured miscreant who sat opposite, coolly rolled his tobacco in his cheek, and squirted the juice into the fire-grate. 'It would be ruin,' said Glossin to himself, 'absolute ruin, if the heir should re-appear—and then what might be the consequence of conniving with these men?—yet there is so little time to take measures—Hark you, Hatteraick; I can't set you at liberty—but I can put you where you may set yourself at liberty—I always like to assist an old friend. I shall confine you in the old castle for to-night, and give these people double allowance of grog. Mac-Guffog will fall in the trap in which he caught you. The stancheons on the window of the strong room, as they call it, are wasted to pieces, and it is not above twelve feet from the level of the ground without, and the snow lies thick.'

'But the darbies,' said Hatteraick, looking upon his fetters.

'Hark ye,' said Glossin, going to a tool chest, and taking out a small file, 'there's a friend for you, and you know the road to the sea by the stairs.' Hatteraick shook his chains in ecstasy, as if he were already at liberty, and strove to extend his fettered hand towards his protector. Glossin laid his finger upon his lips with a cautious glance at the door, and then proceeded in his instructions. 'When you escape, you had better go to the Kaim of Dern-cleugh.'

'Donner! that howff is blown.'

'The devil!—well, then, you may steal my skiff that lies on the beach there, and away. But you must remain snug at the Point of Warroch till I come to see you.'

'The Point of Warroch?' said Hatteraick, his countenance again falling; 'What, in the cave, I suppose?—I would rather it were any where else; —es spuckt da!—they say for certain that he walks —But, donner and blitzen! I never shunned him alive, and I won't shun him dead—Strafe mich helle! it shall never be said Dirk Hatteraick feared either dog or devil!—So I am to wait there till I see you?'

'Ay, ay,' answered Glossin, 'and now I must call in the men.' He did so, accordingly.

'I can make nothing of Captain Janson, as he calls himself, Mac-Guffog, and it's now too late to bundle him off to the county jail. Is there not a strong room up yonder in the old castle?'

'Ay is there, sir; my uncle the constable ance kept a man there for three days in auld Ellangowan's time. But there was an unco dust about it—it was tried in the Inner-house afore the feifteen.'

'I know all that, but this person will not stay there very long—it's only a makeshift for a night, a mere lock-up house till farther examination. There is a small room through which it opens; you may light a fire for yourselves there, and I'll send you plenty of stuff to make you comfortable. But be sure you lock the door upon the prisoner; and, hark ye, let him have a fire in the strong room too; the season requires it. Perhaps he'll make a clean breast to-morrow.'

With these instructions, and with a large allowance of food and liquor, the Justice dismissed his party to keep guard for the night in the old castle, under the full hope and belief that they would neither spend the night in watching nor prayer.

There was little fear that Glossin himself should that night sleep over-sound. His situation was perilous in the extreme, for the schemes of a life of villainy seemed at once to be crumbling around and above him. He laid himself to rest, and tossed upon his pillow for a long time in vain. At length he fell asleep, but it was only to dream of his patron, —now, as he had last seen him, with the paleness of death upon his features, then again transformed into all the vigour and comeliness of youth, approaching to expel him from the mansion-house of his fathers. Then he dreamed, that after wandering long over a wild heath, he came at length to an inn, from which sounded the voice of revelry; and that when he entered, the first person he met was Frank Kennedy, all smashed and gory, as he had lain on the beach at Warroch Point, but with a reeking punch-bowl in his hand. Then the scene changed to a dungeon, where he heard Dirk Hatteraick, whom he imagined to be under sentence of death, confessing his crimes to a clergyman.— ' After the bloody deed was done,' said the penitent, ' we retreated into a cave close beside, the secret of which was known but to one man in the country; we were debating what to do with the child, and we thought of giving it up to the gipsies, when we heard the cries of the pursuers hallooing to each other. One man alone came straight to our

cave, and it was that man who knew the secret—
but we made him our friend at the expense of
half the value of the goods saved. By his advice
we carried off the child to Holland in our consort,
which came the following night to take us from
the coast. That man was——'

'No, I deny it!—it was not I!' said Glossin, in
half-uttered accents; and, struggling in his agony
to express his denial more distinctly, he awoke.

It was, however, conscience that had prepared
this mental phantasmagoria. The truth was, that,
knowing much better than any other person the
haunts of the smugglers, he had, while the others
were searching in different directions, gone straight
to the cave, even before he had learned the murder
of Kennedy, whom he expected to find their
prisoner. He came upon them with some idea
of mediation, but found them in the midst of their
guilty terrors, while the rage, which had hurried
them on to murder, began, with all but Hatteraick,
to sink into remorse and fear. Glossin was then
indigent and greatly in debt, but he was already
possessed of Mr. Bertram's ear, and, aware of the
facility of his disposition, he saw no difficulty in
enriching himself at his expense, provided the heir-
male were removed, in which case the estate became
the unlimited property of the weak and prodigal
father. Stimulated by present gain and the prospect of contingent advantage, he accepted the bribe
which the smugglers offered in their terror, and
connived at, or rather encouraged, their intention
of carrying away the child of his benefactor, who,

if left behind, was old enough to have described the scene of blood which he had witnessed. The only palliative which the ingenuity of Glossin could offer to his conscience was, that the temptation was great, and came suddenly upon him, embracing as it were the very advantages on which his mind had so long rested, and promising to relieve him from distresses which must have otherwise speedily overwhelmed him. Besides, he endeavoured to think that self-preservation rendered his conduct necessary. He was, in some degree, in the power of the robbers, and pleaded hard with his conscience, that, had he declined their offers, the assistance which he could have called for, though not distant, might not have arrived in time to save him from men, who, on less provocation, had just committed murder.

Galled with the anxious forebodings of a guilty conscience, Glossin now arose, and looked out upon the night. The scene which we have already described in the beginning of our first volume, was now covered with snow, and the brilliant, though waste, whiteness of the land, gave to the sea by contrast a dark and livid tinge. A landscape covered with snow, though abstractedly it may be called beautiful, has, both from the association of cold and barrenness, and from its comparative infrequency, a wild, strange, and desolate appearance. Objects, well known to us in their common state, have either disappeared, or are so strangely varied and disguised, that we seem gazing on an unknown world. But it was not with such reflections that the mind of this bad man was occupied. His eye was upon the gigantic and gloomy outlines of the old castle, where, in a flanking tower of enormous size and thickness, glimmered two lights, one from the window of the strong room, where Hatteraick was confined, the other from that of the adjacent apartment occupied by his keepers. 'Has he made his escape, or will he be able to do so?—Have these men watched, who never watched before, in order to complete my ruin?—If morning finds him there, he must be committed to prison; Mac-Morlan or some other person will take the matter up—he will be detected—convicted —and will tell all in revenge!'——

While these racking thoughts glided rapidly through Glossin's mind, he observed one of the lights obscured, as by an opake body placed at the window. What a moment of interest!—'He has got clear of his irons!—he is working at the stancheons of the window—they are surely quite decayed, they must give way—O God! they have fallen outward, I heard them clink among the stones!—the noise cannot fail to wake them—furies seize his Dutch awkwardness!—The light burns free again—they have torn him from the window, and are binding him in the room!—No! he had only retired an instant on the alarm of the falling bars—he is at the window again—and the light is quite obscured now—he is getting out!'——

A heavy sound, as of a body dropped from a height among the snow, announced that Hatteraick had completed his escape, and shortly after Glossin beheld a dark figure, like a shadow, steal along the whitened beach, and reach the spot where the skiff lay. New cause for fear! 'His single strength will be unable to float her,' said Glossin to himself; 'I must go to the rascal's assistance. But no! he has got her off, and now, thank God, her sail is spreading itself against the moon—ay, he has got the breeze now—would to heaven it were a tempest, to sink him to the bottom!'

After this last cordial wish, he continued watching the progress of the boat as it stood away towards the Point of Warroch, until he could no longer distinguish the dusky sail from the gloomy waves over which it glided. Satisfied then that the immediate danger was averted, he retired with somewhat more composure to his guilty pillow.

CHAPTER XXXIV

Why dost not comfort me, and help me out
From this unhallowed and blood-stained hole ?
TITUS ANDRONICUS.

ON the next morning, great was the alarm and confusion of the officers, when they discovered the escape of their prisoner. Mac-Guffog appeared before Glossin with a head perturbed with brandy and fear, and incurred a most severe reprimand for neglect of duty. The resentment of the Justice appeared only to be suspended by his anxiety to recover possession of the prisoner, and the thief-takers, glad to escape from his awful and incensed presence, were sent off in every direction (except the right one) to recover their prisoner, if possible. Glossin particularly recommended a careful search at the Kaim of Derncleugh, which was occasionally occupied under night by vagrants of different descriptions. Having thus dispersed his myrmidons in various directions, he himself hastened by devious paths through the Wood of Warroch, to his appointed interview with Hatteraick, from whom he hoped to learn at more leisure than last night's conference admitted, the circumstances attending the return of the heir of Ellangowan to his native country.

47

With manœuvres like those of a fox when he doubles to avoid the pack, Glossin strove to approach the place of appointment in a manner which should leave no distinct track of his course. 'Would to Heaven it would snow,' he said, looking upward, 'and hide these foot-prints. Should one of the officers light upon them, he would run the scent up like a blood-hound, and surprise us.—I must get down upon the sea-beach, and contrive to creep along beneath the rocks.'

And accordingly, he descended from the cliffs with some difficulty, and scrambled along between the rocks and the advancing tide; now looking up to see if his motions were watched from the rocks above him, now casting a jealous glance to mark if any boat appeared upon the sea, from which his course might be discovered.

But even the feelings of selfish apprehension were for a time superseded, as Glossin passed the spot where Kennedy's body had been found. It was marked by the fragment of rock which had been precipitated from the cliff above, either with the body or after it. The mass was now encrusted with small shell-fish, and tasselled with tangle and sea-weed; but still its shape and substance were different from those of the other rocks which lay scattered around. His voluntary walks, it will readily be believed, had never led to this spot; so that finding himself now there for the first time after the terrible catastrophe, the scene at once recurred to his mind with all its accompaniments of horror. He remembered how, like a guilty thing, gliding from the neighbouring place of concealment, he had mingled with eagerness, yet with caution, among the terrified group who surrounded the corpse, dreading lest any one should ask from whence he came. He remembered, too, with what conscious fear he had avoided gazing upon that ghastly spectacle. The wild scream of his patron, 'My bairn! my bairn!' again rang in his ears. 'Good God!' he exclaimed, 'and is all I have gained worth the agony of that moment, and the thousand anxious fears and horrors which have since embittered my life!—O how I wish that I lay where that wretched man lies, and that he stood here in life and health!—But these regrets are all too late.'

Stifling, therefore, his feelings, he crept forward to the cave, which was so near the spot where the body was found, that the smugglers might have heard from their hiding-place the various conjectures of the by-standers concerning the fate of their victim. But nothing could be more completely concealed than the entrance to their asylum. The opening, not larger than that of a fox-earth, lay in the face of the cliff directly behind a large black rock, or rather upright stone, which served at once to conceal it from strangers, and as a mark to point out its situation to those who used it as a place of retreat. The space between the stone and the cliff was exceedingly narrow, and being heaped with sand and other rubbish, the most minute search would not have discovered the mouth of the cavern, without removing those substances which the tide had drifted before it. For the purpose of farther concealment, it was usual with the contraband traders who frequented this haunt, after they had entered, to stuff the mouth with withered sea-weed, loosely piled together as if carried there by the waves. Dirk Hatteraick had not forgotten this precaution.

Glossin, though a bold and hardy man, felt his heart throb, and his knees knock together, when he prepared to enter this den of secret iniquity, in order to hold conference with a felon, whom he justly accounted one of the most desperate and depraved of men. 'But he has no interest to injure me,' was his consolatory reflection. He examined his pocket-pistols, however, before removing the weeds and entering the cavern, which he did upon hands and knees. The passage, which at first was low and narrow, just admitting entrance to a man in a creeping posture, expanded after a few yards into a high arched vault of considerable width. The bottom, ascending gradually, was covered with the purest sand. Ere Glossin had got upon his feet, the hoarse yet suppressed voice of Hatteraick growled through the recesses of the cave.

'Hagel and donner!—be'st du?'

'Are you in the dark?'

'Dark? der deyvil! ay,' said Dirk Hatteraick; 'where should I have a glim?'

'I have brought light'; and Glossin accordingly produced a tinder-box, and lighted a small lantern.

'You must kindle some fire too, for hold mich der deyvil, Ich bin ganz gefrorne!'

'It is a cold place, to be sure,' said Glossin, gathering together some decayed staves of barrels and pieces of wood, which had perhaps lain in the cavern since Hatteraick was there last.

'Cold?   Snow-wasser and hagel! it's perdition —I could only keep myself alive by rambling up and down this d—d vault, and thinking about the merry rouses we have had in it.'

The flame then began to blaze brightly, and Hatteraick hung his bronzed visage, and expanded his hard and sinewy hands over it, with an avidity resembling that of a famished wretch to whom food is exposed. The light showed his savage and stern features, and the smoke, which in his agony of cold he seemed to endure almost to suffocation, after circling round his head, rose to the dim and rugged roof of the cave, through which it escaped by some secret rents or clefts in the rock; the same doubtless that afforded air to the cavern when the tide was in, at which time the aperture to the sea was filled with water.

'And now I have brought you some breakfast,' said Glossin, producing some cold meat and a flask of spirits. The latter Hatteraick eagerly seized upon, and applied to his mouth; and, after a hearty draught, he exclaimed with great rapture, 'Das schmeckt!—That is good—that warms the liver!' —Then broke into the fragment of a High-Dutch song,

> ' Saufen Bier, und Brante-wein,
>   Schmeissen alle die Fenstern ein;
>   Ich ben liederlich,
>   Du bist liederlich;
>   Sind wir nicht liederlich Leute a!'

' Well said, my hearty Captain!' cried Glossin, endeavouring to catch the tone of revelry,—

> ' Gin by pailfuls, wine in rivers,
>   Dash the window-glass to shivers!
>   For three wild lads were we, brave boys,
>   And three wild lads were we;
>   Thou on the land, and I on the sand,
>   And Jack on the gallows-tree!

That's it, my bully-boy! Why, you're alive again now!—And now let us talk about our business.'

' *Your* business, if you please,' said Hatteraick; ' hagel and donner!—mine was done when I got out of the bilboes.'

' Have patience, my good friend;—I'll convince you our interests are just the same.'

Hatteraick gave a short dry cough, and Glossin, after a pause, proceeded.

' How came you to let the boy escape?'

' Why, fluch and blitzen! he was no charge of mine. Lieutenant Brown gave him to his cousin that's in the Middleburgh house of Vanbeest and Vanbruggen, and told him some goose's gazette about his being taken in a skirmish with the land-sharks—he gave him for a foot-boy. Me let him escape!—the bastard kinchin should have walked the plank ere I troubled myself about him.'

' Well, and was he bred a foot-boy then?'

' Nein, nein; the kinchin got about the old man's heart, and he gave him his own name, and bred him up in the office, and then sent him to India—I believe he would have packed him back here, but his nephew told him it would do up the free trade for many a day, if the youngster got back to Scotland.'

'Do you think the younker knows much of his own origin now?'

'Deyvil!' replied Hatteraick, 'how should I tell what he knows now? But he remembered something of it long. When he was but ten years old, he persuaded another Satan's limb of an English bastard like himself to steal my lugger's khan — boat — what do you call it — to return to his country, as he called it — fire him! Before we could overtake them, they had the skiff out of channel as far as the Deurloo — the boat might have been lost.'

'I wish to Heaven she had—with him in her!' ejaculated Glossin.

'Why, I was so angry myself, that, sapperment! I did give him a tip over the side—but split him— the comical little devil swam like a duck; so I made him swim astern for a mile to teach him manners, and then took him in when he was sinking.—By the knocking Nicholas! he'll plague you, now he's come over the herring-pond! When he was so high, he had the spirit of thunder and lightning.'

'How did he get back from India?'

'Why, how should I know?—the house there was done up, and that gave us a shake at Middleburgh, I think—so they sent me again to see what could be done among my old acquaintances here—for we held old stories were done away and forgotten. So I had got a pretty trade on foot within the last two trips; but that stupid houndsfoot schelm, Brown, has knocked it on the head again, I suppose, with getting himself shot by the colonel-man.'

'Why were not you with them?'

'Why, you see, sapperment! I fear nothing—but it was too far within land, and I might have been scented.'

'True. But to return to this youngster——'

'Ay, ay, donner and blitzen! *he's* your affair,' said the Captain.

'—How do you really know that he is in this country?'

'Why, Gabriel saw him up among the hills.'

'Gabriel! who is he?'

'A fellow from the gipsies, that, about eighteen years since, was pressed on board that d—d fellow Pritchard's sloop-of-war. It was he came off and gave us warning that the Shark was coming round upon us the day Kennedy was done; and he told us how Kennedy had given the information. The gipsies and Kennedy had some quarrel besides. This Gab went to the East Indies in the same ship with your younker, and, sapperment! knew him well, though the other did not remember him. Gab kept out of his eye though, as he had served the States against England, and was a deserter to boot; and he sent us word directly, that we might know of his being here—though it does not concern us a rope's end.'

'So, then, really, and in sober earnest, he is actually in this country, Hatteraick, between friend and friend?' asked Glossin seriously.

'Wetter and donner, yaw! What do you take me for?'

For a blood-thirsty, fearless miscreant! thought Glossin internally; but said aloud, 'And which of your people was it that shot young Hazlewood?'

'Sturm-wetter!' said the Captain, 'do ye think we were mad?—none of *us*, man—Gott! the country was too hot for the trade already with that d—d frolic of Brown's, attacking what you call Woodbourne House.'

'Why, I am told,' said Glossin, 'it was Brown who shot Hazlewood?'

'Not our lieutenant, I promise you; for he was laid six feet deep at Derncleugh the day before the thing happened.—Tausend deyvils, man! do ye think that he could rise out of the earth to shoot another man?'

A light here began to break upon Glossin's confusion of ideas. 'Did you not say that the younker, as you call him, goes by the name of Brown?'

'Of Brown? yaw—Vanbeest Brown; old Vanbeest Brown, of our Vanbeest and Vanbruggen, gave him his own name—he did.'

'Then,' said Glossin, rubbing his hands, 'it is he, by Heaven, who has committed this crime!'

'And what have we to do with that?' demanded Hatteraick.

Glossin · paused, and, fertile in expedients, hastily ran over his project in his own mind, and then drew near the smuggler with a confidential air. 'You know, my dear Hatteraick, it is our principal business to get rid of this young man?'

' Umh ! ' answered Dirk Hatteraick.

' Not,' continued Glossin—'not that I would wish any personal harm to him—if—if—if we can do without. Now, he is liable to be seized upon by justice, both as bearing the same name with your lieutenant, who was engaged in that affair at Woodbourne, and for firing at young Hazlewood with intent to kill or wound.'

' Ay, ay,' said Dirk Hatteraick ; ' but what good will that do you ? He 'll be loose again as soon as he shows himself to carry other colours.'

' True, my dear Dirk ; well noticed, my friend Hatteraick ! But there is ground enough for a temporary imprisonment till he fetch his proofs from England or elsewhere, my good friend. I understand the law, Captain Hatteraick, and I 'll take it upon me, simple Gilbert Glossin of Ellangowan, justice of peace for the county of ——, to refuse his bail, if he should offer the best in the country, until he is brought up for a second examination—now where d' ye think I 'll incarcerate him ? '

' Hagel and wetter ! what do I care ? '

' Stay, my friend—you do care a great deal. Do you know your goods, that were seized and carried to Woodbourne, are now lying in the Custom-house at Portanferry ? (a small fishing - town.) — Now I will commit this younker——'

' When you have caught him ? '

' Ay, ay, when I have caught him ; I shall not be long about that—I will commit him to the Workhouse, or Bridewell, which you know is beside the Custom-house.'

'Yaw, the Rasp-house; I know it very well.'

'I will take care that the red-coats are dispersed through the country; you land at night with the crew of your lugger, receive your own goods, and carry the younker Brown with you back to Flushing. Won't that do?'

'Ay, carry him to Flushing,' said the Captain, 'or—to America?'

'Ay, ay, my friend.'

'Or—to Jericho?'

'Psha! Wherever you have a mind.'

'Ay, or—pitch him overboard?'

'Nay, I advise no violence.'

'Nein, nein—you leave that to me. Sturmwetter! I know you of old. But, hark ye, what am I, Dirk Hatteraick, to be the better of this?'

'Why, is it not your interest as well as mine?' said Glossin; 'besides, I set you free this morning.'

'*You* set me free!—Donner and deyvil! I set myself free. Besides, it was all in the way of your profession, and happened a long time ago, ha, ha, ha!'

'Pshaw! pshaw! don't let us jest; I am not against making a handsome compliment—but it's your affair as well as mine.'

'What do you talk of *my* affair? is it not you that keep the younker's whole estate from him? Dirk Hatteraick never touched a stiver of his rents.'

'Hush — hush — I tell you it shall be a joint business.'

'Why, will ye give me half the kitt?'

'What, half the estate?—d'ye mean we should set up house together at Ellangowan, and take the barony, ridge about?'

'Sturm-wetter, no! but you might give me half the value—half the gelt. Live with you? nein— I would have a lust-haus of mine own on the Middleburgh dyke, and a blumen-garten like a burgomaster's.'

'Ay, and a wooden lion at the door, and a painted sentinel in the garden, with a pipe in his mouth!—But, hark ye, Hatteraick; what will all the tulips, and flower-gardens, and pleasure-houses in the Netherlands do for you, if you are hanged here in Scotland?'

Hatteraick's countenance fell. 'Der deyvil! hanged?'

'Ay, hanged, meinheer Captain. The devil can scarce save Dirk Hatteraick from being hanged for a murderer and kidnapper, if the younker of Ellangowan should settle in this country, and if the gallant Captain chances to be caught here re-establishing his fair trade! And I won't say, but, as peace is now so much talked of, their High Mightinesses may not hand him over to oblige their new allies, even if he remained in fader-land.'

'Poz hagel blitzen and donner! I—I doubt you say true.'

'Not,' said Glossin, perceiving he had made the desired impression, 'not that I am against being civil'; and he slid into Hatteraick's passive hand a bank-note of some value.

'Is this all?' said the smuggler; 'you had the

price of half a cargo for working at our job, and
made us do your business too.'

'But, my good friend, you forget—in this case
you will recover all your own goods.'

'Ay, at the risk of all our own necks—we could
do that without you.'

'I doubt that, Captain Hatteraick,' said Glossin
drily, 'because you would probably find a dozen
red-coats at the Custom-house, whom it must be
my business, if we agree about this matter, to have
removed. Come, come, I will be as liberal as I can,
but you should have a conscience.'

'Now strafe mich der deyfel!—this provokes me
more than all the rest!—You rob and you murder,
and you want me to rob and murder, and play the
silver-cooper, or kidnapper, as you call it, a dozen
times over, and then, hagel and wind-sturm! you
speak to me of conscience!—Can you think of no
fairer way of getting rid of this unlucky lad?'

'No, mein heer; but as I commit him to your
charge——'

'To *my* charge—to the charge of steel and gunpowder! and—well, if it must be, it must—but you
have a tolerably good guess what's like to come
of it.'

'O, my dear friend, I trust no degree of severity
will be necessary,' replied Glossin.

'Severity!' said the fellow, with a kind of groan,
'I wish you had had my dreams when I first came
to this dog-hole, and tried to sleep among the dry
sea-weed.—First, there was that d—d fellow there,
with his broken back, sprawling as he did when

I hurled the rock over a-top on him—ha, ha, you would have sworn he was lying on the floor where you stand, wriggling like a crushed frog — and then——'

'Nay, my friend,' said Glossin, interrupting him, 'what signifies going over this nonsense?—If you are turned chicken-hearted, why, the game's up, that's all—the game's up with us both.'

'Chicken-hearted? — No. I have not lived so long upon the account to start at last, neither for devil nor Dutchman.'

'Well, then, take another schnaps—the cold's at your heart still.—And now tell me, are any of your old crew with you?'

'Nein — all dead, shot, hanged, drowned, and damned. Brown was the last—all dead but Gipsy Gab, and he would go off the country for a spill of money—or he'll be quiet for his own sake—or old Meg, his aunt, will keep him quiet for hers.'

'Which Meg?'

'Meg Merrilies, the old devil's limb of a gipsy witch.'

'Is she still alive?'

'Yaw.'

'And in this country?'

'And in this country. She was at the Kaim of Derncleugh, at Vanbeest Brown's last wake, as they call it, the other night, with two of my people, and some of her own blasted gipsies.'

'That's another breaker ahead, Captain! Will she not squeak, think ye?'

'Not she—she won't start—she swore by the

salmon,* if we did the kinchin no harm, she would never tell how the gauger got it. Why, man, though I gave her a wipe with my hanger in the heat of the matter, and cut her arm, and though she was so long after in trouble about it up at your borough-town there, der deyvil! old Meg was as true as steel.'

' Why, that's true, as you say,' replied Glossin. ' And yet if she could be carried over to Zealand, or Hamburgh, or—or——anywhere else, you know, it were as well.'

Hatteraick jumped upright upon his feet, and looked at Glossin from head to heel.—' I don't see the goat's foot,' he said, ' and yet he must be the very deyvil!—But Meg Merrilies is closer yet with the Kobold than you are—ay, and I had never such weather as after having drawn her blood. Nein, nein, I'll meddle with her no more—she's a witch of the fiend—a real deyvil's kind—but that's her affair. Donner and wetter! I'll neither make nor meddle—that's her work.—But for the rest—why, if I thought the trade would not suffer, I would soon rid you of the younker, if you send me word when he's under embargo.'

In brief and under tones the two worthy associates concerted their enterprise, and agreed at which of his haunts Hatteraick should be heard of. The stay of his lugger on the coast was not difficult, as there were no king's vessels there at the time.

---

* The great and inviolable oath of the strolling tribes.

CHAPTER XXXV

You are one of those that will not serve God if the devil bids you.—
Because we come to do you service, you think we are ruffians.

OTHELLO.

WHEN Glossin returned home, he found, among other letters and papers sent to him, one of considerable importance. It was signed by Mr. Protocol, an attorney in Edinburgh, and, addressing him as the agent for Godfrey Bertram, Esq., late of Ellangowan, and his representatives, acquainted him with the sudden death of Mrs. Margaret Bertram of Singleside, requesting him to inform his clients thereof, in case they should judge it proper to have any person present for their interest at opening the repositories of the deceased. Mr. Glossin perceived at once that the letter-writer was unacquainted with the breach which had taken place between him and his late patron. The estate of the deceased lady should by rights, as he well knew, descend to Lucy Bertram; but it was a thousand to one that the caprice of the old lady might have altered its destination. After running over contingencies and probabilities in his fertile mind, to ascertain what sort of personal advantage might accrue to him from this incident, he could not perceive any mode of availing himself of it, except in so far as it might go to assist his plan of recovering, or rather creating, a character, the want of which he had already experienced, and was likely to feel yet more deeply. I must place myself, he thought, on strong ground, that, if any thing goes wrong with Dirk Hatteraick's project, I may have prepossessions in my favour at least.—Besides, to do Glossin justice, bad as he was, he might feel some desire to compensate to Miss Bertram in a small degree, and in a case in which his own interest did not interfere with hers, the infinite mischief which he had occasioned to her family. He therefore resolved early the next morning to ride over to Woodbourne.

It was not without hesitation that he took this step, having the natural reluctance to face Colonel Mannering, which fraud and villainy have to encounter honour and probity. But he had great confidence in his own *savoir faire*. His talents were naturally acute, and by no means confined to the line of his profession. He had at different times resided a good deal in England, and his address was free both from country rusticity and professional pedantry ; so that he had considerable powers both of address and persuasion, joined to an unshaken effrontery, which he affected to disguise under plainness of manner. Confident, therefore, in himself, he appeared at Woodbourne, about ten in the morning, and was admitted as a gentleman come to wait upon Miss Bertram.

He did not announce himself until he was at the door of the breakfast-parlour, when the servant, by his desire, said aloud,—'Mr. Glossin, to wait upon Miss Bertram.' Lucy, remembering the last scene of her father's existence, turned as pale as death, and had wellnigh fallen from her chair. Julia Mannering flew to her assistance, and they left the room together. There remained Colonel Mannering, Charles Hazlewood, with his arm in a sling, and the Dominie, whose gaunt visage and wall-eyes assumed a most hostile aspect on recognising Glossin.

That honest gentleman, though somewhat abashed by the effect of his first introduction, advanced with confidence, and hoped he did not intrude upon the ladies. Colonel Mannering, in a very upright and stately manner, observed, that he did not know to what he was to impute the honour of a visit from Mr. Glossin.

'Hem! hem! I took the liberty to wait upon Miss Bertram, Colonel Mannering, on account of a matter of business.'

'If it can be communicated to Mr. Mac-Morlan, her agent, sir, I believe it will be more agreeable to Miss Bertram.'

'I beg pardon, Colonel Mannering,' said Glossin, making a wretched attempt at an easy demeanour; 'you are a man of the world—there are some cases in which it is most prudent for all parties to treat with principals.'

'Then,' replied Mannering, with a repulsive air, 'if Mr. Glossin will take the trouble to state his object in a letter, I will answer that Miss Bertram pays proper attention to it.'

'Certainly,' stammered Glossin; 'but there are cases in which a *viva voce* conference — Hem! I perceive—I know—Colonel Mannering has adopted some prejudices which may make my visit appear intrusive; but I submit to his good sense, whether he ought to exclude me from a hearing without knowing the purpose of my visit, or of how much consequence it may be to the young lady whom he honours with his protection.'

'Certainly, sir, I have not the least intention to do so,' replied the Colonel. 'I will learn Miss Bertram's pleasure on the subject, and acquaint Mr. Glossin, if he can spare time to wait for her answer.' So saying, he left the room.

Glossin had still remained standing in the midst of the apartment. Colonel Mannering had made not the slightest motion to invite him to sit, and indeed had remained standing himself during their short interview. When he left the room, however, Glossin seized upon a chair, and threw himself into it with an air between embarrassment and effrontery. He felt the silence of his companions disconcerting and oppressive, and resolved to interrupt it.

'A fine day, Mr. Sampson.'

The Dominie answered with something between an acquiescent grunt and an indignant groan.

'You never come down to see your old acquaintance on the Ellangowan property, Mr. Sampson— You would find most of the old stagers still stationary there. I have too much respect for the late family to disturb old residenters, even under

pretence of improvement. Besides, it's not my
way — I don't like it — I believe, Mr. Sampson,
Scripture particularly condemns those who oppress
the poor, and remove landmarks.'

'Or who devour the substance of orphans,' sub-
joined the Dominie. 'Anathema, Maranatha!' So
saying, he rose, shouldered the folio which he
had been perusing, faced to the right about, and
marched out of the room with the strides of a
grenadier.

Mr. Glossin, no way disconcerted, or at least feeling it necessary not to appear so, turned to young
Hazlewood, who was apparently busy with the
newspaper. 'Any news, sir?' Hazlewood raised
his eyes, looked at him, and pushed the paper
towards him, as if to a stranger in a coffee-house,
then rose, and was about to leave the room. 'I
beg pardon, Mr. Hazlewood—but I can't help wish-
ing you joy of getting so easily over that infernal
accident.' This was answered by a sort of inclination of the head as slight and stiff as could well
be imagined. Yet it encouraged our man of law
to proceed. 'I can promise you, Mr. Hazlewood,
few people have taken the interest in that matter
which I have done, both for the sake of the country,
and on account of my particular respect for your
family, which has so high a stake in it; indeed,
so very high a stake, that, as Mr. Featherhead is
turning old now, and as there's a talk, since his last
stroke, of his taking the Chiltern Hundreds, it
might be worth your while to look about you. I
speak as a friend, Mr. Hazlewood, and as one

who understands the roll; and if in going over it together——'

'I beg pardon, sir, but I have no views in which your assistance could be useful.'

'O very well—perhaps you are right—it's quite time enough, and I love to see a young gentleman cautious. But I was talking of your wound—I think I have got a clew to that business—I think I have—and if I don't bring the fellow to condign punishment!'——

'I beg your pardon, sir, once more; but your zeal outruns my wishes. I have every reason to think the wound was accidental—certainly it was not premeditated. Against ingratitude and premeditated treachery, should you find any one guilty of them, my resentment will be as warm as your own.' This was Hazlewood's answer.

Another rebuff, thought Glossin; I must try him upon the other tack. 'Right, sir; very nobly said! I would have no more mercy on an ungrateful man than I would on a woodcock—And now we talk of sport, (this was a sort of diverting of the conversation which Glossin had learned from his former patron,) I see you often carry a gun, and I hope you will be soon able to take the field again. I observe you confine yourself always to your own side of the Hazleshaws-burn. I hope, my dear sir, you will make no scruple of following your game to the Ellangowan bank : I believe it is rather the best exposure of the two for woodcocks, although both are capital.'

As this offer only excited a cold and constrained

bow, Glossin was obliged to remain silent, and
was presently afterwards somewhat relieved by the
entrance of Colonel Mannering.

'I have detained you some time, I fear, sir,' said
he, addressing Glossin; 'I wished to prevail upon
Miss Bertram to see you, as, in my opinion, her
objections ought to give way to the necessity of
hearing in her own person what is stated to be of
importance that she should know. But I find that
circumstances of recent occurrence, and not easily
to be forgotten, have rendered her so utterly re-
pugnant to a personal interview with Mr. Glossin,
that it would be cruelty to insist upon it: and she
has deputed me to receive his commands, or proposal,
or, in short, whatever he may wish to say to her.'

'Hem, hem! I am sorry, sir—I am very sorry,
Colonel Mannering, that Miss Bertram should
suppose—that any prejudice, in short—or idea
that any thing on my part——'

'Sir,' said the inflexible Colonel, 'where no
accusation is made, excuses or explanations are
unnecessary. Have you any objection to communicate to me, as Miss Bertram's temporary
guardian, the circumstances which you conceive
to interest her?'

'None, Colonel Mannering; she could not choose
a more respectable friend, or one with whom I,
in particular, would more anxiously wish to communicate frankly.'

'Have the goodness to speak to the point, sir,
if you please.'

'Why, sir, it is not so easy all at once—but

Mr. Hazlewood need not leave the room,—I mean so well to Miss Bertram, that I could wish the whole world to hear my part of the conference.'

' My friend Mr. Charles Hazlewood will not probably be anxious, Mr. Glossin, to listen to what cannot concern him—and now, when he has left us alone, let me pray you to be short and explicit in what you have to say. I am a soldier, sir, somewhat impatient of forms and introductions.' So saying, he drew himself up in his chair, and waited for Mr. Glossin's communication.

' Be pleased to look at that letter,' said Glossin, putting Protocol's epistle into Mannering's hand, as the shortest way of stating his business.

The Colonel read it, and returned it, after pencilling the name of the writer in his memorandum-book. ' This, sir, does not seem to require much discussion—I will see that Miss Bertram's interest is attended to.'

' But, sir,—but, Colonel Mannering,' added Glossin, ' there is another matter which no one can explain but myself. This lady—this Mrs. Margaret Bertram, to my certain knowledge, made a general settlement of her affairs in Miss Lucy Bertram's favour while she lived with my old friend, Mr. Bertram, at Ellangowan. The Dominie — that was the name by which my deceased friend always called that very respectable man Mr. Sampson—he and I witnessed the deed. And she had full power at that time to make such a settlement, for she was in fee of the estate of Singleside even then, although it was life-rented by an elder sister. It was a whimsical settlement of old Singleside's, sir; he pitted the two cats his daughters against each other, ha, ha, ha!'

'Well, sir,' said Mannering, without the slightest smile of sympathy, 'but to the purpose. You say that this lady had power to settle her estate on Miss Bertram, and that she did so?'

'Even so, Colonel,' replied Glossin. 'I think I should understand the law—I have followed it for many years, and though I have given it up to retire upon a handsome competence, I did not throw away that knowledge which is pronounced better than house and land, and which I take to be the knowledge of the law, since, as our common rhyme has it,

> 'Tis most excellent,
> To win the land that's gone and spent.

No, no, I love the smack of the whip—I have a little, a very little law yet, at the service of my friends.'

Glossin ran on in this manner, thinking he had made a favourable impression on Mannering. The Colonel indeed reflected that this might be a most important crisis for Miss Bertram's interest, and resolved that his strong inclination to throw Glossin out at window, or at door, should not interfere with it. He put a strong curb on his temper, and resolved to listen with patience at least, if without complacency. He therefore let Mr. Glossin get to the end of his self-congratulations, and then asked him if he knew where the deed was?

' I know—that is, I think—I believe I can recover it—In such cases custodiers have sometimes made a charge.'

' We won't differ as to that, sir,' said the Colonel, taking out his pocket-book.

' But, my dear sir, you take me so very short—I said *some persons might* make such a claim—I mean for payment of the 'expenses of the deed, trouble in the affair, etc. But I, for my own part, only wish Miss Bertram and her friends to be satisfied that I am acting towards her with honour. There's the paper, sir ! It would have been a satisfaction to me to have delivered it into Miss Bertram's own hands, and to have wished her joy of the prospects which it opens. But since her prejudices on the subject are invincible, it only remains for me to transmit her my best wishes through you, Colonel Mannering, and to express that I shall willingly give my testimony in support of that deed when I shall be called upon. I have the honour to wish you a good morning, sir.'

This parting speech was so well got up, and had so much the tone of conscious integrity unjustly suspected, that even Colonel Mannering was staggered in his bad opinion. He followed him two or three steps, and took leave of him with more politeness (though still cold and formal) than he had paid during his visit. Glossin left the house half pleased with the impression he had made, half mortified by the stern caution and proud reluctance with which he had been received. ' Colonel Mannering might have had more politeness,' he said to himself—' it is not every man that can bring a good chance of £400 a-year to a penniless girl. Singleside must be up to £400 a-year now—there's Reilageganbeg, Gillifidget, Loverless, Liealone, and the Spinster's Knowe—good £400 a-year. Some people might have made their own of it in my place—and yet, to own the truth, after much consideration, I don't see how that is possible.'

Glossin was no sooner mounted and gone, than the Colonel dispatched a groom for Mr. Mac-Morlan, and, putting the deed into his hand, requested to know if it was likely to be available to his friend Lucy Bertram. Mac-Morlan perused it with eyes that sparkled with delight, snapped his fingers repeatedly, and at length exclaimed, 'Available!—it 's as tight as a glove—naebody could make better wark than Glossin, when he didna let down a steek on purpose.—But (his countenance falling) the auld b——, that I should say so, might alter at pleasure!'

'Ah! And how shall we know whether she has done so?'

'Somebody must attend on Miss Bertram's part, when the repositories of the deceased are opened.'

'Can you go?' said the Colonel.

'I fear I cannot,' replied Mac-Morlan, 'I must attend a jury trial before our court.'

'Then I will go myself,' said the Colonel, 'I 'll set out to-morrow. Sampson shall go with me—he is witness to this settlement. But I shall want a legal adviser?'

'The gentleman that was lately sheriff of this

county is high in reputation as a barrister; I will give you a card of introduction to him.'

'What I like about you, Mr. Mac-Morlan,' said the Colonel, 'is, that you always come straight to the point. Let me have it instantly—shall we tell Miss Lucy her chance of becoming an heiress?'

'Surely, because you must have some powers from her, which I will instantly draw out. Besides, I will be caution for her prudence, and that she will consider it only in the light of a chance.'

Mac-Morlan judged well. It could not be discerned from Miss Bertram's manner, that she founded exulting hopes upon the prospect thus unexpectedly opening before her. She did indeed, in the course of the evening, ask Mr. Mac-Morlan, as if by accident, what might be the annual income of the Hazlewood property; but shall we therefore aver for certain that she was considering whether an heiress of four hundred a-year might be a suitable match for the young Laird?

CHAPTER XXXVI

Give me a cup of sack, to make mine eyes look red—For I must speak in passion, and I will do it in King Cambyses' vein.

HENRY IV. PART I.

MANNERING, with Sampson for his companion, lost no time in his journey to Edinburgh. They travelled in the Colonel's post-chariot, who, knowing his companion's habits of abstraction, did not choose to lose him out of his own sight, far less to trust him on horseback, where, in all probability, a knavish stable-boy might with little address have contrived to mount him with his face to the tail. Accordingly, with the aid of his valet, who attended on horseback, he contrived to bring Mr. Sampson safe to an inn in Edinburgh,—for hotels in those days there were none,—without any other accident than arose from his straying twice upon the road. On one occasion he was recovered by Barnes, who understood his humour, when, after engaging in close colloquy with the schoolmaster of Moffat, respecting a disputed quantity in Horace's 7th Ode, Book II., the dispute led on to another controversy, concerning the exact meaning of the word *Malobathro*, in that lyric effusion. His second escapade was made for the purpose of visiting the field of Rullion-green, which was dear to his Presbyterian predilections. Having got out of the carriage for an instant, he saw the sepulchral monument of the slain at the distance of about a mile, and was arrested by Barnes in his progress up the Pentland-hills, having on both occasions forgot his friend, patron, and fellow-traveller, as completely, as if he had been in the East Indies. On being reminded that Colonel Mannering was waiting for him, he uttered his usual ejaculation of 'Prodigious!—I was oblivious,' and then strode back to his post. Barnes was surprised at his master's patience on both occasions, knowing by experience how little he brooked neglect or delay; but the Dominie was in every respect a privileged person. His patron and he were never for a moment in each other's way, and it seemed obvious that they were formed to be companions through life. If Mannering wanted a particular book, the Dominie could bring it; if he wished to have accounts summed up, or checked, his assistance was equally ready; if he desired to recall a particular passage in the classics, he could have recourse to the Dominie as to a dictionary; and all the while, this walking statue was neither presuming when noticed, nor sulky when left to himself. To a proud, shy, reserved man, and such in many respects was Mannering, this sort of living catalogue, and animated automaton, had all the advantages of a literary dumb-waiter.

As soon as they arrived in Edinburgh, and were established at the George Inn near Bristo-port, then kept by old Cockburn, (I love to be particular,) the Colonel desired the waiter to procure him a guide to Mr. Pleydell's, the advocate, for whom he had a letter of introduction from Mr. Mac-Morlan. He then commanded Barnes to have an eye to the Dominie, and walked forth with a chairman, who was to usher him to the man of law.

The period was near the end of the American war. The desire of room, of air, and of decent accommodation, had not as yet made very much progress in the capital of Scotland. Some efforts had been made on the south side of the town towards building houses *within themselves*, as they are emphatically termed; and the New Town on the north, since so much extended, was then just commenced. But the great bulk of the better classes, and particularly those connected with the law, still lived in flats or dungeons of the Old Town. The manners also of some of the veterans of the law had not admitted innovation. One or two eminent lawyers still saw their clients in taverns, as was the general custom fifty years before; and although their habits were already considered as old-fashioned by the younger barristers, yet the custom of mixing wine and revelry with serious business was still maintained by those senior counsellors, who loved the old road, either because it was such, or because they had got too well used to it to travel any other. Among those praisers of the past time, who with ostentatious obstinacy affected the manners of a former generation, was this same Paulus Pleydell, Esq., otherwise a good scholar, an excellent lawyer, and a worthy man.

Under the guidance of his trusty attendant,

GUY MANNERING

Colonel Mannering, after threading a dark lane or two, reached the High Street, then clanging with the voices of oyster-women and the bells of pye-men; for it had, as his guide assured him, just 'chappit eight upon the Tron.' It was long since Mannering had been in the street of a crowded metropolis, which, with its noise and clamour, its sounds of trade, of revelry and of license, its variety of lights, and the eternally changing bustle of its hundred groups, offers, by night especially, a spectacle, which, though composed of the most vulgar materials when they are separately considered, has, when they are combined, a striking and powerful effect on the imagination. The extraordinary height of the houses was marked by lights, which, glimmering irregularly along their front, ascended so high among the attics, that they seemed at length to twinkle in the middle sky. This *coup d'œil*, which still subsists in a certain degree, was then more imposing, owing to the uninterrupted range of buildings on each side, which, broken only at the space where the North Bridge joins the main street, formed a superb and uniform Place, extending from the front of the Luckenbooths to the head of the Canongate, and corresponding in breadth and length to the uncommon height of the buildings on either side.

Mannering had not much time to look and to admire. His conductor hurried him across this striking scene, and suddenly dived with him into a very steep paved lane. Turning to the right, they entered a scale stair-case, as it is called, the state of which, so far as it could be judged of by one of his senses, annoyed Mannering's delicacy not a little. When they had ascended cautiously to a considerable height, they heard a heavy rap at a door, still two stories above them. The door opened, and immediately ensued the sharp and worrying bark of a dog, the squalling of a woman, the screams of an assaulted cat, and the hoarse voice of a man, who cried in a most imperative tone, ' Will ye, Mustard ? will ye ? down, sir, down ! '

' Lord preserve us ! ' said the female voice, ' an he had worried our cat, Mr. Pleydell would ne'er hae forgi'en me ! '

' Aweel, my doo, the cat 's no a prin the waur— So he 's no in, ye say ? '

' Na, Mr. Pleydell 's ne'er in the house on Saturday at e'en,' answered the female voice.

' And the morn 's Sabbath too,' said the querist; ' I dinna ken what will be done.'

By this time Mannering appeared, and found a tall strong countryman, clad in a coat of pepper-and-salt-coloured mixture, with huge metal buttons, a glazed hat and boots, and a large horse-whip beneath his arm, in colloquy with a slip-shod damsel, who had in one hand the lock of the door, and in the other a pail of whiting, or *camstane*, as it is called, mixed with water — a circumstance which indicates Saturday night in Edinburgh.

' So Mr. Pleydell is not at home, my good girl ? ' said Mannering.

' Ay, sir, he 's at hame, but he 's no in the house : he 's aye out on Saturday at e'en.'

'But, my good girl, I am a stranger, and my business express—Will you tell me where I can find him?'

'His honour,' said the chairman, 'will be at Clerihugh's about this time—Hersell could hae tell'd ye that, but she thought ye wanted to see his house.'

'Well, then, show me to this tavern—I suppose he will see me, as I come on business of some consequence?'

'I dinna ken, sir,' said the girl, 'he disna like to be disturbed on Saturdays wi' business—but he's aye civil to strangers.'

'I'll gang to the tavern too,' said our friend Dinmont, 'for I am a stranger also, and on business e'en sic like.'

'Na,' said the hand-maiden, 'an he see the gentleman, he'll see the simple body too—but, Lord's sake, dinna say it was me sent ye there!'

'Atweel, I am a simple body, that's true, hinny, but I am no come to steal ony o' his skeel for naething,' said the farmer in his honest pride, and strutted away down stairs, followed by Mannering and the cadie. Mannering could not help admiring the determined stride with which the stranger who preceded them divided the press, shouldering from him, by the mere weight and impetus of his motion, both drunk and sober passengers. 'He'll be a Teviotdale tup tat ane,' said the chairman, 'tat's for keeping ta crown o' ta causeway tat gate—he'll no gang far or he'll get somebody to bell ta cat wi' him.'

His shrewd augury, however, was not fulfilled. Those who recoiled from the colossal weight of Dinmont, on looking up at his size and strength, apparently judged him too heavy metal to be rashly encountered, and suffered him to pursue his course unchallenged. Following in the wake of this first-rate, Mannering proceeded till the farmer made a pause, and, looking back to the chairman, said, ' I 'm thinking this will be the close, friend ? '

' Ay, ay,' replied Donald, ' tat 's ta close.'

Dinmont descended confidently, then turned into a dark alley—then up a dark stair—and then into an open door. While he was whistling shrilly for the waiter, as if he had been one of his collie dogs, Mannering looked round him, and could hardly conceive how a gentleman of a liberal profession, and good society, should choose such a scene for social indulgence. Besides the miserable entrance, the house itself seemed paltry and half ruinous. The passage in which they stood had a window to the close, which admitted a little light during the day-time, and a villainous compound of smells at all times, but more especially towards evening. Corresponding to this window was a borrowed light on the other side of the passage, looking into the kitchen, which had no direct communication with the free air, but received in the day-time, at second hand, such straggling and obscure light as found its way from the lane through the window opposite. At present, the interior of the kitchen was visible by its own huge fires—a sort of Pandemonium, where men and women, half undressed, were busied in baking, broiling, roasting oysters, and preparing devils on the gridiron; the mistress of the place, with her shoes slip-shod, and her hair straggling like that of Megæra from under a round-eared cap, toiling, scolding, receiving orders, giving them, and obeying them all at once, seemed the presiding enchantress of that gloomy and fiery region.

Loud and repeated bursts of laughter, from different quarters of the house, proved that her labours were acceptable, and not unrewarded by a generous public. With some difficulty a waiter was prevailed upon to show Colonel Mannering and Dinmont the room where their friend, learned in the law, held his hebdomadal carousals. The scene which it exhibited, and particularly the attitude of the counsellor himself, the principal figure therein, struck his two clients with amazement.

Mr. Pleydell was a lively, sharp-looking gentleman, with a professional shrewdness in his eye, and, generally speaking, a professional formality in his manners. But this, like his three-tailed wig and black coat, he could slip off on a Saturday evening, when surrounded by a party of jolly companions, and disposed for what he called his altitudes. On the present occasion, the revel had lasted since four o'clock, and, at length, under the direction of a venerable compotator, who had shared the sports and festivity of three generations, the frolicsome company had begun to practise the ancient and now forgotten pastime of *High Jinks*. This game was played in several different ways. Most frequently the dice were thrown by the company, and those upon whom the lot fell were obliged to assume and maintain, for a time, a certain fictitious character, or to repeat a certain number of fescennine verses in a particular order. If they departed from the characters assigned, or if their memory proved treacherous in the repetition, they incurred forfeits, which were either compounded for by swallowing an additional bumper, or by paying a small sum towards the reckoning. At this sport the jovial company were closely engaged, when Mannering entered the room.

Mr. Counsellor Pleydell, such as we have described him, was enthroned, as a monarch, in an elbow-chair, placed on the dining-table, his scratch wig on one side, his head crowned with a bottle-slider, his eye leering with an expression betwixt fun and the effects of wine, while his court around him resounded with such crambo scraps of verse as these:

> Where is Gerunto now? and what's become of him?
> Gerunto's drowned because he could not swim, etc. etc.

Such, O Themis, were anciently the sports of thy Scottish children! Dinmont was first in the room. He stood aghast a moment,—and then exclaimed, 'It's him, sure enough—Deil o' the like o' that ever I saw!'

At the sound of 'Mr. Dinmont and Colonel Mannering wanting to speak to you, sir,' Pleydell turned his head, and blushed a little when he saw the very genteel figure of the English stranger. He was, however, of the opinion of Falstaff, 'Out, ye villains, play out the play!' wisely judging it the better way to appear totally unconcerned. 'Where be our guards?' exclaimed this second Justinian; 'see ye not a stranger knight from foreign parts arrived at this our court of Holyrood,—with our bold yeoman Andrew Dinmont, who has succeeded to the keeping of our royal flocks within the forest of Jedwood, where, thanks to our royal care in the administration of justice, they feed as safe as if they were within the bounds of Fife? Where be our heralds, our pursuivants, our Lyon, our Marchmount, our Carrick, and our Snowdown? Let the strangers be placed at our board, and regaled as beseemeth their quality, and this our high holiday—to-morrow we will hear their tidings.'

'So please you, my liege, to-morrow's Sunday,' said one of the company.

'Sunday, is it? then we will give no offence to the assembly of the kirk—on Monday shall be their audience.'

Mannering, who had stood at first uncertain whether to advance or retreat, now resolved to enter for the moment into the whim of the scene, though internally fretting at Mac-Morlan, for sending him to consult with a crack-brained humourist. He therefore advanced with three profound congees, and craved permission to lay his credentials at the feet of the Scottish monarch, in order to be perused at his best leisure. The gravity with which he accommodated himself to the humour of the moment, and the deep and humble inclination with which he at first declined, and then accepted, a seat presented by the master of the ceremonies, procured him three rounds of applause.

'Deil hae me, if they arena a' mad thegither!' said Dinmont, occupying with less ceremony a seat at the bottom of the table, 'or else they hae taen Yule before it comes, and are gaun a-guisarding.'

A large glass of claret was offered to Mannering, who drank it to the health of the reigning prince. 'You are, I presume to guess,' said the monarch, 'that celebrated Sir Miles Mannering, so renowned in the French wars, and may well pronounce to us if the wines of Gascony lose their flavour in our more northern realm.'

Mannering, agreeably flattered by this allusion to the fame of his celebrated ancestor, replied, by professing himself only a distant relation of the preux chevalier, and added, 'that in his opinion the wine was superlatively good.'

'It's ower cauld for my stamach,' said Dinmont, setting down the glass, (empty, however.)

'We will correct that quality,' answered King Paulus, the first of the name; 'we have not forgotten that the moist and humid air of our valley of Liddel inclines to stronger potations.—Seneschal, let our faithful yeoman have a cup of brandy; it will be more germain to the matter.'

.'And now,' said Mannering, 'since we have unwarily intruded upon your majesty at a moment of mirthful retirement, be pleased to say when you will indulge a stranger with an audience on those affairs of weight which have brought him to your northern capital.'

The monarch opened Mac-Morlan's letter, and, running it hastily over, exclaimed with his natural voice and manner, 'Lucy Bertram of Ellangowan, poor dear lassie!'

'A forfeit! a forfeit!' exclaimed a dozen voices; 'his majesty has forgot his kingly character.'

'Not a whit! not a whit!' replied the king; 'I'll be judged by this courteous knight. May not a monarch love a maid of low degree? Is not King Cophetua and the Beggar-maid, an adjudged case in point?'

'Professional! professional!—another forfeit,' exclaimed the tumultuary nobility.

'Had not our royal predecessors,' continued the monarch, exalting his sovereign voice to drown these disaffected clamours, — 'Had they not their Jean Logies, their Bessie Carmichaels, their Oliphants, their Sandilands, and their Weirs, and shall it be denied to us even to name a maiden whom we delight to honour? Nay, then, sink state and perish sovereignty! for, like a second Charles v., we will abdicate, and seek in the private shades of life those pleasures which are denied to a throne.'

So saying, he flung away his crown, and sprung from his exalted station with more agility than could have been expected from his age, ordered lights and a wash-hand basin and towel, with a cup of green tea, into another room, and made a sign to Mannering to accompany him. In less than two minutes he washed his face and hands, settled his wig in the glass, and, to Mannering's great surprise, looked quite a different man from the childish Bacchanal he had seen a moment before.

'There are folks,' he said, 'Mr. Mannering, before whom one should take care how they play the fool —because they have either too much malice, or too little wit, as the poet says. The best compliment I can pay Colonel Mannering, is to show I am not ashamed to expose myself before him—and truly I think it is a compliment I have not spared to-night on your good-nature.—But what's that great strong fellow wanting?'

Dinmont, who had pushed after Mannering into the room, began with a scrape with his foot and a scratch of his head in unison. 'I am Dandie Dinmont, sir, of the Charlies-hope—the Liddesdale lad —ye'll mind me?—it was for me ye won yon grand plea.'

'What plea, you loggerhead?' said the lawyer, 'd'ye think I can remember all the fools that come to plague me?'

'Lord, sir, it was the grand plea about the grazing o' the Langtae-head!' said the farmer.

'Well, curse thee, never mind; give me the memorial* and come to me on Monday at ten,' replied the learned counsel.

'But, sir, I haena got ony distinct memorial.'

'No memorial, man?' said Pleydell.

'Na, sir, nae memorial,' answered . Dandie; 'for your honour said before, Mr. Pleydell, ye'll mind, that ye liked best to hear us hill-folk tell our ain tale by word o' mouth.'

---

* The Scottish memorial corresponds to the English brief.

'Beshrew my tongue, that said so!' answered the counsellor, 'it will cost my ears a dinning.— Well, say in two words what you've got to say— you see the gentleman waits.'

'Ou, sir, if the gentleman likes he may play his ain spring first; it's a' ane to Dandie.'

'Now, you looby,' said the lawyer, 'cannot you conceive that your business can be nothing to Colonel Mannering, but that he may not choose to have these great ears of thine regaled with his matters?'

'Aweel, sir, just as you and he like—so ye see to my business,' said Dandie, not a whit disconcerted by the roughness of this reception. 'We're at the auld wark o' the marches again, Jock o' Dawston Cleugh and me. Ye see we march on the tap o' Touthop-rigg after we pass the Pomoragrains; for the Pomoragrains, and Slackenspool, and Bloodylaws, they come in there, and they belang to the Peel; but after ye pass Pomoragrains at a muckle great saucer-headed cutlugged stane, that they ca' Charlies Chuckie, there Dawston Cleugh and Charlies-hope they march. Now, I say, the march rins on the tap o' the hill where the wind and water shears; but Jock o' Dawston Cleugh again, he contravenes that, and says, that it hauds down by the auld drove-road that gaes awa by the Knot o' the Gate ower to Keeldar-ward—and that makes an unco difference.'

'And what difference does it make, friend?' said Pleydell. 'How many sheep will it feed?'

'Ou, no mony,' said Dandie, scratching his head,

—' it's lying high and exposed—it may feed a hog, or aiblins twa in a good year.'

' And for this grazing, which may be worth about five shillings a-year, you are willing to throw away a hundred pound or two ? '

' Na, sir, it's no for the value of the grass,' replied Dinmont ; ' it's for justice.'

' My good friend,' said Pleydell, ' justice, like charity, should begin at home. Do you justice to your wife and family, and think no more about the matter.'

Dinmont still lingered, twisting his hat in his hand—' It's no for that, sir—but I would like ill to be bragged wi' him—he threeps he'll bring a score o' witnesses and mair—and I'm sure there's as mony will swear for me as for him, folk that lived a' their days upon the Charlies-hope, and wadna like to see the land lose its right.'

' Zounds, man, if it be a point of honour,' said the lawyer, ' why don't your landlords take it up ? '

' I dinna ken, sir, (scratching his head again,) there's been nae election-dusts lately, and the lairds are unco neighbourly, and Jock and me canna get them to yoke thegither about it a' that we can say—but if ye thought we might keep up the rent——'

' No ! no ! that will never do,' said Pleydell, ' confound you, why don't you take good cudgels and settle it ? '

' Odd, sir,' answered the farmer, ' we tried that three times already—that's twice on the land and ance at Lockerby fair.—But I dinna ken—we're

baith gey good at single-stick, and it couldna weel
be judged.'

'Then take broadswords, and be d—d to you,
as your fathers did before you,' said the counsel
learned in the law.

'Aweel, sir, if ye think it wadna be again the
law, it's a' ane to Dandie.'

'Hold! hold!' exclaimed Pleydell, 'we shall
have another Lord Soulis' mistake—Pr'ythee, man,
comprehend me; I wish you to consider how very
trifling and foolish a lawsuit you wish to engage in.'

'Ay, sir?' said Dandie, in a disappointed tone.
'So ye winna take on wi' me, I'm doubting?'

'Me! not I—go home, go home, take a pint
and agree.' Dandie looked but half contented, and
still remained stationary. 'Any thing more, my
friend?'

'Only, sir, about the succession of this leddy
that's dead, auld Miss Margaret Bertram o' Singleside.'

'Ay, what about her?' said the counsellor, rather
surprised.

'Ou, we have nae connexion at a' wi' the Bertrams,' said Dandie, — 'they were grand folk by
the like o' us — But Jean Liltup, that was auld
Singleside's housekeeper, and the mother of these
twa young ladies that are gane—the last o' them's
dead at a ripe age, I trow—Jean Liltup came out o'
Liddel water, and she was as near our connexion as
second cousin to my mother's half-sister—She drew
up wi' Singleside, nae doubt, when she was his
housekeeper, and it was a sair vex and grief to a'

her kith and kin. But he acknowledged a marriage, and satisfied the kirk—and now I wad ken frae you if we hae not some claim by law?'

'Not the shadow of a claim.'

'Aweel, we're nae puirer,' said Dandie, — 'but she may hae thought on us if she was minded to make a testament.—Weel, sir, I 've said my say— I 'se e'en wish you good night, and——' putting his hand in his pocket.

'No, no, my friend; I never take fees on Saturday nights, or without a memorial — away with you, Dandie.' And Dandie made his reverence, and departed accordingly.

CHAPTER XXXVII

But this poor farce has neither truth, nor art,
To please the fancy or to touch the heart.
Dark but not awful, dismal but yet mean,
With anxious bustle moves the cumbrous scene,
Presents no objects tender or profound,
But spreads its cold unmeaning gloom around.

PARISH REGISTER.

'YOUR majesty,' said Mannering, laughing, 'has solemnized your abdication by an act of mercy and charity—That fellow will scarce think of going to law.'

'O, you are quite wrong,' said the experienced lawyer. 'The only difference is, I have lost my client and my fee. He'll never rest till he finds somebody to encourage him to commit the folly he has predetermined—No! no! I have only shown you another weakness of my character—I always speak truth of a Saturday night.'

'And sometimes through the week, I should think,' said Mannering, continuing the same tone.

'Why, yes; as far as my vocation will permit. I am, as Hamlet says, indifferent honest, when my clients and their solicitors do not make me the medium of conveying their double-distilled lies to the bench. But *oportet vivere!* it is a sad thing.— And now to our business. I am glad my old friend

Mac-Morlan has sent you to me; he is an active, honest, and intelligent man, long sheriff-substitute of the county of —— under me, and still holds the office. He knows I have a regard for that unfortunate family of Ellangowan, and for poor Lucy. I have not seen her since she was twelve years old, and she was then a sweet pretty girl under the management of a very silly father. But my interest in her is of an early date. I was called upon, Mr. Mannering, being then sheriff of that county, to investigate the particulars of a murder which had been committed near Ellangowan the day on which this poor child was born; and which, by a strange combination that I was unhappily not able to trace, involved the death or abstraction of her only brother, a boy of about five years old. No, Colonel, I shall never forget the misery of the house of Ellangowan that morning!—the father half-distracted— the mother dead in premature travail—the helpless infant, with scarce any one to attend it, coming wawling and crying into this miserable world at such a moment of unutterable misery. We lawyers are not of iron, sir, or of brass, any more than you soldiers are of steel. We are conversant with the crimes and distresses of civil society, as you are with those that occur in a state of war, and to do our duty in either case a little apathy is perhaps necessary—But the devil take a soldier whose heart can be as hard as his sword, and his dam catch the lawyer who bronzes his bosom instead of his forehead!—But come, I am losing my Saturday at e'en —will you have the kindness to trust me with these

papers which relate to Miss Bertram's business?—
and stay—to-morrow you'll take a bachelor's dinner
with an old lawyer,—I insist upon it, at three
precisely—and come an hour sooner.—The old lady
is to be buried on Monday; it is the orphan's cause,
and we'll borrow an hour from the Sunday to talk
over this business—although I fear nothing can be
done if she has altered her settlement—unless
perhaps it occurs within the sixty days, and then
if Miss Bertram can show that she possesses the
character of heir-at-law, why——

'But, hark! my lieges are impatient of their
interregnum—I do not invite you to rejoin us,
Colonel; it would be a trespass on your complaisance, unless you had begun the day with us,
and gradually glided on from wisdom to mirth,
and from mirth to—to—to—extravagance.—Good
night—Harry, go home with Mr. Mannering to
his lodging—Colonel, I expect you at a little past
two to-morrow.'

The Colonel returned to his inn, equally surprised
at the childish frolics in which he had found his
learned counsellor engaged, at the candour and
sound sense which he had in a moment summoned
up to meet the exigencies of his profession, and
at the tone of feeling which he displayed when he
spoke of the friendless orphan.

In the morning, while the Colonel and his most
quiet and silent of all retainers, Dominie Sampson,
were finishing the breakfast which Barnes had made
and poured out, after the Dominie had scalded himself in the attempt, Mr. Pleydell was suddenly

ushered in. A nicely dressed bob-wig, upon every hair of which a zealous and careful barber had bestowed its proper allowance of powder; a well-brushed black suit, with very clean shoes and gold buckles and stock-buckle; a manner rather reserved and formal than intrusive, but, withal, showing only the formality of manner, by no means that of awkwardness; a countenance, the expressive and somewhat comic features of which were in complete repose, — all showed a being perfectly different from the choice spirit of the evening before. A glance of shrewd and piercing fire in his eye was the only marked expression which recalled the man of 'Saturday at e'en.'

'I am come,' said he, with a very polite address, 'to use my regal authority in your behalf in spirituals as well as temporals—can I accompany you to the Presbyterian kirk, or Episcopal meeting-house?—*Tros Tyriusve*, a lawyer, you know, is of both religions, or rather I should say of both forms —or can I assist in passing the forenoon otherwise? You'll excuse my old-fashioned importunity—I was born in a time when a Scotchman was thought inhospitable if he left a guest alone a moment except when he slept—but I trust you will tell me at once if I intrude.'

'Not at all, my dear sir,' answered Colonel Mannering—'I am delighted to put myself under your pilotage. I should wish much to hear some of your Scottish preachers whose talents have done such honour to your country — your Blair, your Robertson, or your Henry; and I embrace your

kind offer with all my heart—Only,' drawing the
lawyer a little aside, and turning his eye towards
Sampson, 'my worthy friend there in the reverie
is a little helpless and abstracted, and my servant,
Barnes, who is his pilot in ordinary, cannot well
assist him here, especially as he has expressed his
determination of going to some of your darker and
more remote places of worship.'

The lawyer's eye glanced at Dominie Sampson.
'A curiosity worth preserving—and I'll find you
a fit custodier.—Here you, sir, (to the waiter) go
to Luckie Finlayson's in the Cowgate for Miles
Macfin the cadie, he'll be there about this time, and
tell him I wish to speak to him.'

The person wanted soon arrived. 'I will commit
your friend to this man's charge,' said Pleydell;
'he'll attend him, or conduct him, wherever he
chooses to go, with a happy indifference as to kirk
or market, meeting or court of justice, or—any
other place whatever—and bring him safe home at
whatever hour you appoint; so that Mr. Barnes
there may be left to the freedom of his own will.'

This was easily arranged, and the Colonel committed the Dominie to the charge of this man while
they should remain in Edinburgh.

'And now, sir, if you please, we shall go to the
Greyfriars' church, to hear our historian of Scotland,
of the Continent, and of America.'

They were disappointed—he did not preach that
morning.—'Never mind,' said the counsellor, 'have
a moment's patience, and we shall do very well.'

The colleague of Dr. Robertson ascended the

pulpit.* His external appearance was not prepossessing. A remarkably fair complexion, strangely contrasted with a black wig without a grain of powder; a narrow chest and a stooping posture; hands which, placed like props on either side of the pulpit, seemed necessary rather to support the person than to assist the gesticulation of the preacher,—no gown, not even that of Geneva, a tumbled band, and a gesture which seemed scarce voluntary, were the first circumstances which struck a stranger. 'The preacher seems a very ungainly person,' whispered Mannering to his new friend.

'Never fear, he's the son of an excellent Scottish lawyer†—he'll show blood, I'll warrant him.'

The learned counsellor predicted truly. A lecture was delivered, fraught with new, striking, and entertaining views of Scripture history—a sermon, in which the Calvinism of the Kirk of Scotland was ably supported, yet made the basis of a sound system of practical morals, which should neither shelter the sinner under the cloak of speculative faith or of peculiarity of opinion, nor leave him loose to the waves of unbelief and schism. Something there was of an antiquated turn of argument and metaphor, but it only served to give zest and peculiarity to the style of elocution. The sermon was not read—a scrap of paper containing the heads of

* This was the celebrated Dr. Erskine, a distinguished clergyman, and a most excellent man.

† The father of Dr. Erskine was an eminent lawyer, and his Institutes of the Law of Scotland are to this day the text-book of students of that science.

the discourse was occasionally referred to, and the enunciation, which at first seemed imperfect and embarrassed, became, as the preacher warmed in his progress, animated and distinct; and although the discourse could not be quoted as a correct specimen of pulpit eloquence, yet Mannering had seldom heard so much learning, metaphysical acuteness, and energy of argument, brought into the service of Christianity.

' Such,' he said, going out of the church, ' must have been the preachers, to whose unfearing minds, and acute, though sometimes rudely exercised talents, we owe the Reformation.'

' And yet that reverend gentleman,' said Pleydell, ' whom I love for his father's sake and his own, has nothing of the sour or pharisaical pride which has been imputed to some of the early fathers of the Calvinistic Kirk of Scotland. His colleague and he differ, and head different parties in the kirk, about particular points of church discipline; but without for a moment losing personal regard or respect for each other, or suffering malignity to interfere in an opposition, steady, constant, and apparently conscientious on both sides.'

' And you, Mr. Pleydell, what do you think of their points of difference ? '

' Why, I hope, Colonel, a plain man may go to heaven without thinking about them at all— besides, *inter nos*, I am a member of the suffering and Episcopal Church of Scotland—the shadow of a shade now, and fortunately so—but I love to pray where my fathers prayed before me, without thinking worse of the Presbyterian forms, because they do not affect me with the same associations.' And with this remark they parted until dinner-time.

From the awkward access to the lawyer's mansion, Mannering was induced to form very moderate expectations of the entertainment which he was to receive. The approach looked even more dismal by day-light than on the preceding evening. The houses on each side of the lane were so close, that the neighbours might have shaken hands with each other from the different sides, and occasionally the space between was traversed by wooden galleries, and thus entirely closed up. The stair, the scale-stair, was not well cleaned; and on entering the house, Mannering was struck with the narrowness and meanness of the wainscotted passage. But the library, into which he was shown by an elderly respectable-looking man-servant, was a complete contrast to these unpromising appearances. It was a well-proportioned room, hung with a portrait or two of Scottish characters of eminence, by Jamieson, the Caledonian Vandyke, and surrounded with books, the best editions of the best authors, and in particular, an admirable collection of classics.

'These,' said Pleydell, 'are my tools of trade. A lawyer without history or literature is a mechanic, a mere working mason; if he possesses some knowledge of these, he may venture to call himself an architect.'

But Mannering was chiefly delighted with the

view from the windows, which commanded that incomparable prospect of the ground between Edinburgh and the sea; the Frith of Forth, with its islands; the embayment which is terminated by the Law of North Berwick; and the varied shores of Fife to the northward, indenting with a hilly outline the clear blue horizon.

When Mr. Pleydell had sufficiently enjoyed the surprise of his guest, he called his attention to Miss Bertram's affairs. ' I was in hopes,' he said, ' though but faint, to have discovered some means of ascertaining her indefeasible right to this property of Singleside; but my researches have been in vain. The old lady was certainly absolute fiar, and might dispose of it in full right of property. All that we have to hope is, that the devil may not have tempted her to alter this very proper settlement. You must attend the old girl's funeral to-morrow, to which you will receive an invitation, for I have acquainted her agent with your being here on Miss Bertram's part; and I will meet you afterwards at the house she inhabited, and be present to see fair play at the opening of the settlement. The old cat had a little girl, the orphan of some relation, who lived with her as a kind of slavish companion. I hope she has had the conscience to make her independent, in consideration of the *peine forte et dure* to which she subjected her during her life-time.'

Three gentlemen now appeared, and were introduced to the stranger. They were men of good sense, gaiety, and general information, so that the day passed very pleasantly over; and Colonel

Mannering assisted, about eight o'clock at night, in discussing the landlord's bottle, which was, of course, a *magnum*. Upon his return to the inn, he found a card inviting him to the funeral of Miss Margaret Bertram, late of Singleside, which was to proceed from her own house to the place of interment in the Greyfriars' churchyard, at one o'clock afternoon.

At the appointed hour, Mannering went to a small house in the suburbs to the southward of the city, where he found the place of mourning, indicated, as usual in Scotland, by two rueful figures with long black cloaks, white crapes and hat-bands, holding in their hands poles, adorned with melancholy streamers of the same description. By two other mutes, who, from their visages, seemed suffering under the pressure of some strange calamity, he was ushered into the dining-parlour of the defunct, where the company were assembled for the funeral.

In Scotland, the custom, now disused in England, of inviting the relations of the deceased to the interment, is universally retained. On many occasions this has a singular and striking effect, but it degenerates into mere empty form and grimace, in cases where the defunct has had the misfortune to live unbeloved and die unlamented. The English service for the dead, one of the most beautiful and impressive parts of the ritual of the church, would have, in such cases, the effect of fixing the attention, and uniting the thoughts and feelings of the audience present, in an exercise of devotion so peculiarly adapted to such an occasion. But according to the Scottish custom, if there be not real feeling among the assistants, there is nothing to supply the deficiency, and exalt or rouse the attention; so that a sense of tedious form, and almost hypocritical restraint, is too apt to pervade the company assembled for the mournful solemnity. Mrs. Margaret Bertram was unluckily one of those whose good qualities had attached no general friendship. She had no near relations who might have mourned from natural affection, and therefore her funeral exhibited merely the exterior trappings of sorrow.

Mannering, therefore, stood among this lugubrious company of cousins in the third, fourth, fifth, and sixth degree, composing his countenance to the decent solemnity of all who were around him, and looking as much concerned on Mrs. Margaret Bertram's account, as if the deceased lady of Singleside had been his own sister or mother. After a deep and awful pause, the company began to talk aside—under their breaths, however, and as if in the chamber of a dying person.

'Our poor friend,' said one grave gentleman, scarcely opening his mouth, for fear of deranging the necessary solemnity of his features, and sliding his whisper from between his lips, which were as little unclosed as possible,—'Our poor friend has died well to pass in the world.'

'Nae doubt,' answered the person addressed, with half-closed eyes; 'poor Mrs. Margaret was aye careful of the gear.'

'Any news to-day, Colonel Mannering?' said one of the gentlemen whom he had dined with the day before, but in a tone which might, for its impressive gravity, have communicated the death of his whole generation.

'Nothing particular, I believe, sir,' said Mannering, in the cadence which was, he observed, appropriated to the house of mourning.

'I understand,' continued the first speaker, emphatically, and with the air of one who is well informed—'I understand there *is* a settlement.'

'And what does little Jenny Gibson get?'

'A hundred, and the auld repeater.'

'That's but sma' gear, puir thing; she had a sair time o't with the auld leddy. But it's ill waiting for dead folk's shoon.'

'I am afraid,' said the politician, who was close by Mannering, 'we have not done with your old friend Tippoo Saib yet—I doubt he'll give the Company more plague; and I am told, but you'll know for certain, that East India Stock is not rising.'

'I trust it will, sir, soon.'

'Mrs. Margaret,' said another person, mingling in the conversation, 'had some India bonds. I know that, for I drew the interest for her—it would be desirable now for the trustees and legatees to have the Colonel's advice about the time and mode of converting them into money. For my part I think—But there's Mr. Mortcloke to tell us they are gaun to lift.'

Mr. Mortcloke the undertaker did accordingly, with a visage of professional length and most grievous solemnity, distribute among the pall-bearers little cards, assigning their respective situations in attendance upon the coffin. As this precedence is supposed to be regulated by propinquity to the defunct, the undertaker, however skilful a master of these lugubrious ceremonies, did not escape giving some offence. To be related to Mrs. Bertram was to be of kin to the lands of Singleside, and was a propinquity of which each relative present at that moment was particularly jealous. Some murmurs there were on the occasion, and our friend Dinmont gave more open offence, being unable either to repress his discontent, or to utter it in the key properly modulated to the solemnity. 'I think ye might hae at least gi'en me a leg o' her to carry,' he exclaimed, in a voice considerably louder than propriety admitted; 'God! an it hadna been for the rigs o' land, I would hae gotten her a' to carry mysell, for as mony gentles as are here.'

A score of frowning and reproving brows were bent upon the unappalled yeoman, who, having given vent to his displeasure, stalked sturdily down stairs with the rest of the company, totally disregarding the censures of those whom his remarks had scandalized.

And then the funeral pomp set forth; saulies with their batons, and gumphions of tarnished white crape, in honour of the well-preserved maiden fame of Mrs. Margaret Bertram. Six starved horses, themselves the very emblems of mortality, well cloaked and plumed, lugging along the hearse with its dismal emblazonry, crept in slow state towards the place of interment, preceded by Jamie Duff, an idiot, who, with weepers and gravat made of white paper, attended on every funeral, and followed by six mourning coaches, filled with the company. Many of these now gave more free loose to their tongues, and discussed with unrestrained earnestness the amount of the succession, and the probability of its destination. The principal expectants, however, kept a prudent silence, indeed ashamed to express hopes which might prove fallacious; and the agent, or man of business, who alone knew exactly how matters stood, maintained a countenance of mysterious importance, as if determined to preserve the full interest of anxiety and suspense.

At length they arrived at the churchyard gates, and from thence, amid the gaping of two or three dozen of idle women with infants in their arms, and accompanied by some twenty children, who ran gambolling and screaming alongside of the sable procession, they finally arrived at the burial place of the Singleside family. This was a square enclosure in the Greyfriars' churchyard, guarded on one side by a veteran angel, without a nose, and having only one wing, who had the merit of having maintained his post for a century, while his comrade cherub, who had stood sentinel on the corresponding pedestal, lay a broken trunk among the hemlock, burdock, and nettles, which grew in gigantic luxuriance around the walls of the mausoleum. A moss-grown and broken inscription informed the reader, that in the year 1650 Captain Andrew Bertram, first of Singleside, descended of the very ancient and honourable house of Ellangowan, had caused this monument to be erected for himself and his descendants. A reasonable number of scythes and hour-glasses, and death's heads, and cross bones, garnished the following sprig of sepulchral poetry, to the memory of the founder of the mausoleum :

> Nathaniel's heart, Bezaleel's hand,
>   If ever any had,
> These boldly do I say had he,
>   Who lieth in this bed.

Here then, amid the deep black fat loam into which her ancestors were now resolved, they deposited the body of Mrs. Margaret Bertram; and, like soldiers returning from a military funeral, the nearest relations who might be interested in the settlements of the lady, urged the dog-cattle of the hackney coaches to all the speed of which they were capable, in order to put an end to farther suspense on that interesting topic.

CHAPTER XXXVIII

Die and endow a college or a cat.
POPE.

THERE is a fable told by Lucian, that while a troop of monkeys, well drilled by an intelligent manager, were performing a tragedy with great applause, the decorum of the whole scene was at once destroyed, and the natural passions of the actors called forth into very indecent and active emulation, by a wag who threw a handful of nuts upon the stage. In like manner, the approaching crisis stirred up among the expectants feelings of a nature very different from those of which, under the superintendence of Mr. Mortcloke, they had but now been endeavouring to imitate the expression. Those eyes which were lately devoutly cast up to heaven, or with greater humility bent solemnly upon earth, were now sharply and alertly darting their glances through shuttles, and trunks, and drawers, and cabinets, and all the odd corners of an old maiden lady's repositories. Nor was their search without interest, though they did not find the will of which they were in quest.

Here was a promissory note for £20 by the minister of the nonjuring chapel, interest marked as paid to Martinmas last, carefully folded up in a new set of words to the old tune of 'Over the

Water to Charlie ';—there, was a curious love correspondence between the deceased and a certain Lieutenant O'Kean of a marching regiment of foot; and
tied up with the letters was a document, which at
once explained to the relatives why a connexion that
boded them little good had been suddenly broken
off, being the Lieutenant's bond for two hundred
pounds, upon which *no* interest whatever appeared
to have been paid. Other bills and bonds to a
larger amount, and signed by better names (I mean
commercially) than those of the worthy divine and
gallant soldier, also occurred in the course of their
researches, besides a hoard of coins of every size
and denomination, and scraps of broken gold and
silver, old ear-rings, hinges of cracked snuff-boxes,
mountings of spectacles, etc. etc. etc. Still no
will made its appearance, and Colonel Mannering
began full well to hope that the settlement which
he had obtained from Glossin contained the ultimate
arrangement of the old lady's affairs. But his friend
Pleydell, who now came into the room, cautioned
him against entertaining this belief.

'I am well acquainted with the gentleman,' he
said, 'who is conducting the search, and I guess
from his manner that he knows something more of
the matter than any of us.' Meantime, while the
search proceeds, let us take a brief glance at one or
two of the company, who seem most interested.

Of Dinmont, who, with his large hunting-whip
under his arm, stood poking his great round face
over the shoulder of the *homme d'affaires*, it is unnecessary to say any thing. That thin-looking

oldish person, in a most correct and gentleman-like suit of mourning, is Mac-Casquil, formerly of Drumquag, who was ruined by having a legacy bequeathed to him of two shares in the Ayr bank. His hopes on the present occasion are founded on a very distant relationship, upon his sitting in the same pew with the deceased every Sunday, and upon his playing at cribbage with her regularly on the Saturday evenings—taking great care never to come off a winner. That other coarse-looking man, wearing his own greasy hair tied in a leathern cue more greasy still, is a tobacconist, a relation of Mrs. Bertram's mother, who, having a good stock in trade when the colonial war broke out, trebled the price of his commodity to all the world, Mrs. Bertram alone excepted, whose tortoise-shell snuff-box was weekly filled with the best rappee at the old prices, because the maid brought it to the shop with Mrs. Bertram's respects to her cousin Mr. Quid. That young fellow, who has not had the decency to put off his boots and buckskins, might have stood as forward as most of them in the graces of the old lady, who loved to look upon a comely young man; but it is thought he has forfeited the moment of fortune, by sometimes neglecting her tea-table when solemnly invited; sometimes appearing there, when he had been dining with blither company; twice treading upon her cat's tail, and once affronting her parrot.

To Mannering, the most interesting of the group was the poor girl, who had been a sort of humble companion of the deceased, as a subject

upon whom she could at all times expectorate her
bad humour. She was for form's sake dragged into
the room by the deceased's favourite female attendant, where, shrinking into a corner as soon as
possible, she saw with wonder and affright the intrusive researches of the strangers amongst those
recesses to which from childhood she had looked
with awful veneration. This girl was regarded
with an unfavourable eye by all the competitors,
honest Dinmont only excepted; the rest conceived
they should find in her a formidable competitor,
whose claims might at least encumber and diminish
their chance of succession. Yet she was the only
person present who seemed really to feel sorrow
for the deceased. Mrs. Bertram had been her pro-
tectress, although from selfish motives, and her
capricious tyranny was forgotten at the moment
while the tears followed each other fast down the
cheeks of her frightened and friendless dependent.
'There's ower muckle saut water there, Drumquag,' said the tobacconist to the ex-proprietor,
'to bode ither folk muckle gude. Folk seldom
greet that gate but they ken what it's for.' Mr.
Mac-Casquil only replied with a nod, feeling the
propriety of asserting his superior gentry in presence
of Mr. Pleydell and Colonel Mannering.

'Very queer if there suld be nae will after a',
friend,' said Dinmont, who began to grow impatient, to the man of business.

'A moment's patience, if you please—she was a
good and prudent woman, Mrs. Margaret Bertram—
a good and prudent and well-judging woman, and

knew how to choose friends and depositories—she may have put her last will and testament, or rather her *mortis causa* settlement, as it relates to heritage, into the hands of some safe friend.'

'I'll bet a rump and dozen,' said Pleydell, whispering to the Colonel, 'he has got it in his own pocket';—then addressing the man of law, 'Come, sir, we'll cut this short if you please—here is a settlement of the estate of Singleside, executed several years ago, in favour of Miss Lucy Bertram of Ellangowan——' The company stared fearfully wild. 'You, I presume, Mr. Protocol, can inform us if there is a later deed?'

'Please to favour me, Mr. Pleydell';—and so saying, he took the deed out of the learned counsel's hand, and glanced his eye over the contents.

'Too cool,' said Pleydell, 'too cool by half—he has another deed in his pocket still.'

'Why does he not show it then, and be d—d to him!' said the military gentleman, whose patience began to wax threadbare.

'Why, how should I know?' answered the barrister,—'why does a cat not kill a mouse when she takes him?—the consciousness of power and the love of teasing, I suppose.—Well, Mr. Protocol, what say you to that deed?'

'Why, Mr. Pleydell, the deed is a well-drawn deed, properly authenticated and tested in forms of the statute.'

'But recalled or superseded by another of posterior date in your possession, eh?' said the counsellor.

' Something of the sort, I confess, Mr. Pleydell,' rejoined the man of business, producing a bundle tied with tape, and sealed at each fold and ligation with black wax. ' That deed, Mr. Pleydell, which you produce and found upon, is dated 1st June 17—; but this '—breaking the seals and unfolding the document slowly—' is dated the 20th—no, I see it is the 21st, of April of this present year, being ten years posterior.'

' Marry, hang her, brock !' said the counsellor, borrowing an exclamation from Sir Toby Belch, ' just the month in which Ellangowan's distresses became generally public. But let us hear what she has done.'

Mr. Protocol accordingly, having required silence, began to read the settlement aloud in a slow, steady, business-like tone. The group around, in whose eyes hope alternately awakened and faded, and who were straining their apprehensions to get at the drift of the testator's meaning through the mist of technical language in which the conveyance had involved it, might have made a study for Hogarth.

The deed was of an unexpected nature. It set forth with conveying and disponing all and whole the estate and lands of Singleside and others, with the lands of Loverless, Liealone, Spinster's Knowe, and heaven knows what beside, ' to and in favours of (here the reader softened his voice to a gentle and modest piano) Peter Protocol, clerk to the signet, having the fullest confidence in his capacity and integrity,' (these are the very words which my worthy deceased friend insisted upon my inserting,)

'But in TRUST always,' (here the reader recovered his voice and style, and the visages of several of the hearers, which had attained a longitude that Mr. Mortcloke might have envied, were perceptibly shortened), 'in TRUST always, and for the uses, ends, and purposes herein after-mentioned.'

In these 'uses, ends, and purposes,' lay the cream of the affair. The first was introduced by a preamble setting forth, that the testatrix was lineally descended from the ancient house of Ellangowan, her respected great-grandfather, Andrew Bertram, first of Singleside, of happy memory, having been second son to Allan Bertram, fifteenth Baron of Ellangowan. It proceeded to state, that Henry Bertram, son and heir of Godfrey Bertram, now of Ellangowan, had been stolen from his parents in infancy, but that she, the testatrix, *was well assured that he was yet alive in foreign parts, and by the providence of heaven would be restored to the possessions of his ancestors*—in which case the said Peter Protocol was bound and obliged, like as he bound and obliged himself, by acceptance of these presents, to denude himself of the said lands of Singleside and others, and of all the other effects thereby conveyed (excepting always a proper gratification for his own trouble) to and in favour of the said Henry Bertram upon his return to his native country. And during the time of his residing in foreign parts, or in case of his never again returning to Scotland, Mr. Peter Protocol, the trustee, was directed to distribute the rents of the land, and interest of the other funds, (deducting always a proper gratification for his trouble in the premises) in equal portions, among four charitable establishments pointed out in the will. The power of management, of letting leases, of raising and lending out money, in short, the full authority of a proprietor, was vested in this confidential trustee, and, in the event of his death, went to certain official persons named in the deed. There were only two legacies; one of a hundred pounds to a favourite waiting-maid, another of the like sum to Janet Gibson (whom the deed stated to have been supported by the charity of the testatrix) for the purpose of binding her an apprentice to some honest trade.

A settlement in mortmain is in Scotland termed a *mortification*, and in one great borough (Aberdeen, if I remember rightly) there is a municipal officer who takes care of these public endowments, and is thence called the Master of Mortifications. One would almost presume, that the term had its origin in the effect which such settlements usually produce upon the kinsmen of those by whom they are executed. Heavy at least was the mortification which befell the audience, who, in the late Mrs. Margaret Bertram's parlour, had listened to this unexpected destination of the lands of Singleside. There was a profound silence after the deed had been read over.

Mr. Pleydell was the first to speak. He begged to look at the deed, and having satisfied himself that it was correctly drawn and executed, he returned it without any observation, only saying aside to Mannering, 'Protocol is not worse than other people, I believe; but this old lady has determined that, if he do not turn rogue, it shall not be for want of temptation.'

'I really think,' said Mr. Mac-Casquil of Drumquag, who, having gulped down one half of his vexation, determined to give vent to the rest, 'I really think this is an extraordinary case! I should like now to know from Mr. Protocol, who, being sole and unlimited trustee, must have been consulted upon this occasion; I should like, I say, to know, how Mrs. Bertram could possibly believe in the existence of a boy, that a' the world kens was murdered many a year since?'

'Really, sir,' said Mr. Protocol, 'I do not conceive it is possible for me to explain her motives more than she has done herself. Our excellent deceased friend was a good woman, sir—a pious woman — and might have grounds for confidence in the boy's safety which are not accessible to us, sir.'

'Hout,' said the tobacconist, 'I ken very weel what were her grounds for confidence. There's Mrs. Rebecca (the maid) sitting there, has tell'd me a hundred times in my ain shop, there was nae kenning how her leddy wad settle her affairs, for an auld gipsy witch wife at Gilsland had possessed her with a notion, that the callant—Harry Bertram ca's she him?—would come alive again some day after a'—ye'll no deny that, Mrs. Rebecca?—though I dare to say ye forgot to put your mistress in mind of what ye promised to say when I gied

ye mony a half-crown—But ye 'll no deny what I
am saying now, lass ? '

' I ken naething at a' about it,' answered Rebecca,
doggedly, and looking straight forward with the firm
countenance of one not disposed to be compelled to
remember more than was agreeable to her.

' Weel said, Rebecca ! ye 're satisfied wi' your ain
share ony way,' rejoined the tobacconist.

The buck of the second-head, for a buck of the
first-head he was not, had hitherto been slapping
his boots with his switch-whip, and looking like a
spoiled child that has lost its supper.   His murmurs,
however, were all vented inwardly, or at most in
a soliloquy such as this—' I am sorry, by G—d, I
ever plagued myself about her—I came here, by
G—d, one night to drink tea, and I left King, and
the Duke's rider Will Hack.   They were toasting
a round of running horses ; by G—d, I might have
got leave to wear the jacket as well as other folk,
if I had carried it on with them—and she has not
so much as left me that hundred ! '

' We 'll make the payment of the note quite
agreeable,' said Mr. Protocol, who had no wish to
increase at that moment the odium attached to his
office—' And now, gentlemen, I fancy we have no
more to wait for here, and—I shall put the settlement of my excellent and worthy friend on record
to-morrow, that every gentleman may examine the
contents, and have free access to take an extract ;
and '—he proceeded to lock up the repositories of
the deceased with more speed than he had opened
them—' Mrs. Rebecca, ye 'll be so kind as to keep

all right here until we can let the house—I had
an offer from a tenant this morning, if such a thing
should be, and if I was to have any management.'

Our friend Dinmont, having had his hopes as
well as another, had hitherto sate sulky enough in
the arm-chair formerly appropriated to the deceased,
and in which she would have been not a little
scandalized to have seen this colossal specimen of
the masculine gender lolling at length. His em-
ployment had been rolling up, into the form of a
coiled snake, the long lash of his horse-whip, and
then by a jerk causing it to unroll itself into the
middle of the floor. The first words he said when
he had digested the shock, contained a magnani-
mous declaration, which he probably was not conscious of having uttered aloud—'Weel—blude's
thicker than water—she's welcome to the cheeses
and the hams just the same.' But when the
trustee had made the above-mentioned motion for
the mourners to depart, and talked of the house
being immediately let, honest Dinmont got upon
his feet, and stunned the company with this blunt
question, 'And what's to come o' this poor lassie
then, Jenny Gibson? Sae mony o' us as thought
oursells sib to the family when the gear was parting,
we may do something for her amang us surely.'

This proposal seemed to dispose most of the assembly instantly to evacuate the premises, although
upon Mr. Protocol's motion they had lingered as
if around the grave of their disappointed hopes.
Drumquag said, or rather muttered, something of
having a family of his own, and took precedence,

in virtue of his gentle blood, to depart as fast as possible. The tobacconist sturdily stood forward, and scouted the motion—' A little huzzie, like that, was weel enough provided for already; and Mr. Protocol at ony rate was the proper person to take direction of her, as he had charge of her legacy'; and after uttering such his opinion in a steady and decisive tone of voice, he also left the place. The buck made a stupid and brutal attempt at a jest upon Mrs. Bertram's recommendation that the poor girl should be taught some honest trade; but encountered a scowl from Colonel Mannering's darkening eye (to whom, in his ignorance of the tone of good society, he had looked for applause) that made him ache to the very back-bone. He shuffled down stairs, therefore, as fast as possible.

Protocol, who was really a good sort of man, next expressed his intention to take a temporary charge of the young lady, under protest always, that his so doing should be considered as merely eleemosynary; when Dinmont at length got up, and, having shaken his huge dreadnought great-coat, as a Newfoundland dog does his shaggy hide when he comes out of the water, ejaculated, ' Weel, deil hae me then, if ye hae ony fash wi' her, Mr. Protocol, if she likes to gang hame wi' me, that is. Ye see, Ailie and me we 're weel to pass, and we would like the lassies to hae a wee bit mair lair than oursells, and to be neighbour-like—that wad we.—And ye see Jenny canna miss but to ken manners, and the like o' reading books, and sewing seams—having lived sae lang wi' a grand lady like

Lady Singleside; or if she disna ken ony thing about it, I 'm jealous that our bairns will like her a' the better.   And I 'll take care o' the bits o' claes, and what spending siller she maun hae, so the hundred pound may rin on in your hands, Mr. Protocol, and I 'll be adding something till 't, till she 'll may be get a Liddesdale joe that wants something to help to buy the hirsel.*—What d' ye say to that, hinny ?   I 'll take out a ticket for ye in the fly to Jethart—odd, but ye maun take a powny after that o'er the Limestane-rig—deil a wheeled carriage ever gaed into Liddesdale : †—And I 'll be very glad if Mrs. Rebecca comes wi' you, hinny, and stays a month or twa while ye 're stranger like.'

While Mrs. Rebecca was curtsying, and endeavouring to make the poor orphan girl curtsy instead of crying, and while Dandie, in his rough way, was encouraging them both, old Pleydell had recourse to his snuff-box.   ' It 's meat and drink to me, now, Colonel,' he said, as he recovered himself, ' to see a clown like this—I must gratify him in his own way, —must assist him to ruin himself—there 's no help for it.   Here, you Liddesdale—Dandie—Charlieshope—what do they call you ? '

The farmer turned, infinitely gratified even by

---

* The stock of sheep.

† The roads of Liddesdale, in Dandie Dinmont's days, could not be said to exist, and the district was only accessible through a succession of tremendous morasses.   About thirty years ago, the author himself was the first person who ever drove a little open carriage into these wilds : the excellent roads by which they are now traversed being then in some progress.   The people stared with no small wonder at a sight which many of them had never witnessed in their lives before.

this sort of notice; for in his heart, next to his own landlord, he honoured a lawyer in high practice.

'So you will not be advised against trying that question about your marches?'

'No—no, sir—naebody likes to lose their right, and to be laughed at down the haill water. But since your honour's no agreeable, and is may be a friend to the other side like, we maun try some other advocate.'

'There—I told you so, Colonel Mannering!— Well, sir, if you must needs be a fool, the business is to give you the luxury of a lawsuit at the least possible expense, and to bring you off conqueror if possible. Let Mr. Protocol send me your papers, and I will advise him how to conduct your cause. I don't see, after all, why you should not have your lawsuits too, and your feuds in the Court of Session, as well as your forefathers had their manslaughters and fire-raisings.'

'Very natural, to be sure, sir. We wad just take the auld gate as readily, if it werena for the law. And as the law binds us, the law should loose us. Besides, a man's aye the better thought o' in our country for having been afore the feifteen.'

'Excellently argued, my friend! Away with you, and send your papers to me.—Come, Colonel, we have no more to do here.'

'God, we'll ding Jock o' Dawston Cleugh now after a'!' said Dinmont, slapping his thigh in great exultation.

CHAPTER XXXIX

I am going to the parliament ;
You understand this bag : If you have any business
Depending there, be short, and let me hear it,
And pay your fees.

LITTLE FRENCH LAWYER.

'SHALL you be able to carry this honest fellow's cause for him ?' said Mannering.

'Why, I don't know; the battle is not to the strong, but he shall come off triumphant over Jock of Dawston if we can make it out. I owe him something. It is the pest of our profession, that we seldom see the best side of human nature. People come to us with every selfish feeling newly pointed and grinded; they turn down the very caulkers of their animosities and prejudices, as smiths do with horses' shoes in a white frost. Many a man has come to my garret yonder, that I have at first longed to pitch out at the window, and yet, at length, have discovered that he was only doing as I might have done in his case, being very angry, and, of course, very unreasonable. I have now satisfied myself, that if our profession sees more of human folly and human roguery than others, it is because we witness them acting in that channel in which they can most freely vent themselves. In civilized society, law is the chimney through which all that smoke discharges itself that used to circulate through the whole house, and put every one's eyes out — no wonder, therefore, that the vent itself should sometimes get a little sooty. But we will take care our Liddesdale-man's cause is well conducted and well argued, so all unnecessary expense will be saved — he shall have his pine-apple at wholesale price.'

'Will you do me the pleasure,' said Mannering, as they parted, 'to dine with me at my lodgings? my landlord says he has a bit of red-deer venison, and some excellent wine.'

'Venison—eh?' answered the counsellor alertly, but presently added—'But no! it's impossible— and I can't ask you home neither. Monday's a sacred day—so's Tuesday—and Wednesday, we are to be heard in the great teind case in presence —but stay—it's frosty weather, and if you don't leave town, and that venison would keep till Thursday——'

'You will dine with me that day?'

'Under certification.'

'Well, then, I will indulge a thought I had of spending a week here; and if the venison will not keep, why we will see what else our landlord can do for us.'

'O, the venison *will* keep,' said Pleydell; 'and now good-by—look at these two or three notes, and deliver them if you like the addresses. I wrote them for you this morning—farewell, my clerk has been waiting this hour to begin a d—d information.'—And away walked Mr. Pleydell with great activity, diving through closes and ascending covered stairs, in order to attain the High-Street by an access, which, compared to the common route, was what the Straits of Magellan are to the more open, but circuitous passage round Cape Horn.

On looking at the notes of introduction which Pleydell had thrust into his hand, Mannering was gratified with seeing that they were addressed to some of the first literary characters of Scotland. 'To David Hume, Esq.' 'To John Home, Esq.' 'To Dr. Ferguson.' 'To Dr. Black.' 'To Lord Kaimes.' 'To Mr. Hutton.' 'To John Clerk, Esq. of Eldin.' 'To Adam Smith, Esq.' 'To Dr. Robertson.'

'Upon my word, my legal friend has a good selection of acquaintances—these are names pretty widely blown indeed—an East-Indian must rub up his faculties a little, and put his mind in order, before he enters this sort of society.'

Mannering gladly availed himself of these introductions; and we regret deeply it is not in our power to give the reader an account of the pleasure and information which he received, in admission to a circle never closed against strangers of sense and information, and which has perhaps at no period been equalled, considering the depth and variety of talent which it embraced and concentrated.

Upon the Thursday appointed, Mr. Pleydell made his appearance at the inn where Colonel Mannering lodged. The venison proved in high order, the claret excellent, and the learned counsel, a professed amateur in the affairs of the table, did

distinguished honour to both. I am uncertain, however, if even the good cheer gave him more satisfaction than the presence of Dominie Sampson, from
whom, in his own juridical style of wit, he contrived to extract great amusement, both for himself and one or two friends whom the Colonel
regaled on the same occasion. The grave and
laconic simplicity of Sampson's answers to the
insidious questions of the barrister, placed the *bonhomie* of his character in a more luminous point
of view than Mannering had yet seen it. Upon
the same occasion he drew forth a strange quantity
of miscellaneous and abstruse, though, generally
speaking, useless learning. The lawyer afterwards
compared his mind to the magazine of a pawn-
broker, stowed with goods of every description,
but so cumbrously piled together, and in such
total disorganization, that the owner can never
lay his hands upon any one article at the moment
he has occasion for it.

As for the advocate himself, he afforded at least
as much exercise to Sampson as he extracted amusement from him. When the man of law began to
get into his altitudes, and his wit, naturally shrewd
and dry, became more lively and poignant, the
Dominie looked upon him with that sort of surprise
with which we can conceive a tame bear might
regard his future associate, the monkey, on their
being first introduced to each other. It was Mr.
Pleydell's delight to state in grave and serious argument some position which he knew the Dominie
would be inclined to dispute. He then beheld

with exquisite pleasure the internal labour with which the honest man arranged his ideas for reply, and tasked his inert and sluggish powers to bring up all the heavy artillery of his learning for demolishing the schismatic or heretical opinion which had been stated— -when, behold, before the ordnance could be discharged, the foe had quitted the post, and appeared in a new position of annoyance on the Dominie's flank or rear. Often did he exclaim 'Prodigious!' when, marching up to the enemy in full confidence of victory, he found the field evacuated, and it may be supposed that it cost him no little labour to attempt a new formation. 'He was like a native Indian army,' the Colonel said, 'formidable by numerical strength and size of ordnance, but liable to be thrown into irreparable confusion by a movement to take them in flank.'—On the whole, however, the Dominie, though somewhat fatigued with these mental exertions, made at unusual speed and upon the pressure of the moment, reckoned this one of the white days of his life, and always mentioned Mr. Pleydell as a very erudite and fa-ce-ti-ous person.

By degrees the rest of the party dropped off, and left these three gentlemen together. Their conversation turned to Mrs. Bertram's settlements. 'Now what could drive it into the noddle of that old harridan,' said Pleydell, 'to disinherit poor Lucy Bertram, under pretence of settling her property on a boy who has been so long dead and gone?—I ask your pardon, Mr. Sampson, I forgot what an affecting case this was for you—I remember taking your examination upon it—and I never had so much trouble to make any one speak three words consecutively—You may talk of your Pythagoreans, or your silent Bramins, Colonel,—go to, I tell you this learned gentleman beats them all in taciturnity—but the words of the wise are precious, and not to be thrown away lightly.'

'Of a surety,' said the Dominie, taking his blue-checqued handkerchief from his eyes, 'that was a bitter day with me indeed; ay, and a day of grief hard to be borne—but He giveth strength who layeth on the load.'

Colonel Mannering took this opportunity to request Mr. Pleydell to inform him of the particulars attending the loss of the boy; and the counsellor, who was fond of talking upon subjects of criminal jurisprudence, especially when connécted with his own experience, went through the circumstances at full length. 'And what is your opinion upon the result of the whole?'

'O, that Kennedy was murdered: it's an old case which has occurred on that coast before now—the case of Smuggler *versus* Exciseman.'

'What then is your conjecture concerning the fate of the child?'

'O, murdered too, doubtless,' answered Pleydell. 'He was old enough to tell what he had seen, and these ruthless scoundrels would not scruple committing a second Bethlehem massacre if they thought their interest required it.'

The Dominie groaned deeply, and ejaculated, 'Enormous!'

'Yet there was mention of gipsies in the business too, counsellor,' said Mannering, 'and from what that vulgar-looking fellow said after the funeral——'

'Mrs. Margaret Bertram's idea that the child was alive was founded upon the report of a gipsy,' said Pleydell, catching at the half-spoken hint—'I envy you the concatenation, Colonel—it is a shame to me not to have drawn the same conclusion. We'll follow this business up instantly—Here, hark ye, waiter, go down to Luckie Wood's in the Cowgate; ye'll find my clerk Driver; he'll be set down to High-Jinks by this time; (for we and our retainers, Colonel, are exceedingly regular in our irregularities;) tell him to come here instantly, and I will pay his forfeits.'

'He won't appear in character, will he?' said Mannering.

'Ah! no more of that, Hal, an thou lovest me,' said Pleydell. 'But we must have some news from the land of Egypt, if possible. O, if I had but hold of the slightest thread of this complicated skein, you should see how I would unravel it!—I would work the truth out of your Bohemian, as the French call them, better than a *Monitoire*, or a *Plainte de Tournelle*; I know how to manage a refractory witness.'

While Mr. Pleydell was thus vaunting his knowledge of his profession, the waiter re-entered with Mr. Driver, his mouth still greasy with mutton pies, and the froth of the last draught of twopenny yet unsubsided on his upper lip, with such speed had he obeyed the commands of his principal.—' Driver, you must go instantly and find out the woman who was old Mrs. Margaret Bertram's maid. Inquire for her every where, but if you find it necessary to have recourse to Protocol, Quid the tobacconist, or any other of these folks, you will take care not to appear yourself, but send some woman of your acquaintance—I dare say you know enough that may be so condescending as to oblige you. When you have found her out, engage her to come to my chambers to-morrow at eight o'clock precisely.'

' What shall I say to make her forthcoming ? ' asked the aide-de-camp.

' Any thing you choose,' replied the lawyer. ' Is it my business to make lies for you, do you think ? But let her be *in præsentia* by eight o'clock, as I have said before.' The clerk grinned, made his reverence, and exit.

' That 's a useful fellow,' said the counsellor ; ' I don't believe his match ever carried a process. He 'll write to my dictating three nights in the week without sleep, or, what 's the same thing, he writes as well and correctly when he 's asleep as when he 's awake. Then he 's such a steady fellow —some of them are always changing their ale-houses, so that they have twenty cadies sweating after them, like the bare-headed captains traversing the taverns of East-Cheap in search of Sir John Falstaff. But this is a complete fixture—he has his winter seat by the fire, and his summer seat by the window, in Luckie Wood's, betwixt which seats are his only migrations ; there he 's to be found at all times when he is off duty. It is my opinion he never puts off his clothes or goes to sleep—sheer ale supports him under every thing. It is meat, drink, and clothing, bed, board, and washing.'

'And is he always fit for duty upon a sudden turn-out? I should distrust it, considering his quarters.'

'O, drink never disturbs him, Colonel; he can write for hours after he cannot speak. I remember being called suddenly to draw an appeal case. I had been dining, and it was Saturday night, and I had ill will to begin to it—however, they got me down to Clerihugh's and there we sat birling till I had a fair tappit hen* under my belt, and then they persuaded me to draw the paper. Then we had to seek Driver, and it was all that two men could do to bear him in, for, when found, he was, as it happened, both motionless and speechless. But no sooner was his pen put between his fingers, his paper stretched before him, and he heard my voice, than he began to write like a scrivener—and, excepting that we were obliged to have somebody to dip his pen in the ink, for he could not see the standish, I never saw a thing scrolled more handsomely.'

'But how did your joint production look the next morning?' said the Colonel.

'Wheugh! capital — not three words required to be altered;† it was sent off by that day's post.

---

* See Note F. Tappit Hen.
† See Note G. Convivial Habits of the Scottish Bar.

But you'll come and breakfast with me to-morrow, and hear this woman's examination?'

'Why, your hour is rather early.'

'Can't make it later. If I were not on the boards of the outer-house precisely as the nine-hours bell rings, there would be a report that I had got an apoplexy, and I should feel the effects of it all the rest of the session.'

'Well, I will make an exertion to wait upon you.'

Here the company broke up for the evening.

In the morning Colonel Mannering appeared at the counsellor's chambers, although cursing the raw air of a Scottish morning in December. Mr. Pleydell had got Mrs. Rebecca installed on one side of his fire, accommodated her with a cup of chocolate, and was already deeply engaged in conversation with her. 'O, no, I assure you, Mrs. Rebecca, there is no intention to challenge your mistress's will; and I give you my word of honour that your legacy is quite safe. You have deserved it by your conduct to your mistress, and I wish it had been twice as much.'

'Why, to be sure, sir, it's no right to mention what is said before ane—ye heard how that dirty body Quid cast up to me the bits o' compliments he gied me, and tell'd ower again ony loose cracks I might hae had wi' him; now if ane was talking loosely to your honour, there's nae saying what might come o't.'

'I assure you, my good Rebecca, my character and your own age and appearance are your security, if you should talk as loosely as an amatory poet.'

'Aweel, if your honour thinks I am safe—the story is just this.—Ye see, about a year ago, or no just sae lang, my leddy was advised to go to Gilsland for a while, for her spirits were distressing her sair. Ellangowan's troubles began to be spoken o' publicly, and sair vexed she was—for she was proud o' her family. For Ellangowan himsell and her, they sometimes 'greed, and sometimes no—but at last they didna 'gree at a' for twa or three year— for he was aye wanting to borrow siller, and that was what she couldna bide at no hand, and she was aye wanting it paid back again, and that the Laird he liked as little. So, at last, they were clean aff thegither. And then some of the company at Gilsland tells her that the estate was to be sell'd; and ye wad hae thought she had taen an ill will at Miss Lucy Bertram frae that moment, for mony a time she cried to me, " O Becky, O Becky, if that useless peenging thing o' a lassie there, at Ellangowan, that canna keep her ne'er-do-weel father within bounds — if she had been but a lad-bairn, they couldna hae sell'd the auld inheritance for that fool-body's debts ';—and she would rin on that way till I was just wearied and sick to hear her ban the puir lassie, as if she wadna hae been a lad-bairn, and keepit the land, if it had been in her will to change her sect. And ae day at the spaw-well below the craig at Gilsland, she was seeing a very bonny family o' bairns—they belanged to ane Mac-Crosky—and she broke out—" Is not it an odd like

thing that ilka waf carle * in the country has a
son and heir, and that the house of Ellangowan is
without male succession ? " There was a gipsy
wife stood ahint and heard her—a muckle sture
fearsome - looking wife she was as ever I set een
on.—"Wha is it," says she, "that dare say the
house of Ellangowan will perish without male succession ? " My mistress just turned on her—she
was a high-spirited woman, and aye ready wi' an
answer to a' body. " It's me that says it," says
she, "that may say it with a sad heart." Wi'
that the gipsy wife gripped till her hand; " I ken
you weel eneuch," says she, " though ye kenna
me—But as sure as that sun's in heaven, and as
sure as that water's rinning to the sea, and as
sure as there's an ee that sees, and an ear that
hears us baith—Harry Bertram, that was thought
to perish at Warroch Point, never did die there—
he was to have a weary weird o't till his ane-
and - twentieth year, that was aye said o' him—
but if ye live and I live, ye'll hear mair o' him
this winter before the snaw lies twa days on the
Dun of Singleside—I want nane o' your siller," she
said, "to make ye think I am blearing your ee—
fare ye weel till after Martinmas";—and there she
left us standing.'

'Was she a very tall woman?' interrupted
Mannering.

'Had she black hair, black eyes, and a cut above
the brow?' added the lawyer.

---

* Every insignificant churl.

'She was the tallest woman I ever saw, and her hair was as black as midnight, unless where it was grey, and she had a scar abune the brow, that ye might hae laid the lith of your finger in. Naebody that's seen her will ever forget her; and I am morally sure that it was on the ground o' what that gipsy-woman said that my mistress made her will, having taen a dislike at the young leddy o' Ellangowan; and she liked her far waur after she was obliged to send her £20—for she said, Miss Bertram, no content wi' letting the Ellangowan property pass into strange hands, owing to her being a lass and no a lad, was coming, by her poverty, to be a burden and a disgrace to Singleside too.—But I hope my mistress's is a good will for a' that, for it would be hard on me to lose the wee bit legacy—I served for little fee and bountith, weel I wot.'

The counsellor relieved her fears on this head, then inquired after Jenny Gibson, and understood she had accepted Mr. Dinmont's offer; 'and I have done sae mysell too, since he was sae discreet as to ask me,' said Mrs. Rebecca; 'they are very decent folk the Dinmonts, though my lady didna dow to hear muckle about the friends on that side the house. But she liked the Charlies-hope hams, and the cheeses, and the muir-fowl, that they were aye sending, and the lamb's-wool hose and mittens —she liked them weel eneuch.'

Mr. Pleydell now dismissed Mrs. Rebecca. When she was gone, 'I think I know the gipsy woman,' said the lawyer.

'I was just going to say the same,' replied Mannering.

'And her name,' said Pleydell——

'Is Meg Merrilies,' answered the Colonel.

'Are you avised of that?' said the counsellor, looking at his military friend with a comic expression of surprise.

Mannering answered, that he had known such a woman when he was at Ellangowan upwards of twenty years before; and then made his learned friend acquainted with all the remarkable particulars of his first visit there.

Mr. Pleydell listened with great attention, and then replied, 'I congratulated myself upon having made the acquaintance of a profound theologian in your chaplain; but I really did not expect to find a pupil of Albumazar or Messahala in his patron. I have a notion, however, this gipsy could tell us some more of the matter than she derives from astrology or second-sight—I had her through hands once, and could then make little of her, but I must write to Mac-Morlan to stir heaven and earth to find her out. I will gladly come to —— shire myself to assist at her examination—I am still in the commission of the peace there, though I have ceased to be sheriff—I never had anything more at heart in my life than tracing that murder, and the fate of the child. I must write to the Sheriff of Roxburghshire too, and to an active justice of peace in Cumberland.'

'I hope when you come to the country you will make Woodbourne your head-quarters?'

'Certainly; I was afraid you were going to forbid me—but we must go to breakfast now, or I shall be too late.'

On the following day the new friends parted, and the Colonel rejoined his family without any adventure worthy of being detailed in these chapters.

CHAPTER XL

Can no rest find me, no private place secure me,
But still my miseries like bloodhounds haunt me ?
Unfortunate young man, which way now guides thee,
Guides thee from death ?   The country's laid around for thee.
WOMEN PLEASED.

OUR narrative now recalls us for a moment to the
period when young Hazlewood received his wound.
That accident had no sooner happened, than the
consequences to Miss Mannering and to himself
rushed upon Brown's mind. From the manner in
which the muzzle of the piece was pointed when
it went off, he had no great fear that the consequences would be fatal. But an arrest in a strange
country, and while he was unprovided with any
means of establishing his rank and character, was
at least to be avoided. He therefore resolved to
escape for the present to the neighbouring coast of
England, and to remain concealed there, if possible,
until he should receive letters from his regimental
friends, and remittances from his agent; and then
to resume his own character, and offer to young
Hazlewood and his friends any explanation or satisfaction they might desire. With this purpose he
walked stoutly forward, after leaving the spot where
the accident had happened, and reached without
adventure the village which we have called Portan-

ferry, (but which the reader will in vain seek for under that name in the county map.) A large open boat was just about to leave the quay, bound for the little seaport of Allonby, in Cumberland. In this vessel Brown embarked, and resolved to make that place his temporary abode, until he should receive letters and money from England.

In the course of their short voyage he entered into some conversation with the steersman, who was also owner of the boat, a jolly old man, who had occasionally been engaged in the smuggling trade, like most fishers on the coast. After talking about objects of less interest, Brown endeavoured to turn the discourse toward the Mannering family. The sailor had heard of the attack upon the house at Woodbourne, but disapproved of the smugglers' proceedings.

'Hands off is fair play; zounds, they 'll bring the whole country down upon them—na, na! when I was in that way I played at giff-gaff with the officers—here a cargo taen—vera weel, that was their luck;—there another carried clean through, that was mine—na, na! hawks shouldna pike out hawks een.'

'And this Colonel Mannering?' said Brown.

'Troth, he 's nae wise man neither, to interfere—no that I blame him for saving the gaugers' lives—that was very right; but it wasna like a gentleman to be fighting about the poor folk's pocks o' tea and brandy kegs—however, he 's a grand man and an officer man, and they do what they like wi' the like o' us.'

'And his daughter,' said Brown, with a throbbing heart, 'is going to be married into a great family too, as I have heard?'

'What, into the Hazlewoods'?' said the pilot. 'Na, na, that's but idle clashes—every Sabbath day, as regularly as it came round, did the young man ride hame wi' the daughter of the late Ellangowan—and my daughter Peggy's in the service up at Woodbourne, and she says she's sure young Hazlewood thinks nae mair of Miss Mannering than you do.'

Bitterly censuring his own precipitate adoption of a contrary belief, Brown yet heard with delight that the suspicions of Julia's fidelity, upon which he had so rashly acted, were probably void of foundation. How must he in the meantime be suffering in her opinion? or what could she suppose of conduct, which must have made him appear to her regardless alike of her peace of mind, and of the interests of their affection? The old man's connexion with the family at Woodbourne seemed to offer a safe mode of communication, of which he determined to avail himself.

'Your daughter is a maid-servant at Woodbourne?—I knew Miss Mannering in India, and though I am at present in an inferior rank of life, I have great reason to hope she would interest herself in my favour. I had a quarrel unfortunately with her father, who was my commanding officer, and I am sure the young lady would endeavour to reconcile him to me. Perhaps your daughter could deliver a letter to her upon the subject, without making mischief between her father and her ? '

The old man, a friend to smuggling of every kind, readily answered for the letter's being faithfully and secretly delivered; and, accordingly, as soon as they arrived at Allonby, Brown wrote to Miss Mannering, stating the utmost contrition for what had happened through his rashness, and conjuring her to let him have an opportunity of pleading his own cause, and obtaining forgiveness for his indiscretion. He did not judge it safe to go into any detail concerning the circumstances by which he had been misled, and upon the whole endeavoured to express himself with such ambiguity, that if the letter should fall into wrong hands, it would be difficult either to understand its real purport, or to trace the writer. This letter the old man undertook faithfully to deliver to his daughter at Woodbourne; and, as his trade would speedily again bring him or his boat to Allonby, he promised farther to take charge of any answer with which the young lady might intrust him.

And now our persecuted traveller landed at Allonby, and sought for such accommodations as might at once suit his temporary poverty, and his desire of remaining as much unobserved as possible. With this view he assumed the name and profession of his friend Dudley, having command enough of the pencil to verify his pretended character to his host of Allonby. His baggage he pretended to expect from Wigton; and keeping himself as much within doors as possible, awaited the return of the letters which he had sent to his agent, to Delaserre, and to his Lieutenant-Colonel. From the first he requested a supply of money; he conjured Delaserre, if possible, to join him in Scotland; and from the Lieutenant-Colonel he required such testimony of his rank and conduct in the regiment, as should place his character as a gentleman and officer beyond the power of question. The inconvenience of being run short in his finances struck him so strongly, that he wrote to Dinmont on that subject, requesting a small temporary loan, having no doubt that, being within sixty or seventy miles of his residence, he should receive a speedy as well as favourable answer to his request of pecuniary accommodation, which was owing, as he stated, to his having been robbed after their parting. And then, with impatience enough, though without any serious apprehension, he waited the answers of these various letters.

It must be observed, in excuse of his correspondents, that the post was then much more tardy than since Mr. Palmer's ingenious invention has taken place; and with respect to honest Dinmont in particular, as he rarely received above one letter a-quarter, (unless during the time of his being engaged in a law-suit, when he regularly sent to the post-town,) his correspondence usually remained for a month or two sticking in the postmaster's window, among pamphlets, gingerbread, rolls, or ballads, according to the trade which the said postmaster exercised. Besides, there was then a custom, not yet wholly obsolete, of causing a letter, from

one town to another, perhaps within the distance of
thirty miles, perform a circuit of two hundred miles
before delivery; which had the combined advantage
of airing the epistle thoroughly, of adding some
pence to the revenue of the post-office, and of exer-
cising the patience of the correspondents. Owing
to these circumstances, Brown remained several days
in Allonby without any answers whatever, and his
stock of money, though husbanded with the utmost
economy, began to wear very low, when he received,
by the hands of a young fisherman, the following
letter :—

'You have acted with the most cruel indiscretion; you have shown how little I can trust to your
declarations that my peace and happiness are dear
to you; and your rashness has nearly occasioned
the death of a young man of the highest worth and
honour. Must I say more?—must I add, that I
have been myself very ill in consequence of your
violence, and its effects? And, alas! need I say
still farther, that I have thought anxiously upon
them as they are likely to affect you, although you
have given me such slight cause to do so? The
C. is gone from home for several days; Mr. H. is
almost quite recovered; and I have reason to think
that the blame is laid in a quarter different from
that where it is deserved. Yet do not think of
venturing here. Our fate has been crossed by
accidents of a nature too violent and terrible to
permit me to think of renewing a correspondence
which has so often threatened the most dreadful

catastrophe. Farewell, therefore, and believe that no one can wish your happiness more sincerely than
'J. M.'

This letter contained that species of advice, which is frequently given for the precise purpose that it may lead to a directly opposite conduct from that which it recommends. At least so thought Brown, who immediately asked the young fisherman if he came from Portanferry.

'Ay,' said the lad; 'I am auld Willie Johnstone's son, and I got that letter frae my sister Peggy, that's laundry-maid at Woodbourne.'

'My good friend, when do you sail?'

'With the tide this evening.'

'I'll return with you; but as I do not desire to go to Portanferry, I wish you could put me on shore somewhere on the coast.'

'We can easily do that,' said the lad.

Although the price of provisions, etc., was then very moderate, the discharging his lodgings, and the expense of his living, together with that of a change of dress, which safety as well as a proper regard to his external appearance · rendered necessary, brought Brown's purse to a very low ebb. He left directions at the post-office that his letters should be forwarded to Kippletringan, whither he resolved to proceed, and reclaim the treasure which he had deposited in the hands of Mrs. Mac-Candlish. He also felt it would be his duty to assume his proper character as soon as he should receive the necessary evidence for supporting it, and, as an officer in the king's service, give and receive every explanation which might be necessary with young Hazlewood. If he is not very wrong-headed indeed, he thought, he must allow the manner in which I acted to have been the necessary consequence of his own overbearing conduct.

And now we must suppose him once more embarked on the Solway frith. The wind was adverse, attended by some rain, and they struggled against it without much assistance from the tide. The boat was heavily laden with goods, (part of which were probably contraband), and laboured deep in the sea. Brown, who had been bred a sailor, and was indeed skilled in most athletic exercises, gave his powerful and effectual assistance in rowing, or occasionally in steering the boat, and his advice in the management, which became the more delicate as the wind increased, and, being opposed to the very rapid tides of that coast, made the voyage perilous. At length, after spending the whole night upon the frith, they were at morning within sight of a beautiful bay upon the Scottish coast. The weather was now more mild. The snow, which had been for some time waning, had given way entirely under the fresh gale of the preceding night. The more distant hills, indeed, retained their snowy mantle, but all the open country was cleared, unless where a few white patches indicated that it had been drifted to an uncommon depth. Even under its wintry appearance, the shore was highly interesting. The line of sea-coast, with all its varied curves, indentures, and embayments, swept away from the

sight on either hand, in that varied, intricate, yet graceful and easy line, which the eye loves so well to pursue. And it was no less relieved and varied in elevation than in outline, by the different forms of the shore; the beach in some places being edged by steep rocks, and in others rising smoothly from the sands in easy and swelling slopes. Buildings of different kinds caught and reflected the wintry sunbeams of a December morning, and the woods, though now leafless, gave relief and variety to the landscape. Brown felt that lively and awakening interest which taste and sensibility always derive from the beauties of nature, when opening suddenly to the eye, after the dulness and gloom of a night voyage. Perhaps,—for who can presume to analyze that inexplicable feeling which binds the person born in a mountainous country to his native hills,— perhaps some early associations, retaining their effect long after the cause was forgotten, mingled in the feelings of pleasure with which he regarded the scene before him.

'And what,' said Brown to the boatman, 'is the name of that fine cape, that stretches into the sea with its sloping banks and hillocks of wood, and forms the right side of the bay?'

'Warroch Point,' answered the lad.

'And that old castle, my friend, with the modern house situated just beneath it? It seems at this distance a very large building.'

'That's the Auld Place, sir; and that's the New Place below it. We'll land you there if you like.'

' I should like it of all things. I must visit that ruin before I continue my journey.'

' Ay, it 's a queer auld bit,' said the fisherman ; ' and that highest tower is a gude land - mark as far as Ramsey in Man, and the Point of Ayr— there was muckle fighting about the place lang syne.'

Brown would have inquired into farther particulars, but a fisherman is seldom an antiquary. His boatman's local knowledge was summed up in the information already given, ' that it was a grand land-mark, and that there had been muckle fighting about the bit lang syne.'

' I shall learn more of it,' said Brown to himself, ' when I get ashore.'

The boat continued its course close under the point upon which the castle was situated, which frowned from the summit of its rocky site upon the still agitated waves of the bay beneath. ' I believe,' said the steersman, ' ye 'll get ashore here as dry as ony gate. There 's a place where their berlins and galleys, as they ca'd them, used to lie in lang syne, but it 's no used now, because it 's ill carrying gudes up the narrow stairs, or ower the rocks. Whiles of a moonlight night I have landed article there, though.'

While he thus spoke, they pulled round a point of rock, and found a very small harbour, partly formed by nature, partly by the indefatigable labour of the ancient inhabitants of the castle, who, as the fisherman observed, had found it essential for the protection of their boats and small craft, though it could not receive vessels of any burden. The two points of rock which formed the access approached each other so nearly, that only one boat could enter at a time. On each side were still remaining two immense iron rings, deeply morticed into the solid rock. Through these, according to tradition, there was nightly drawn a huge chain, secured by an immense padlock, for the protection of the haven, and the armada which it contained. A ledge of rock had, by the assistance of the chisel and pick-axe, been formed into a sort of quay. The rock was of extremely hard consistence, and the task so difficult, that, according to the fisherman, a labourer who wrought at the work might in the evening have carried home in his bonnet all the shivers which he had struck from the mass in the course of the day. This little quay communicated with a rude staircase, already repeatedly mentioned, which descended from the old castle. There was also a communication between the beach and the quay, by scrambling over the rocks.

'Ye had better land here,' said the lad, 'for the surf's running high at the Shellicoat-stane, and there will no be a dry thread amang us or we get the cargo out.—Na! na! (in answer to an offer of money) ye have wrought for your passage, and wrought far better than ony o' us. Gude day to ye: I wuss ye weel.'

So saying, he pushed off in order to land his cargo on the opposite side of the bay; and Brown, with a small bundle in his hand, containing the trifling stock of necessaries which he had been obliged to purchase at Allonby, was left on the rocks beneath the ruin.

And thus, unconscious as the most absolute stranger, and in circumstances, which, if not destitute, were for the present highly embarrassing; without the countenance of a friend within the circle of several hundred miles; accused of a heavy crime, and, what was as bad as all the rest, being nearly penniless, did the harassed wanderer for the first time, after the interval of so many years, approach the remains of the castle, where his ancestors had exercised all but regal dominion.

CHAPTER XLI

Yes, ye moss-green walls,
Ye towers defenceless, I revisit ye
Shame-stricken !   Where are all your trophies now ?
Your throngèd courts, the revelry, the tumult,
That spoke the grandeur of my house, the homage
Of neighbouring Barons ?

MYSTERIOUS MOTHER.

ENTERING the castle of Ellangowan by a postern
door-way, which showed symptoms of having been
once secured with the most jealous care, Brown
(whom, since he has set foot upon the property of
his fathers, we shall hereafter call by his father's
name of Bertram) wandered from one ruined apartment to another, surprised at the massive strength
of some parts of the building, the rude and impressive magnificence of others, and the great extent of
the whole.   In two of these rooms, close beside each
other, he saw signs of recent habitation.   In one
small apartment were empty bottles, half-gnawed
bones, and dried fragments of bread.   In the vault
which adjoined, and which was defended by a strong
door, then left open, he observed a considerable
quantity of straw, and in both were the relics of
recent fires.   How little was it possible for Bertram
to conceive, that such trivial circumstances were

closely connected with incidents, affecting his prosperity, his honour, perhaps his life!

After satisfying his curiosity by a hasty glance through the interior of the castle, Bertram now advanced through the great gate-way which opened to the land, and paused to look upon the noble landscape which it commanded. Having in vain endeavoured to guess the position of Woodbourne, and having nearly ascertained that of Kippletringan, he turned to take a parting look at the stately ruins which he had just traversed. He admired the massive and picturesque effect of the huge round towers, which, flanking the gateway, gave a double portion of depth and majesty to the high yet gloomy arch under which it opened. The carved stone escutcheon of the ancient family, bearing for their arms three wolves' heads, was hung diagonally beneath the helmet and crest, the latter being a wolf couchant pierced with an arrow. On either side stood as supporters, in full human size, or larger, a salvage man *proper*, to use the language of heraldry, *wreathed and cinctured*, and holding in his hand an oak tree *eradicated*, that is, torn up by the roots.

And the powerful barons who owned this blazonry, thought Bertram, pursuing the usual train of ideas which flows upon the mind at such scenes, — do their posterity continue to possess the lands which they had laboured to fortify so strongly? or are they wanderers, ignorant perhaps even of the fame or power of their forefathers, while their hereditary possessions are held by a race of strangers?

Why is it, he thought, continuing to follow out the succession of ideas which the scene prompted— Why is it that some scenes awaken thoughts, which belong as it were to dreams of early and shadowy recollection, such as my old Bramin Moonshie would have ascribed to a state of previous existence? Is it the visions of our sleep that float confusedly in our memory, and are recalled by the appearance of such real objects as in any respect correspond to the phantoms they presented to our imagination? How often do we find ourselves in society which we have never before met, and yet feel impressed with a mysterious and ill-defined consciousness, that neither the scene, the speakers, nor the subject are entirely new; nay, feel as if we could anticipate that part of the conversation which has not yet taken place! It is even so with me while I gaze upon that ruin; nor can I divest myself of the idea, that these massive towers, and that dark gate-way, retiring through its deep-vaulted and ribbed arches, and dimly lighted by the court-yard beyond, are not entirely strange to me. Can it be that they have been familiar to me in infancy, and that I am to seek in their vicinity those friends of whom my childhood has still a tender though faint remembrance, and whom I early exchanged for such severe task-masters? Yet Brown, who I think would not have deceived me, always told me I was brought off from the eastern coast, after a skirmish in which my father was killed; and I do remember enough of a horrid scene of violence to strengthen his account.—

It happened that the spot upon which young Bertram chanced to station himself for the better viewing the castle, was nearly the same on which his father had died. It was marked by a large old oak-tree, the only one on the esplanade, and which, having been used for executions by the barons of Ellangowan, was called the Justice-Tree. It chanced, and the coincidence was remarkable, that Glossin was this morning engaged with a person, whom he was in the habit of consulting in such matters, concerning some projected repairs, and a large addition to the house of Ellangowan, and that, having no great pleasure in remains so intimately connected with the grandeur of the former inhabitants, he had resolved to use the stones of the ruinous castle in his new edifice. Accordingly he came up the bank, followed by the land-surveyor mentioned on a former occasion, who was also in the habit of acting as a sort of architect in case of necessity. In drawing the plans, etc., Glossin was in the custom of relying upon his own skill. Bertram's back was towards them as they came up the ascent, and he was quite shrouded by the branches of the large tree, so that Glossin was not aware of the presence of the stranger till he was close upon him.

' Yes, sir, as I have often said before to you, the Old Place is a perfect quarry of hewn stone, and it would be better for the estate if it were all down, since it is only a den for smugglers.' At this instant Bertram turned short round upon

Glossin at the distance of two yards only, and said —' Would you destroy this fine old castle, sir ? '

His face, person, and voice, were so exactly those of his father in his best days, that Glossin, hearing his exclamation, and seeing such a sudden apparition in the shape of his patron, and on nearly the very spot where he had expired, almost thought the grave had given up its dead !—He staggered back two or three paces, as if he had received a sudden and deadly wound. He instantly recovered, however, his presence of mind, stimulated by the thrilling reflection that it was no inhabitant of the other world which stood before him, but an injured man, whom the slightest want of dexterity on his part might lead to acquaintance with his rights, and the means of asserting them to his utter destruction. Yet his ideas were so much confused by the shock he had received, that his first question partook of the alarm.

' In the name of God how came you here ! ' said Glossin.

' How came I here ? ' repeated Bertram, surprised at the solemnity of the address. ' I landed a quarter of an hour since in the little harbour beneath the castle, and was employing a moment's leisure in viewing these fine ruins. I trust there is no intrusion ? '

' Intrusion, sir ?—no, sir,' said Glossin, in some degree recovering his breath, and then whispered a few words into his companion's ear, who imme-

diately left him and descended towards the house.
' Intrusion, sir?—no, sir,—you or any gentleman
are welcome to satisfy your curiosity.'

' I thank you, sir,' said Bertram.   ' They call this
the Old Place, I am informed?'

' Yes, sir; in distinction to the New Place, my
house there below.'

Glossin, it must be remarked, was, during the
following dialogue, on the one hand eager to learn
what local recollections young Bertram had retained
of the scenes of his infancy, and, on the other,
compelled to be extremely cautious in his replies,
lest he should awaken or assist, by some name,
phrase, or anecdote, the slumbering train of association.   He suffered, indeed, during the whole scene,
the agonies which he so richly deserved; yet his
pride and interest, like the fortitude of a North
American Indian, manned him to sustain the
tortures inflicted at once by the contending stings
of a guilty conscience, of hatred, of fear, and of
suspicion.

' I wish to ask the name, sir,' said Bertram, ' of
the family to whom this stately ruin belongs?'

' It is my property, sir; my name is Glossin.'

' Glossin—Glossin?' repeated Bertram, as if the
answer were somewhat different from what he
expected; ' I beg your pardon, Mr. Glossin; I am
apt to be very absent.—May I ask if the castle has
been long in your family?'

' It was built, I believe, long ago, by a family
called Mac-Dingawaie,' answered Glossin; suppress-
ing for obvious reasons the more familiar sound of

Bertram, which might have awakened the recollections which he was anxious to lull to rest, and slurring with an evasive answer the question concerning the endurance of his own possession.

'And how do you read the half-defaced motto, sir,' said Bertram, 'which is upon that scroll above the entablature with the arms?'

'I—I—I really do not exactly know,' replied Glossin.

'I should be apt to make it out, *Our Right makes our Might.*'

'I believe it is something of that kind,' said Glossin.

'May I ask, sir,' said the stranger, 'if it is your family motto?'

'N—n—no—no—not ours. That is, I believe, the motto of the former people—mine is—mine is—in fact I have had some correspondence with Mr. Cumming of the Lyon Office in Edinburgh, about mine. He writes me the Glossins anciently bore for a motto, "He who takes it, makes it."'

'If there be any uncertainty, sir, and the case were mine,' said Bertram, 'I would assume the old motto, which seems to me the better of the two.'

Glossin, whose tongue by this time clove to the roof of his mouth, only answered by a nod.

'It is odd enough,' said Bertram, fixing his eye upon the arms and gate-way, and partly addressing Glossin, partly as it were thinking aloud—'it is odd the tricks which our memory plays us. The remnants of an old prophecy, or song, or rhyme, of some kind or other, return to my recollection on hearing that motto — stay — it is a strange jingle of sounds :

> "The dark shall be light,
> And the wrong made right,
> When Bertram's right and Bertram's might
> Shall meet on——"

I cannot remember the last line—on some particular *height*—height is the rhyme, I am sure; but I cannot hit upon the preceding word.'

' Confound your memory,' muttered Glossin; ' you remember by far too much of it ! '

' There are other rhymes connected with these early recollections,' continued the young man : ' Pray, sir, is there any song current in this part of the world respecting a daughter of the King of the Isle of Man eloping with a Scottish knight ? '

' I am the worst person in the world to consult upon legendary antiquities,' answered Glossin.

' I could sing such a ballad,' said Bertram, ' from one end to another, when I was a boy. You must know I left Scotland, which is my native country, very young, and those who brought me up discouraged all my attempts to preserve recollection of my native land, on account, I believe, of a boyish wish which I had to escape from their charge.'

' Very natural,' said Glossin, but speaking as if his utmost efforts were unable to unseal his lips beyond the width of a quarter of an inch, so that his whole utterance was a kind of compressed muttering, very different from the round bold bullying voice with which he usually spoke. Indeed his appearance and demeanour during all this conversation seemed to diminish even his strength and stature; so that he appeared to wither into the shadow of himself, now advancing one foot, now the other, now stooping and wriggling his shoulders, now fumbling with the buttons of his waistcoat, now clasping his hands together,—in short, he was the picture of a mean-spirited shuffling rascal in the very agonies of detection. To these appearances Bertram was totally inattentive, being dragged on as it were by the current of his own associations. Indeed, although he addressed Glossin, he was not so much thinking of him, as arguing upon the embarrassing state of his own feelings and recollection. 'Yes,' he said, 'I preserved my language among the sailors, most of whom spoke English, and when I could get into a corner by myself, I used to sing all that song over from beginning to end—I have forgot it all now—but I remember the tune well, though I cannot guess what should at present so strongly recall it to my memory.'

He took his flageolet from his pocket, and played a simple melody. Apparently the tune awoke the corresponding associations of a damsel, who, close beside a fine spring about half way down the descent, and which had once supplied the castle with water, was engaged in bleaching linen. She immediately took up the song:

> ' Are these the Links of Forth, she said,
>   Or are they the crooks of Dee,
>   Or the bonnie woods of Warroch-head
>   That I so fain would see ? '

'By heaven,' said Bertram, 'it is the very ballad! I must learn these words from the girl.'

Confusion! thought Glossin; if I cannot put a stop to this, all will be out. O the devil take all ballads, and ballad-makers, and ballad-singers! and that d——d jade too, to set up her pipe!—'You will have time enough for this on some other occasion,' he said aloud; 'at present'—(for now he saw his emissary with two or three men coming up the bank,) 'at present we must have some more serious conversation together.'

'How do you mean, sir?' said Bertram, turning short upon him, and not liking the tone which he made use of.

'Why, sir, as to that—I believe your name is Brown?' said Glossin.

'And what of that, sir?'

Glossin looked over his shoulder to see how near his party had approached; they were coming fast on. 'Vanbeest Brown? if I mistake not.'

'And what of that, sir?' said Bertram, with increasing astonishment and displeasure.

'Why, in that case,' said Glossin, observing his friends had now got upon the level space close beside them—'in that case you are my prisoner in the king's name!'—At the same time he stretched his hand towards Bertram's collar, while two of the men who had come up seized upon his arms; he shook himself, however, free of their grasp by a violent effort, in which he pitched the most per-tinacious down the bank, and, drawing his cutlass, stood on the defensive, while those who had felt his strength recoiled from his presence, and gazed at a safe distance. 'Observe,' he called out at the same time, 'that I have no purpose to resist legal authority; satisfy me that you have a magistrate's warrant, and are authorised to make this arrest, and I will obey it quietly; but let no man who loves his life venture to approach me, till I am satisfied for what crime, and by whose authority, I am apprehended.'

Glossin then caused one of the officers to show a warrant for the apprehension of Vanbeest Brown, accused of the crime of wilfully and maliciously shooting at Charles Hazlewood, younger of Hazlewood, with an intent to kill, and also of other crimes and misdemeanours, and which appointed him, having been so apprehended, to be brought before the next magistrate for examination. The warrant being formal, and the fact such as he could not deny, Bertram threw down his weapon, and submitted himself to the officers, who, flying on him with eagerness corresponding to their former pusillanimity, were about to load him with irons, alleging the strength and activity which he had displayed, as a justification of this severity. But Glossin was ashamed or afraid to permit this unnecessary insult, and directed the prisoner to be treated with all the decency, and even respect, that was consistent with safety. Afraid, however, to introduce him into his own house, where still further subjects of recollection might have been suggested, and anxious at the same time to cover his own proceedings by the sanction of another's authority, he ordered his carriage (for he had lately set up a carriage) to be got ready, and in the meantime directed refreshments to be given to the prisoner and the officers, who were consigned to one of the rooms in the old castle, until the means of conveyance for examination before a magistrate should be provided.

CHAPTER XLII

Bring in the evidence——
Thou robed man of justice, take thy place,
And thou, his yoke-fellow of equity,
Bench by his side—you are of the commission,
Sit you too.

KING LEAR.

WHILE the carriage was getting ready, Glossin had a letter to compose, about which he wasted no small time. It was to his neighbour, as he was fond of calling him, Sir Robert Hazlewood of Hazlewood, the head of an ancient and powerful interest in the county, which had in the decadence of the Ellangowan family gradually succeeded to much of their authority and influence. The present representative of the family was an elderly man, dotingly fond of his own family, which was limited to an only son and daughter, and stoically indifferent to the fate of all mankind besides. For the rest, he was honourable in his general dealings, because he was afraid to suffer the censure of the world, and just from a better motive. He was presumptuously over-conceited on the score of family pride and importance, a feeling considerably enhanced by his late succession to the title of a Nova Scotia Baronet; and he hated the memory of the Ellangowan family, though now a memory only, because a certain baron of that house was traditionally reported to have caused the founder of the Hazlewood family hold his stirrup until he mounted into his saddle. In his general deportment he was pompous and important, affecting a species of florid elocution, which often became ridiculous from his misarranging the triads and quaternions with which he loaded his sentences.

To this personage Glossin was now to write in such a conciliatory style as might be most acceptable to his vanity and family pride, and the following was the form of his note.

' Mr. Gilbert Glossin ' (he longed to add of Ellangowan, but prudence prevailed, and he suppressed that territorial designation)—' Mr. Gilbert Glossin has the honour to offer his most respectful compliments to Sir Robert Hazlewood, and to inform him, that he has this morning been fortunate enough to secure the person who wounded Mr. C. Hazlewood. As Sir Robert Hazlewood may probably choose to conduct the examination of this criminal himself, Mr. G. Glossin will cause the man to be carried to the inn at Kippletringan, or to Hazlewood - house, as Sir Robert Hazlewood may be pleased to direct: And, with Sir Robert Hazlewood's permission, Mr. G. Glossin will attend him at either of these places with the proofs and declarations which he has been so fortunate as to collect respecting this atrocious business.'

Addressed,

' SIR ROBERT HAZLEWOOD of Hazlewood, Bart.

' Hazlewood-house, etc. etc.

' ELL^{N.} G^{N.}, Tuesday.'

This note he dispatched by a servant on horse-back, and having given the man some time to get a-head, and desired him to ride fast, he ordered two officers of justice to get into the carriage with Bertram; and he himself, mounting his horse, accompanied them at a slow pace to the point where the roads to Kippletringan and Hazlewood-house separated, and there awaited the return of his messenger, in order that his farther route might be determined by the answer he should receive from the Baronet. In about half an hour his servant returned with the following answer, hand-somely folded, and sealed with the Hazlewood arms, having the Nova Scotia badge depending from the shield.

'Sir Robert Hazlewood of Hazlewood returns Mr. G. Glossin's compliments, and thanks him for the trouble he has taken in a matter affecting the safety of Sir Robert's family. Sir R. H. requests Mr. G. G. will have the goodness to bring the prisoner to Hazlewood-house for examination, with the other proofs or declarations which he mentions. And after the business is over, in case Mr. G. G. is not otherwise engaged, Sir R. and Lady Hazle-wood request his company to dinner.'

Addressed,

'MR. GILBERT GLOSSIN, etc.

' HAZLEWOOD-HOUSE, }
    Tuesday.'   }

Soh! thought Mr. Glossin, here is one finger in at least, and that I will make the means of intro-

ducing my whole hand. But I must first get clear
of this wretched young fellow. — I think I can
manage Sir Robert. He is dull and pompous, and
will be alike disposed to listen to my suggestions
upon the law of the case, and to assume the credit
of acting upon them as his own proper motion. So
I shall have the advantage of being the real magistrate, without the odium of responsibility.—

As he cherished these hopes and expectations,
the carriage approached Hazlewood-house, through
a noble avenue of old oaks, which shrouded the
ancient abbey-resembling building so called. It
was a large edifice built at different periods, part
having actually been a priory, upon the suppression
of which, in the time of Queen Mary, the first of
the family had obtained a gift of the house and sur-
rounding lands from the crown. It was pleasantly
situated in a large deer-park, on the banks of the
river we have before mentioned. The scenery
around was of a dark, solemn, and somewhat
melancholy cast, according well with the architecture of the house. Every thing appeared to be
kept in the highest possible order, and announced
the opulence and rank of the proprietor.

As Mr. Glossin's carriage stopped at the door of
the hall, Sir Robert reconnoitred the new vehicle
from the windows. According to his aristocratic
feelings, there was a degree of presumption in this
novus homo, this Mr. Gilbert Glossin, late writer
in ——, presuming to set up such an accommodation at all; but his wrath was mitigated when he
observed that the mantle upon the panels only bore

a plain cipher of G. G. This apparent modesty was
indeed solely owing to the delay of Mr. Cumming
of the Lyon Office, who, being at that time engaged
in discovering and matriculating the arms of two
commissaries from North America, three English-
Irish peers, and two great Jamaica traders, had been
more slow than usual in finding an escutcheon for
the new Laird of Ellangowan. But his delay told
to the advantage of Glossin in the opinion of the
proud Baronet.

While the officers of justice detained their prisoner in a sort of steward's room, Mr. Glossin was
ushered into what was called the great oak-parlour,
a long room, panelled with well-varnished wainscot,
and adorned with the grim portraits of Sir Robert
Hazlewood's ancestry. The visitor, who had no
internal consciousness of worth to balance that of
meanness of birth, felt his inferiority, and by the
depth of his bow and the obsequiousness of his
demeanour, showed that the Laird of Ellangowan
was sunk for the time in the old and submissive
habits of the quondam retainer of the law. He
would have persuaded himself, indeed, that he was
only humouring the pride of the old Baronet, for
the purpose of turning it to his own advantage; but
his feelings were of a mingled nature, and he felt
the influence of those very prejudices which he
pretended to flatter.

The Baronet received his visitor with that condescending parade which was meant at once to
assert his own vast superiority, and to show the
generosity and courtesy with which he could waive

it, and descend to the level of ordinary conversation with ordinary men. He thanked Glossin for his attention to a matter in which 'young Hazlewood' was so intimately concerned, and, pointing to his family pictures, observed, with a gracious smile, 'Indeed these venerable gentlemen, Mr. Glossin, are as much obliged as I am in this case, for the labour, pains, care, and trouble which you have taken in their behalf; and I have no doubt, were they capable of expressing themselves, would join me, sir, in thanking you for the favour you have conferred upon the house of Hazlewood, by taking care, and trouble, sir, and interest, in behalf of the young gentleman who is to continue their name and family.'

Thrice bowed Glossin, and each time more profoundly than before; once in honour of the knight who stood upright before him, once in respect to the quiet personages who patiently hung upon the wainscot, and a third time in deference to the young gentleman who was to carry on the name and family. *Roturier* as he was, Sir Robert was gratified by the homage which he rendered, and proceeded in a tone of gracious familiarity: 'And now, Mr. Glossin, my exceeding good friend, you must allow me to avail myself of your knowledge of law in our proceedings in this matter. I am not much in the habit of acting as a justice of the peace; it suits better with other gentlemen, whose domestic and family affairs require less constant superintendence, attention, and management, than mine.'

Of course, whatever small assistance Mr. Glossin

could render was entirely at Sir Robert Hazlewood's service; but, as Sir Robert Hazlewood's name stood high in the list of the faculty, the said Mr. Glossin could not presume to hope it could be either necessary or useful.

'Why, my good sir, you will understand me only to mean, that I am something deficient in the practical knowledge of the ordinary details of justice-business. I was indeed educated to the bar, and might boast perhaps at one time, that I had made some progress in the speculative, and abstract, and abstruse doctrines of our municipal code; but there is in the present day so little opportunity of a man of family and fortune rising to that eminence at the bar, which is attained by adventurers who are as willing to plead for John a Nokes as for the first noble of the land, that I was really early disgusted with practice. The first case, indeed, which was laid on my table, quite sickened me; it respected a bargain, sir, of tallow, between a butcher and a candle-maker; and I found it was expected that I should grease my mouth, not only with their vulgar names, but with all the technical terms, and phrases, and peculiar language, of their dirty arts. Upon my honour, my good sir, I have never been able to bear the smell of a tallow-candle since.'

Pitying, as seemed to be expected, the mean use to which the Baronet's faculties had been degraded on this melancholy occasion, Mr. Glossin offered to officiate as clerk or assessor, or in any way in which he could be most useful. 'And with a view to possessing you of the whole business, and in the first place, there will, I believe, be no difficulty in proving the main fact, that this was the person who fired the unhappy piece. Should he deny it, it can be proved by Mr. Hazlewood, I presume?'

'Young Hazlewood is not at home to-day, Mr. Glossin.'

'But we can have the oath of the servant who attended him,' said the ready Mr. Glossin; 'indeed I hardly think the fact will be disputed. I am more apprehensive, that, from the too favourable and indulgent manner in which I have understood that Mr. Hazlewood has been pleased to represent the business, the assault may be considered as accidental, and the injury as unintentional, so that the fellow may be immediately set at liberty, to do more mischief.'

'I have not the honour to know the gentleman who now holds the office of king's advocate,' replied Sir Robert, gravely; 'but I presume, sir— nay, I am confident, that he will consider the mere fact of having wounded young Hazlewood of Hazlewood, even by inadvertency, to take the matter in its mildest and gentlest, and in its most favourable and improbable light, as a crime which will be too easily atoned by imprisonment, and as more deserving of deportation.'

'Indeed, Sir Robert,' said his assenting brother in justice, 'I am entirely of your opinion; but, I don't know how it is, I have observed the Edinburgh gentlemen of the bar, and even the officers of the crown, pique themselves upon an indifferent administration of justice, without respect to rank and family; and I should fear——'

166

'How, sir, without respect to rank and family?
Will you tell me *that* doctrine can be held by men
of birth and legal education? No, sir; if a trifle
stolen in the street is termed mere pickery, but is
elevated into sacrilege if the crime be committed
in a church, so, according to the just gradations of
society, the guilt of an injury is enhanced by the
rank of the person to whom it is offered, done, or
perpetrated, sir.'

Glossin bowed low to this declaration *ex cathedra*,
but observed, that in case of the very worst, and
of such unnatural doctrines being actually held as
he had already hinted, 'the law had another hold
on Mr. Vanbeest Brown.'

'Vanbeest Brown! is that the fellow's name?
Good God! that young Hazlewood of Hazlewood
should have had his life endangered, the clavicle of
his right shoulder considerably lacerated and dis-
lodged, several large drops or slugs deposited in
the acromion process, as the account of the family
surgeon expressly bears, and all by an obscure
wretch named Vanbeest Brown!'

'Why, really, Sir Robert, it is a thing which
one can hardly bear to think of; but, begging ten
thousand pardons for resuming what I was about
to say, a person of the same name is, as appears
from these papers, (producing Dirk Hatteraick's
pocket-book,) mate to the smuggling vessel who
offered such violence at Woodbourne, and I have
no doubt that this is the same individual; which,
however, your acute discrimination will easily be
able to ascertain.'

'The same, my good sir, he must assuredly be—
it would be injustice even to the meanest of the
people, to suppose there could be found among them
two persons doomed to bear a name so shocking to
one's ears as this of Vanbeest Brown.'

'True, Sir Robert; most unquestionably; there
cannot be a shadow of doubt of it. But you see
farther, that this circumstance accounts for the
man's desperate conduct. You, Sir Robert, will
discover the motive for his crime—you, I say, will
discover it without difficulty, on your giving your
mind to the examination; for my part, I cannot
help suspecting the moving spring to have been
revenge for the gallantry with which Mr. Hazlewood, with all the spirit of his renowned forefathers,
defended the house at Woodbourne against this
villain and his lawless companions.'

'I will inquire into it, my good sir,' said the
learned Baronet. 'Yet even now I venture to
conjecture that I shall adopt the solution or explanation of this riddle, enigma, or mystery, which you
have in some degree thus started. Yes! revenge
it must be—and, good Heaven! entertained by and
against whom?—entertained, fostered, cherished,
against young Hazlewood of Hazlewood, and in
part carried into effect, executed, and implemented,
by the hand of Vanbeest Brown! These are dreadful days indeed, my worthy neighbour (this epithet
indicated a rapid advance in the Baronet's good
graces)—days when the bulwarks of society are
shaken to their mighty base, and that rank, which
forms, as it were, its highest grace and ornament,

is mingled and confused with the viler parts of the architecture. O, my good Mr. Gilbert Glossin, in my time, sir, the use of swords and pistols, and such honourable arms, was reserved by the nobility and gentry to themselves, and the disputes of the vulgar were decided by the weapons which nature had given them, or by cudgels cut, broken, or hewed out of the next wood. But now, sir, the clouted shoe of the peasant galls the kibe of the courtier. The lower ranks have their quarrels, sir, and their points of honour, and their revenges, which they must bring, forsooth, to fatal arbitrement. But well, well! it will last my time—let us have in this fellow, this Vanbeest Brown, and make an end of him at least for the present.'

CHAPTER XLIII

'Twas he
Gave heat unto the injury, which returned,
Like a petard ill lighted, into the bosom
Of him gave fire to't.   Yet I hope his hurt
Is not so dangerous but he may recover.

FAIR MAID OF THE INN.

THE prisoner was now presented before the two worshipful magistrates. Glossin, partly from some compunctious visitings, and partly out of his cautious resolution to suffer Sir Robert Hazlewood to be the ostensible manager of the whole examination, looked down upon the table, and busied himself with reading and arranging the papers respecting the business, only now and then throwing in a skilful catchword as prompter, when he saw the principal, and apparently most active magistrate, stand in need of a hint. As for Sir Robert Hazlewood, he assumed on his part a happy mixture of the austerity of the justice, combined with the display of personal dignity appertaining to the baronet of ancient family.

'There, constables, let him stand there at the bottom of the table.—Be so good as look me in the face, sir, and raise your voice as you answer the questions which I am going to put to you.'

'May I beg, in the first place, to know, sir, who

170

it is that takes the trouble to interrogate me?' said the prisoner; 'for the honest gentlemen who have brought me here have not been pleased to furnish any information upon that point.'

'And pray, sir,' answered Sir Robert, 'what has my name and quality to do with the questions I am about to ask you?'

'Nothing, perhaps, sir,' replied Bertram; 'but it may considerably influence my disposition to answer them.'

'Why, then, sir, you will please to be informed that you are in presence of Sir Robert Hazlewood of Hazlewood, and another justice of peace for this county—that's all.'

As this intimation produced a less stunning effect upon the prisoner than he had anticipated, Sir Robert proceeded in his investigation with an increasing dislike to the object of it.

'Is your name Vanbeest Brown, sir?'

'It is,' answered the prisoner.

'So far well;—and how are we to design you farther, sir?' demanded the Justice.

'Captain in his majesty's —— regiment of horse,' answered Bertram.

The Baronet's ears received this intimation with astonishment; but he was refreshed in courage by an incredulous look from Glossin, and by hearing him gently utter a sort of interjectional whistle, in a note of surprise and contempt. 'I believe, my friend,' said Sir Robert, 'we shall find for you, before we part, a more humble title.'

'If you do, sir,' replied his prisoner, 'I shall

willingly submit to any punishment which such an imposture shall be thought to deserve.'

'Well, sir, we shall see,' continued Sir Robert. 'Do you know young Hazlewood of Hazlewood?'

'I never saw the gentleman who I am informed bears that name excepting once, and I regret that it was under very unpleasant circumstances.'

'You mean to acknowledge, then,' said the Baronet, 'that you inflicted upon young Hazlewood of Hazlewood that wound which endangered his life, considerably lacerated the clavicle of his right shoulder, and deposited, as the family surgeon declares, several large drops or slugs in the acromion process?'

'Why, sir,' replied Bertram, 'I can only say I am equally ignorant of and sorry for the extent of the damage which the young gentleman has sustained. I met him in a narrow path, walking with two ladies and a servant, and before I could either pass them or address them, this young Hazlewood took his gun from his servant, presented it against my body, and commanded me in the most haughty tone to stand back. I was neither inclined to submit to his authority, nor to leave him in possession of the means to injure me, which he seemed disposed to use with such rashness. I therefore closed with him for the purpose of disarming him; and just as I had nearly effected my purpose, the piece went off accidentally, and, to my regret then and since, inflicted upon the young gentleman a severer chastisement than I desired, though I am glad to understand it is like to prove no more than his unprovoked folly deserved.'

'And so, sir,' said the Baronet, every feature swoln with offended dignity,—'You, sir, admit, sir, that it was your purpose, sir, and your intention, sir, and the real jet and object of your assault, sir, to disarm young Hazlewood of Hazlewood of his gun, sir, or his fowling-piece, or his fuzee, or whatever you please to call it, sir, upon the king's highway, sir?—I think this will do, my worthy neighbour! I think he should stand committed?'

'You are by far the best judge, Sir Robert,' said Glossin, in his most insinuating tone; 'but if I might presume to hint, there was something about these smugglers.'

'Very true, good sir.—And besides, sir, you, Vanbeest Brown, who call yourself a captain in his majesty's service, are no better or worse than a rascally mate of a smuggler!'

'Really, sir,' said Bertram, 'you are an old gentleman, and acting under some strange delusion, otherwise I should be very angry with you.'

'Old gentleman, sir! strange delusion, sir!' said Sir Robert, colouring with indignation. 'I protest and declare——Why, sir, have you any papers or letters that can establish your pretended rank, and estate, and commission?'

'None at present, sir,' answered Bertram; 'but in the return of a post or two——'

'And how do you, sir,' continued the Baronet, if you are a captain in his majesty's service, how do you chance to be travelling in Scotland without letters of introduction, credentials, baggage, or any thing belonging to your pretended rank, estate, and condition, as I said before?'

'Sir,' replied the prisoner, 'I had the misfortune to be robbed of my clothes and baggage.'

'Oho! then you are the gentleman who took a post-chaise from —— to Kippletringan, gave the boy the slip on the road, and sent two of your accomplices to beat the boy and bring away the baggage?'

'I was, sir, in a carriage as you describe, was obliged to alight in the snow, and lost my way endeavouring to find the road to Kippletringan. The landlady of the inn will inform you that on my arrival there the next day, my first inquiries were after the boy.'

'Then give me leave to ask where you spent the night—not in the snow, I presume? you do not suppose that will pass, or be taken, credited, and received?'

'I beg leave,' said Bertram, his recollection turning to the gipsy female, and to the promise he had given her, 'I beg leave to decline answering that question.'

'I thought as much,' said Sir Robert.—'Were you not during that night in the ruins of Derncleugh?—in the ruins of Derncleugh, sir?'

'I have told you that I do not intend answering that question,' replied Bertram.

'Well, sir, then you will stand committed, sir,' said Sir Robert, 'and be sent to prison, sir, that's all, sir,—Have the goodness to look at these papers; are you the Vanbeest Brown who is there mentioned?'

It must be remarked that Glossin had shuffled among the papers some writings which really did belong to Bertram, and which had been found by the officers in the old vault where his portmanteau was ransacked.

'Some of these papers,' said Bertram, looking over them, 'are mine, and were in my portfolio when it was stolen from the post-chaise. They are memoranda of little value, and, I see, have been carefully selected as affording no evidence of my rank or character, which many of the other papers would have established fully. They are mingled with ship-accounts and other papers, belonging apparently to a person of the same name.'

'And wilt thou attempt to persuade me, friend,' demanded Sir Robert, 'that there are *two* persons in this country, at the same time, of thy very uncommon and awkwardly sounding name?'

'I really do not see, sir, as there is an old Hazlewood and a young Hazlewood, why there should not be an old and a young Vanbeest Brown. And, to speak seriously, I was educated in Holland, and I know that this name, however uncouth it may sound in British ears——'

Glossin, conscious that the prisoner was now about to enter upon dangerous ground, interfered, though the interruption was unnecessary, for the purpose of diverting the attention of Sir Robert Hazlewood, who was speechless and motionless with indignation at the presumptuous comparison

implied in Bertram's last speech. In fact, the veins
of his throat and of his temples swelled almost
to bursting, and he sat with the indignant and
disconcerted air of one who has received a mortal
insult from a quarter, to which he holds it unmeet
and indecorous to make any reply. While with
a bent brow and an angry eye he was drawing in
his breath slowly and majestically, and puffing it
forth again with deep and solemn exertion, Glossin
stepped in to his assistance. 'I should think now,
Sir Robert, with great submission, that this matter
may be closed. One of the constables, besides the
pregnant proof already produced, offers to make
oath, that the sword of which the prisoner was
this morning deprived (while using it, by the way,
in resistance to a legal warrant) was a cutlass
taken from him in a fray between the officers and
smugglers, just previous to their attack upon Woodbourne. And yet,' he added, 'I would not have
you form any rash construction upon that subject;
perhaps the young man can explain how he came
by that weapon.'

'That question, sir,' said Bertram, 'I shall also
leave unanswered.'

'There is yet another circumstance to be inquired
into, always under Sir Robert's leave,' insinuated
Glossin. 'This prisoner put into the hands of Mrs.
Mac-Candlish of Kippletringan, a parcel containing
a variety of gold coins and valuable articles of
different kinds. Perhaps, Sir Robert, you might
think it right to ask, how he came by property of
a description which seldom occurs?'

'You, sir, Mr. Vanbeest Brown, sir, you hear the question, sir, which the gentleman asks you?'

'I have particular reasons for declining to answer that question,' answered Bertram.

'Then I am afraid, sir,' said Glossin, who had brought matters to the point he desired to reach, 'our duty must lay us under the necessity to sign a warrant of committal.'

'As you please, sir,' answered Bertram; 'take care, however, what you do. Observe that I inform you that I am a captain in his majesty's ——— regiment, and that I am just returned from India, and therefore cannot possibly be connected with any of those contraband traders you talk of; that my Lieutenant-Colonel is now at Nottingham, the Major, with the officers of my corps, at Kingston-upon-Thames. I offer before you both to submit to any degree of ignominy, if, within the return of the Kingston and Nottingham posts, I am not able to establish these points. Or you may write to the agent for the regiment, if you please, and———'

'This is all very well, sir,' said Glossin, beginning to fear lest the firm expostulation of Bertram should make some impression on Sir Robert, who would almost have died of shame at committing such a solecism as sending a captain of horse to jail—'This is all very well, sir; but is there no person nearer whom you could refer to?'

'There are only two persons in this country who know any thing of me,' replied the prisoner. 'One is a plain Liddesdale sheep-farmer, called Dinmont of Charlies-hope; but he knows nothing more of me than what I told him, and what I now tell you.'

'Why, this is well enough, Sir Robert!' said Glossin. 'I suppose he would bring forward this thick-skulled fellow to give his oath of credulity, Sir Robert, ha, ha, ha!'

'And what is your other witness, friend?' said the Baronet.

'A gentleman whom I have some reluctance to mention, because of certain private reasons; but under whose command I served some time in India, and who is too much a man of honour to refuse his testimony to my character as a soldier and gentleman.'

'And who is this doughty witness, pray, sir?' said Sir Robert,—'some half-pay quarter-master or sergeant, I suppose?'

'Colonel Guy Mannering, late of the —— regiment, in which, as I told you, I have a troop.'

Colonel Guy Mannering! thought Glossin,—who the devil could have guessed this?

'Colonel Guy Mannering?' echoed the Baronet, considerably shaken in his opinion,—'My good sir,' —apart to Glossin, 'the young man with a dreadfully plebeian name, and a good deal of modest assurance, has nevertheless something of the tone, and manners, and feeling of a gentleman, of one at least who has lived in good society—they do give commissions very loosely and carelessly, and inaccurately, in India—I think we had better pause till Colonel Mannering shall return; he is now, I believe, at Edinburgh.'

'You are in every respect the best judge, Sir Robert,' answered Glossin, 'in every possible respect. I would only submit to you, that we are certainly hardly entitled to dismiss this man upon an assertion which cannot be satisfied by proof, and that we shall incur a heavy responsibility by detaining him in private custody, without committing him to a public jail. Undoubtedly, however, you are the best judge, Sir Robert;—and I would only say, for my own part, that I very lately incurred severe censure by detaining a person in a place which I thought perfectly secure, and under the custody of the proper officers. The man made his escape, and I have no doubt my own character for attention and circumspection as a magistrate has in some degree suffered—I only hint this—I will join in any step you, Sir Robert, think most advisable.' But Mr. Glossin was well aware that such a hint was of power sufficient to decide the motions of his self-important, but not self-relying colleague. So that Sir Robert Hazlewood summed up the business in the following speech, which proceeded partly upon the supposition of the prisoner being really a gentleman, and partly upon the opposite belief that he was a villain and an assassin.

'Sir, Mr. Vanbeest Brown—I would call you Captain Brown if there was the least reason, or cause, or grounds to suppose that you are a captain, or had a troop in the very respectable corps you mention, or indeed in any other corps in his majesty's service, as to which circumstance I beg to

be understood to give no positive, settled, or un-
alterable judgment, declaration, or opinion. I say
therefore, sir, Mr. Brown, we have determined, considering the unpleasant predicament in which you
now stand, having been robbed, as you say, an
assertion as to which I suspend my opinion, and
being possessed of much and valuable treasure, and
of a brass-handled cutlass besides, as to your obtaining which you will favour us with no explanation—
I say, sir, we have determined and resolved, and
made up our minds, to commit you to jail, or rather
to assign you an apartment therein, in order that
you may be forthcoming upon Colonel Mannering's
return from Edinburgh.'

'With humble submission, Sir Robert,' said Glossin, 'may I inquire if it is your purpose to send this
young gentleman to the county jail?—for if that
were not your settled intention, I would take the
liberty to hint, that there would be less hardship in
sending him to the Bridewell at Portanferry, where
he can be secured without public exposure; a circumstance which, on the mere chance of his story
being really true, is much to be avoided.'

'Why, there is a guard of soldiers at Portanferry, to be sure, for protection of the goods in the
Custom-house; and upon the whole, considering
every thing, and that the place is comfortable for
such a place, I say all things considered, we will
commit this person, I would rather say authorize
him to be detained, in the workhouse at Portanferry.'

The warrant was made out accordingly, and

Bertram was informed he was next morning to be removed to his place of confinement, as Sir Robert had determined he should not be taken there under cloud of night, for fear of rescue. He was, during the interval, to be detained at Hazle-wood-house.

It cannot be so hard as my imprisonment by the Looties in India, he thought; nor can it last so long. But the deuce take the old formal dunder-head, and his more sly associate, who speaks always under his breath,—they cannot understand a plain man's story when it is told them.

In the meanwhile Glossin took leave of the Baronet, with a thousand respectful bows and cring-ing apologies for not accepting his invitation to dinner, and venturing to hope he might be pardoned in paying his respects to him, Lady Hazlewood, and young Mr. Hazlewood, on some future occasion.

'Certainly, sir,' said the Baronet, very graci-ously. 'I hope our family was never at any time deficient in civility to our neighbours; and when I ride that way, good Mr. Glossin, I will convince you of this by calling at your house as familiarly as is consistent — that is, as can be hoped or expected.'

'And now,' said Glossin to himself, 'to find Dirk Hatteraick and his people,—to get the guard sent off from the Custom-house,—and then for the grand cast of the dice. Every thing must depend upon speed. How lucky that Mannering has betaken himself to Edinburgh! His knowledge of this young fellow is a most perilous addition to my

dangers,'—here he suffered his horse to slacken his
pace—'What if I should try to compound with
the heir?—It's likely he might be brought to pay
a round sum for restitution, and I could give up
Hatteraick—But no, no, no! there were too many
eyes on me, Hatteraick himself, and the gipsy
sailor, and that old hag—No, no! I must stick to
my original plan.' And with that he struck his
spurs against his horse's flanks, and rode forward
at a hard trot to put his machines in motion.

CHAPTER XLIV

A prison is a house of care,
A place where none can thrive,
A touchstone true to try a friend,
A grave for one alive.
Sometimes a place of right,
Sometimes a place of wrong,
Sometimes a place of rogues and thieves,
And honest men among.

INSCRIPTION ON EDINBURGH TOLBOOTH.

EARLY on the following morning, the carriage which had brought Bertram to Hazlewood-house, was, with his two silent and surly attendants, appointed to convey him to his place of confinement at Portanferry. This building adjoined to the Custom-house established at that little seaport, and both were situated so close to the sea-beach, that it was necessary to defend the back part with a large and strong rampart or bulwark of huge stones, disposed in a slope towards the surf, which often reached and broke upon them. The front was surrounded by a high wall, enclosing a small courtyard, within which the miserable inmates of the mansion were occasionally permitted to take exercise and air. The prison was used as a House of Correction, and sometimes as a chapel of ease to the county jail, which was old, and far from being conveniently situated with reference to the Kippletringan district of the county. Mac-Guffog, the officer by whom Bertram had at first been apprehended, and who was now in attendance upon him, was keeper of this palace of little-ease. He caused the carriage to be drawn close up to the outer gate, and got out himself to summon the warders. The noise of his rap alarmed some twenty or thirty ragged boys, who left off sailing their mimic sloops and frigates in the little pools of salt water left by the receding tide, and hastily crowded round the vehicle to see what luckless being was to be delivered to the prison-house out of 'Glossin's braw new carriage.' The door of the court-yard, after the heavy clanking of many chains and bars, was opened by Mrs. Mac-Guffog, an awful spectacle, being a woman for strength and resolution capable of maintaining order among her riotous inmates, and of administering the discipline of the house, as it was called, during the absence of her husband, or when he chanced to have taken an over-dose of the creature. The growling voice of this Amazon, which rivalled in harshness the crashing music of her own bolts and bars, soon dispersed in every direction the little varlets who had thronged around her threshold, and she next addressed her amiable help-mate :—

'Be sharp, man, and get out the swell, canst thou not ?'

'Hold your tongue and be d—d, you ——,' answered her loving husband, with two additional epithets of great energy, but which we beg to be excused from repeating. Then, addressing Bertram,—

'Come, will you get out, my handy lad, or must we lend you a lift?'

Bertram came out of the carriage, and, collared by the constable as he put his foot on the ground, was dragged, though he offered no resistance, across the threshold, amid the continued shouts of the little *sans-culottes*, who looked on at such distance as their fear of Mrs. Mac-Guffog permitted. The instant his foot had crossed the fatal porch, the portress again dropped her chains, drew her bolts, and turning with both hands an immense key, took it from the lock, and thrust it into a huge side-pocket of red cloth.

Bertram was now in the small court already mentioned. Two or three prisoners were sauntering along the pavement, and deriving as it were a feeling of refreshment from the momentary glimpse with which the opening door had extended their prospect to the other side of a dirty street. Nor can this be thought surprising, when it is considered, that, unless on such occasions, their view was confined to the grated front of their prison, the high and sable walls of the court-yard, the heaven above them, and the pavement beneath their feet; a sameness of landscape, which, to use the poet's expression, 'lay like a load on the wearied eye,' and had fostered in some a callous and dull misanthropy, in others that sickness of the heart which induces him who is immured already in a living grave, to wish for a sepulchre yet more calm and sequestered.

Mac-Guffog, when they entered the court-yard, suffered Bertram to pause for a minute, and look upon his companions in affliction. When he had cast his eye around, on faces on which guilt, and despondence, and low excess, had fixed their stigma; upon the spendthrift, and the swindler, and the thief, the bankrupt debtor, the 'moping idiot, and the madman gay,' whom a paltry spirit of economy congregated to share this dismal habitation, he felt his heart recoil with inexpressible loathing from enduring the contamination of their society even for a moment.

' I hope, sir,' he said to the keeper, ' you intend to assign me a place of confinement apart ? '

' And what should I be the better of that ? '

' Why, sir, I can but be detained here a day or two, and it would be very disagreeable to me to mix in the sort of company this place affords.'

' And what do I care for that ? '

' Why, then, sir, to speak to your feelings,' said Bertram, ' I shall be willing to make you a handsome compliment for this indulgence.'

' Ay, but when, Captain ? when and how ? that 's the question, or rather the twa questions,' said the jailor.

' When I am delivered, and get my remittances from England,' answered the prisoner.

Mac-Guffog shook his head incredulously.

' Why, friend, you do not pretend to believe that I am really a malefactor ? ' said Bertram.

' Why, I no ken,' said the fellow; ' but if you *are* on the account, ye 're nae sharp ane, that 's the day-light o't.'

'And why do you say I am no sharp one?'

'Why, wha but a crack-brained greenhorn wad hae let them keep up the siller that ye left at the Gordon Arms?' said the constable. 'Deil fetch me, but I wad have had it out o' their wames! Ye had nae right to be strippit o' your money and sent to jail without a mark to pay your fees; they might have keepit the rest o' the articles for evidence. But why, for a blind bottle-head, did not ye ask the guineas? and I kept winking and nodding a' the time, and the donnert deevil wad never ance look my way!'

'Well, sir,' replied Bertram, 'if I have a title to have that property delivered up to me, I shall apply for it; and there is a good deal more than enough to pay any demand you can set up.'

'I dinna ken a bit about that,' said Mac-Guffog; 'ye may be here lang eneugh. And then the gieing credit maun be considered in the fees. But, however, as ye *do* seem to be a chap by common, though my wife says I lose by my good-nature, if ye gie me an order for my fees upon that money— I dare say Glossin will make it forthcoming—I ken something about an escape from Ellangowan—ay, ay, he 'll be glad to carry me through, and be neigh-bour-like.'

'Well, sir,' replied Bertram, 'if I am not fur-nished in a day or two otherwise, you shall have such an order.'

'Weel, weel, then ye shall be put up like a prince,' said Mac-Guffog. 'But mark ye me, friend, that we may have nae colly-shangie afterhend, these

are the fees that I always charge a swell that must
have his lib-ken to himself—Thirty shillings a-week
for lodgings, and a guinea for garnish; half-a-guinea
a-week for a single bed,—and I dinna get the
whole of it, for I must gie half-a-crown out of it to
Donald Laider that's in for sheep-stealing, that
should sleep with you by rule, and he'll expect clean
strae, and maybe some whisky beside. So I make
little upon that.'

'Well, sir, go on.'

'Then for meat and liquor, ye may have the best,
and I never charge abune twenty per cent ower
tavern price for pleasing a gentleman that way—
and that's little eneugh for sending in and sending
out, and wearing the lassie's shoon out. And then
if ye're dowie, I will sit wi' you a gliff in the
evening mysell, man, and help ye out wi' your
bottle.—I have drank mony a glass wi' Glossin,
man, that did you up, though he's a justice now.
And then I'se warrant ye'll be for fire thir cauld
nights, or if ye want candle, that's an expensive
article, for it's against the rules. And now I've
tell'd ye the head articles of the charge, and I dinna
think there's muckle mair, though there will aye
be some odd expenses ower and abune.'

'Well, sir, I must trust to your conscience, if
ever you happened to hear of such a thing—I
cannot help myself.'

'Na, na, sir,' answered the cautious jailor, 'I'll
no permit you to be saying that—I'm forcing
naething upon ye;—an ye dinna like the price, ye
needna take the article—I force no man; I was

only explaining what civility was; but if ye like to take the common run of the house, it's a' ane to me—I'll be saved trouble, that's a'.'

'Nay, my friend, I have, as I suppose you may easily guess, no inclination to dispute your terms upon such a penalty,' answered Bertram. 'Come, show me where I am to be, for I would fain be alone for a little while.'

'Ay, ay, come along then, Captain,' said the fellow, with a contortion of visage which he intended to be a smile; 'and I'll tell you now,—to show you that I *have* a conscience, as ye ca't, d—n me if I charge ye abune sixpence a-day for the freedom o' the court, and ye may walk in't very near three hours a-day, and play at pitch-and-toss, and handba', and what not.'

With this gracious promise, he ushered Bertram into the house, and showed him up a steep and narrow stone staircase, at the top of which was a strong door, clenched with iron and studded with nails. Beyond this door was a narrow passage or gallery, having three cells on each side, wretched vaults, with iron bed-frames and straw mattresses. But at the farther end was a small apartment, of rather a more decent appearance, that is, having less the air of a place of confinement, since, unless for the large lock and chain upon the door, and the crossed and ponderous stanchions upon the window, it rather resembled the ' worst inn's worst room.' It was designed as a sort of infirmary for prisoners whose state of health required some indulgence; and, in fact, Donald Laider, Bertram's destined chum, had been just dragged out of one of the two beds which it contained, to try whether clean straw and whisky might not have a better chance to cure his intermitting fever. This process of ejection had been carried into force by Mrs. Mac-Guffog while her husband parleyed with Bertram in the courtyard, that good lady having a distinct presentiment of the manner in which the treaty must necessarily terminate. Apparently the expulsion had not taken place without some application of the strong hand, for one of the bed-posts of a sort of tent-bed was broken down, so that the tester and curtains hung forward into the middle of the narrow chamber, like the banner of a chieftain, half-sinking amid the confusion of a combat.

' Never mind that being out o' sorts, Captain,' said Mrs. Mac-Guffog, who now followed them into the room; then, turning her back to the prisoner, with as much delicacy as the action admitted, she whipped from her knee her ferret garter, and applied it to splicing and fastening the broken bed-post—then used more pins than her apparel could well spare to fasten up the bed-curtains in festoons —then shook the bed-clothes into something like form—then flung over all a tattered patch-work quilt, and pronounced that things were now ' something purpose-like.' 'And there 's your bed, Captain,' pointing to a massy four-posted hulk, which, owing to the inequality of the floor that had sunk considerably, (the house, though new, having been built by contract,) stood on three legs, and held the fourth aloft as if pawing the air, and in the attitude of advancing like an elephant passant upon the panel of a coach—'There's your bed and the blankets; but if ye want sheets, or bowster, or pillow, or ony sort o' nappery for the table, or for your hands, ye'll hae to speak to me about it, for that's out o' the gudeman's line, (Mac-Guffog had by this time left the room, to avoid, probably, any appeal which might be made to him upon this new exaction,) and he never engages for ony thing like that.'

'In God's name,' said Bertram, 'let me have what is decent, and make any charge you please.'

'Aweel, aweel, that's sune settled; we'll no excise you neither, though we live sae near the Custom-house. And I maun see to get you some fire and some dinner too, I'se warrant; but your dinner will be but a puir ane the day, no expecting company that would be nice and fashious.'—So saying, and in all haste, Mrs. Mac-Guffog fetched a scuttle of live coals, and having replenished 'the rusty grate, unconscious of a fire' for months before, she proceeded with unwashed hands to arrange the stipulated bed-linen, (alas, how different from Ailie Dinmont's!) and, muttering to herself as she discharged her task, seemed, in inveterate spleen of temper, to grudge even those accommodations for which she was to receive payment. At length, however, she departed, grumbling between her teeth, that 'she wad rather lock up a haill ward than be fiking about thae niff-naffy gentles that gae sae muckle fash wi' their fancies.'

When she was gone, Bertram found himself reduced to the alternative of pacing his little apartment for exercise, or gazing out upon the sea in such proportions as could be seen from the narrow panes of his window, obscured by dirt and by close iron-bars, or reading over the records of brutal wit and blackguardism which despair had scrawled upon the half-whitened walls. The sounds were as uncomfortable as the objects of sight; the sullen dash of the tide, which was now retreating, and the occasional opening and shutting of a door, with all its accompaniments of jarring bolts and creaking hinges, mingling occasionally with the dull monotony of the retiring ocean. Sometimes, too, he could hear the hoarse growl of the keeper, or the shriller strain of his helpmate, almost always in the tone of discontent, anger, or insolence. At other times the large mastiff, chained in the courtyard, answered with furious bark the insults of the idle loiterers who made a sport of incensing him.

At length the tædium of this weary space was broken by the entrance of a dirty-looking serving wench, who made some preparations for dinner by laying a half-dirty cloth upon a whole-dirty deal table. A knife and fork, which had not been worn out by overcleaning, flanked a cracked delf plate ; a nearly empty mustard-pot, placed on one side of the table, balanced a saltcellar, containing an article of a greyish, or rather a blackish mixture, upon the other, both of stone-ware, and bearing too obvious marks of recent service. Shortly after, the same Hebe brought up a plate of beef-collops, done in the frying-pan, with a huge allowance of grease floating in an ocean of lukewarm water ; and having added a coarse loaf to these savoury viands, she requested to know what liquors the gentleman chose to order. The appearance of this fare was not very inviting; but Bertram endeavoured to mend his commons by ordering wine, which he found tolerably good, and, with the assistance of some indifferent cheese, made his dinner chiefly off the brown loaf. When his meal was over, the girl presented her master's compliments, and, if agreeable to the gentleman, he would help him to spend the evening. Bertram desired to be excused, and begged, instead of this gracious society, that he might be furnished with paper, pen, ink, and candles. The light appeared in the shape of one long broken tallow - candle, inclining over a tin candlestick coated with grease; as for the writing materials, the prisoner was informed that he might have them the next day if he chose to send out to buy them. Bertram next desired the maid to procure him a book, and enforced his request with a shilling; in consequence of which, after long absence, she re-appeared with two odd volumes of the Newgate Calendar, which she had borrowed from Sam Silverquill, an idle apprentice, who was imprisoned under a charge of forgery. Having laid the books on the table she retired, and left Bertram to studies which were not ill adapted to his present melancholy situation.

CHAPTER XLV

But if thou shouldst be dragg'd in scorn
To yonder ignominious tree,
Thou shalt not want one faithful friend
To share the cruel fates' decree.
SHENSTONE.

PLUNGED in the gloomy reflections which were
naturally excited by his dismal reading, and disconsolate situation, Bertram, for the first time in
his life, felt himself affected with a disposition to
low spirits. ' I have been in worse situations than
this too,' he said;—' more dangerous, for here is
no danger; more dismal in prospect, for my present
confinement must necessarily be short; more intolerable for the time, for here, at least, I have
fire, food, and shelter.   Yet, with reading these
bloody tales of crime and misery, in a place so
corresponding to the ideas which they excite, and
in listening to these sad sounds, I feel a stronger
disposition to melancholy than in my life I ever experienced.   But I will not give way to it—Begone,
thou record of guilt and infamy!' he said, flinging
the book upon the spare bed; ' a Scottish jail shall
not break, on the very first day, the spirits which
have resisted climate, and want, and penury, and
disease, and imprisonment, in a foreign land.   I

have fought many a hard battle with Dame Fortune, and she shall not beat me now if I can
help it.'

Then bending his mind to a strong effort, he
endeavoured to view his situation in the most
favourable light. Delaserre must soon be in Scotland; the certificates from his commanding officer
must soon arrive; nay, if Mannering were first
applied to, who could say but the effect might
be a reconciliation between them? He had often
observed, and now remembered, that when his
former colonel took the part of any one, it was
never by halves, and that he seemed to love those
persons most who had lain under obligation to him.
In the present case, a favour, which could be asked
with honour and granted with readiness, might be
the means of reconciling them to each other. From
this his feelings naturally turned towards Julia;
and, without very nicely measuring the distance
between a soldier of fortune, who expected that
her father's attestation would deliver him from
confinement, and the heiress of that father's wealth
and expectations, he was building the gayest castle
in the clouds, and varnishing it with all the tints
of a summer-evening sky, when his labour was interrupted by a loud knocking at the outer-gate,
answered by the barking of the gaunt half-starved
mastiff, which was quartered in the court-yard as
an addition to the garrison. After much scrupulous
precaution the gate was opened, and some person
admitted. The house-door was next unbarred,
unlocked, and unchained, a dog's feet pattered up

stairs in great haste, and the animal was heard
scratching and whining at the door of the room.
Next a heavy step was heard lumbering up, and
Mac-Guffog's voice in the character of pilot—'This
way, this way; take care of the step;—that's the
room.'—Bertram's door was then unbolted, and,
to his great surprise and joy, his terrier, Wasp,
rushed into the apartment, and almost devoured
him with caresses, followed by the massy form of
his friend from Charlies-hope.

'Eh whow! Eh whow!' ejaculated the honest
farmer, as he looked round upon his friend's
miserable apartment and wretched accommodation—'What's this o't! what's this o't!'

'Just a trick of fortune, my good friend,' said
Bertram, rising and shaking him heartily by the
hand, 'that's all.'

'But what will be done about it?—or what *can*
be done about it?' said honest Dandie—'is't for
debt, or what is't for?'

'Why, it is not for debt,' answered Bertram;
'and if you have time to sit down, I'll tell you all
I know of the matter myself.'

'If I hae time?' said Dandie, with an accent
on the word that sounded like a howl of derision
—'Ou, what the deevil am I come here for, man,
but just ance errand to see about it? But ye'll
no be the waur o' something to eat, I trow;—it's
getting late at e'en—I tell'd the folk at the Change,
where I put up Dumple, to send ower my supper
here, and the chield Mac-Guffog is agreeable to let
it in—I hae settled a' that.—And now let's hear

your story—Whisht, Wasp, man! wow but he's glad to see you, poor thing!'

Bertram's story, being confined to the accident of Hazlewood, and the confusion made between his own identity and that of one of the smugglers, who had been active in the assault of Woodbourne, and chanced to bear the same name, was soon told. Dinmont listened very attentively. 'Aweel,' he said, 'this suld be nae sic dooms-desperate business surely—the lad's doing weel again that was hurt, and what signifies twa or three lead draps in his shouther? if ye had putten out his ee it would hae been another case. But eh, as I wuss auld Sherra Pleydell was to the fore here!—odd, he was the man for sorting them, and the queerest rough-spoken deevil too that ever ye heard!'

'But now tell me, my excellent friend, how did you find out I was here?'

'Odd, lad, queerly eneugh,' said Dandie; 'but I'll tell ye that after we are done wi' our supper, for it will maybe no be sae weel to speak about it while that lang-lugged limmer o' a lass is gaun flisking in and out o' the room.'

Bertram's curiosity was in some degree put to rest by the appearance of the supper which his friend had ordered, which, although homely enough, had the appetizing cleanliness in which Mrs. Mac-Guffog's cookery was so eminently deficient. Dinmont also, premising he had ridden the whole day since breakfast-time, without tasting any thing 'to speak of,' which qualifying phrase related to about three pounds of cold roast mutton which he had discussed at his mid-day stage,—Dinmont, I say, fell stoutly upon the good cheer, and, like one of Homer's heroes, said little, either good or bad, till the rage of thirst and hunger was appeased. At length, after a draught of home-brewed ale, he began by observing, 'Aweel, aweel, that hen,' looking upon the lamentable relics of what had been once a large fowl, 'wasna a bad ane to be bred at a town end, though it's no like our barn-door chuckies at Charlies-hope—and I am glad to see that this vexing job hasna taen awa your appetite, Captain.'

'Why, really, my dinner was not so excellent, Mr. Dinmont, as to spoil my supper.'

'I dare say no, I dare say no,' said Dandie:— 'But now, hinny, that ye hae brought us the brandy, and the mug wi' the het water, and the sugar, and a' right, ye may steek the door, ye see, for we wad hae some o' our ain cracks.' The damsel accordingly retired, and shut the door of the apartment, to which she added the precaution of drawing a large bolt on the outside.

As soon as she was gone, Dandie reconnoitred the premises, listened at the key-hole as if he had been listening for the blowing of an otter, and having satisfied himself that there were no eaves-droppers, returned to the table; and making himself what he called a gey stiff cheerer, poked the fire, and began his story in an under tone of gravity and importance not very usual with him.

'Ye see, Captain, I had been in Edinbro' for twa or three days, looking after the burial of a friend that we hae lost, and may be I suld hae had something for my ride; but there's disappointments in a' things, and wha can help the like o' that? And I had a wee bit law business besides, but that's neither here nor there. In short, I had got my matters settled, and hame I cam; and the morn awa to the muirs to see what the herds had been about, and I thought I might as weel gie a look to the Tout-hope head, where Jock o' Dawston and me has the outcast about a march.—Weel, just as I was coming upon the bit, I saw a man afore me that I kenn'd was nane o' our herds, and it's a wild bit to meet ony other body, so when I cam up to him, it was Tod Gabriel the fox-hunter. So I says to him, rather surprised like, "What are ye doing up amang the craws here, without your hounds, man? are ye seeking the fox without the dogs?" So he said, "Na, gudeman, but I wanted to see yoursell."

'"Ay," said I, "and ye'll be wanting eilding now, or something to pit ower the winter?"

'"Na, na," quo' he, "it's no that I'm seeking; but ye tak an unco concern in that Captain Brown that was staying wi' you, d'ye no?"

'"Troth do I, Gabriel," says I; "and what about him, lad?"

'Says he, "There's mair tak an interest in him than you, and some that I am bound to obey; and it's no just on my ain will that I'm here to tell you something about him that will no please you."

' " Faith, naething will please me," quo' I, " that's no pleasing to him."

' " And then," quo' he, " ye 'll be ill-sorted to hear that he's like to be in the prison at Portanferry, if he disna tak a' the better care o' himsell, for there's been warrants out to tak him as soon as he comes ower the water frae Allonby. And now, gudeman, an ever ye wish him weel, ye maun ride down to Portanferry, and let nae grass grow at the nag's heels; and if ye find him in confinement, ye maun stay beside him night and day, for a day or twa, for he'll want friends that hae baith heart and hand; and if ye neglect this ye 'll never rue but ance, for it will be for a' your life."

' " But, safe us, man," quo' I, " how did ye learn a' this? it's an unco way between this and Portanferry."

'" Never ye mind that," quo' he, "them that brought us the news rade night and day, and ye maun be aff instantly if ye wad do ony gude—and sae I have naething mair to tell ye."—Sae he sat himsell doun and hirselled doun into the glen, where it wad hae been ill following him wi' the beast, and I cam back to Charlies-hope to tell the gudewife, for I was un- certain what to do. It wad look unco-like, I thought, just to be sent out on a hunt-the-gowk errand wi' a land-louper like that. But, Lord! as the gude- wife set up her throat about it, and said what a shame it wad be if ye was to come to ony wrang, an I could help ye; and then in cam your letter that confirmed it. So I took to the kist, and out wi' the pickle notes in case they should be needed, and a' the bairns ran to saddle Dumple. By great luck I had taen the other beast to Edinbro', sae Dumple was as fresh as a rose. Sae aff I set, and Wasp wi' me, for ye wad really hae thought he kenn'd where I was gaun, puir beast; and here I am after a trot o' sixty mile, or near by. But Wasp rade thirty o' them afore me on the saddle, and the puir doggie balanced itsell as ane of the weans wad hae dune, whether I trotted or cantered.'

In this strange story Bertram obviously saw, supposing the warning to be true, some intimation of danger more violent and imminent than could be likely to arise from a few days' imprisonment. At the same time it was equally evident that some unknown friend was working in his behalf. 'Did you not say,' he asked Dinmont, 'that this man Gabriel was of gipsy blood?'

'It was e'en judged sae,' said Dinmont, 'and I think this maks it likely; for they aye ken where the gangs o' ilk ither are to be found, and they can gar news flee like a foot-ba' through the country an they like. An' I forgat to tell ye, there's been an unco inquiry after the auld wife that we saw in Bewcastle; the sheriff's had folk ower the Lime-stane Edge after her, and down the Hermitage and Liddel, and a' gates, and a reward offered for her to appear, o' fifty pounds sterling, nae less; and Justice Forster, he's had out warrants, as I am tell'd, in Cumberland, and an unco ranging and ripeing they have had a' gates seeking for her; but she'll no be taen wi' them unless she likes, for a' that.'

'And how comes that?' said Bertram.

'Ou, I dinna ken; I daur say it's nonsense, but they say she has gathered the fern-seed, and can gang ony gate she likes, like Jock-the-Giant-killer in the ballant, wi' his coat o' darkness and his shoon o' swiftness. Ony way she's a kind o' queen amang the gipsies; she is mair than a hundred year auld, folk say, and minds the coming in o' the moss-troopers in the troublesome times when the Stewarts were put awa. Sae, if she canna hide hersell, she kens them that can hide her weel eneugh, ye needna doubt that. Odd, an I had kenn'd it had been Meg Merrilies yon night at Tib Mumps's, I wad taen care how I crossed her.'

Bertram listened with great attention to this account, which tallied so well in many points with what he had himself seen of this gipsy sibyl. After a moment's consideration, he concluded it would be no breach of faith to mention what he had seen at Derncleugh to a person who held Meg in such reverence as Dinmont obviously did. He told his story accordingly, often interrupted by ejaculations, such as, 'Weel, the like o' that now!' or, 'Na, deil an that's no something now!'

When our Liddesdale friend had heard the whole to an end, he shook his great black head—'Weel, I'll uphaud there's baith gude and ill amang the gipsies, and if they deal wi' the Enemy, it's a' their ain business and no ours.—I ken what the streeking the corpse wad be, weel eneugh. Thae smuggler deevils, when ony o' them's killed in a fray, they'll send for a wife like Meg far eneugh to dress the corpse; odd, it's a' the burial they ever think o'!

and then to be put into the ground without ony decency, just like dogs. But they stick to it, that they'll be streekit, and hae an auld wife when they're dying to rhyme ower prayers, and ballants, and charms, as they ca' them, rather than they'll hae a minister to come and pray wi' them—that's an auld threep o' theirs; and I am thinking the man that died will hae been ane o' the folk that was shot when they burnt Woodbourne.'

'But, my good friend, Woodbourne is not burnt,' said Bertram.

'Weel, the better for them that bides in't,' answered the store-farmer. 'Odd, we had it up the water wi' us, that there wasna a stane on the tap o' anither. But there was fighting, ony way; I daur to say, it would be fine fun! And, as I said, ye may take it on trust, that that's been ane o' the men killed there, and that it's been the gipsies that took your pockmanky when they fand the chaise stickin' in the snaw—they wadna pass the like o' that—it wad just come to their hand like the bowl o' a pint stoup.'*

'But if this woman is a sovereign among them, why was she not able to afford me open protection, and to get me back my property?'

'Ou, wha kens? she has muckle to say wi' them, but whiles they'll tak their ain way for a' that, when they're under temptation. And then there's the smugglers that they're aye leagued wi', she maybe

---

* The handle of a stoup of liquor; than which, our proverb seems to infer, there is nothing comes more readily to the grasp.

couldna manage them sae weel—they 're aye banded thegither — I 've heard, that the gipsies ken when the smugglers will come aff, and where they 're to land, better than the very merchants that deal wi' them. And then, to the boot o' that, she 's whiles crack-brained, and has a bee in her head; they say that whether her spaeings and fortune-tellings be true or no, for certain she believes in them a' hersell, and is aye guiding hersell by some queer prophecy or anither. So she disna aye gang the straight road to the well.—But deil o' sic a story as yours, wi' glamour and dead folk and losing ane's gate, I ever heard out o' the tale-books ! — But whisht, I hear the keeper coming.'

Mac-Guffog accordingly interrupted their discourse by the harsh harmony of the bolts and bars, and showed his bloated visage at the opening door. 'Come, Mr. Dinmont, we have put off locking up for an hour to oblige ye; ye must go to your quarters.'

'Quarters, man ? I intend to sleep here the night. There 's a spare bed in the Captain's room.'

'It 's impossible !' answered the keeper.

'But I say it *is* possible, and that I winna stir— and there 's a dram t' ye.'

Mac-Guffog drank off the spirits, and resumed his objection. 'But it 's against rule, sir; ye have committed nae malefaction.'

'I 'll break your head,' said the sturdy Liddesdale man, 'if ye say ony mair about it, and that will be malefaction eneugh to entitle me to ae night's lodging wi' you, ony way.'

'But I tell ye, Mr. Dinmont,' reiterated the keeper, 'it's against rule, and I behoved to lose my post.'

'Weel, Mac-Guffog,' said Dandie, 'I hae just twa things to say. Ye ken wha I am weel eneugh, and that I wadna loose a prisoner.'

'And how do I ken that?' answered the jailor.

'Weel, if ye dinna ken that,' said the resolute farmer, 'ye ken this;—ye ken ye're whiles obliged to be up our water in the way o' your business; now, if ye let me stay quietly here the night wi' the Captain, I'se pay ye double fees for the room; and if ye say no, ye shall hae the best sark-fu' o' sair banes that ever ye had in your life, the first time ye set a foot by Liddel-moat!'

'Aweel, aweel, gudeman,' said Mac-Guffog, 'a wilfu' man maun hae his way; but if I am challenged for it by the justices, I ken wha sall bear the wyte';—and having sealed this observation with a deep oath or two, he retired to bed, after carefully securing all the doors of the Bridewell. The bell from the town steeple tolled nine just as the ceremony was concluded.

'Although it's but early hours,' said the farmer, who had observed that his friend looked somewhat pale and fatigued, 'I think we had better lie down, Captain, if ye're no agreeable to another cheerer. But troth, ye're nae glass-breaker; and neither am I, unless it be a screed wi' the neighbours, or when I'm on a ramble.'

Bertram readily assented to the motion of his faithful friend, but, on looking at the bed, felt repugnance to trust himself undressed to Mrs. Mac-Guffog's clean sheets.

'I'm muckle o' your opinion, Captain,' said Dandie. 'Odd, this bed looks as if a' the colliers in Sanquhar had been in't thegither. But it'll no win through my muckle coat.' So saying, he flung himself upon the frail bed with a force that made all its timbers crack, and in a few moments gave audible signal that he was fast asleep. Bertram slipped off his coat and boots, and occupied the other dormitory. The strangeness of his destiny, and the mysteries which appeared to thicken around him, while he seemed alike to be persecuted and protected by secret enemies and friends, arising out of a class of people with whom he had no previous connexion, for some time occupied his thoughts. Fatigue, however, gradually composed his mind, and in a short time he was as fast asleep as his companion. And in this comfortable state of oblivion we must leave them, until we acquaint the reader with some other circumstances which occurred about the same period.

CHAPTER XLVI

Say from whence
You owe this strange intelligence ? or why
Upon this blasted heath you stop our way
With such prophetic greeting ?—
Speak, I charge you.

MACBETH.

UPON the evening of the day when Bertram's examination had taken place, Colonel Mannering arrived at Woodbourne from Edinburgh. He found his family in their usual state, which probably, so far as Julia was concerned, would not have been the case had she learned the news of Bertram's arrest. But as, during the Colonel's absence, the two young ladies lived much retired, this circumstance fortunately had not reached Woodbourne. A letter had already made Miss Bertram acquainted with the downfall of the expectations which had been formed upon the bequest of her kinswoman. Whatever hopes that news might have dispelled, the disappointment did not prevent her from joining her friend in affording a cheerful reception to the Colonel, to whom she thus endeavoured to express the deep sense she entertained of his paternal kindness. She touched on her regret, that at such a season of the year he should have made, upon her account, a journey so fruitless.

'That it was fruitless to you, my dear,' said the Colonel, 'I do most deeply lament; but for my own share, I have made some valuable acquaintances, and have spent the time I have been absent in Edinburgh with peculiar satisfaction; so that, on that score, there is nothing to be regretted. Even our friend the Dominie is returned thrice the man he was, from having sharpened his wits in controversy with the geniuses of the northern metropolis.'

'Of a surety,' said the Dominie, with great complacency, 'I did wrestle, and was not overcome, though my adversary was cunning in his art.'

'I presume,' said Miss Mannering, 'the contest was somewhat fatiguing, Mr. Sampson?'

'Very much, young lady—howbeit I girded up my loins and strove against him.'

'I can bear witness,' said the Colonel; 'I never saw an affair better contested. The enemy was like the Mahratta cavalry; he assailed on all sides, and presented no fair mark for artillery; but Mr. Sampson stood to his guns, notwithstanding, and fired away, now upon the enemy, and now upon the dust which he had raised. But we must not fight our battles over again to-night—to-morrow we shall have the whole at breakfast.'

The next morning at breakfast, however, the Dominie did not make his appearance. He had walked out, a servant said, early in the morning. It was so common for him to forget his meals, that his absence never deranged the family. The house-keeper, a decent old-fashioned Presbyterian matron, having, as such, the highest respect for Sampson's theological acquisitions, had it in charge on these occasions to take care that he was no sufferer by his absence of mind, and therefore usually way-laid him on his return, to remind him of his sub-lunary wants, and to minister to their relief. It seldom, however, happened that he was absent from two meals together, as was the case in the present instance. We must explain the cause of this unusual occurrence.

The conversation which Mr. Pleydell had held with Mr. Mannering on the subject of the loss of Harry Bertram, had awakened all the painful sensa-tions which that event had inflicted upon Sampson. The affectionate heart of the poor Dominie had always reproached him, that his negligence in leaving the child in the care of Frank Kennedy had been the proximate cause of the murder of the one, the loss of the other, the death of Mrs. Bertram, and the ruin of the family of his patron. It was a subject which he never conversed upon,— if indeed his mode of speech could be called con-versation at any time,—but it was often present to his imagination. The sort of hope so strongly affirmed and asserted in Mrs. Bertram's last settle-ment, had excited a corresponding feeling in the Dominie's bosom, which was exasperated into a sort of sickening anxiety, by the discredit with which Pleydell had treated it.—Assuredly, thought Samp-son to himself, he is a man of erudition, and well skilled in the weighty matters of the law; but he is also a man of humorous levity and inconsistency of speech; and wherefore should he pronounce *ex cathedra*, as it were, on the hope expressed by worthy Madam Margaret Bertram of Singleside?—

All this, I say, the Dominie *thought* to himself; for had he uttered half the sentence, his jaws would have ached for a month under the unusual fatigue of such a continued exertion. The result of these cogitations was a resolution to go and visit the scene of the tragedy at Warroch Point, where he had not been for many years — not, indeed, since the fatal accident had happened. The walk was a long one, for the Point of Warroch lay on the farther side of the Ellangowan property, which was interposed between it and Woodbourne. Besides, the Dominie went astray more than once, and met with brooks swoln into torrents by the melting of the snow, where he, honest man, had only the summer-recollection of little trickling rills.

At length, however, he reached the woods which he had made the object of his excursion, and traversed them with care, muddling his disturbed brains with vague efforts to recall every circumstance of the catastrophe. It will readily be supposed that the influence of local situation and association was inadequate to produce conclusions different from those which he had formed under the immediate pressure of the occurrences themselves. ' With many a weary sigh, therefore, and many a groan,' the poor Dominie returned from his hopeless pilgrimage, and weariedly plodded his way towards Woodbourne, debating at times in his altered mind a question which was forced upon him by the cravings of an appetite rather of the keenest, namely, whether he had breakfasted that morning or no ?—It was in this twilight humour, now thinking of the loss of the child, then involuntarily compelled to meditate upon the somewhat incongruous subject of hung-beef, rolls, and butter, that his route, which was different from that which he had taken in the morning, conducted him past the small ruined tower, or rather vestige of a tower, called by the country people the Kaim of Derncleugh.

The reader may recollect the description of this ruin in the twenty-seventh chapter of last volume, as the vault in which young Bertram, under the auspices of Meg Merrilies, witnessed the death of Hatteraick's lieutenant. The tradition of the country added ghostly terrors to the natural awe inspired by the situation of this place, which terrors the gipsies, who so long inhabited the vicinity, had probably invented, or at least propagated, for their own advantage. It was said that, during the times of the Galwegian independence, one Hanlon Mac-Dingawaie, brother to the reigning chief, Knarth Mac-Dingawaie, murdered his brother and sovereign, in order to usurp the principality from his infant nephew, and that being pursued for vengeance by the faithful allies and retainers of the house, who espoused the cause of the lawful heir, he was compelled to retreat, with a few followers whom he had involved in his

crime, to this impregnable tower called the Kaim
of Derncleugh, where he defended himself until
nearly reduced by famine, when, setting fire to the
place, he and the small remaining garrison desperately perished by their own swords, rather than fall
into the hands of their exasperated enemies. This
tragedy, which, considering the wild times wherein
it was placed, might have some foundation in truth,
was larded with many legends of superstition and
diablerie, so that most of the peasants of the
neighbourhood, if benighted, would rather have
chosen to make a considerable circuit, than pass
these haunted walls. The lights, often seen around
the tower when used as the rendezvous of the
lawless characters by whom it was occasionally
frequented, were accounted for, under authority
of the tales of witchery, in a manner at once
convenient for the private parties concerned, and
satisfactory to the public.

Now it must be confessed, that our friend
Sampson, although a profound scholar and mathe-
matician, had not travelled so far in philosophy as to
doubt the reality of witchcraft or apparitions. Born
indeed at a time when a doubt in the existence of
witches was interpreted as equivalent to a justification of their infernal practices, a belief of such
legends had been impressed upon the Dominie as
an article indivisible from his religious faith, and
perhaps it would have been equally difficult to have
induced him to doubt the one as the other. With
these feelings, and in a thick misty day, which was
already drawing to its close, Dominie Sampson did

not pass the Kaim of Derncleugh without some feelings of tacit horror.

What then was his astonishment, when, on passing the door—that door which was supposed to have been placed there by one of the latter Lairds of Ellangowan to prevent presumptuous strangers from incurring the dangers of the haunted vault—that door, supposed to be always locked, and the key of which was popularly said to be deposited with the presbytery—that door, that very door, opened suddenly, and the figure of Meg Merrilies, well known, though not seen for many a revolving year, was placed at once before the eyes of the startled Dominie! She stood immediately before him in the foot-path, confronting him so absolutely, that he could not avoid her except by fairly turning back, which his manhood prevented him from thinking of.

'I kenn'd ye wad be here,' she said with her harsh and hollow voice: 'I ken wha ye seek; but ye maun do my bidding.'

'Get thee behind me!' said the alarmed Dominie —'Avoid ye!—*Conjuro te, scelestissima—nequissima —spurcissima—iniquissima—atque miserrima—conjuro te! ! !*'—

Meg stood her ground against this tremendous volley of superlatives, which Sampson hawked up from the pit of his stomach, and hurled at her in thunder. 'Is the carle daft,' she said, 'wi' his glamour?'

'*Conjuro,*' continued the Dominie, '*abjuro, contestor, atque viriliter impero tibi!*'——

'What, in the name of Sathan, are ye feared for, wi' your French gibberish, that would make a dog sick? Listen, ye stickit stibbler, to what I tell ye, or ye sall rue it while there's a limb o' ye hings to anither!—Tell Colonel Mannering that I ken he's seeking me. He kens, and I ken, that the blood will be wiped out, and the lost will be found,

> And Bertram's right and Bertram's might
> Shall meet on Ellangowan height.

Hae, there's a letter to him; I was gaun to send it in another way.—I canna write mysell; but I hae them that will baith write and read, and ride and rin for me. Tell him the time's coming now, and the weird's dreed, and the wheel's turning. Bid him look at the stars as he has looked at them before.—Will ye mind a' this?'

'Assuredly,' said the Dominie, 'I am dubious—for, woman, I am perturbed at thy words, and my flesh quakes to hear thee.'

'They'll do you nae ill though, and maybe muckle gude.'

'Avoid ye! I desire no good that comes by unlawful means.'

'Fule-body that thou art,' said Meg, stepping up to him with a frown of indignation that made her dark eyes flash like lamps from under her bent brows,—'Fule-body! if I meant ye wrang, couldna I clod ye ower that craig, and wad man ken how ye cam by your end mair than Frank Kennedy? Hear ye that, ye worricow?'

'In the name of all that is good,' said the

Dominie, recoiling, and pointing his long pewter-headed walking cane like a javelin at the supposed sorceress,—'in the name of all that is good, bide off hands! I will not be handled—woman, stand off, upon thine own proper peril!—desist, I say—I am strong—lo, I will resist!'—Here his speech was cut short; for Meg, armed with supernatural strength (as the Dominie asserted), broke in upon his guard, put by a thrust which he made at her with his cane, and lifted him into the vault, 'as easily,' said he, 'as I could sway a Kitchen's Atlas.'

'Sit down there,' she said, pushing the half-throttled preacher with some violence against a broken chair,—'sit down there, and gather your wind and your senses, ye black barrow-tram o' the kirk that ye are—Are ye fou or fasting?'

'Fasting—from all but sin,' answered the Dominie, who, recovering his voice, and finding his exorcisms only served to exasperate the intractable sorceress, thought it best to affect complaisance and submission, inwardly conning over, however, the wholesome conjurations which he durst no longer utter aloud. But as the Dominie's brain was by no means equal to carry on two trains of ideas at the same time, a word or two of his mental exercise sometimes escaped, and mingled with his uttered speech in a manner ludicrous enough, especially as the poor man shrunk himself together after every escape of the kind, from terror of the effect it might produce upon the irritable feelings of the witch.

Meg, in the meanwhile, went to a great black
cauldron that was boiling on a fire on the floor,
and, lifting the lid, an odour was diffused through
the vault, which, if the vapours of a witch's
cauldron could in aught be trusted, promised
better things than the hell-broth which such vessels
are usually supposed to contain. It was in fact the
savour of a goodly stew, composed of fowls, hares,
partridges, and moor-game, boiled in a large mess
with potatoes, onions, and leeks, and from the size
of the cauldron, appeared to be prepared for half
a dozen of people at least. 'So ye hae eat naething a' day?' said Meg, heaving a large portion
of this mess into a brown dish, and strewing it
savourily with salt and pepper.*

'Nothing,' answered the Dominie—'*scelestissima!*
—that is—gudewife.'

'Hae then,' said she, placing the dish before him,
'there's what will warm your heart.'

'I do not hunger—*malefica*—that is to say—Mrs.
Merrilies!' for he said unto himself, 'the savour

---

* We must again have recourse to the contribution to Blackwood's
Magazine, April 1817 :—

'To the admirers of good eating, gipsy cookery seems to have little
to recommend it. I can assure you, however, that the cook of a noble-
man of high distinction, a person who never reads even a novel without
an eye to the enlargement of the culinary science, has added to the
Almanach des Gourmands, a certain *Potage à la Meg Merrilies de Derncleugh*, consisting of game and poultry of all kinds, stewed with vege-
tables into a soup, which rivals in savour and richness the gallant messes
of Camacho's wedding ; and which the Baron of Bradwardine would
certainly have reckoned among the *Epulæ lautiores*.'

The artist alluded to in this passage, is Mons. Florence, cook to
Henry and Charles, late Dukes of Buccleuch, and of high distinction in
his profession.

is sweet, but it hath been cooked by a Canidia or an Ericthoe.'

'If ye dinna eat instantly, and put some saul in ye, by the bread and the salt, I'll put it down your throat wi' the cutty spoon, scaulding as it is, and whether ye will or no. Gape, sinner, and swallow!'

Sampson, afraid of eye of newt, and toe of frog, tigers' chaudrons, and so forth, had determined not to venture; but the smell of the stew was fast melting his obstinacy, which flowed from his chops as it were in streams of water, and the witch's threats decided him to feed. Hunger and fear are excellent casuists.

'Saul,' said Hunger, 'feasted with the witch of Endor.'—'And,' quoth Fear, 'the salt which she sprinkled upon the food showeth plainly it is not a necromantic banquet, in which that seasoning never occurs.'—'And, besides,' says Hunger, after the first spoonful, 'it is savoury and refreshing viands.'

'So ye like the meat?' said the hostess.

'Yea,' answered the Dominie, 'and I give thee thanks — *sceleratissima!*—which means — Mrs. Margaret.'

'Aweel, eat your fill; but an ye kenn'd how it was gotten, ye maybe wadna like it sae weel.' Sampson's spoon dropped, in the act of conveying its load to his mouth. 'There's been mony a moonlight watch to bring a' that trade thegither,' continued Meg, — 'the folk that are to eat that dinner thought little o' your game-laws.'

Is that all? thought Sampson, resuming his spoon, and shovelling away manfully; I will not lack my food upon that argument.

'Now, ye maun tak a dram?'

'I will,' quoth Sampson—'*conjuro te*—that is, I thank you heartily,' for he thought to himself, in for a penny, in for a pound; and he fairly drank the witch's health, in a cupful of brandy. When he had put this cope-stone upon Meg's good cheer, he felt, as he said, 'mightily elevated, and afraid of no evil which could befall unto him.'

'Will ye remember my errand now?' said Meg Merrilies; 'I ken by the cast o' your ee that ye're anither man than when you cam in.'

'I will, Mrs. Margaret,' repeated Sampson stoutly; 'I will deliver unto him the sealed yepistle, and will add what you please to send by word of mouth.'

'Then I'll make it short,' says Meg. 'Tell him to look at the stars without fail this night, and to do what I desire him in that letter, as he would wish

> That Bertram's right and Bertram's might
> Should meet on Ellangowan height.

I have seen him twice when he saw na me; I ken when he was in this country first, and I ken what's brought him back again. Up, an' to the gate! ye're ower lang here—follow me.'

Sampson followed the sibyl accordingly, who guided him about a quarter of a mile through the woods, by a shorter cut than he could have found for himself; they then entered upon the common, Meg still marching before him at a great pace, until she gained the top of a small hillock which overhung the road.

'Here,' she said, 'stand still here. Look how the setting sun breaks through yon cloud that's been darkening the lift a' day. See where the first stream o' light fa's—it's upon Donagild's round tower—the auldest tower in the Castle o' Ellangowan—that's no for naething!—See as it's glooming to seaward abune yon sloop in the bay—that's no for naething neither. — Here I stood on this very spot,' said she, drawing herself up so as not to lose one hair-breadth of her uncommon height, and stretching out her long sinewy arm, and clenched hand, 'Here I stood, when I tauld the last Laird o' Ellangowan what was coming on his house—and did that fa' to the ground?—na—it hit even ower sair!—And here, where I brake the wand of peace ower him—here I stand again—to bid God bless and prosper the just heir of Ellangowan that will sune be brought to his ain; and the best laird he shall be that Ellangowan has seen for three hundred years.—I'll no live to see it, maybe; but there will be mony a blithe ee see it though mine be closed. And now, Abel Sampson, as ever ye lo'ed the house of Ellangowan, away wi' my message to the English Colonel, as if life and death were upon your haste!'

So saying, she turned suddenly from the amazed Dominie, and regained with swift and long strides the shelter of the wood from which she had issued, at the point where it most encroached upon the common. Sampson gazed after her for a moment in utter astonishment, and then obeyed her directions, hurrying to Woodbourne at a pace very unusual for him, exclaiming three times, ' Prodigious! prodigious ! pro-di-gi-ous ! '

CHAPTER XLVII

It is not madness
That I have utter'd ; bring me to the test,
And I the matter will re-word ; which madness
Would gambol from.

HAMLET.

As Mr. Sampson crossed the hall with a be-wildered look, Mrs. Allan, the good housekeeper, who, with the reverent attention which is usually rendered to the clergy in Scotland, was on the watch for his return, sallied forth to meet him—
' What 's this o't now, Mr. Sampson, this is waur than ever !—ye 'll really do yoursell some injury wi' these lang fasts—naething 's sae hurtful to the stamach, Mr. Sampson ;—if ye would but put some peppermint draps in your pocket, or let Barnes cut ye a sandwich.'

' Avoid thee !' quoth the Dominie, his mind running still upon his interview with Meg Merri-lies, and making for the dining parlour.

' Na, ye needna gang in there, the cloth 's been removed an hour syne, and the Colonel 's at his wine ; but just step into my room, I have a nice steak that the cook will do in a moment.'

'*Exorciso te !*' said Sampson,—' that is, I have dined.'

'Dined! it's impossible—wha can ye hae dined wi', you that gangs out nae gate?'

'With Beelzebub, I believe,' said the minister.

'Na, then he's bewitched for certain,' said the housekeeper, letting go her hold; 'he's bewitched, or he's daft, and ony way the Colonel maun just guide him his ain gate—Wae's me! Hech, sirs! It's a sair thing to see learning bring folk to this!' And with this compassionate ejaculation, she retreated into her own premises.

The object of her commiseration had by this time entered the dining parlour, where his appearance gave great surprise. He was mud up to the shoulders, and the natural paleness of his hue was twice as cadaverous as usual, through terror, fatigue, and perturbation of mind. 'What on earth is the meaning of this, Mr. Sampson?' said Mannering, who observed Miss Bertram looking much alarmed for her simple but attached friend.

'*Exorciso*,'—said the Dominie.

'How, sir?' replied the astonished Colonel.

'I crave pardon, honourable sir! but my wits——'

'Are gone a wool-gathering, I think—pray, Mr. Sampson, collect yourself, and let me know the meaning of all this.'

Sampson was about to reply, but finding his Latin *formula* of exorcism still came most readily to his tongue, he prudently desisted from the attempt, and put the scrap of paper which he had received from the gipsy into Mannering's hand, who broke the seal and read it with surprise. 'This seems to be some jest,' he said, 'and a very dull one.'

'It came from no jesting person,' said Mr. Sampson.

'From whom then did it come?' demanded Mannering.

The Dominie, who often displayed some delicacy of recollection in cases where Miss Bertram had an interest, remembered the painful circumstances connected with Meg Merrilies, looked at the young ladies, and remained silent. 'We will join you at the tea-table in an instant, Julia,' said the Colonel; 'I see that Mr. Sampson wishes to speak to me alone.—And now they are gone, what, in Heaven's name, Mr. Sampson, is the meaning of all this?'

'It may be a message from Heaven,' said the Dominie, 'but it came by Beelzebub's postmistress. It was that witch, Meg Merrilies, who should have been burned with a tar-barrel twenty years since, for a harlot, thief, witch, and gipsy.'

'Are you sure it was she?' said the Colonel with great interest.

'Sure, honoured sir?—Of a truth she is one not to be forgotten—the like o' Meg Merrilies is not to be seen in any land.'

The Colonel paced the room rapidly, cogitating with himself. 'To send out to apprehend her—but it is too distant to send to Mac-Morlan, and Sir Robert Hazlewood is a pompous coxcomb; besides the chance of not finding her upon the spot, or that the humour of silence that seized her before may again return;—no, I will not, to save being thought a fool, neglect the course she points out. Many of her class set out by being impostors, and end by becoming enthusiasts, or hold a kind of darkling conduct between both lines, unconscious almost when they are cheating themselves, or when imposing on others.—Well, my course is a plain one at any rate; and if my efforts are fruitless, it shall not be owing to over-jealousy of my own character for wisdom.'

With this he rang the bell, and ordering Barnes into his private sitting-room, gave him some orders, with the result of which the reader may be made hereafter acquainted. We must now take up another adventure, which is also to be woven into the story of this remarkable day.

Charles Hazlewood had not ventured to make a visit at Woodbourne during the absence of the Colonel. Indeed Mannering's whole behaviour had impressed upon him an opinion that this would be disagreeable; and such was the ascendency which the successful soldier and accomplished gentleman had attained over the young man's conduct, that in no respect would he have ventured to offend him. He saw, or thought he saw, in Colonel Mannering's general conduct, an approbation of his attachment to Miss Bertram. But then he saw still more plainly the impropriety of any attempt at a private correspondence, of which his parents could not be supposed to approve, and he respected this barrier interposed betwixt them, both on Mannering's account, and as he was the liberal and zealous protector of Miss Bertram. 'No,' said he to himself, 'I will not endanger the comfort of my Lucy's present retreat, until I can offer her a home of her own.'

With this valorous resolution, which he maintained, although his horse, from constant habit, turned his head down the avenue of Woodbourne, and although he himself passed the lodge twice every day, Charles Hazlewood withstood a strong inclination to ride down, just to ask how the young ladies were, and whether he could be of any service to them during Colonel Mannering's absence. But on the second occasion he felt the temptation so severe, that he resolved not to expose himself to it a third time; and, contenting himself with sending hopes and inquiries, and so forth, to Woodbourne, he resolved to make a visit long promised to a family at some distance, and to return in such time as to be one of the earliest among Mannering's visitors, who should congratulate his safe arrival from his distant and hazardous expedition to Edinburgh. Accordingly, he made out his visit, and having arranged matters so as to be informed within a few hours after Colonel Mannering reached home, he finally resolved to take leave of the friends with whom he had spent the intervening time, with the intention of dining at Woodbourne, where he was in a great measure domesticated; and this (for he thought much more deeply on the subject than was necessary) would, he flattered himself, appear a simple, natural, and easy mode of conducting himself.

Fate, however, of which lovers make so many complaints, was, in this case, unfavourable to Charles

Hazlewood. His horse's shoes required an altera-
tion, in consequence of the fresh weather having
decidedly commenced. The lady of the house, where
he was a visitor, chose to indulge in her own room
till a very late breakfast hour. His friend also
insisted on showing him a litter of puppies, which
his favourite pointer bitch had produced that morning. The colours had occasioned some doubts about
the paternity, a weighty question of legitimacy, to
the decision of which Hazlewood's opinion was
called in as arbiter between his friend and his groom,
and which inferred in its consequences, which of
the litter should be drowned, which saved. Besides,
the Laird himself delayed our young lover's departure for a considerable time, endeavouring, with
long and superfluous rhetoric, to insinuate to Sir
Robert Hazlewood, through the medium of his son,
his own particular ideas respecting the line of a
meditated turnpike road. It is greatly to the shame
of our young lover's apprehension, that after the
tenth reiterated account of the matter, he could
not see the advantage to be obtained by the proposed road passing over the Lang-hirst, Windy-
knowe, the Goodhouse-park, Hailziecroft, and then
crossing the river at Simon's Pool, and so by the
road to Kippletringan ; and the less eligible line
pointed out by the English surveyor, which would
go clear through the main enclosures at Hazlewood,
and cut within a mile, or nearly so, of the house
itself, destroying the privacy and pleasure, as his
informer contended, of the grounds.

In short, the adviser (whose actual interest was

to have the bridge built as near as possible to a farm of his own) failed in every effort to attract young Hazlewood's attention, until he mentioned by chance that the proposed line was favoured by 'that fellow Glossin,' who pretended to take a lead in the county. On a sudden young Hazlewood became attentive and interested; and having satisfied himself which was the line that Glossin patronised, assured his friend it should not be his fault if his father did not countenance any other instead of that. But these various interruptions consumed the morning. Hazlewood got on horseback at least three hours later than he intended, and, cursing fine ladies, pointers, puppies, and turnpike acts of parliament, saw himself detained beyond the time when he could, with propriety, intrude upon the family at Woodbourne.

He had passed, therefore, the turn of the road which led to that mansion, only edified by the distant appearance of the blue smoke, curling against the pale sky of the winter evening, when he thought he beheld the Dominie taking a footpath for the house through the woods. He called after him, but in vain; for that honest gentleman, never the most susceptible of extraneous impressions, had just that moment parted from Meg Merrilies, and was too deeply wrapt up in pondering upon her vaticinations, to make any answer to Hazlewood's call. He was, therefore, obliged to let him proceed without inquiry after the health of the young ladies, or any other fishing question, to which he might, by good chance, have had an answer returned wherein Miss

Bertram's name might have been mentioned. All cause for haste was now over, and, slackening the reins upon his horse's neck, he permitted the animal to ascend at his own leisure the steep sandy track between two high banks, which, rising to a considerable height, commanded, at length, an extensive view of the neighbouring country.

Hazlewood was, however, so far from eagerly looking forward to this prospect, though it had the recommendation, that great part of the land was his father's, and must necessarily be his own, that his head still turned backward towards the chimneys of Woodbourne, although at every step his horse made the difficulty of employing his eyes in that direction became greater. From the reverie in which he was sunk, he was suddenly roused by a voice too harsh to be called female, yet too shrill for a man:—'What's kept you on the road sae lang?—maun ither folk do your wark?'

He looked up; the spokeswoman was very tall, had a voluminous handkerchief rolled round her head, grizzled hair flowing in elf-locks from beneath it, a long red cloak, and a staff in her hand, headed with a sort of spear-point—it was, in short, Meg Merrilies. Hazlewood had never seen this remarkable figure before; he drew up his reins in astonishment at her appearance, and made a full stop. 'I think,' continued she, 'they that hae taen interest in the house of Ellangowan suld sleep nane this night; three men hae been seeking ye, and you are gaun hame to sleep in your bed—d'ye think if the lad-bairn fa's, the sister will do weel? na, na!'

' I don't understand you, good woman,' said Hazlewood : ' If you speak of Miss——I mean of any of the late Ellangowan family, tell me what I can do for them.'

' Of the late Ellangowan family ? ' she answered with great vehemence ; ' of the *late* Ellangowan family ! and when was there ever, or when will there ever be, a family of Ellangowan, but bearing the gallant name of the bauld Bertrams ? '

' But what do you mean, good woman ? '

' I am nae good woman—a' the country kens I am bad eneugh, and baith they and I may be sorry eneugh that I am nae better. But I can do what good women canna, and daurna do. I can do what would freeze the blood o' them that is bred in biggit wa's for naething but to bind bairns' heads, and to hap them in the cradle. Hear me—the guard's drawn off at the Custom-house at Portanferry, and it's brought up to Hazlewood-house by your father's orders, because he thinks his house is to be attacked this night by the smugglers ;—there's naebody means to touch his house ; he has gude blood and gentle blood—I say little o' him for himsell, but there's naebody thinks him worth meddling wi'. Send the horsemen back to their post, cannily and quietly—see an they winna hae wark the night —ay will they—the guns will flash and the swords will glitter in the braw moon.'

' Good God ! what do you mean ? ' said young Hazlewood ; ' your words and manner would persuade me you are mad, and yet there is a strange combination in what you say.'

'I am not mad!' exclaimed the gipsy; 'I have been imprisoned for mad — scourged for mad— banished for mad—but mad I am not. Hear ye, Charles Hazlewood of Hazlewood: d'ye bear malice against him that wounded you?'

'No, dame, God forbid; my arm is quite well, and I have always said the shot was discharged by accident. I should be glad to tell the young man so himself.'

'Then do what I bid ye,' answered Meg Merrilies, 'and ye'll do him mair gude than ever he did you ill; for if he was left to his ill-wishers he would be a bloody corpse ere morn, or a banished man—but there's ane abune a'.—Do as I bid you; send back the soldiers to Portanferry. There's nae mair fear o' Hazlewood-house than there's o' Cruffel-fell.' And she vanished with her usual celerity of pace.

It would seem that the appearance of this female, and the mixture of frenzy and enthusiasm in her manner, seldom failed to produce the strongest impression upon those whom she addressed. Her words, though wild, were too plain and intelligible for actual madness, and yet too vehement and extravagant for sober-minded communication. She seemed acting under the influence of an imagination rather strongly excited than deranged; and it is wonderful how palpably the difference, in such cases, is impressed upon the mind of the auditor. This may account for the attention with which her strange and mysterious hints were heard and acted upon. It is certain, at least, that young Hazlewood was strongly impressed by her sudden appearance and imperative tone. He rode to Hazlewood at a brisk pace. It had been dark for some time before he reached the house, and on his arrival there, he saw a confirmation of what the sibyl had hinted.

Thirty dragoon horses stood under a shed near the offices, with their bridles linked together. Three or four soldiers attended as a guard, while others stamped up and down with their long broadswords and heavy boots in front of the house. Hazlewood asked a non-commissioned officer from whence they came?

'From Portanferry.'

'Had they left any guard there?'

'No; they had been drawn off by order of Sir Robert Hazlewood for defence of his house, against an attack which was threatened by the smugglers.'

Charles Hazlewood instantly went in quest of his father, and, having paid his respects to him upon his return, requested to know upon what account he had thought it necessary to send for a military escort. Sir Robert assured his son in reply, that from the information, intelligence, and tidings, which had been communicated to, and laid before him, he had the deepest reason to believe, credit, and be convinced, that a riotous assault would that night be attempted and perpetrated against Hazlewood-house, by a set of smugglers, gipsies, and other desperadoes.

'And what, my dear sir,' said his son, 'should

direct the fury of such persons against ours rather than any other house in the country?'

'I should rather think, suppose, and be of opinion, sir,' answered Sir Robert, 'with deference to your wisdom and experience, that on these occasions and times, the vengeance of such persons is directed or levelled against the most important and distinguished in point of rank, talent, birth, and situation, who have checked, interfered with, and discountenanced their unlawful and illegal and criminal actions or deeds.'

Young Hazlewood, who knew his father's foible, answered, that the cause of his surprise did not lie where Sir Robert apprehended, but that he only wondered they should think of attacking a house where there were so many servants, and where a signal to the neighbouring tenants could call in such strong assistance; and added, that he doubted much whether the reputation of the family would not in some degree suffer from calling soldiers from their duty at the Custom-house, to protect them, as if they were not sufficiently strong to defend themselves upon any ordinary occasion. He even hinted, that in case their house's enemies should observe that this precaution had been taken unnecessarily, there would be no end of their sarcasms.

Sir Robert Hazlewood was rather puzzled at this intimation, for, like most dull men, he heartily hated and feared ridicule. He gathered himself up and looked with a sort of pompous embarrassment, as if he wished to be thought to despise the opinion of the public, which in reality he dreaded.

'I really should have thought,' he said, 'that the injury which had already been aimed at my house in your person, being the next heir and representative of the Hazlewood family, failing me —I should have thought and believed, I say, that this would have justified me sufficiently in the eyes of the most respectable and the greater part of the people, for taking such precautions as are calculated to prevent and impede a repetition of outrage.'

'Really, sir,' said Charles, 'I must remind you of what I have often said before, that I am positive the discharge of the piece was accidental.'

'Sir, it was not accidental,' said his father angrily; 'but you will be wiser than your elders.'

'Really, sir,' replied Hazlewood, 'in what so intimately concerns myself——'

'Sir, it does not concern you but in a very secondary degree—that is, it does not concern you, as a giddy young fellow, who takes pleasure in contradicting his father; but it concerns the country, sir; and the county, sir; and the public, sir; and the kingdom of Scotland, in so far as the interest of the Hazlewood family, sir, is committed, and interested, and put in peril, in, by, and through you, sir. And the fellow is in safe custody, and Mr. Glossin thinks——'

'Mr. Glossin, sir?'

'Yes, sir, the gentleman who has purchased Ellangowan—you know who I mean, I suppose?'

'Yes, sir,' answered the young man, 'but I should hardly have expected to hear you quote

such authority.   Why, this fellow—all the world
knows him to be sordid, mean, tricking, and I
suspect him to be worse.   And you yourself, my
dear sir, when did you call such a person a gentleman in your life before?'

'Why, Charles, I did not mean gentleman in the
precise sense and meaning, and restricted and proper
use, to which, no doubt, the phrase ought legiti-
mately to be confined; but I meant to use it rela-
tively, as marking something of that state to which
he has elevated and raised himself—as designing,
in short, a decent and wealthy and estimable sort
of a person.'

'Allow me to ask, sir,' said Charles, 'if it was
by this man's orders that the guard was drawn from
Portanferry?'

'Sir,' replied the Baronet, 'I do apprehend that
Mr. Glossin would not presume to give orders, or
even an opinion, unless asked, in a matter in which
Hazlewood-house and the house of Hazlewood—
meaning by the one this mansion-house of my
family, and by the other, typically, metaphorically,
and parabolically, the family itself—I say then where
the house of Hazlewood, or Hazlewood-house, was
so immediately concerned.'

'I presume, however, sir,' said the son, 'this
Glossin approved of the proposal?'

'Sir,' replied his father, 'I thought it decent and
right and proper to consult him as the nearest
magistrate, as soon as report of the intended outrage reached my ears; and although he declined,
out of deference and respect, as became our relative

situations, to concur in the order, yet he did entirely approve of my arrangement.'

At this moment a horse's feet were heard coming very fast up the avenue. In a few minutes the door opened, and Mr. Mac-Morlan presented himself. ' I am under great concern to intrude, Sir Robert, but——'

' Give me leave, Mr. Mac - Morlan,' said Sir Robert, with a gracious flourish of welcome; ' this is no intrusion, sir; for your situation as Sheriff-substitute calling upon you to attend to the peace of the county, (and you, doubtless, feeling yourself particularly called upon to protect Hazlewood-house,) you have an acknowledged, and admitted, and undeniable right, sir, to enter the house of the first gentleman in Scotland, uninvited—always presuming you to be called there by the duty of your office.'

' It is indeed the duty of my office,' said Mac-Morlan, who waited with impatience an opportunity to speak, ' that makes me an intruder.'

' No intrusion!' reiterated the Baronet, gracefully waving his hand.

' But permit me to say, Sir Robert,' said the Sheriff-Substitute, ' I do not come with the purpose of remaining here, but to recall these soldiers to Portanferry, and to assure you that I will answer for the safety of your house.'

' To withdraw the guard from Hazlewood-house!' exclaimed the proprietor in mingled displeasure and surprise; ' and *you* will be answerable for it! And, pray, who are you, sir, that I should take your security, and caution, and pledge, official or personal, for the safety of Hazlewood-house?—I think, sir, and believe, sir, and am of opinion, sir, that if any one of these family pictures were deranged, or destroyed, or injured, it would be difficult for me to make up the loss upon the guarantee which *you* so obligingly offer me.'

'In that case I shall be sorry for it, Sir Robert,' answered the downright Mac - Morlan; 'but I presume I may escape the pain of feeling my conduct the cause of such irreparable loss, as I can assure you there will be no attempt upon Hazlewood-house whatever, and I have received information which induces me to suspect that the rumour was put afloat merely in order to occasion the removal of the soldiers from Portanferry. And under this strong belief and conviction, I must exert my authority as sheriff and chief magistrate of police, to order the whole, or greater part of them, back again. I regret much, that by my accidental absence, a good deal of delay has already taken place, and we shall not now reach Portanferry until it is late.'

As Mr. Mac-Morlan was the superior magistrate, and expressed himself peremptory in the purpose of acting as such, the Baronet, though highly offended, could only say, 'Very well, sir, it is very well. Nay, sir, take them all with you—I am far from desiring any to be left here, sir. We, sir, can protect ourselves, sir. But you will have the goodness to observe, sir, that you are acting on your own proper risk, sir, and peril, sir, and responsibility, sir, if any thing shall happen or befall to Hazlewood-house, sir, or the inhabitants, sir, or to the furniture and paintings, sir.'

'I am acting to the best of my judgment and information, Sir Robert,' said Mac-Morlan, 'and I must pray of you to believe so, and to pardon me accordingly. I beg you to observe it is no time for ceremony—it is already very late.'

But Sir Robert, without deigning to listen to his apologies, immediately employed himself with much parade in arming and arraying his domestics. Charles Hazlewood longed to accompany the military, which were about to depart for Portanferry, and which were now drawn up and mounted by direction and under the guidance of Mr. Mac-Morlan, as the civil magistrate. But it would have given just pain and offence to his father to have left him at a moment when he conceived himself and his mansion-house in danger. Young Hazlewood therefore gazed from a window with suppressed regret and displeasure, until he heard the officer give the word of command—'From the right to the front, by files, m-a-rch. Leading file, to the right wheel—Trot.'—The whole party of soldiers then getting into a sharp and uniform pace, were soon lost among the trees, and the noise of the hoofs died speedily away in the distance.

CHAPTER XLVIII

Wi' coulters and wi' forehammers
We garr'd the bars bang merrily,
Until we came to the inner prison,
Where Willie o' Kinmont he did lie.

OLD BORDER BALLAD.

WE return to Portanferry, and to Bertram and his honest-hearted friend, whom we left most innocent inhabitants of a place built for the guilty. The slumbers of the farmer were as sound as it was possible.

But Bertram's first heavy sleep passed away long before midnight, nor could he again recover that state of oblivion. Added to the uncertain and uncomfortable state of his mind, his body felt feverish and oppressed. This was chiefly owing to the close and confined air of the small apartment in which they slept. After enduring for some time the broiling and suffocating feeling attendant upon such an atmosphere, he rose to endeavour to open the window of the apartment, and thus to procure a change of air. Alas! the first trial reminded him that .he was in jail, and that the building being contrived for security, not comfort, the means of procuring fresh air were not left at the disposal of the wretched inhabitants.

Disappointed in this attempt, he stood by the

238

unmanageable window for some time. Little Wasp, though oppressed with the fatigue of his journey on the preceding day, crept out of bed after his master, and stood by him rubbing his shaggy coat against his legs, and expressing, by a murmuring sound, the delight which he felt at being restored to him. Thus accompanied, and waiting until the feverish feeling which at present agitated his blood should subside into a desire for warmth and slumber, Bertram remained for some time looking out upon the sea.

The tide was now nearly full, and dashed hoarse and near below the base of the building. Now and then a large wave reached even the barrier or bulwark which defended the foundation of the house, and was flung upon it with greater force and noise than those which only broke upon the sand. Far in the distance, under the indistinct light of a hazy and often over-clouded moon, the ocean rolled its multitudinous complication of waves, crossing, bursting, and mingling with each other.

' A wild and dim spectacle,' said Bertram to himself, ' like those crossing tides of fate which have tossed me about the world from my infancy upwards. When will this uncertainty cease, and how soon shall I be permitted to look out for a tranquil home, where I may cultivate in quiet, and without dread and perplexity, those arts of peace from which my cares have been hitherto so forcibly diverted ? The ear of Fancy, it is said, can discover the voice of sea-nymphs and tritons amid the bursting murmurs of the ocean ; would that I could do so, and that some siren or Proteus would arise from these billows, to unriddle for me the strange maze of fate in which I am so deeply entangled!— Happy friend!' he said, looking at the bed where Dinmont had deposited his bulky person, 'thy cares are confined to the narrow round of a healthy and thriving occupation! Thou canst lay them aside at pleasure, and enjoy the deep repose of body and mind which wholesome labour has prepared for thee!'

At this moment his reflections were broken by little Wasp, who, attempting to spring up against the window, began to yelp and bark most furiously. The sounds reached Dinmont's ears, but without dissipating the illusion which had transported him from this wretched apartment to the free air of his own green hills. 'Hoy, Yarrow, man—far yaud—far yaud,' he muttered between his teeth, imagining, doubtless, that he was calling to his sheep-dog, and hounding him, in shepherds' phrase, against some intruders on the grazing. The continued barking of the terrier within was answered by the angry challenge of the mastiff in the court-yard, which had for a long time been silent, excepting only an occasional short and deep note, uttered when the moon shone suddenly from among the clouds. Now, his clamour was continued and furious, and seemed to be excited by some disturbance distinct from the barking of Wasp, which had first given him the alarm, and which, with much trouble, his master had contrived to still into an angry note of low growling.

GUY MANNERING

At last Bertram, whose attention was now fully awakened, conceived that he saw a boat upon the sea, and heard in good earnest the sound of oars and of human voices, mingling with the dash of the billows. Some benighted fishermen, he thought, or perhaps some of the desperate traders from the Isle of Man. They are very hardy, however, to approach so near to the Custom-house, where there must be sentinels. It is a large boat, like a long-boat, and full of people; perhaps it belongs to the revenue service. — Bertram was confirmed in this last opinion, by observing that the boat made for a little quay which ran into the sea behind the Custom-house, and, jumping ashore one after another, the crew, to the number of twenty hands, glided secretly up a small lane which divided the Custom-house from the Bridewell, and disappeared from his sight, leaving only two persons to take care of the boat.

The dash of these men's oars at first, and latterly the suppressed sounds of their voices, had excited the wrath of the wakeful sentinel in the courtyard, who now exalted his deep voice into such a horrid and continuous din, that it awakened his brute master, as savage a ban-dog as himself. His cry from a window, of ' How now, Tearum, what 's the matter, sir ?—down, d—n ye, down !' produced no abatement of Tearum's vociferation, which in part prevented his master from hearing the sounds of alarm which his ferocious vigilance was in the act of challenging. But the mate of the two-legged Cerberus was gifted with sharper ears than her husband. She also was now at the window; 'B—t ye, gae down and let loose the dog,' she said, 'they're sporting the door of the Custom-house, and the auld sap at Hazlewood-house has ordered off the guard. But ye hae nae mair heart than a cat.' And down the Amazon sallied to perform the task herself, while her help-mate, more jealous of insurrection within doors, than of storm from without, went from cell to cell to see that the inhabitants of each were carefully secured.

These latter sounds, with which we have made the reader acquainted, had their origin in front of the house, and were consequently imperfectly heard by Bertram, whose apartment, as we have already noticed, looked from the back part of the building upon the sea. He heard, however, a stir and tumult in the house, which did not seem to accord with the stern seclusion of a prison at the hour of midnight, and, connecting them with the arrival of an armed boat at that dead hour, could not but suppose that something extraordinary was about to take place. In this belief he shook Dinmont by the shoulder—'Eh!—Ay!—Oh!—Ailie, woman, it's no time to get up yet,' groaned the sleeping man of the mountains. More roughly shaken, however, he gathered himself up, shook his ears, and asked, 'In the name of Providence, what's the matter?'

'That I can't tell you,' replied Bertram; 'but either the place is on fire, or some extraordinary thing is about to happen. Are you not sensible of a smell of fire? Do you not hear what a noise there is of clashing doors within the house, and of hoarse voices, murmurs, and distant shouts on the outside? Upon my word, I believe something very extraordinary has taken place—Get up, for the love of Heaven, and let us be on our guard.'

Dinmont rose at the idea of danger, as intrepid and undismayed as any of his ancestors when the beacon-light was kindled. 'Odd, Captain, this is a queer place! they winna let ye out in the day, and they winna let ye sleep in the night. Deil, but it wad break my heart in a fortnight. But, Lordsake, what a racket they're making now!—Odd, I wish we had some light.—Wasp—Wasp, whisht, hinny—whisht, my bonnie man, and let's hear what they're doing.—Deil's in ye, will ye whisht?'

They sought in vain among the embers the means of lighting their candle, and the noise without still continued. Dinmont in his turn had recourse to the window—'Lordsake, Captain! come here.— Odd, they hae broken the Custom-house!'

Bertram hastened to the window, and plainly saw a miscellaneous crowd of smugglers, and blackguards of different descriptions, some carrying lighted torches, others bearing packages and barrels down the lane to the boat that was lying at the quay, to which two or three other fisher-boats were now brought round. They were loading each of these in their turn, and one or two had already put off to seaward. 'This speaks for itself,' said Bertram; 'but I fear something worse has happened. Do you perceive a strong smell of smoke, or is it my fancy?'

'Fancy?' answered Dinmont, 'there's a reek like a killogie. Odd, if they burn the Custom-house it will catch here, and we'll lunt like a tar-barrel a' thegither.—Eh! it wad be fearsome to be burnt alive for naething, like as if ane had been a warlock!—Mac-Guffog, hear ye!'—roaring at the top of his voice; 'an ye wad ever hae a haill bane in your skin, let's out, man! let's out!'

The fire began now to rise high, and thick clouds of smoke rolled past the window, at which Bertram and Dinmont were stationed. Sometimes, as the wind pleased, the dim shroud of vapour hid every thing from their sight; sometimes a red glare illuminated both land and sea, and shone full on the stern and fierce figures, who, wild with ferocious activity, were engaged in loading the boats. The fire was at length triumphant, and spouted in jets of flame out at each window of the burning building, while huge flakes of flaming materials came driving on the wind against the adjoining prison, and rolling a dark canopy of smoke over all the neighbourhood. The shouts of a furious mob resounded far and wide; for the smugglers, in their triumph, were joined by all the rabble of the little town and neighbourhood, now aroused, and in complete agitation, notwithstanding the lateness of the hour; some from interest in the free trade, and most from the general love of mischief and tumult, natural to a vulgar populace.

Bertram began to be seriously anxious for their fate. There was no stir in the house; it seemed as if the jailor had deserted his charge, and left the prison with its wretched inhabitants to the mercy of the conflagration which was spreading towards them. In the meantime a new and fierce attack was heard upon the outer gate of the Correction-house, which, battered with sledge-hammers and crows, was soon forced. The keeper, as great a coward as a bully, with his more ferocious wife, had fled; their servants readily surrendered the keys. The liberated prisoners, celebrating their deliverance with the wildest yells of joy, mingled among the mob which had given them freedom.

In the midst of the confusion that ensued, three or four of the principal smugglers hurried to the apartment of Bertram with lighted torches, and armed with cutlasses and pistols. — 'Der deyvil,' said the leader, 'here's our mark!' and two of them seized on Bertram; but one whispered in his ear, 'Make no resistance till you are in the street.' The same individual found an instant to say to Dinmont—'Follow your friend, and help when you see the time come.'

In the hurry of the moment, Dinmont obeyed and followed close. The two smugglers dragged Bertram along the passage, down stairs, through the court-yard, now illuminated by the glare of fire, and into the narrow street to which the gate opened, where, in the confusion, the gang were necessarily in some degree separated from each other. A rapid noise, as of a body of horse advancing, seemed to add to the disturbance. 'Hagel and wetter, what is that?' said the leader; 'keep together, kinder, look to the prisoner.'—But in spite of his charge, the two who held Bertram were the last of the party.

The sounds and signs of violence were heard in front. The press became furiously agitated, while some endeavoured to defend themselves, others to escape; shots were fired, and the glittering broad-swords of the dragoons began to appear flashing above the heads of the rioters. 'Now,' said the warning whisper of the man who held Bertram's left arm, the same who had spoken before, 'shake off that fellow, and follow me.'

Bertram, exerting his strength suddenly and effectually, easily burst from the grasp of the man who held his collar on the right side. The fellow attempted to draw a pistol, but was prostrated by a blow of Dinmont's fist, which an ox could hardly have received without the same humiliation. 'Follow me quick,' said the friendly partisan, and dived through a very narrow and dirty lane which led from the main street.

No pursuit took place. The attention of the smugglers had been otherwise and very disagree-ably engaged by the sudden appearance of Mac-Morlan and the party of horse. The loud manly voice of the provincial magistrate, was heard pro-claiming the riot act, and charging 'all those unlawfully assembled, to disperse at their own proper peril.' This interruption would indeed have happened in time sufficient to have prevented the attempt, had not the magistrate received upon the road some false information, which led him to think that the smugglers were to land at the Bay of

Ellangowan. Nearly two hours were lost in consequence of this false intelligence, which it may be no lack of charity to suppose that Glossin, so deeply interested in the issue of that night's daring attempt, had contrived to throw in Mac-Morlan's way, availing himself of the knowledge that the soldiers had left Hazlewood-house, which would soon reach an ear so anxious as his.

In the mean time, Bertram followed his guide, and was in his turn followed by Dinmont. The shouts of the mob, the trampling of the horses, the dropping pistol-shots, sunk more and more faintly upon their ears; when at the end of the dark lane they found a post-chaise with four horses. 'Are you here, in God's name?' said the guide to the postilion who drove the leaders.

'Ay, troth am I,' answered Jock Jabos, 'and I wish I were ony gate else.'

'Open the carriage, then—You, gentlemen, get into it—in a short time you 'll be in a place of safety—and (to Bertram) remember your promise to the gipsy wife!'

Bertram, resolving to be passive in the hands of a person who had just rendered him such a distinguished piece of service, got into the chaise as directed. Dinmont followed; Wasp, who had kept close by them, sprung in at the same time, and the carriage drove off very fast. 'Have a care o' me,' said Dinmont, 'but this is the queerest thing yet!—Odd, I trust they 'll no coup us—and then what 's to come o' Dumple?—I would rather be on his back than in the Deuke's coach, God bless him.'

Bertram observed, that they could not go at that rapid rate to any very great distance without changing horses, and that they might insist upon remaining till day-light at the first inn they stopped at, or at least upon being made acquainted with the purpose and termination of their journey, and Mr. Dinmont might there give directions about his faithful horse, which would probably be safe at the stables where he had left him.—' Aweel, aweel, e'en sae be it for Dandie.—Odd, if we were ance out o' this trindling kist o' a thing, I am thinking they wad find it hard wark to gar us gang ony gate but where we liked oursells.'

While he thus spoke, the carriage making a sudden turn, showed them, through the left window, the village at some distance, still widely beaconed by the fire, which, having reached a storehouse wherein spirits were deposited, now rose high into the air, a wavering column of brilliant light. They had not long time to admire this spectacle, for another turn of the road carried them into a close lane between plantations, through which the chaise proceeded in nearly total darkness, but with un-abated speed.

CHAPTER XLIX

The night drave on wi' sangs and clatter,
And aye the ale was growing better.

TAM O' SHANTER.

WE must now return to Woodbourne, which, it may be remembered, we left just after the Colonel had given some directions to his confidential servant. When he returned, his absence of mind, and an unusual expression of thought and anxiety upon his features, struck the ladies whom he joined in the drawing-room. Mannering was not, however, a man to be questioned, even by those whom he most loved, upon the cause of the mental agitation which these signs expressed. The hour of tea arrived, and the party were partaking of that refreshment in silence, when a carriage drove up to the door, and the bell announced the arrival of a visitor. 'Surely,' said Mannering, 'it is too soon by some hours.'—

There was a short pause, when Barnes, opening the door of the saloon, announced Mr. Pleydell. In marched the lawyer, whose well-brushed black coat, and well-powdered wig, together with his point ruffles, brown silk stockings, highly varnished shoes, and gold buckles, exhibited the pains which the old gentleman had taken to prepare his person for the

ladies' society. He was welcomed by Mannering
with a hearty shake by the hand. 'The very man
I wished to see at this moment!'

'Yes,' said the counsellor, 'I told you I would
take the first opportunity; so I have ventured to
leave the Court for a week in session time—no
common sacrifice—but I had a notion I could be
useful, and I was to attend a proof here about the
same time. But will you not introduce me to the
young ladies?—Ah! there is one I should have
known at once, from her family likeness! Miss
Lucy Bertram, my love, I am most happy to see
you.'—And he folded her in his arms, and gave
her a hearty kiss on each side of the face, to which
Lucy submitted in blushing resignation.

'*On ne s'arrête pas dans un si beau chemin*,' continued the gay old gentleman, and, as the Colonel
presented him to Julia, took the same liberty with
that fair lady's cheek. Julia laughed, coloured, and
disengaged herself. 'I beg a thousand pardons,'
said the lawyer, with a bow which was not at all
professionally awkward; 'age and old fashions give
privileges, and I can hardly say whether I am most
sorry just now at being too well entitled to claim
them at all, or happy in having such an opportunity
to exercise them so agreeably.'

'Upon my word, sir,' said Miss Mannering,
laughing, 'if you make such flattering apologies,
we shall begin to doubt whether we can admit
you to shelter yourself under your alleged quali-
fications.'

'I can assure you, Julia,' said the Colonel,

'you are perfectly right; my friend the counsellor is a dangerous person; the last time I had the pleasure of seeing him, he was closeted with a fair lady, who had granted him a *tête-à-tête* at eight in the morning.'

'Ay, but, Colonel,' said the counsellor, 'you should add, I was more indebted to my chocolate than my charms for so distinguished a favour, from a person of such propriety of demeanour as Mrs. Rebecca.'

'And that should remind me, Mr. Pleydell,' said Julia, 'to offer you tea—that is, supposing you have dined.'

'Any thing, Miss Mannering, from your hands,' answered the gallant jurisconsult; 'yes, I have dined—that is to say, as people dine at a Scotch inn.'

'And that is indifferently enough,' said the Colonel, with his hand upon the bell-handle; 'give me leave to order something.'

'Why, to say truth,' replied Mr. Pleydell, 'I had rather not; I have been inquiring into that matter, for you must know I stopped an instant below to pull off my boot-hose, "a world too wide for my shrunk shanks,"' glancing down with some complacency upon limbs which looked very well for his time of life, 'and I had some conversation with your Barnes, and a very intelligent person whom I presume to be the housekeeper; and it was settled among us—*tota re perspecta*—I beg Miss Mannering's pardon for my Latin—that the old lady should add to your light family-supper the more substantial refreshment of a brace of wild-ducks. I told her (always under deep submission) my poor thoughts about the sauce, which concurred exactly with her own; and, if you please, I would rather wait till they are ready before eating any thing solid.'

'And we will anticipate our usual hour of supper,' said the Colonel.

'With all my heart,' said Pleydell, 'providing I do not lose the ladies' company a moment the sooner. I am of counsel with my old friend Burnet;* I love the *cœna*, the supper of the ancients, the pleasant meal and social glass that wash out of one's mind the cobwebs that business or gloom have been spinning in our brains all day.'

The vivacity of Mr. Pleydell's look and manner, and the quietness with which he made himself at home on the subject of his little epicurean comforts, amused the ladies, but particularly Miss Mannering, who immediately gave the counsellor a great deal of flattering attention; and more pretty things were said on both sides during the service of the tea-table than we have leisure to repeat.

As soon as this was over, Mannering led the counsellor by the arm into a small study which opened from the saloon, and where, according to the custom of the family, there were always lights and a good fire in the evening.

'I see,' said Mr. Pleydell, 'you have got something to tell me about the Ellangowan business—

* See Note H.   Lord Monboddo.

Is it terrestrial or celestial? What says my military Albumazar? Have you calculated the course of futurity? have you consulted your Ephemerides, your Almochoden, your Almuten?'

'No, truly, counsellor,' replied Mannering, 'you are the only Ptolemy I intend to resort to upon the present occasion — a second Prospero, I have broken my staff, and drowned my book far beyond plummet depth. But I have great news notwithstanding. Meg Merrilies, our Egyptian sibyl, has appeared to the Dominie this very day, and, as I conjecture, has frightened the honest man not a little.'

'Indeed?'

'Ay, and she has done me the honour to open a correspondence with me, supposing me to be as deep in astrological mysteries as when we first met. Here is her scroll, delivered to me by the Dominie.'

Pleydell put on his spectacles. 'A vile greasy scrawl, indeed—and the letters are uncial or semi-uncial, as somebody calls your large text hand, and in size and perpendicularity resemble the ribs of a roasted pig—I can hardly make it out.'

'Read aloud,' said Mannering.

'I will try,' answered the lawyer. '"*You are a good seeker, but a bad finder; you set yourself to prop a falling house, but had a gey guess it would rise again. Lend your hand to the wark that's near, as you lent your ee to the weird that was far. Have a carriage this night by ten o'clock, at the end of the Crooked Dykes at Portanferry, and let it bring the folk to Woodbourne that shall ask them, if they be there* IN GOD'S NAME."—Stay, here follows some poetry—

> " *Dark shall be light,*
> *And wrong done to right,*
> *When Bertram's right and Bertram's might*
> *Shall meet on Ellangowan's height.*"

A most mystic epistle truly, and closes in a vein of poetry worthy of the Cumæan sibyl—And what have you done?'

'Why,' said Mannering, rather reluctantly, ' I was loth to risk any opportunity of throwing light on this business. The woman is perhaps crazed, and these effusions may arise only from visions of her imagination; — but you were of opinion that she knew more of that strange story than she ever told.'

'And so,' said Pleydell, 'you sent a carriage to the place named?'

'You will laugh at me if I own I did,' replied the Colonel.

'Who, I?' replied the advocate. 'No, truly, I think it was the wisest thing you could do.'

'Yes,' answered Mannering, well pleased to have escaped the ridicule he apprehended; 'you know the worst is paying the chaise-hire—I sent a post-chaise and four from Kippletringan, with instructions corresponding to the letter—the horses will have a long and cold station on the out-post to-night if our intelligence be false.'

'Ay, but I think it will prove otherwise,' said the lawyer. 'This woman has played a part till she believes it; or, if she be a thorough-paced impostor, without a single grain of self-delusion to qualify her knavery, still she may think herself bound to act in character — this I know, that I could get nothing out of her by the common modes of interrogation, and the wisest thing we can do is to give her an opportunity of making the discovery her own way. And now have you more to say, or shall we go to the ladies?'

'Why, my mind is uncommonly agitated,' answered the Colonel, 'and — but I really have no more to say—only I shall count the minutes till the carriage returns; but you cannot be expected to be so anxious.'

'Why, no—use is all in all,' said the more experienced lawyer,—' I am much interested certainly, but I think I shall be able to survive the interval, if the ladies will afford us some music.'

'And with the assistance of the wild-ducks, by and by?' suggested Mannering.

'True, Colonel; a lawyer's anxiety about the fate of the most interesting cause has seldom spoiled either his sleep or digestion.* And yet I shall be very eager to hear the rattle of these wheels on their return, notwithstanding.'

So saying, he rose and led the way into the next room, where Miss Mannering, at his request, took her seat at the harpsichord. Lucy Bertram, who sung her native melodies very sweetly, was accompanied by her friend upon the instrument, and Julia

---

* See Note I.   Lawyers' Sleepless Nights.

afterwards performed some of Scarlatti's sonatas with great brilliancy. The old lawyer, scraping a little upon the violoncello, and being a member of the gentlemen's concert in Edinburgh, was so greatly delighted with this mode of spending the evening, that I doubt if he once thought of the wild-ducks until Barnes informed the company that supper was ready.

'Tell Mrs. Allan to have something in readiness,' said the Colonel—'I expect—that is, I hope—perhaps some company may be here to-night; and let the men sit up, and do not lock the upper gate on the lawn until I desire you.'

'Lord, sir,' said Julia, 'whom can you possibly expect to-night?'

'Why, some persons, strangers to me, talked of calling in the evening on business,' answered her father, not without embarrassment, for he would have little brooked a disappointment which might have thrown ridicule on his judgment; 'it is quite uncertain.'

'Well, we shall not pardon them for disturbing our party,' said Julia, 'unless they bring as much good-humour, and as susceptible hearts, as my friend and admirer, for so he has dubbed himself, Mr. Pleydell.'

'Ah, Miss Julia,' said Pleydell, offering his arm with an air of gallantry to conduct her into the eating-room, 'the time has been—when I returned from Utrecht in the year 1738—'

'Pray don't talk of it,' answered the young lady—'we like you much better as you are—

Utrecht, in heaven's name!—I dare say you have spent all the intervening years in getting rid so completely of the effects of your Dutch education.'

'O forgive me, Miss Mannering,' said the lawyer; 'the Dutch are a much more accomplished people in point of gallantry than their volatile neighbours are willing to admit. They are constant as clockwork in their attentions.'

'I should tire of that,' said Julia.

'Imperturbable in their good temper,' continued Pleydell.

'Worse and worse,' said the young lady.

'And then,' said the old *beau garçon*, 'although for six times three hundred and sixty-five days, your swain has placed the capuchin round your neck, and the stove under your feet, and driven your little sledge upon the ice in winter, and your cabriole through the dust in summer, you may dismiss him at once, without reason or apology, upon the two thousand one hundred and ninetieth day, which, according to my hasty calculation, and without reckoning leap-years, will complete the cycle of the supposed adoration, and that without your amiable feelings having the slightest occasion to be alarmed for the consequences to those of Mynheer.'

'Well,' replied Julia, 'that last is truly a Dutch recommendation, Mr. Pleydell—crystal and hearts would lose all their merit in the world, if it were not for their fragility.'

'Why, upon that point of the argument, Miss Mannering, it is as difficult to find a heart that will break, as a glass that will not; and for that reason I would press the value of mine own—were it not that I see Mr. Sampson's eyes have been closed, and his hands clasped for some time, attending the end of our conference to begin the grace—And, to say the truth, the appearance of the wild-ducks is very appetizing.' So saying, the worthy counsellor sat himself to table, and laid aside his gallantry for awhile, to do honour to the good things placed before him. Nothing further is recorded of him for some time, excepting an observation that the ducks were roasted to a single turn, and that Mrs. Allan's sauce of claret, lemon, and cayenne, was beyond praise.

'I see,' said Miss Mannering, 'I have a formidable rival in Mr. Pleydell's favour, even on the very first night of his avowed admiration.'

'Pardon me, my fair lady,' answered the counsellor, 'your avowed rigour alone has induced me to commit the solecism of eating a good supper in your presence; how shall I support your frowns without reinforcing my strength? Upon the same principle, and no other, I will ask permission to drink wine with you.'

'This is the fashion of Utrecht also, I suppose, Mr. Pleydell?'

'Forgive me, madam,' answered the counsellor; 'the French themselves, the patterns of all that is gallant, term their tavern-keepers *restaurateurs*, alluding, doubtless, to the relief they afford the disconsolate lover, when bowed down to the earth by his mistress's severity. My own case requires so much relief, that I must trouble you for that other wing, Mr. Sampson, without prejudice to my afterwards applying to Miss Bertram for a tart;—be pleased to tear the wing, sir, instead of cutting it off—Mr. Barnes will assist you, Mr. Sampson,—thank you, sir—and, Mr. Barnes, a glass of ale, if you please.'

While the old gentleman, pleased with Miss Mannering's liveliness and attention, rattled away for her amusement and his own, the impatience of Colonel Mannering began to exceed all bounds. He declined sitting down at table, under pretence that he never eat supper; and traversed the parlour, in which they were, with hasty and impatient steps, now throwing up the window to gaze upon the dark lawn, now listening for the remote sound of the carriage advancing up the avenue. At length, in a feeling of uncontrollable impatience, he left the room, took his hat and cloak, and pursued his walk up the avenue, as if his so doing would hasten the approach of those whom he desired to see. 'I really wish,' said Miss Bertram, 'Colonel Mannering would not venture out after night-fall. You must have heard, Mr. Pleydell, what a cruel fright we had.'

'O, with the smugglers?' replied the advocate —'they are old friends of mine. I was the means of bringing some of them to justice a long time since, when sheriff of this county.'

'And then the alarm we had immediately afterwards,' added Miss Bertram, 'from the vengeance of one of these wretches.'

'When young Hazlewood was hurt—I heard of that too.'

'Imagine, my dear Mr. Pleydell,' continued Lucy, 'how much Miss Mannering and I were alarmed, when a ruffian, equally dreadful for his great strength, and the sternness of his features, rushed out upon us!'

'You must know, Mr. Pleydell,' said Julia, unable to suppress her resentment at this undesigned aspersion of her admirer, 'that young Hazlewood is so handsome in the eyes of the young ladies of this country, that they think every person shocking who comes near him.'

Oho! thought Pleydell, who was by profession an observer of tones and gestures, there's something wrong here between my young friends.— 'Well, Miss Mannering, I have not seen young Hazlewood since he was a boy, so the ladies may be perfectly right; but I can assure you, in spite of your scorn, that if you want to see handsome men you must go to Holland; the prettiest fellow I ever saw was a Dutchman, in spite of his being called Vanbost, or Vanbuster, or some such barbarous name. He will not be quite so handsome now, to be sure.'

It was now Julia's turn to look a little out of countenance at the chance hit of her learned admirer, but that instant the Colonel entered the room. 'I can hear nothing of them yet,' he said; 'still, however, we will not separate—Where is Dominie Sampson?'

'Here, honoured sir.'

' What is that book you hold in your hand, Mr. Sampson ? '

' It's even the learned De Lyra, sir—I would crave his honour Mr. Pleydell's judgment, always with his best leisure, to expound a disputed passage. '

' I am not in the vein, Mr. Sampson,' answered Pleydell; ' here's metal more attractive—I do not despair to engage these two young ladies in a glee or a catch, wherein I, even I myself, will adventure myself for the bass part—Hang de Lyra, man; keep him for a fitter season. '

The disappointed Dominie shut his ponderous tome, much marvelling in his mind how a person, possessed of the lawyer's erudition, could give his mind to these frivolous toys. But the counsellor, indifferent to the high character for learning which he was trifling away, filled himself a large glass of Burgundy, and after preluding a little with a voice somewhat the worse for the wear, gave the ladies a courageous invitation to join in ' We be three poor Mariners,' and accomplished his own part therein with great eclat.

' Are you not withering your roses with sitting up so late, my young ladies ? ' said the Colonel.

' Not a bit, sir,' answered Julia; ' your friend, Mr. Pleydell, threatens to become a pupil of Mr. Sampson's to-morrow, so we must make the most of our conquest to-night. '

This led to another musical trial of skill, and that to lively conversation. At length, when the solitary sound of one o'clock had long since resounded on the ebon ear of night, and the next signal of the advance of time was close approaching, Mannering, whose impatience had long subsided into disappointment and despair, looked at his watch, and said, ' We must now give them up ' — when at that instant — But what then befell will require a separate chapter.

CHAPTER L

Justice. *This does indeed confirm each circumstance*
The gipsy told !————————
No orphan, nor without a friend art thou——
I am thy father, here's *thy mother,* there
Thy uncle——This *thy first cousin, and* these
Are all thy near relations !

THE CRITIC.

As Mannering replaced his watch, he heard a distant
and hollow sound—'It is a carriage for certain—
no, it is but the sound of the wind among the leafless trees. Do come to the window, Mr. Pleydell.'
The counsellor, who, with his large silk handkerchief
in his hand, was expatiating away to Julia upon
some subject which he thought was interesting,
obeyed, however, the summons, first wrapping the
handkerchief round his neck by way of precaution
against the cold air. The sound of wheels became
now very perceptible, and Pleydell, as if he had
reserved all his curiosity till that moment, ran out
to the hall. The Colonel rung for Barnes to desire
that the persons who came in the carriage might be
shown into a separate room, being altogether uncertain whom it might contain. It stopped, however, at the door, before his purpose could be fully
explained. A moment after, Mr. Pleydell called
out, ' Here's our Liddesdale friend, I protest, with

a strapping young fellow of the same calibre.' His voice arrested Dinmont, who recognised him with equal surprise and pleasure. 'Odd, if it's your honour, we'll a' be as right and tight as thack and rape can make us.'*

But while the farmer stopped to make his bow, Bertram, dizzied with the sudden glare of light, and bewildered with the circumstances of his situation, almost unconsciously entered the open door of the parlour, and confronted the Colonel, who was just advancing towards it. The strong light of the apartment left no doubt of his identity, and he himself was as much confounded with the appearance of those to whom he so unexpectedly presented himself, as they were by the sight of so utterly unlooked-for an object. It must be remembered that each individual present had their own peculiar reasons for looking with terror upon what seemed at first sight a spectral apparition. Mannering saw before him the man whom he supposed he had killed in India; Julia beheld her lover in a most peculiar and hazardous situation; and Lucy Bertram at once knew the person who had fired upon young Hazlewood. Bertram, who interpreted the fixed and motionless astonishment of the Colonel into displeasure at his intrusion, hastened to say that it was involuntary, since he had been hurried hither without even knowing whither he was to be transported.

---

* When a farmer's crop is got safely into the barn-yard, it is said to be made fast with thack and rape—Anglicé, straw and rope.

'Mr. Brown, I believe?' said Colonel Mannering.

'Yes, sir,' replied the young man modestly, but with firmness, 'the same you knew in India; and who ventures to hope, that what you did then know of him is not such as should prevent his requesting you would favour him with your attestation to his character, as a gentleman and man of honour.'

'Mr. Brown—I have been seldom—never—so much surprised—certainly, sir, in whatever passed between us, you have a right to command my favourable testimony.'

At this critical moment entered the counsellor and Dinmont. The former beheld, to his astonishment, the Colonel but just recovering from his first surprise, Lucy Bertram ready to faint with terror, and Miss Mannering in an agony of doubt and apprehension, which she in vain endeavoured to disguise or suppress. 'What is the meaning of all this?' said he; 'has this young fellow brought the Gorgon's head in his hand?—let me look at him.—By heaven!' he muttered to himself, 'the very image of old Ellangowan!—Yes, the same manly form and handsome features, but with a world of more intelligence in the face—Yes!—the witch has kept her word.' Then instantly passing to Lucy, 'Look at that man, Miss Bertram, my dear; have you never seen any one like him?'

Lucy had only ventured one glance at this object of terror, by which, however, from his remarkable height and appearance, she at once recognised the supposed assassin of young Hazlewood; a conviction which excluded, of course, the more favourable association of ideas which might have occurred on a closer view.—'Don't ask me about him, sir,' said she, turning away her eyes; 'send him away, for heaven's sake! we shall all be murdered!'

'Murdered! where's the poker?' said the advocate in some alarm; 'but nonsense! we are three men besides the servants, and there is honest Liddesdale worth half-a-dozen to boot—we have the *major vis* upon our side—however, here, my friend Dandie —Davie—what do they call you?—keep between that fellow and us for the protection of the ladies.'

'Lord! Mr. Pleydell,' said the astonished farmer, 'that's Captain Brown; d'ye no ken the Captain?'

'Nay, if he's a friend of yours, we may be safe enough,' answered Pleydell; 'but keep near him.'

All this passed with such rapidity, that it was over before the Dominie had recovered himself from a fit of absence, shut the book which he had been studying in a corner, and advancing to obtain a sight of the strangers, exclaimed at once, upon beholding Bertram, 'If the grave can give up the dead, that is my dear and honoured master!'

'We're right, after all, by Heaven! I was sure I was right,' said the lawyer; 'he is the very image of his father.—Come, Colonel, what do you think of, that you do not bid your guest welcome? I think—I believe—I trust we're right—never saw such a likeness!—But patience—Dominie, say not a word.—Sit down, young gentleman.'

'I beg pardon, sir; if I am, as I understand, in Colonel Mannering's house, I should wish first to know if my accidental appearance here gives offence, or if I am welcome ? '

Mannering instantly made an effort. ' Welcome ? most certainly, especially if you can point out how I can serve you. I believe I may have some wrongs to repair towards you—I have often suspected so ; but your sudden and unexpected appearance, connected with painful recollections, prevented my saying at first, as I now say, that whatever has procured me the honour of this visit, it is an acceptable one.'

Bertram bowed with an air of distant, yet civil acknowledgment, to the grave courtesy of Mannering.

' Julia, my love, you had better retire. Mr. Brown, you will excuse my daughter ; there are circumstances which I perceive rush upon her recollection. '

Miss Mannering rose and retired accordingly ; yet, as she passed Bertram, could not suppress the words, ' Infatuated ! a second time ! ' but so pronounced as to be heard by him alone. Miss Bertram accompanied her friend, much surprised, but without venturing a second glance at the object of her terror. Some mistake she saw there was, and was unwilling to increase it by denouncing the stranger as an assassin. He was known, she saw, to the Colonel, and received as a gentleman ; certainly he either was not the person she suspected, or Hazlewood was right in supposing the shot accidental.

The remaining part of the company would have

formed no bad group for a skilful painter. Each
was too much embarrassed with his own sensations
to observe those of the others. Bertram most unexpectedly found himself in the house of one, whom
he was alternately disposed to dislike as his personal
enemy, and to respect as the father of Julia; Mannering was struggling between his high sense of
courtesy and hospitality, his joy at finding himself
relieved from the guilt of having shed life in a
private quarrel, and the former feelings of dislike
and prejudice, which revived in his haughty mind
at the sight of the object against whom he had
entertained them; Sampson, supporting his shaking
limbs by leaning on the back of a chair, fixed his
eyes upon Bertram, with a staring expression of
nervous anxiety which convulsed his whole visage;
Dinmont, enveloped in his loose shaggy great-coat,
and resembling a huge bear erect upon his hinder
legs, stared on the whole scene with great round
eyes that witnessed his amazement.

The counsellor alone was in his element, shrewd,
prompt, and active; he already calculated the prospect of brilliant success in a strange, eventful, and
mysterious law-suit, and no young monarch, flushed
with hopes, and at the head of a gallant army, could
experience more glee when taking the field on his
first campaign. He bustled about with great
energy, and took the arrangement of the whole
explanation upon himself.

' Come, come, gentlemen, sit down; this is all in
my province: you must let me arrange it for you.
Sit down, my dear Colonel, and let me manage;

sit down, Mr. Brown, *aut quocunque alio nomine vocaris* — Dominie, take your seat — draw in your chair, honest Liddesdale.'

' I dinna ken, Mr. Pleydell,' said Dinmont, looking at his dreadnought-coat, then at the handsome furniture of the room, ' I had maybe better gang some gate else, and leave ye till your cracks—I 'm no just that weel put on.'

The Colonel, who by this time recognised Dandie, immediately went up and bid him heartily welcome; assuring him, that from what he had seen of him in Edinburgh, he was sure his rough coat and thick-soled boots would honour a royal drawing-room.

' Na, na, Colonel, we 're just plain up-the-country folk; but nae doubt I would fain hear o' ony pleasure that was gaun to happen the Captain, and I 'm sure a' will gae right if Mr. Pleydell will take his bit job in hand.'

' You 're right, Dandie — spoke like a Hieland * oracle — and now be silent.—Well, you are all seated at last; take a glass of wine till I begin my catechism methodically. And now,' turning to Bertram, ' my dear boy, do you know who or what you are ? '

In spite of his perplexity, the catechumen could not help laughing at this commencement, and answered, ' Indeed, sir, I formerly thought I did;

---

* It may not be unnecessary to tell southern readers, that the mountainous country in the south-western borders of Scotland, is called Hïeland, though totally different from the much more mountainous and more extensive districts of the north, usually accented Hïelands.

but I own late circumstances have made me somewhat uncertain.'

'Then tell us what you formerly thought yourself.'

'Why, I was in the habit of thinking and calling myself Vanbeest Brown, who served as a cadet or volunteer under Colonel Mannering, when he commanded the —— regiment, in which capacity I was not unknown to him.'

'There,' said the Colonel, 'I can assure Mr. Brown of his identity; and add, what his modesty may have forgotten, that he was distinguished as a young man of talent and spirit.'

'So much the better, my dear sir,' said Mr. Pleydell; 'but that is to general character—Mr. Brown must tell us where he was born.'

'In Scotland, I believe, but the place uncertain.'

'Where educated?'

'In Holland, certainly.'

'Do you remember nothing of your early life before you left Scotland?'

'Very imperfectly; yet I have a strong idea, perhaps more deeply impressed upon me by subsequent hard usage, that I was during my childhood the object of much solicitude and affection. I have an indistinct remembrance of a good-looking man whom I used to call papa, and of a lady who was infirm in health, and who, I think, must have been my mother; but it is an imperfect and confused recollection. I remember too a tall thin kind-tempered man in black, who used to teach me my letters and walk out with me;—and I think the very last time——'

Here the Dominie could contain no longer. While every succeeding word served to prove that the child of his benefactor stood before him, he had struggled with the utmost difficulty to suppress his emotions; but, when the juvenile recollections of Bertram turned towards his tutor and his precepts, he was compelled to give way to his feelings. He rose hastily from his chair, and with clasped hands, trembling limbs, and streaming eyes, called out aloud, 'Harry Bertram!—look at me—was I not the man?'

'Yes!' said Bertram, starting from his seat as if a sudden light had burst in upon his mind,— 'Yes—that was my name!—and that is the voice and the figure of my kind old master!'

The Dominie threw himself into his arms, pressed him a thousand times to his bosom in convulsions of transport, which shook his whole frame, sobbed hysterically, and, at length, in the emphatic language of Scripture, lifted up his voice and wept aloud. Colonel Mannering had recourse to his handkerchief; Pleydell made wry faces, and wiped the glasses of his spectacles; and honest Dinmont, after two loud blubbering explosions, exclaimed, 'Deil's in the man! he's garred me do that I haena done since my auld mither died.'

'Come, come,' said the counsellor at last, 'silence in the court.—We have a clever party to contend with; we must lose no time in gathering our information—for any thing I know, there may be something to be done before day-break.'

'I will order a horse to be saddled, if you please,' said the Colonel.

'No, no, time enough—time enough—but come, Dominie, I have allowed you a competent space to express your feelings. I must circumduce the term—you must let me proceed in my examination.'

The Dominie was habitually obedient to any one who chose to impose commands upon him; he sunk back into his chair, spread his checked handkerchief over his face, to serve, as I suppose, for the Grecian painter's veil, and, from the action of his folded hands, appeared for a time engaged in the act of mental thanksgiving. He then raised his eyes over the screen, as if to be assured that the pleasing apparition had not melted into air—then again sunk them to resume his internal act of devotion, until he felt himself compelled to give attention to the counsellor, from the interest which his questions excited.

'And now,' said Mr. Pleydell, after several minute inquiries concerning his recollection of early events—'And now, Mr. Bertram, for I think we ought in future to call you by your own proper name, will you have the goodness to let us know every particular which you can recollect concerning the mode of your leaving Scotland?'

'Indeed, sir, to say the truth, though the terrible outlines of that day are strongly impressed upon my memory, yet somehow the very terror which fixed them there has in a great measure confounded and confused the details. I recollect, however, that I was walking somewhere or other—in a wood, I think——'

'O yes, it was in Warroch-wood, my dear,' said the Dominie.

'Hush, Mr. Sampson,' said the lawyer.

'Yes, it was in a wood,' continued Bertram, as long past and confused ideas arranged themselves in his reviving recollection; 'and some one was with me—this worthy and affectionate gentleman, I think.'

'O, ay, ay, Harry, Lord bless thee—it was even I myself.'

'Be silent, Dominie, and don't interrupt the evidence,' said Pleydell.—'And so, sir?' to Bertram.

'And so, sir,' continued Bertram, 'like one of the changes of a dream, I thought I was on horseback before my guide.'

'No, no,' exclaimed Sampson, 'never did I put my own limbs, not to say thine, into such peril.'

'On my word, this is intolerable!—Look ye, Dominie, if you speak another word till I give you leave, I will read three sentences out of the Black Acts, whisk my cane round my head three times, undo all the magic of this night's work, and conjure Harry Bertram back again into Vanbeest Brown.'

'Honoured and worthy sir,' groaned out the Dominie, 'I humbly crave pardon—it was but *verbum volans*.'

'Well, *nolens volens*, you must hold your tongue,' said Pleydell.

'Pray, be silent, Mr. Sampson,' said the Colonel; 'it is of great consequence to your recovered friend, that you permit Mr. Pleydell to proceed in his inquiries.'

'I am mute,' said the rebuked Dominie.

'On a sudden,' continued Bertram, 'two or three men sprung out upon us, and we were pulled from horseback. I have little recollection of any thing else, but that I tried to escape in the midst of a desperate scuffle, and fell into the arms of a very tall woman who started from the bushes, and protected me for some time—the rest is all confusion and dread—a dim recollection of a sea-beach, and a cave, and of some strong potion which lulled me to sleep for a length of time. In short, it is all a blank in my memory, until I recollect myself first an ill-used and half-starved cabin-boy aboard a sloop, and then a school-boy in Holland under the protection of an old merchant, who had taken some fancy for me.'

'And what account,' said Mr. Pleydell, 'did your guardian give of your parentage?'

'A very brief one,' answered Bertram, 'and a charge to inquire no farther. I was given to understand, that my father was concerned in the smuggling trade carried on on the eastern coast of Scotland, and was killed in a skirmish with the revenue officers; that his correspondents in Holland had a vessel on the coast at the time, part of the crew of which were engaged in the affair, and that they brought me off after it was over, from a motive of compassion, as I was left destitute by my father's death. As I grew older there was much of this story seemed inconsistent with my own recollections, but what could I do? I had no means of ascertaining my doubts, nor a single friend with whom I could communicate or canvass them. The rest of my story is known to Colonel Mannering: I went out to India to be a clerk in a Dutch house; their affairs fell into confusion—I betook myself to the military profession, and, I trust, as yet I have not disgraced it.'

'Thou art a fine young fellow, I 'll be bound for thee,' said Pleydell, 'and since you have wanted a father so long, I wish from my heart I could claim the paternity myself. But this affair of young Hazlewood——'

'Was merely accidental,' said Bertram. 'I was travelling in Scotland for pleasure, and after a week's residence with my friend, Mr. Dinmont, with whom I had the good fortune to form an accidental acquaintance——'

'It was my gude fortune that,' said Dinmont; 'odd, my brains wad hae been knockit out by twa blackguards, if it hadna been for his four quarters.'

'Shortly after we parted at the town of ——, I lost my baggage by thieves, and it was while residing at Kippletringan I accidentally met the young gentleman. As I was approaching to pay my respects to Miss Mannering, whom I had known in India, Mr. Hazlewood, conceiving my appearance none of the most respectable, commanded me rather haughtily to stand back, and so gave occasion to the fray in which I had the misfortune to be the accidental means of wounding him.—And now, sir, that I have answered all your questions——'

'No, no, not quite all,' said Pleydell, winking sagaciously; 'there are some interrogatories which I shall delay till to-morrow, for it is time, I believe, to close the sederunt for this night, or rather morning.'

'Well, then, sir,' said the young man, 'to vary the phrase, since I have answered all the questions which you have chosen to ask to-night, will you be so good as to tell me who you are that take such interest in my affairs, and whom you take me to be, since my arrival has occasioned such commotion?'

'Why, sir, for myself,' replied the counsellor, 'I am Paulus Pleydell, an advocate at the Scottish bar; and for you, it is not easy to say distinctly who you are at present; but I trust in a short time to hail you by the title of Henry Bertram, Esq., representative of one of the oldest families in Scotland, and heir of tailzie and provision to the estate of Ellangowan—Ay,' continued he, shutting his eyes and speaking to himself, 'we must pass over his father, and serve him heir to his grandfather Lewis, the entailer—the only wise man of his family that I ever heard of.'

They had now risen to retire to their apartments for the night, when Colonel Mannering walked up to Bertram, as he stood astonished at the counsellor's words. 'I give you joy,' he said, 'of the prospects which fate has opened before you. I was an early friend of your father, and chanced to be in the house of Ellangowan as unexpectedly as you are now in mine, upon the very night in which you were born. I little knew this circumstance when—

but I trust unkindness will be forgotten between us. Believe me, your appearance here, as Mr. Brown, alive and well, has relieved me from most painful sensations; and your right to the name of an old friend renders your presence, as Mr. Bertram, doubly welcome.'

' And my parents ? ' said Bertram.

' Are both no more—and the family property has been sold, but I trust may be recovered. Whatever is wanted to make your right effectual, I shall be most happy to supply.'

' Nay, you may leave all that to me,' said the counsellor; ' 'tis my vocation, Hal, I shall make money of it.'

' I 'm sure it 's no for the like o' me,' observed Dinmont, ' to speak to you gentlefolks ; but if siller would help on the Captain's plea, and they say nae plea gangs on weel without it——'

' Except on Saturday night,' said Pleydell.

' Ay, but when your honour wadna take your fee ye wadna hae the cause neither, sae I 'll ne'er fash you on a Saturday at e'en again—but I was saying, there 's some siller in the spleuchan* that 's like the Captain's ain, for we 've aye counted it such, baith Ailie and me.'

' No, no, Liddesdale — no occasion, no occasion whatever—keep thy cash to stock thy farm.'

' To stock my farm ? Mr. Pleydell, your honour kens mony things, but ye dinna ken the farm o' Charlies-hope — it 's sae weel stockit already, that

---

* A spleuchan is a tobacco pouch, occasionally used as a purse.

we sell maybe sax hundred pounds off it ilka year, flesh and fell thegither—na, na.'

' Can't you take another, then ? '

' I dinna ken—the Deuke's no that fond o' led farms, and he canna bide to put away the auld tenantry; and then I wadna like, mysell, to gang about whistling * and raising the rent on my neighbours.'

' What, not upon thy neighbour at Dawston—Devilstone—how d' ye call the place ? '

' What, on Jock o' Dawston ? hout na—he's a camsteary † chield, and fasheous ‡ about marches, and we 've had some bits o' splores thegither; but deil o' me if I wad wrang Jock o' Dawston neither.'

' Thou 'rt an honest fellow,' said the lawyer ; ' get thee to bed. Thou wilt sleep sounder, I warrant thee, than many a man that throws off an embroidered coat, and puts on a laced night-cap.—Colonel, I see you are busy with our *Enfant trouvé*. But Barnes must give me a summons of wakening at seven to-morrow morning, for my servant's a sleepy-headed fellow; and I dare say my clerk, Driver, has had Clarence's fate, and is drowned by this time in a butt of your ale; for Mrs. Allan promised to make him comfortable, and she 'll soon discover what he expects from that engagement.

---

* Whistling, among the tenantry of a large estate, is, when an individual gives such information to the proprietor, or his managers, as to occasion the rent of his neighbour's farms being raised, which, for obvious reasons, is held a very unpopular practice.

† Obstinate and unruly.

‡ Troublesome.

Good night, Colonel—good night, Dominie Sampson —good night, Dinmont the downright—good night, last of all, to the new-found representative of the Bertrams, and the Mac-Dingawaies, the Knarths, the Arths, the Godfreys, the Dennises, and the Rolands, and, last and dearest title, heir of tailzie and provision of the lands and barony of Ellangowan, under the settlement of Lewis Bertram, Esq., whose representative you are.'

And so saying, the old gentleman took his candle and left the room; and the company dispersed, after the Dominie had once more hugged and embraced his 'little Harry Bertram,' as he continued to call the young soldier of six feet high.

CHAPTER LI

My imagination
Carries no favour in it but Bertram's;
I am undone; there is no living, none,
If Bertram be away.——
ALL'S WELL THAT ENDS WELL.

At the hour which he had appointed the preceding evening, the indefatigable lawyer was seated by a good fire, and a pair of wax candles, with a velvet cap on his head, and a quilted silk night-gown on his person, busy arranging his *memoranda* of proofs and indications concerning the murder of Frank Kennedy. An express had also been dispatched to Mr. Mac-Morlan, requesting his attendance at Woodbourne as soon as possible, on business of importance. Dinmont, fatigued with the events of the evening before, and finding the accommodations of Woodbourne much preferable to those of Mac-Guffog, was in no hurry to rise. The impatience of Bertram might have put him earlier in motion, but Colonel Mannering had intimated an intention to visit him in his apartment in the morning, and he did not choose to leave it. Before this interview he had dressed himself, Barnes having, by his master's orders, supplied him with every accommodation of linen, etc., and he now anxiously waited the promised visit of his landlord.

280

In a short time a gentle tap announced the Colonel, with whom Bertram held a long and satisfactory conversation. Each, however, concealed from the other one circumstance. Mannering could not bring himself to acknowledge the astrological prediction; and Bertram was, from motives which may be easily conceived, silent respecting his love for Julia. In other respects, their intercourse was frank and grateful to both, and had latterly, upon the Colonel's part, even an approach to cordiality. Bertram carefully measured his own conduct by that of his host, and seemed rather to receive his offered kindness with gratitude and pleasure, than to press for it with solicitation.

Miss Bertram was in the breakfast parlour when Sampson shuffled in, his face all radiant with smiles; a circumstance so uncommon, that Lucy's first idea was, that somebody had been bantering him with an imposition, which had thrown him into this ecstasy. Having sate for some time rolling his eyes and gaping with his mouth like the great wooden head at Merlin's exhibition, he at length began—'And what do you think of him, Miss Lucy?'

'Think of whom, Mr. Sampson?' asked the young lady.

'Of Har—no—of him that you know about?' again demanded the Dominie.

'That I know about?' replied Lucy, totally at a loss to comprehend his meaning.

'Yes, the stranger, you know, that came last evening in the post vehicle—he who shot young

Hazlewood—ha, ha, ho!' burst forth the Dominie, with a laugh that sounded like neighing.

'Indeed, Mr. Sampson,' said his pupil, 'you have chosen a strange subject for mirth—I think nothing about the man, only I hope the outrage was accidental, and that we need not fear a repetition of it.'

'Accidental! ho, ho, ha!' again whinnied Sampson.

'Really, Mr. Sampson,' said Lucy, somewhat piqued, 'you are unusually gay this morning.'

'Yes, of a surety I am! ha, ha, ho! face-ti-ous—ho, ho, ha!'

'So unusually facetious, my dear sir,' pursued the young lady, 'that I would wish rather to know the meaning of your mirth, than to be amused with its effects only.'

'You shall know it, Miss Lucy,' replied poor Abel—'Do you remember your brother?'

'Good God! how can you ask me?—no one knows better than you, he was lost the very day I was born.'

'Very true, very true,' answered the Dominie, saddening at the recollection; 'I was strangely oblivious—ay, ay—too true—But you remember your worthy father?'

'How should you doubt it, Mr. Sampson? it is not so many weeks since——'

'True, true—ay, too true,' replied the Dominie, his Houyhnhnm laugh sinking into a hysterical giggle,—'I will be facetious no more under these remembrances—but look at that young man!'

Bertram at this instant entered the room. 'Yes, look at him well—he is your father's living image; and as God has deprived you of your dear parents— O my children, love one another!'

'It is indeed my father's face and form,' said Lucy, turning very pale; Bertram ran to support her—the Dominie to fetch water to throw upon her face — (which in his haste he took from the boiling tea-urn) when fortunately her colour returning rapidly, saved her from the application of this ill-judged remedy. 'I conjure you to tell me, Mr. Sampson,' she said, in an interrupted, yet solemn voice, 'is this my brother?'

'It is—it is!—Miss Lucy, it is little Harry Bertram, as sure as God's sun is in that Heaven!'

'And this is my sister?' said Bertram, giving way to all that family affection, which had so long slumbered in his bosom for want of an object to expand itself upon——

'It is—it is!—it is Miss Lucy Bertram,' ejaculated Sampson, 'whom by my poor aid you will find perfect in the tongues of France, and Italy, and even of Spain—in reading and writing her vernacular tongue, and in arithmetic and book-keeping by double and single entry — I say nothing of her talents of shaping, and hemming, and governing a household, which, to give every one their due, she acquired not from me, but from the housekeeper— nor do I take merit for her performance upon stringed instruments, whereunto the instructions of an honourable young lady of virtue and modesty, and very facetious withal—Miss Julia Mannering

—hath not meanly contributed—*Suum cuique tri-buito.*'

'You, then,' said Bertram to his sister, 'are all that remains to me!—Last night, but more fully this morning, Colonel Mannering gave me an account of our family misfortunes, though without saying I should find my sister here.'

'That,' said Lucy, 'he left to this gentleman to tell you, one of the kindest and most faithful of friends, who soothed my father's long sickness, witnessed his dying moments, and amid the heaviest clouds of fortune would not desert his orphan.'

'God bless him for it!' said Bertram, shaking the Dominie's hand; 'he deserves the love with which I have always regarded even that dim and imperfect shadow of his memory which my childhood retained.'

'And God bless you both, my dear children,' said Sampson; 'if it had not been for your sake, I would have been contented (had Heaven's pleasure so been) to lay my head upon the turf beside my patron.'

'But I trust,' said Bertram, 'I am encouraged to hope we shall all see better days. All our wrongs shall be redressed, since Heaven has sent me means and friends to assert my right.'

'Friends indeed!' echoed the Dominie, 'and sent, as you truly say, by HIM, to whom I early taught you to look up as the source of all that is good. There is the great Colonel Mannering from the Eastern Indies, a man of war from his birth

upwards, but who is not the less a man of great erudition, considering his imperfect opportunities; and
there is, moreover, the great advocate Mr. Pleydell,
who is also a man of great erudition, but who
descendeth to trifles unbeseeming thereof; and
there is Mr. Andrew Dinmont, whom I do not
understand to have possession of much erudition,
but who, like the patriarchs of old, is cunning in
that which belongeth to flocks and herds—Lastly,
there is even I myself, whose opportunities of
collecting erudition, as they have been greater
than those of the aforesaid valuable persons, have
not, if it becomes me to speak, been pretermitted
by me, in so far as my poor faculties have enabled
me to profit by them. Of a surety, little Harry,
we must speedily resume our studies. I will begin
from the foundation—Yes, I will reform your education upward from the true knowledge of English
grammar, even to that of the Hebrew or Chaldaic
tongue.'

The reader may observe, that, upon this occasion,
Sampson was infinitely more profuse of words than
he had hitherto exhibited himself. The reason was,
that in recovering his pupil his mind went instantly
back to their original connexion, and he had, in his
confusion of ideas, the strongest desire in the world
to resume spelling lessons and half-text with young
Bertram. This was the more ridiculous, as towards
Lucy he assumed no such powers of tuition. But
she had grown up under his eye, and had been
gradually emancipated from his government by
increase in years and knowledge, and a latent

sense of his own inferior tact in manners, whereas his first ideas went to take up Harry pretty nearly where he had left him. From the same feelings of reviving authority, he indulged himself in what was to him a profusion of language; and as people seldom speak more than usual without exposing themselves, he gave those whom he addressed plainly to understand, that while he deferred implicitly to the opinions and commands, if they chose to impose them, of almost every one whom he met with, it was under an internal conviction, that in the article of eru-di-ti-on, as he usually pronounced the word, he was infinitely superior to them all put together. At present, however, this intimation fell upon heedless ears, for the brother and sister were too deeply engaged in asking and receiving intelligence concerning their former fortunes to attend much to the worthy Dominie.

When Colonel Mannering left Bertram, he went to Julia's dressing-room, and dismissed her attendant. 'My dear sir,' she said as he entered, 'you have forgot our vigils last night, and have hardly allowed me time to comb my hair, although you must be sensible how it stood on end at the various wonders which took place.'

'It is with the inside of your head that I have some business at present, Julia; I will return the outside to the care of your Mrs. Mincing in a few minutes.'

'Lord, papa,' replied Miss Mannering, 'think how entangled all my ideas are, and you to propose to comb them out in a few minutes! If Mincing were to do so in her department, she would tear half the hair out of my head.'

'Well then, tell me,' said the Colonel, 'where the entanglement lies, which I will try to extricate with due gentleness?'

'O, everywhere,' said the young lady—'the whole is a wild dream.'

'Well then, I will try to unriddle it.'—He gave a brief sketch of the fate and prospects of Bertram, to which Julia listened with an interest which she in vain endeavoured to disguise—'Well,' concluded her father, 'are your ideas on the subject more luminous?'

'More confused than ever, my dear sir,' said Julia.—'Here is this young man come from India, after he had been supposed dead, like Aboulfouaris the great voyager to his sister Canzade and his provident brother Hour. I am wrong in the story, I believe—Canzade was his wife—but Lucy may represent the one, and the Dominie the other. And then this lively crack-brained Scotch lawyer appears like a pantomime at the end of a tragedy— And then how delightful it will be if Lucy gets back her fortune!'

'Now I think,' said the Colonel, 'that the most mysterious part of the business is, that Miss Julia Mannering, who must have known her father's anxiety about the fate of this young man Brown, or Bertram, as we must now call him, should have met him when Hazlewood's accident took place, and never once mentioned to her father a word of the matter, but suffered the search to proceed against this young gentleman as a suspicious character and assassin.'

Julia, much of whose courage had been hastily assumed to meet the interview with her father, was now unable to rally herself; she hung down her head in silence, after in vain attempting to utter a denial that she recollected Brown when she met him.

'No answer!—Well, Julia,' continued her father, gravely but kindly, 'allow me to ask you, Is this the only time you have seen Brown since his return from India?—Still no answer. I must then naturally suppose that it is *not* the first time—Still no reply. Julia Mannering, will you have the kindness to answer me? Was it this young man who came under your window and conversed with you during your residence at Mervyn-Hall? Julia—I command—I entreat you to be candid.'

Miss Mannering raised her head. 'I have been, sir—I believe I am still very foolish—and it is perhaps more hard upon me that I must meet this gentleman, who has been, though not the cause entirely, yet the accomplice of my folly, in your presence.'—Here she made a full stop.

'I am to understand, then,' said Mannering, 'that this was the author of the serenade at Mervyn-Hall?'

There was something in this allusive change of epithet, that gave Julia a little more courage—'He was indeed, sir; and if I am very wrong, as I have often thought, I have some apology.'

'And what is that?' answered the Colonel,

speaking quick, and with something of harsh-ness.

'I will not venture to name it, sir—but'—She opened a small cabinet, and put some letters into his hands; 'I will give you these, that you may see how this intimacy began, and by whom it was encouraged.'

Mannering took the packet to the window—his pride forbade a more distant retreat—he glanced at some passages of the letters with an unsteady eye and an agitated mind—his stoicism, however, came in time to his aid; that philosophy, which, rooted in pride, yet frequently bears the fruits of virtue. He returned towards his daughter with as firm an air as his feelings permitted him to assume.

'There is great apology for you, Julia, as far as I can judge from a glance at these letters—you have obeyed at least one parent. Let us adopt a Scotch proverb the Dominie quoted the other day—"Let bygones be bygones, and fair play for the future."—I will never upbraid you with your past want of con-fidence—do you judge of my future intentions by my actions, of which hitherto you have surely had no reason to complain. Keep these letters—they were never intended for my eye, and I would not willingly read more of them than I have done, at your desire and for your exculpation. And now, are we friends? Or rather, do you understand me?'

'O my dear, generous father,' said Julia, throw-ing herself into his arms, 'why have I ever for an instant misunderstood you?'

'No more of that, Julia,' said the Colonel; 'we have both been to blame. He that is too proud to vindicate the affection and confidence which he conceives should be given without solicitation, must meet much, and perhaps deserved disappointment. It is enough that one dearest and most regretted member of my family has gone to the grave without knowing me; let me not lose the confidence of a child, who ought to love me if she really loves herself.'

'O no danger—no fear!' answered Julia; 'let me but have your approbation and my own, and there is no rule you can prescribe so severe that I will not follow.'

'Well, my love,' kissing her forehead, 'I trust we shall not call upon you for any thing too heroic. With respect to this young gentleman's addresses, I expect in the first place that all clandestine correspondence—which no young woman can entertain for a moment without lessening herself in her own eyes, and in those of her lover—I request, I say, that clandestine correspondence of every kind may be given up, and that you will refer Mr. Bertram to me for the reason. You will naturally wish to know what is to be the issue of such a reference. In the first place, I desire to observe this young gentleman's character more closely than circumstances, and perhaps my own prejudices, have permitted formerly—I should also be glad to see his birth established. Not that I am anxious about his getting the estate of Ellangowan, though such a subject is held in absolute indifference nowhere except in a novel; but certainly Henry Bertram, heir of Ellangowan, whether possessed of the property of his ancestors or not, is a very different person from Vanbeest Brown, the son of nobody at all. His fathers, Mr. Pleydell tells me, are distinguished in history as following the banners of their native princes, while our own fought at Cressy and Poictiers. In short, I neither give nor withhold my approbation, but I expect you will redeem past errors; and as you can now unfortunately only have recourse to *one* parent, that you will show the duty of a child, by reposing that confidence in me, which I will say my inclination to make you happy renders a filial debt upon your part.'

The first part of this speech affected Julia a good deal; the comparative merit of the ancestors of the Bertrams and Mannerings excited a secret smile, but the conclusion was such as to soften a heart peculiarly open to the feelings of generosity. 'No, my dear sir,' she said, extending her hand, 'receive my faith, that from this moment you shall be the first person consulted respecting what shall pass in future between Brown—I mean Bertram—and me; and that no engagement shall be undertaken by me, excepting what you shall immediately know and approve of. May I ask—if Mr. Bertram is to continue a guest at Woodbourne?'

'Certainly,' said the Colonel, 'while his affairs render it advisable.'

'Then, sir, you must be sensible, considering what is already past, that he will expect some reason for my withdrawing—I believe I must say the encouragement, which he may think I have given.'

'I expect, Julia,' answered Mannering, 'that he will respect my roof, and entertain some sense perhaps of the services I am desirous to render him, and so will not insist upon any course of conduct of which I might have reason to complain; and I expect of you, that you will make him sensible of what is due to both.'

'Then, sir, I understand you, and you shall be implicitly obeyed.'

'Thank you, my love; my anxiety (kissing her) is on your account.—Now wipe these witnesses from your eyes, and so to breakfast.'

CHAPTER LII

And, Sheriff, I will engage my word to you,
That I will by to-morrow dinner time,
Send him to answer thee, or any man,
For any thing he shall be charged withal.

HENRY IV. PART I.

WHEN the several by-plays, as they may be termed, had taken place among the individuals of the Woodbourne family, as we have intimated in the preceding chapter, the breakfast party at length assembled, Dandie excepted, who had consulted his taste in viands, and perhaps in society, by partaking of a cup of tea with Mrs. Allan, just laced with two tea-spoonfuls of Cogniac, and reinforced with various slices from a huge round of beef. He had a kind of feeling that he could eat twice as much, and speak twice as much, with this good dame and Barnes, as with the grand folk in the parlour. Indeed, the meal of this less distinguished party was much more mirthful than that in the higher circle, where there was an obvious air of constraint on the greater part of the assistants. Julia dared not raise her voice in asking Bertram if he chose another cup of tea. Bertram felt embarrassed while eating his toast and butter under the eye of Mannering. Lucy, while she indulged to the uttermost her affection for her recovered brother, began to think of the quarrel betwixt him and Hazlewood. The Colonel felt the painful anxiety natural to a proud mind, when it deems its slightest action subject for a moment to the watchful construction of others. The lawyer, while sedulously buttering his roll, had an aspect of unwonted gravity, arising, perhaps, from the severity of his morning studies. As for the Dominie, his state of mind was ecstatic!—He looked at Bertram—he looked at Lucy—he whimpered—he sniggled—he grinned—he committed all manner of solecisms in point of form—poured the whole cream (no unlucky mistake) upon the plate of porridge, which was his own usual breakfast—threw the slops of what he called his 'crowning dish of tea' into the sugar-dish instead of the slop-basin, and concluded with spilling the scalded liquor upon old Plato, the Colonel's favourite spaniel, who received the libation with a howl that did little honour to his philosophy.

The Colonel's equanimity was rather shaken by this last blunder. 'Upon my word, my good friend, Mr. Sampson, you forget the difference between Plato and Zenocrates.'

'The former was chief of the Academics, the latter of the Stoics,' said the Dominie, with some scorn of the supposition.

'Yes, my dear sir, but it was Zenocrates, not Plato, who denied that pain was an evil.'

'I should have thought,' said Pleydell, 'that very respectable quadruped, which is just now limping out of the room upon three of his four legs, was rather of the Cynic school.'

'Very well hit off——But here comes an answer from Mac-Morlan.'

It was unfavourable. Mrs. Mac-Morlan sent her respectful compliments, and her husband had been, and was, detained, by some alarming disturbances which had taken place the preceding night at Portanferry, and the necessary investigation which they had occasioned.

'What's to be done, now, counsellor?' said the Colonel to Pleydell.

'Why, I wish we could have seen Mac-Morlan,' said the counsellor, 'who is a sensible fellow himself, and would besides have acted under my advice. But there is little harm. Our friend here must be made *sui juris*—he is at present an escaped prisoner; the law has an awkward claim upon him; he must be placed *rectus in curia*, that is the first object. For which purpose, Colonel, I will accompany you in your carriage down to Hazlewood-house. The distance is not great; we will offer our bail; and I am confident I can easily show Mr.——I beg his pardon—Sir Robert Hazlewood, the necessity of receiving it.'

'With all my heart,' said the Colonel; and, ringing the bell, gave the necessary orders. 'And what is next to be done?'

'We must get hold of Mac-Morlan, and look out for more proof.'

'Proof!' said the Colonel, 'the thing is as clear as day-light — here are Mr. Sampson and Miss

Bertram, and you yourself, at once recognise the
young gentleman as his father's image; and he himself recollects all the very peculiar circumstances
preceding his leaving this country — What else is
necessary to conviction?'

'To moral conviction nothing more, perhaps,'
said the experienced lawyer, 'but for legal proof
a great deal. Mr. Bertram's recollections are his
own recollections merely, and therefore are not
evidence in his own favour; Miss Bertram, the
learned Mr. Sampson, and I, can only say, what
every one who knew the late Ellangowan will
readily agree in, that this gentleman is his very
picture—But that will not make him Ellangowan's
son, and give him the estate.'

'And what will do so?' said the Colonel.

'Why, we must have a distinct probation.—
There are these gipsies,—but then, alas! they are
almost infamous in the eye of law—scarce capable
of bearing evidence, and Meg Merrilies utterly so,
by the various accounts which she formerly gave of
the matter, and her impudent denial of all knowledge of the fact when I myself examined her
respecting it.'

'What must be done then?' asked Mannering.

'We must try,' answered the legal sage, 'what
proof can be got at in Holland, among the persons
by whom our young friend was educated.—But then
the fear of being called in question for the murder of
the gauger may make them silent; or if they speak,
they are either foreigners or outlawed smugglers.
In short, I see doubts.'

'Under favour, most learned and honoured sir,' said the Dominie, 'I trust HE, who hath restored little Harry Bertram to his friends, will not leave his own work imperfect.'

'I trust so too, Mr. Sampson,' said Pleydell; 'but we must use the means; and I am afraid we shall have more difficulty in procuring them than I at first thought.—But a faint heart never won a fair lady—and, by the way, (apart to Miss Mannering, while Bertram was engaged with his sister,) there's a vindication of Holland for you! what smart fellows do you think Leyden and Utrecht must send forth, when such a very genteel and handsome young man comes from the paltry schools of Middleburgh?'

'Of a verity,' said the Dominie, jealous of the reputation of the Dutch seminary,—'of a verity, Mr. Pleydell, but I make it known to you that I myself laid the foundation of his education.'

'True, my dear Dominie,' answered the advocate; 'that accounts for his proficiency in the graces, without question—but here comes your carriage, Colonel. Adieu, young folks: Miss Julia, keep your heart till I come back again—let there be nothing done to prejudice my right, whilst I am *non valens agere.*'

Their reception at Hazlewood-house was more cold and formal than usual; for in general the Baronet expressed great respect for Colonel Mannering, and Mr. Pleydell, besides being a man of good family and of high general estimation, was Sir Robert's old friend. But now he seemed dry and embarrassed in his manner. 'He would willingly,' he said, 'receive bail, notwithstanding that the offence had been directly perpetrated, committed, and done, against young Hazlewood of Hazlewood; but the young man had given himself a fictitious description, and was altogether that sort of person, who should not be liberated, discharged, or let loose upon society; and therefore——'

'I hope, Sir Robert Hazlewood,' said the Colonel, 'you do not mean to doubt my word, when I assure you that he served under me as cadet in India?'

'By no means or account whatsoever. But you call him a cadet; now he says, avers, and upholds, that he was a captain, or held a troop in your regiment.'

'He was promoted since I gave up the command.'

'But you must have heard of it?'

'No. I returned on account of family circumstances from India, and have not since been solicitous to hear particular news from the regiment; the name of Brown, too, is so common, that I might have seen his promotion in the Gazette without noticing it. But a day or two will bring letters from his commanding officer.'

'But I am told and informed, Mr. Pleydell,' answered Sir Robert, still hesitating, 'that he does not mean to abide by this name of Brown, but is to set up a claim to the estate of Ellangowan, under the name of Bertram.'

'Ay, who says that?' said the counsellor.

'Or,' demanded the soldier, 'whoever says so, does that give a right to keep him in prison?'

'Hush, Colonel,' said the lawyer; 'I am sure you would not, any more than I, countenance him, if he prove an impostor—And, among friends, who informed you of this, Sir Robert?'

'Why, a person, Mr. Pleydell,' answered the Baronet, 'who is peculiarly interested in investigating, sifting, and clearing out this business to the bottom—you will excuse my being more particular.'

'O, certainly,' replied Pleydell—'well, and he says——?'

'He says that it is whispered about among tinkers, gipsies, and other idle persons, that there is such a plan as I mentioned to you, and that this young man, who is a bastard or natural son of the late Ellangowan, is pitched upon as the impostor, from his strong family likeness.'

'And was there such a natural son, Sir Robert?' demanded the counsellor.

'O, certainly, to my own positive knowledge. Ellangowan had him placed as cabin-boy or powder-monkey on board an armed sloop or yacht belonging to the revenue, through the interest of the late Commissioner Bertram, a kinsman of his own.'

'Well, Sir Robert,' said the lawyer, taking the word out of the mouth of the impatient soldier—'you have told me news; I shall investigate them, and if I find them true, certainly Colonel Mannering and I will not countenance this young man. In the meanwhile, as we are all willing to make him forthcoming, to answer all complaints against him, I do assure you, you will act most illegally, and incur heavy responsibility, if you refuse our bail.'

'Why, Mr. Pleydell,' said Sir Robert, who knew the high authority of the counsellor's opinion, 'as you must know best, and as you promise to give up this young man——'

'If he proves an impostor,' replied the lawyer, with some emphasis.

'Ay, certainly—under that condition I will take your bail; though I must say, an obliging, well-disposed, and civil neighbour of mine, who was himself bred to the law, gave me a hint or caution this morning against doing so. It was from him I learned that this youth was liberated and had come abroad, or rather had broken prison.—But where shall we find one to draw the bail-bond?'

'Here,' said the counsellor, applying himself to the bell, 'send up my clerk, Mr. Driver—it will not do my character harm if I dictate the needful myself.' It was written accordingly and signed, and, the Justice having subscribed a regular warrant for Bertram *alias* Brown's discharge, the visitors took their leave.

Each threw himself into his own corner of the post-chariot, and said nothing for some time. The Colonel first broke silence: 'So you intend to give up this poor young fellow at the first brush?'

'Who, I?' replied the counsellor; 'I will not give up one hair of his head, though I should follow them to the court of last resort in his behalf—but what signified mooting points and showing

one's hand to that old ass? Much better he should report to his prompter, Glossin, that we are in-different or lukewarm in the matter. Besides, I wished to have a peep at the enemies' game.'

'Indeed!' said the soldier. 'Then I see there are stratagems in law as well as war. Well, and how do you like their line of battle?'

'Ingenious,' said Mr. Pleydell, 'but I think desperate—they are finessing too much; a common fault on such occasions.'

During this discourse the carriage rolled rapidly towards Woodbourne without any thing occurring worthy of the reader's notice, excepting their meeting with young Hazlewood, to whom the Colonel told the extraordinary history of Bertram's re-appearance, which he heard with high delight, and then rode on before to pay Miss Bertram his compliments on an event so happy and so unexpected.

We return to the party at Woodbourne. After the departure of Mannering, the conversation related chiefly to the fortunes of the Ellangowan family, their domains, and their former power. 'It was, then, under the towers of my fathers,' said Bertram, 'that I landed some days since, in circumstances much resembling those of a vagabond? Its moulder-ing turrets and darksome arches even then awakened thoughts of the deepest interest, and recollections which I was unable to decipher. I will now visit them again with other feelings, and, I trust, other and better hopes.'

'Do not go there now,' said his sister. 'The house of our ancestors is at present the habitation of a wretch as insidious as dangerous, whose arts and villainy accomplished the ruin and broke the heart of our unhappy father.'

'You increase my anxiety,' replied her brother, 'to confront this miscreant, even in the den he has constructed for himself—I think I have seen him.'

'But you' must consider,' said Julia, 'that you are now left under Lucy's guard and mine, and are responsible to us for all your motions—consider I have not been a lawyer's mistress twelve hours for nothing, and I assure you it would be madness to attempt to go to Ellangowan just now.—The utmost to which I can consent, is, that we shall walk in a body to the head of the Woodbourne avenue, and from that perhaps we may indulge you with our company as far as a rising ground in the common, whence your eyes may be blessed with a distant prospect of those gloomy towers, which struck so strongly your sympathetic imagination.'

The party was speedily agreed upon; and the ladies, having taken their cloaks, followed the route proposed, under the escort of Captain Bertram. It was a pleasant winter morning, and the cool breeze served only to freshen, not to chill, the fair walkers. A secret though unacknowledged bond of kindness combined the two ladies, and Bertram, now hearing the interesting accounts of his own family, now communicating his adventures in Europe and in India, repaid the pleasure which he received. Lucy felt proud of her brother, as well from the bold and manly turn of his sentiments, as from the dangers he had encountered, and the spirit with which he had surmounted them. And Julia, while she pondered on her father's words, could not help entertaining hopes, that the independent spirit which had seemed to her father presumption in the humble and plebeian Brown, would have the grace of courage, noble bearing, and high blood, in the far-descended heir of Ellangowan.

They reached at length the little eminence or knoll upon the highest part of the common, called Gibbie's-knowe—a spot repeatedly mentioned in this history, as being on the skirts of the Ellangowan estate. It commanded a fair variety of hill and dale, bordered with natural woods, whose naked boughs at this season relieved the general colour of the landscape with a dark purple hue; while in other places the prospect was more formally intersected by lines of plantation, where the Scotch firs displayed their variety of dusky green. At the distance of two or three miles lay the bay of Ellangowan, its waves rippling under the influence of the western breeze. The towers of the ruined castle, seen high over every object in the neighbourhood, received a brighter colouring from the wintry sun.

'There,' said Lucy Bertram, pointing them out in the distance, 'there is the seat of our ancestors. God knows, my dear brother, I do not covet in your behalf the extensive power which the lords of these ruins are said to have possessed so long, and sometimes to have used so ill. But, O that I might see you in possession of such relics of their fortune as should give you an honourable independence,

and enable you to stretch your hand for the protection of the old and destitute dependents of our
family, whom our poor father's death——'

'True, my dearest Lucy,' answered the young
heir of Ellangowan; 'and I trust, with the assistance of Heaven, which has so far guided us, and
with that of these good friends, whom their own
generous hearts have interested in my behalf, such
a consummation of my hard adventures is now not
unlikely.—But as a soldier, I must look with some
interest upon that worm-eaten hold of ragged stone;
and if this undermining scoundrel, who is now in
possession, dare to displace a pebble of it——'

He was here interrupted by Dinmont, who came
hastily after them up the road, unseen till he was
near the party:—'Captain, Captain! ye're wanted—
Ye're wanted by her ye ken o'.'

And immediately Meg Merrilies, as if emerging
out of the earth, ascended from the hollow way,
and stood before them. 'I sought ye at the
house,' she said, 'and found but him, (pointing to
Dinmont,) but ye are right, and I was wrang. It
is *here* we should meet, on this very spot, where
my eyes last saw your father. Remember your
promise, and follow me.'

CHAPTER LIII

THE fairy bride of Sir Gawaine, while under the
influence of the spell of her wicked step-mother,
was more decrepit probably, and what is commonly
called more ugly, than Meg Merrilies; but I doubt
if she possessed that wild sublimity which an excited
imagination communicated to features, marked and
expressive in their own peculiar character, and to
the gestures of a form, which, her sex considered,
might be termed gigantic. Accordingly, the Knights
of the Round Table did not recoil with more terror
from the apparition of the loathly lady placed
between 'an oak and a green holly,' than Lucy
Bertram and Julia Mannering did from the appearance of this Galwegian sibyl upon the common of
Ellangowan.

' For God's sake,' said Julia, pulling out her purse,
' give that dreadful woman something, and bid her
go away.'

' I cannot,' said Bertram ; ' I must not offend her.'

' What keeps you here ? ' said Meg, exalting the harsh and rough tones of her hollow voice ; ' Why do you not follow ? — Must your hour call you twice ? — Do you remember your oath ? — were it at kirk or market, wedding or burial,' — and she held high her skinny forefinger in a menacing attitude.

Bertram turned round to his terrified companions. ' Excuse me for a moment ; I am engaged by a promise to follow this woman.'

' Good heavens ! engaged to a madwoman ? ' said Julia.

' Or to a gipsy, who has her band in the wood ready to murder you ! ' said Lucy.

' That was not spoken like a bairn of Ellangowan,' said Meg, frowning upon Miss Bertram. ' It is the ill-doers are ill-dreaders.'

' In short, I must go,' said Bertram ; ' it is absolutely necessary ; wait for me five minutes on this spot.'

' Five minutes ? ' said the gipsy, ' five hours may not bring you here again.'

' Do you hear that ? ' said Julia ; ' for Heaven's sake do not go ! '

' I must, I must—Mr. Dinmont will protect you back to the house.'

' No,' said Meg, ' he must come with you ; it is for that he is here. He maun take part wi' hand and heart ; and weel his part it is, for redding his quarrel might have cost you dear.'

' Troth, Luckie, it's very true,' said the steady

farmer; 'and ere I turn back frae the Captain's side, I 'll show that I haena forgotten 't.'

'O, yes,' exclaimed both the ladies at once, 'let Mr. Dinmont go with you, if go you must, on this strange summons.'

'Indeed I must,' answered Bertram, 'but you see I am safely guarded—Adieu for a short time; go home as fast as you can.'

He pressed his sister's hand, and took a yet more affectionate farewell of Julia with his eyes. Almost stupified with surprise and fear, the young ladies watched with anxious looks the course of Bertram, his companion, and their extraordinary guide. Her tall figure moved across the wintry heath with steps so swift, so long, and so steady, that she appeared rather to glide than to walk. Bertram and Dinmont, both tall men, apparently scarce equalled her in height, owing to her longer dress and high head-gear. She proceeded straight across the common, without turning aside to the winding path, by which passengers avoided the inequalities and little rills that traversed it in different directions. Thus the diminishing figures often disappeared from the eye, as they dived into such broken ground, and again ascended to sight when they were past the hollow. There was something frightful and unearthly, as it were, in the rapid and undeviating course which she pursued, undeterred by any of the impediments which usually incline a traveller from the direct path. Her way was as straight, and nearly as swift, as that of a bird through the air. At length they reached those thickets of natural wood which extended from the skirts of the common towards the glades and brook of Derncleugh, and were there lost to the view.

'This is very extraordinary,' said Lucy after a pause, and turning round to her companion; 'What can he have to do with that old hag?'

'It is very frightful,' answered Julia, 'and almost reminds me of the tales of sorceresses, witches, and evil genii, which I have heard in India. They believe there in a fascination of the eye, by which those who possess it control the will and dictate the motions of their victims. What can your brother have in common with that fearful woman, that he should leave us, obviously against his will, to attend to her commands?'

'At least,' said Lucy, 'we may hold him safe from harm; for she would never have summoned that faithful creature Dinmont, of whose strength, courage, and steadiness, Henry said so much, to attend upon an expedition where she projected evil to the person of his friend. And now let us go back to the house till the Colonel returns— perhaps Bertram may be back first; at any rate, the Colonel will judge what is to be done.'

Leaning then upon each other's arm, but yet occasionally stumbling, between fear and the disorder of their nerves, they at length reached the head of the avenue, when they heard the tread of a horse behind. They started, for their ears were awake to every sound, and beheld to their great pleasure young Hazlewood. 'The Colonel will be here immediately,' he said; 'I galloped on before to pay my

respects to Miss Bertram, with the sincerest con-
gratulations upon the joyful event which has taken
place in her family. I long to be introduced to Captain Bertram, and to thank him for the well-deserved
lesson he gave to my rashness and indiscretion.'

'He has left us just now,' said Lucy, 'and in a
manner that has frightened us very much.'

Just at that moment the Colonel's carriage drove
up, and, on observing the ladies, stopped, while
Mannering and his learned counsel alighted and
joined them. They instantly communicated the
new cause of alarm.

'Meg Merrilies again!' said the Colonel; 'she
certainly is a most mysterious and unaccountable
personage; but I think she must have something
to impart to Bertram, to which she does not mean
we should be privy.'

'The devil take the bedlamite old woman,' said
the counsellor; 'will she not let things take their
course, *prout de lege*, but must always be putting
in her oar in her own way?—Then I fear from the
direction they took they are going upon the Ellangowan estate — that rascal Glossin has shown us
what ruffians he has at his disposal. I wish honest
Liddesdale may be guard sufficient.'

'If you please,' said Hazlewood, 'I should be
most happy to ride in the direction which they have
taken. I am so well known in the country, that
I scarce think any outrage will be offered in my
presence, and I shall keep at such a cautious distance
as not to appear to watch Meg, or interrupt any
communication which she may make.'

'Upon my word,' said Pleydell, (aside,) 'to be a sprig, whom I remember with a whey face and a satchel not so very many years ago, I think young Hazlewood grows a fine fellow. I am more afraid of a new attempt at legal oppression than at open violence, and from that this young man's presence would deter both Glossin and his understrappers.— Hie away then, my boy — peer out — peer out— you'll find them somewhere about Derncleugh, or very probably in Warroch-wood.'

Hazlewood turned his horse. 'Come back to us to dinner, Hazlewood,' cried the Colonel. He bowed, spurred his horse, and galloped off.

We now return to Bertram and Dinmont, who continued to follow their mysterious guide through the woods and dingles, between the open common and the ruined hamlet of Derncleugh. As she led the way, she never looked back upon her followers, unless to chide them for loitering, though the sweat, in spite of the season, poured from their brows. At other times she spoke to herself in such broken expressions as these:—' It is to rebuild the auld house —it is to lay the corner stone—and did I not warn him ? — I tell'd him I was born to do it, if my father's head had been the stepping - stane, let alane his. I was doomed—still I kept my purpose in the cage and in the stocks;—I was banished—I kept it in an unco land;—I was scourged —I was branded—My resolution lay deeper than scourge or red iron could reach—and now the hour is come.'

'Captain,' said Dinmont, in a half whisper, 'I

GUY MANNERING

wish she binna uncanny! her words dinna seem to
come in God's name, or like other folk's. Odd, they
threep in our country that there *are* sic things.'

'Don't be afraid, my friend,' whispered Bertram
in return.

'.Fear'd! fient a haet care I,' said the dauntless
farmer, 'be she witch or deevil; it's a' ane to
Dandie Dinmont.'

'Haud your peace, gudeman,' said Meg, looking
sternly over her shoulder; 'is this a time or place
for you to speak, think ye?'

'But, my good friend,' said Bertram, 'as I have
no doubt in your good faith, or kindness, which I
have experienced; you should in return have some
confidence in me—I wish to know where you are
leading us.'

'There's but ae answer to that, Henry Bertram,'
said the sibyl.—'I swore my tongue should never
tell, but I never said my finger should never show.
Go on and meet your fortune, or turn back and lose
it—that's a' I hae to say.'

'Go on then,' answered Bertram; 'I will ask no
more questions.'

They descended into the glen about the same
place where Meg had formerly parted from Bertram.
She paused an instant beneath the tall rock where
he had witnessed the burial of a dead body, and
stamped upon the ground, which, notwithstanding
all the care that had been taken, showed vestiges
of having been recently moved. 'Here rests ane,'
she said; 'he'll maybe hae neibors sune.'

She then moved up the brook until she came to

the ruined hamlet, where, pausing with a look of peculiar and softened interest before one of the gables which was still standing, she said in a tone less abrupt, though as solemn as before, 'Do you see that blackit and broken end of a shealing?— there my kettle boiled for forty years — there I bore twelve buirdly sons and daughters—where are they now?—where are the leaves that were on that auld ash-tree at Martinmas!—the west wind has made it bare—and I'm stripped too.—Do you see that saugh-tree?—it's but a blackened rotten stump now—I've sate under it mony a bonnie summer afternoon, when it hung its gay garlands ower the poppling water. — I've sat there, and,' elevating her voice, 'I've held you on my knee, Henry Bertram, and sung ye sangs of the auld barons and their bloody wars—It will ne'er be green again, and Meg Merrilies will never sing sangs mair, be they blithe or sad. But ye'll no forget her, and ye'll gar big up the auld wa's for her sake?—and let somebody live there that's ower gude to fear them of another warld—For if ever the dead came back amang the living, I'll be seen in this glen mony a night after these crazed banes are in the mould.'

The mixture of insanity and wild pathos with which she spoke these last words, with her right arm bare and extended, her left bent and shrouded beneath the dark red drapery of her mantle, might have been a study worthy of our Siddons herself. 'And now,' she said, resuming at once the short, stern, and hasty tone which was most ordinary to her—'let us to the wark—let us to the wark.'

She then led the way to the promontory on which the Kaim of Derncleugh was situated, produced a large key from her pocket, and unlocked the door. The interior of this place was in better order than formerly. 'I have made things decent,' she said; 'I may be streekit here or night.—There will be few, few at Meg's lykewake, for mony of our folk will blame what I hae done, and am to do!'

She then pointed to a table, upon which was some cold meat, arranged with more attention to neatness than could have been expected from Meg's habits. 'Eat,' she said, 'eat; ye'll need it this night yet.'

Bertram, in complaisance, eat a morsel or two; and Dinmont, whose appetite was unabated either by wonder, apprehension, or the meal of the morning, made his usual figure as a trencher-man. She then offered each a single glass of spirits, which Bertram drank diluted, and his companion plain.

'Will ye taste naething yoursell, Luckie?' said Dinmont.

'I shall not need it,' replied their mysterious hostess. 'And now,' she said, 'ye maun hae arms — ye maunna gang on dry-handed—but use them not rashly—take captive, but save life—let the law hae its ain—he maun speak ere he die.'

'Who is to be taken?—who is to speak?' said Bertram in astonishment, receiving a pair of pistols which she offered him, and which, upon examining, he found loaded and locked.

'The flints are gude,' she said, 'and the powder dry—I ken this wark weel.'

Then, without answering his questions, she armed Dinmont also with a large pistol, and desired them to choose sticks for themselves out of a parcel of very suspicious-looking bludgeons, which she brought from a corner. Bertram took a stout sapling, and Dandie selected a club which might have served Hercules himself. They then left the hut together, and, in doing so, Bertram took an opportunity to whisper to Dinmont, 'There's something inexplicable in all this—But we need not use these arms unless we see necessity and lawful occasion—take care to do as you see me do.'

Dinmont gave a sagacious nod; and they continued to follow, over wet and over dry, through bog and through fallow, the footsteps of their conductress. She guided them to the wood of Warroch by the same track which the late Ellangowan had used when riding to Derncleugh in quest of his child, on the miserable evening of Kennedy's murder.

When Meg Merrilies had attained these groves, through which the wintry sea-wind was now whistling hoarse and shrill, she seemed to pause a moment as if to recollect the way. 'We maun go the precise track,' she said, and continued to go forward, but rather in a zigzag and involved course than according to her former steady and direct line of motion. At length she guided them through the mazes of the wood to a little open glade of about a quarter of an acre, surrounded by trees and bushes, which made a wild and irregular boundary. Even in winter it was a sheltered and snugly sequestered spot; but when arrayed in the verdure of spring, the earth sending forth all its wild flowers, the shrubs spreading their waste of blossom around it, and the weeping birches, which towered over the underwood, drooping their long and leafy fibres to intercept the sun, it must have seemed a place for a youthful poet to study his earliest sonnet, or a pair of lovers to exchange their first mutual avowal of affection. Apparently it now awakened very different recollections. Bertram's brow, when he had looked round the spot, became gloomy and embarrassed. Meg, after uttering to herself, ' This is the very spot!' looked at him with a ghastly side-glance,—' D'ye mind it?'

' Yes!' answered Bertram, ' imperfectly I do.'

' Ay!' pursued his guide, ' on this very spot the man fell from his horse — I was behind that bourtree-bush at the very moment. Sair, sair he strove, and sair he cried for mercy—but he was in the hands of them that never kenn'd the word!— Now will I show you the further track—the last time ye travelled it was in these arms.'

She led them accordingly by a long and winding passage almost overgrown with brushwood, until, without any very perceptible descent, they suddenly found themselves by the sea-side. Meg then walked very fast on between the surf and the rocks, until she came to a remarkable fragment of rock detached from the rest. ' Here,' she said in a low and scarcely audible whisper, ' here the corpse was found.'

' And the cave,' said Bertram, in the same

tone, 'is close beside it — are you guiding us there?'

'Yes,' said the gipsy in a decided tone. 'Bend up both your hearts—follow me as I creep in—I have placed the fire-wood so as to screen you. Bide behind it for a gliff till I say, *The hour and the man are baith come;* then rin in on him, take his arms, and bind him till the blood burst frae his finger nails.'

'I will, by my soul,' said Henry—'if he is the man I suppose—Jansen?'

'Ay, Jansen, Hatteraick, and twenty mair names are his.'

'Dinmont, you must stand by me now,' said Bertram, 'for this fellow is a devil.'

'Ye needna doubt that,' said the stout yeoman— 'but I wish I could mind a bit prayer or I creep after the witch into that hole that she's opening— It wad be a sair thing to leave the blessed sun, and the free air, and gang and be killed, like a tod that's run to earth, in a dungeon like that. But, my sooth, they will be hard-bitten terriers will worry Dandie; so, as I said, deil hae me if I baulk you.' This was uttered in the lowest tone of voice possible. The entrance was now open. Meg crept in upon her hands and knees, Bertram followed, and Dinmont, after giving a rueful glance toward the daylight, whose blessings he was abandoning, brought up the rear.

CHAPTER LIV

Die, prophet ! in thy speech;
For this, among the rest, was I ordained.

HENRY VI. PART III.

THE progress of the Borderer, who, as we have said, was the last of the party, was fearfully arrested by a hand, which caught hold of his leg as he dragged his long limbs after him in silence and perturbation through the low and narrow entrance of the subterranean passage. The steel heart of the bold yeoman had wellnigh given way, and he suppressed with difficulty a shout, which, in the defenceless posture and situation which they then occupied, might have cost all their lives. He contented himself, however, with extricating his foot from the grasp of this unexpected follower. 'Be still,' said a voice behind him, releasing him; 'I am a friend—Charles Hazlewood.'

These words were uttered in a very low voice, but they produced sound enough to startle Meg Merrilies, who led the van, and who, having already gained the place where the cavern expanded, had risen upon her feet. She began, as if to confound any listening ear, to growl, to mutter, and to sing aloud, and at the same time to make a bustle among some brushwood which was now heaped in the cave.

317

'Here — beldam — Deyvil's kind,' growled the harsh voice of Dirk Hatteraick from the inside of his den, 'what makest thou there?'

'Laying the roughies* to keep the cauld wind frae you, ye desperate do-nae-good—Ye're e'en ower weel off, and wots na; it will be otherwise soon.'

'Have you brought me the brandy, and any news of my people?' said Dirk Hatteraick.

'There's the flask for ye. Your people—dispersed—broken—gone—or cut to ribbands by the red coats.'

'Der Deyvil!—this coast is fatal to me.'

'Ye may hae mair reason to say sae.'

While this dialogue went forward, Bertram and Dinmont had both gained the interior of the cave, and assumed an erect position. The only light which illuminated its rugged and sable precincts was a quantity of wood burnt to charcoal in an iron grate, such as they use in spearing salmon by night. On these red embers Hatteraick from time to time threw a handful of twigs or splintered wood; but these, even when they blazed up, afforded a light much disproportioned to the extent of the cavern; and, as its principal inhabitant lay upon the side of the grate most remote from the entrance, it was not easy for him to discover distinctly objects which lay in that direction. The intruders, therefore, whose number was now augmented unexpectedly to three, stood behind the loosely-piled branches

---

* Withered boughs.

with little risk of discovery. Dinmont had the sense to keep back Hazlewood with one hand till he whispered to Bertram, ' A friend—young Hazlewood.'

It was no time for following up the introduction, and they all stood as still as the rocks around them, obscured behind the pile of brushwood, which had been probably placed there to break the cold wind from the sea, without totally intercepting the supply of air. The branches were laid so loosely above each other, that, looking through them towards the light of the fire-grate, they could easily discover what passed in its vicinity, although a much stronger degree of illumination than it afforded, would not have enabled the persons placed near the bottom of the cave to have descried them in the position which they occupied.

The scene, independent of the peculiar moral interest and personal danger which attended it, had, from the effect of the light and shade on the uncommon objects which it exhibited, an appearance emphatically dismal. The light in the fire-grate was the dark-red glare of charcoal in a state of ignition, relieved from time to time by a transient flame of a more vivid or duskier light, as the fuel with which Dirk Hatteraick fed his fire was better or worse fitted for his purpose. Now a dark cloud of stifling smoke rose up to the roof of the cavern, and then lighted into a reluctant and sullen blaze, which flashed wavering up the pillar of smoke, and was suddenly rendered brighter and more lively by some drier fuel, or perhaps some splintered fir-timber, which at once converted the smoke into flame. By such fitful irradiation, they could see, more or less distinctly, the form of Hatteraick, whose savage and rugged cast of features, now rendered yet more ferocious by the circumstances of his situation, and the deep gloom of his mind, assorted well with the rugged and broken vault, which rose in a rude arch over and around him. The form of Meg Merrilies, which stalked about him, sometimes in the light, sometimes partially obscured in the smoke or darkness, contrasted strongly with the sitting figure of Hatteraick as he bent over the flame, and from his stationary posture was constantly visible to the spectator, while that of the female flitted around, appearing or disappearing like a spectre.

Bertram felt his blood boil at the sight of Hatteraick. He remembered him well under the name of Jansen, which the smuggler had adopted after the death of Kennedy; and he remembered also, that this Jansen, and his mate Brown, the same who was shot at Woodbourne, had been the brutal tyrants of his infancy. Bertram knew farther, from piecing his own imperfect recollections with the narratives of Mannering and Pleydell, that this man was the prime agent in the act of violence which tore him from his family and country, and had exposed him to so many distresses and dangers. A thousand exasperating reflections rose within his bosom; and he could hardly refrain from rushing upon Hatteraick and blowing his brains out.

At the same time this would have been no safe
adventure. The flame, as it rose and fell, while it
displayed the strong, muscular, and broad-chested
frame of the ruffian, glanced also upon two brace
of pistols in his belt, and upon the hilt of his
cutlass; it was not to be doubted that his despera-
tion was commensurate with his personal strength
and means of resistance. Both, indeed, were inadequate to encounter the combined power of two
such men as Bertram himself and his friend Dinmont, without reckoning their unexpected assistant
Hazlewood, who was unarmed, and of a slighter
make; but Bertram felt, on a moment's reflection,
that there would be neither sense nor valour in
anticipating the hangman's office, and he considered
the importance of making Hatteraick prisoner alive.
He therefore repressed his indignation, and awaited
what should pass between the ruffian and his gipsy
guide.

'And how are ye now?' said the harsh and
discordant tones of his female attendant: 'Said I
not it would come upon you—ay, and in this very
cave, where ye harboured after the deed?'

'Wetter and sturm, ye hag!' replied Hatteraick,
'keep your deyvil's matins till they're wanted.
Have you seen Glossin?'

'No,' replied Meg Merrilies: 'you've missed your
blow, ye blood-spiller! and ye have nothing to
expect from the tempter.'

'Hagel!' exclaimed the ruffian, 'if I had him
but by the throat!—and what am I to do
then?'

' Do ? ' answered the gipsy; ' Die like a man, or be hanged like a dog ! '

' Hanged, ye hag of Satan !—the hemp 's not sown that shall hang me.'

' It 's sown, and it 's grown, and it 's heckled, and it 's twisted. Did I not tell ye, when ye wad take away the boy Harry Bertram, in spite of my prayers,—Did I not say he would come back when he had dree'd his weird in foreign land till his twenty-first year ?—Did I not say the auld fire would burn down to a spark, but wad kindle again ? '

' Well, mother, you did say so,' said Hatteraick, in a tone that had something of despair in its accents; ' and, donner and blitzen ! I believe you spoke the truth—that younker of Ellangowan has been a rock ahead to me all my life ! and now, with Glossin's cursed contrivance, my crew have been cut off, my boats destroyed, and I dare say the lugger 's taken—there were not men enough left on board to work her, far less to fight her—a dredge-boat might have taken her. And what will the owners say ?—Hagel and sturm ! I shall never dare go back again to Flushing.'

' You 'll never need,' said the gipsy.

' What are you doing there,' said her companion, ' and what makes you say that ? '

During this dialogue, Meg was heaping some flax loosely together. Before answer to this question, she dropped a fire-brand upon the flax, which had been previously steeped in some spirituous liquor, for it instantly caught fire, and rose in a vivid pyramid of the most brilliant light up to the very top of the vault. As it ascended, Meg answered the ruffian's question in a firm and steady voice:— '*Because the Hour's come, and the Man.*'

At the appointed signal, Bertram and Dinmont sprung over the brushwood, and rushed upon Hatteraick. Hazlewood, unacquainted with their plan of assault, was a moment later. The ruffian, who instantly saw he was betrayed, turned his first vengeance on Meg Merrilies, at whom he discharged a pistol. She fell, with a piercing and dreadful cry, between the shriek of pain and the sound of laughter, when at its highest and most suffocating height. ' I kenn'd it would be this way,' she said.

Bertram, in his haste, slipped his foot upon the uneven rock which floored the cave; a fortunate stumble, for Hatteraick's second bullet whistled over him with so true and steady an aim, that had he been standing upright, it must have lodged in his brain. Ere the smuggler could draw another pistol, Dinmont closed with him, and endeavoured by main force to pinion down his arms. Such, however, was the wretch's personal strength, joined to the efforts of his despair, that, in spite of the gigantic force with which the Borderer grappled him, he dragged Dinmont through the blazing flax, and had almost succeeded in drawing a third pistol, which might have proved fatal to the honest farmer, had not Bertram, as well as Hazlewood, come to his assistance, when, by main force, and no ordinary exertion of it, they threw Hatteraick on the ground, disarmed him, and bound him.

This scuffle, though it takes up some time in the narrative, passed in less than a single minute. When he was fairly mastered, after one or two desperate and almost convulsionary struggles, the ruffian lay perfectly still and silent. 'He's gaun to die game ony how,' said Dinmont; 'weel, I like him na the waur for that.'

This observation honest Dandie made while he was shaking the blazing flax from his rough coat and shaggy black hair, some of which had been singed in the scuffle. 'He is quiet now,' said Bertram; 'stay by him, and do not permit him to stir till I see whether the poor woman be alive or dead.' With Hazlewood's assistance he raised Meg Merrilies.

'I kenn'd it would be this way,' she muttered, 'and it's e'en this way that it should be.'

The ball had penetrated the breast below the throat. It did not bleed much externally; but Bertram, accustomed to see gun-shot wounds, thought it the more alarming. 'Good God! what shall we do for this poor woman?' said he to Hazlewood, the circumstances superseding the necessity of previous explanation or introduction to each other.

'My horse stands tied above in the wood,' said Hazlewood. 'I have been watching you these two hours—I will ride off for some assistants that may be trusted. Meanwhile, you had better defend the mouth of the cavern against every one until I return.' He hastened away. Bertram, after binding Meg Merrilies's wound as well as he could, took station near the mouth of the cave with a cocked pistol in his hand; Dinmont continued to watch Hatteraick, keeping a grasp, like that of Hercules, on his breast. There was a dead silence in the cavern, only interrupted by the low and suppressed moaning of the wounded female, and by the hard breathing of the prisoner.

CHAPTER LV

For though, seduced and led astray,
  Thou'st travelled far and wander'd long,
Thy God hath seen thee all the way,
  And all the turns that led thee wrong.

THE HALL OF JUSTICE.

AFTER the space of about three quarters of an hour, which the uncertainty and danger of their situation made seem almost thrice as long, the voice of young Hazlewood was heard without. 'Here I am,' he cried, 'with a sufficient party.'

'Come in then,' answered Bertram, not a little pleased to find his guard relieved. Hazlewood then entered, followed by two or three countrymen, one of whom acted as a peace-officer. They lifted Hatteraick up, and carried him in their arms as far as the entrance of the vault was high enough to permit them; then laid him on his back, and dragged him along as well as they could, for no persuasion would induce him to assist the trans-portation by any exertion of his own. He lay as silent and inactive in their hands as a dead corpse, incapable of opposing, but in no way aiding, their operations. When he was dragged into day-light, and placed erect upon his feet among three or four assistants, who had remained without the cave, he seemed stupified and dazzled by the sudden change from the darkness of his cavern. While others were superintending the removal of Meg Merrilies, those who remained with Hatteraick attempted to make him sit down upon a fragment of rock which lay close upon the high-water mark. A strong shuddering convulsed his iron frame for an instant, as he resisted their purpose. 'Not there—Hagel!—you would not make me sit *there*?'

These were the only words he spoke; but their import, and the deep tone of horror in which they were uttered, served to show what was passing in his mind.

When Meg Merrilies had also been removed from the cavern, with all the care for her safety that circumstances admitted, they consulted where she should be carried. Hazlewood had sent for a surgeon, and proposed that she should be lifted in the meantime to the nearest cottage. But the patient exclaimed with great earnestness, 'Na, na, na! To the Kaim o' Derncleugh—the Kaim o' Derncleugh—the spirit will not free itself o' the flesh but there.'

'You must indulge her, I believe,' said Bertram; 'her troubled imagination will otherwise aggravate the fever of the wound.'

They bore her accordingly to the vault. On the way her mind seemed to run more upon the scene which had just passed, than on her own approaching death. 'There were three of them set upon him—I brought the twasome—but wha was the third?—It would be *himsell*, returned to work his ain vengeance!'

It was evident that the unexpected appearance
of Hazlewood, whose person the outrage of Hatteraick left her no time to recognise, had produced a
strong effect on her imagination. She often recurred to it. Hazlewood accounted for his unexpected arrival to Bertram, by saying, that he had
kept them in view for some time by the direction
of Mannering; that, observing them disappear into
the cave, he had crept after them, meaning to
announce himself and his errand, when his hand
in the darkness encountering the leg of Dinmont,
had nearly produced a catastrophe, which, indeed,
nothing but the presence of mind and fortitude of
the bold yeoman could have averted.

When the gipsy arrived at the hut, she produced
the key; and when they entered, and were about
to deposit her upon the bed, she said, in an anxious
tone, ' Na, na! not that way, the feet to the east ';
and appeared gratified when they reversed her
posture accordingly, and placed her in that appro-
priate to a dead body.

' Is there no clergyman near,' said Bertram, ' to
assist this unhappy woman's devotions ? '

A gentleman, the minister of the parish, who had
been Charles Hazlewood's tutor, had, with many
others, caught the alarm, that the murderer of
Kennedy was taken on the spot where the deed
had been done so many years before, and that a
woman was mortally wounded. From curiosity, or
rather from the feeling that his duty called him to
scenes of distress, this gentleman had come to the
Kaim of Derncleugh, and now presented himself.

The surgeon arrived at the same time, and was about to probe the wound; but Meg resisted the assistance of either. ' It 's no what man can do, that will heal my body, or save my spirit. Let me speak what I have to say, and then ye may work your will; I 'se be nae hindrance.—But where 's Henry Bertram ? ' — The assistants, to whom this name had been long a stranger, gazed upon each other. —' Yes ! ' she said, in a stronger and harsher tone, ' I said *Henry Bertram of Ellangowan.* Stand from the light and let me see him.'

All eyes were turned towards Bertram, who approached the wretched couch. The wounded woman took hold of his hand. ' Look at him,' she said, ' all that ever saw his father or his grandfather, and bear witness if he is not their living image ? ' A murmur went through the crowd—the resemblance was too striking to be denied. ' And now hear me—and let that man,' pointing to Hatteraick, who was seated with his keepers on a sea-chest at some distance—' let him deny what I say, if he can. That is Henry Bertram, son to Godfrey Bertram, umquhile of Ellangowan; that young man is the very lad-bairn that Dirk Hatteraick carried off from Warroch wood the day that he murdered the gauger. I was there like a wandering spirit—for I longed to see that wood or we left the country. I saved the bairn's life, and sair, sair I prigged and prayed they would leave him wi' me —But they bore him away, and he 's been lang ower the sea, and now he 's come for his ain, and what should withstand him ?—I swore to keep the secret

till he was ane-an'-twenty—I kenn'd he behoved
to dree his weird till that day cam—I keepit that
oath which I took to them—but I made another
vow to mysell, that if I lived to see the day of his
return, I would set him in his father's seat, if every
step was on a dead man. I have keepit that oath
too; I will be ae step mysell—He (pointing to
Hatteraick) will soon be another, and there will be
ane mair yet.'

The clergyman, now interposing, remarked it was
a pity this deposition was not regularly taken and
written down, and the surgeon urged the necessity
of examining the wound, previously to exhausting
her by questions. When she saw them removing
Hatteraick, in order to clear the room and leave
the surgeon to his operations, she called out aloud,
raising herself at the same time upon the couch,
'Dirk Hatteraick, you and I will never meet again
until we are before the judgment-seat—Will ye
own to what I have said, or will you dare deny
it?' He turned his hardened brow upon her, with
a look of dumb and inflexible defiance. 'Dirk
Hatteraick, dare ye deny, with my blood upon
your hands, one word of what my dying breath
is uttering?'—He looked at her with the same
expression of hardihood and dogged stubbornness,
and moved his lips, but uttered no sound. 'Then
fareweel!' she said, 'and God forgive you! your
hand has sealed my evidence.—When I was in life,
I was the mad randy gipsy, that had been scourged,
and banished, and branded—that had begged from
door to door, and been hounded like a stray tike

from parish to parish—wha would hae minded *her* tale?—But now I am a dying woman, and my words will not fall to the ground, any more than the earth will cover my blood!'

She here paused, and all left the hut except the surgeon and two or three women. After a very short examination, he shook his head, and resigned his post by the dying woman's side to the clergyman.

A chaise returning empty to Kippletringan had been stopped on the high-road by a constable, who foresaw it would be necessary to convey Hatteraick to jail. The driver, understanding what was going on at Derncleugh, left his horses to the care of a blackguard boy, confiding, it is to be supposed, rather in the years and discretion of the cattle, than in those of their keeper, and set off full speed to see, as he expressed himself, 'whaten a sort o' fun was gaun on.' He arrived just as the group of tenants and peasants, whose numbers increased every moment, satiated with gazing upon the rugged features of Hatteraick, had turned their attention towards Bertram. Almost all of them, especially the aged men who had seen Ellangowan in his better days, felt and acknowledged the justice of Meg Merrilies's appeal. But the Scotch are a cautious people; they remembered there was another in possession of the estate, and they as yet only expressed their feelings in low whispers to each other. Our friend Jock Jabos, the postilion, forced his way into the middle of the circle; but no sooner cast his eyes upon Bertram, than he started back in amazement, with a solemn exclamation, 'As sure as there's breath in man, it's auld Ellangowan arisen from the dead!'

This public declaration of an unprejudiced witness was just the spark wanted to give fire to the popular feeling, which burst forth in three distinct shouts:—'Bertram for ever!'—'Long life to the heir of Ellangowan!'—'God send him his ain, and to live among us as his forebears did of yore!'

'I hae been seventy years on the land,' said one person.

'I and mine hae been seventy and seventy to that,' said another; 'I have a right to ken the glance of a Bertram.'

'I and mine hae been three hundred years here,' said another old man, 'and I sall sell my last cow, but I'll see the young laird placed in his right.'

The women, ever delighted with the marvellous, and not less so when a handsome young man is the subject of the tale, added their shrill acclamations to the general all-hail. 'Blessings on him—he's the very picture o' his father!—the Bertrams were aye the wale o' the country side!'

'Eh! that his puir mother, that died in grief and in doubt about him, had but lived to see this day!' exclaimed some female voices.

'But we'll help him to his ain, kimmers,' cried others; 'and before Glossin sall keep the Place of Ellangowan, we'll howk him out o't wi' our nails!'

Others crowded around Dinmont, who was nothing loth to tell what he knew of his friend, and to boast

GUY MANNERING

the honour which he had in contributing to the
discovery.   As he was known to several of the
principal farmers present, his testimony afforded an
additional motive to the general enthusiasm.   In
short it was one of those moments of intense feeling,
when the frost of the Scottish people melts like a
snow-wreath, and the dissolving torrent carries dam
and dyke before it.

The sudden shouts interrupted the devotions of
the clergyman; and Meg, who was in one of those
dozing fits of stupefaction that precede the close
of existence, suddenly started—' Dinna ye hear?—
dinna ye hear? — he's owned! — he's owned! — I
lived but for this.—I am a sinfu' woman; but if
my curse brought it down, my blessing has taen it
off!   And now I wad hae liked to hae said mair.
But it canna be.   Stay'—she continued, stretching
her head towards the gleam of light that shot
through the narrow slit which served for a window,
' Is he not there?—stand out o' the light, and let
me look upon him ance mair.   But the darkness is
in my ain een,' she said, sinking back, after an
earnest gaze upon vacuity—' it's a' ended now,

" Pass breath,
Come death!"'

And, sinking back upon her couch of straw, she
expired without a groan.   The clergyman and the
surgeon carefully noted down all that she had said,
now deeply regretting they had not examined her
more minutely, but both remaining morally convinced of the truth of her disclosure.

Hazlewood was the first to compliment Bertram upon the near prospect of his being restored to his name and rank in society. The people around, who now learned from Jabos that Bertram was the person who had wounded him, were struck with his generosity, and added his name to Bertram's in their exulting acclamations.

Some, however, demanded of the postilion how he had not recognised Bertram when he saw him some time before at Kippletringan? to which he gave the very natural answer,—'Hout, what was I thinking about Ellangowan then?—It was the cry that was rising e'en now that the young laird was found, that put me on finding out the likeness —There was nae missing it ance ane was set to look for 't.'

The obduracy of Hatteraick, during the latter part of this scene, was in some slight degree shaken. He was observed to twinkle with his eyelids—to attempt to raise his bound hands for the purpose of pulling his hat over his brow—to look angrily and impatiently to the road, as if anxious for the vehicle which was to remove him from the spot. At length Mr. Hazlewood, apprehensive that the popular ferment might take a direction towards the prisoner, directed he should be taken to the post-chaise, and so removed to the town of Kippletringan to be at Mr. Mac-Morlan's disposal; at the same time he sent an express to warn that gentleman of what had happened. 'And now,' he said to Bertram, 'I should be happy if you would accompany me to Hazlewood-house; but as that might

not be so agreeable just now as I trust it will be
in a day or two, you must allow me to return with
you to Woodbourne. But you are on foot.'—'O if
the young laird would take my horse!'—'Or mine'
—'Or mine,' said half a dozen voices—'Or mine;
he can trot ten mile an hour without whip or spur,
and he's the young laird's frae this moment, if he
likes to take him for a herezeld,* as they ca'd it
lang syne.'—Bertram readily accepted the horse as a
loan, and poured forth his thanks· to the assembled
crowd for their good wishes, which they repaid with
shouts and vows of attachment.

While the happy owner was directing one lad to
'gae doun for the new saddle'; another, 'just to
rin the beast ower wi' a dry wisp o' strae'; a third,
'to hie doun and borrow Dan Dunkieson's plated
stirrups,' and expressing his regret, 'that there
was nae time to gie the nag a feed, that the young
laird might ken his mettle,' Bertram, taking the
clergyman by the arm, walked into the vault, and
shut the door immediately after them. He gazed
in silence for some minutes upon the body of Meg
Merrilies, as it lay before him, with the features
sharpened by death, yet still retaining the stern and
energetic character, which had maintained in life
her superiority as the wild chieftainess of the lawless

---

* This hard word is placed in the mouth of one of the aged tenants.
In the old feudal tenures, the herezeld constituted the best horse or
other animal on the vassals' lands, become the right of the superior.
The only remnant of this custom is what is called the sasine, or a fee
of certain estimated value, paid to the sheriff of the county, who gives
possession to the vassals of the crown.

people amongst whom she was born. The young soldier dried the tears which involuntarily rose on viewing this wreck of one, who might be said to have died a victim to her fidelity to his person and family. He then took the clergyman's hand, and asked solemnly, if she appeared able to give that attention to his devotions which befitted a departing person.

'My dear sir,' said the good minister, 'I trust this poor woman had remaining sense to feel and join in the import of my prayers. But let us humbly hope we are judged of by our opportunities of religious and moral instruction. In some degree she might be considered as an uninstructed heathen, even in the bosom of a Christian country; and let us remember, that the errors and vices of an ignorant life were balanced by instances of disinterested attachment, amounting almost to heroism. To HIM, who can alone weigh our crimes and errors against our efforts towards virtue, we consign her with awe, but not without hope.'

'May I request,' said Bertram, 'that you will see every decent solemnity attended to in behalf of this poor woman? I have some property belonging to her in my hands—at all events I will be answerable for the expense—you will hear of me at Woodbourne.'

Dinmont, who had been furnished with a horse by one of his acquaintance, now loudly called out that all was ready for their return; and Bertram and Hazlewood, after a strict exhortation to the crowd, which was now increased to several hundreds, to preserve good order in their rejoicing, as the least ungoverned zeal might be turned to the disadvantage of the young Laird, as they termed him, took their leave amid the shouts of the multitude.

As they rode past the ruined cottages at Derncleugh, Dinmont said, ' I 'm sure when ye come to your ain, Captain, ye 'll no forget to bigg a bit cot-house there? Deil be in me but I wad do 't mysell, an it werena in better hands.—I wadna like to live in 't though, after what she said. Odd, I wad put in auld Elspeth, the bedral's widow—the like o' them 's used wi' graves and ghaists, and thae things.'

A short but brisk ride brought them to Woodbourne. The news of their exploit had already flown far and wide, and the whole inhabitants of the vicinity met them on the lawn with shouts of congratulation. ' That you have seen me alive,' said Bertram to Lucy, who first ran up to him, though Julia's eyes even anticipated hers, ' you must thank these kind friends.'

With a blush expressing at once pleasure, gratitude, and bashfulness, Lucy curtsied to Hazlewood, but to Dinmont she frankly extended her hand. The honest farmer, in the extravagance of his joy, carried his freedom farther than the hint warranted, for he imprinted his thanks on the lady's lips, and was instantly shocked at the rudeness of his own conduct. ' Lord sake, madam, I ask your pardon,' he said; ' I forgot but ye had been a bairn o' my ain—the Captain's sae hamely, he gars ane forget himsell.'

Old Pleydell now advanced: 'Nay, if fees like these are going,' he said——

'Stop, stop, Mr. Pleydell,' said Julia, 'you had your fees beforehand—remember last night.'

'Why, I do confess a retainer,' said the barrister; 'but if I don't deserve double fees from both Miss Bertram and you when I conclude my examination of Dirk Hatteraick to-morrow — Gad, I will so supple him!—You shall see, Colonel, and you, my saucy misses, though you may not see, shall hear.'

'Ay, that's if we choose to listen, counsellor,' replied Julia.

'And you think,' said Pleydell, 'it's two to one you won't choose that?—But you have curiosity that teaches you the use of your ears now and then.'

'I declare, counsellor,' answered the lively damsel, 'that such saucy bachelors as you would teach us the use of our fingers now and then.'

'Reserve them for the harpsichord, my love,' said the counsellor. 'Better for all parties.'

While this idle chat ran on, Colonel Mannering introduced to Bertram a plain good-looking man, in a grey coat and waistcoat, buckskin breeches, and boots. 'This, my dear sir, is Mr. Mac-Morlan.'

'To whom,' said Bertram, embracing him cordially, 'my sister was indebted for a home, when deserted by all her natural friends and relations.'

The Dominie then pressed forward, grinned, chuckled, made a diabolical sound in attempting to whistle, and finally, unable to stifle his emotions, ran away to empty the feelings of his heart at his eyes.

We shall not attempt to describe the expansion of heart and glee of this happy evening.

CHAPTER LVI

How like a hateful ape,
Detected grinning 'midst his pilfer'd hoard,
A cunning man appears, whose secret frauds
Are open'd to the day !——

COUNT BASIL.

THERE was a great movement at Woodbourne
early on the following morning, to attend the examination at Kippletringan. Mr. Pleydell, from
the investigation which he had formerly bestowed
on the dark affair of Kennedy's death, as well as
from the general deference due to his professional
abilities, was requested by Mr. Mac-Morlan and
Sir Robert Hazlewood, and another justice of peace
who attended, to take the situation of chairman,
and the lead in the examination. Colonel Mannering was invited to sit down with them. The examination, being previous to trial, was private in
other respects.

The counsellor resumed and re-interrogated former
evidence. He then examined the clergyman and
surgeon respecting the dying declaration of Meg
Merrilies. They stated, that she distinctly, posi-
tively, and repeatedly, declared herself an eye-
witness of Kennedy's death by the hands of
Hatteraick, and two or three of his crew; that
her presence was accidental; that she believed their

resentment at meeting him, when they were in the
act of losing their vessel through the means of his
information, led to the commission of the crime;
that she said there was one witness of the murder,
but who refused to participate in it, still alive,—
her nephew, Gabriel Faa; and she had hinted at
another person, who was an accessory after, not
before, the fact; but her strength there failed her.
They did not forget to mention her declaration,
that she had saved the child, and that he was torn
from her by the smugglers, for the purpose of
carrying him to Holland.—All these particulars
were carefully reduced to writing.

Dirk Hatteraick was then brought in, heavily
ironed; for he had been strictly secured and
guarded, owing to his former escape. He was
asked his name; he made no answer:—His profession; he was silent:—Several other questions
were put; to none of which he returned any reply.
Pleydell wiped the glasses of his spectacles, and
considered the prisoner very attentively. 'A very
truculent-looking fellow,' he whispered to Mannering; 'but, as Dogberry says, I'll go cunningly
to work with him.—Here, call in Soles—Soles
the shoemaker.—Soles, do you remember measuring some footsteps imprinted on the mud at the
wood of Warroch, on —— November 17—, by my
orders?' Soles remembered the circumstance perfectly. 'Look at that paper—is that your note of
the measurement?'—Soles verified the memoran-
dum—'Now, there stands a pair of shoes on that
table; measure them, and see if they correspond

with any of the marks you have noted there.' The shoemaker obeyed, and declared, 'that they answered exactly to the largest of the foot-prints.'

'We shall prove,' said the counsellor, aside to Mannering, 'that these shoes, which were found in the ruins at Derncleugh, belonged to Brown, the fellow whom you shot on the lawn at Woodbourne.—Now, Soles, measure that prisoner's feet very accurately.'

Mannering observed Hatteraick strictly, and could notice a visible tremor. 'Do these measurements correspond with any of the foot-prints?'

The man looked at the note, then at his foot-rule and measure—then verified his former measurement by a second. 'They correspond,' he said, 'within a hair-breadth, to a foot-mark broader and shorter than the former.'

Hatteraick's genius here deserted him — 'Der deyvil!' he broke out, 'how could there be a foot-mark on the ground, when it was a frost as hard as the heart of a Memel log?'

'In the evening, I grant you, Captain Hatteraick,' said Pleydell, 'but not in the forenoon—will you favour me with information where you were upon the day you remember so exactly?'

Hatteraick saw his blunder, and again screwed up his hard features for obstinate silence—'Put down his observation, however,' said Pleydell to the clerk.

At this moment the door opened, and, much to the surprise of most present, Mr. Gilbert Glossin made his appearance. That worthy gentleman had, by dint of watching and eaves-dropping, ascertained that he was not mentioned by name in Meg Merrilies' dying declaration, a circumstance, certainly not owing to any favourable disposition towards him, but to the delay of taking her regular examination, and to the rapid approach of death. He therefore supposed himself safe from all evidence but such as might arise from Hatteraick's confession; to prevent which he resolved to push a bold face, and join his brethren of the bench during his examination.—I shall be able, he thought, to make the rascal sensible his safety lies in keeping his own counsel and mine; and my presence, besides, will be a proof of confidence and innocence. If I must lose the estate, I must—but I trust better things.—

He entered with a profound salutation to Sir Robert Hazlewood. Sir Robert, who had rather begun to suspect that his plebeian neighbour had made a cat's paw of him, inclined his head stiffly, took snuff, and looked another way.

'Mr. Corsand,' said Glossin to the other yokefellow of justice, 'your most humble servant.'

'Your humble servant, Mr. Glossin,' answered Mr. Corsand drily, composing his countenance *regis ad exemplar*, that is to say, after the fashion of the Baronet.

'Mac-Morlan, my worthy friend,' continued Glossin, 'how d'ye do—always on your duty?'

'Umph,' said honest Mac-Morlan, with little respect either to the compliment or salutation. 'Colonel Mannering (a low bow slightly returned) and Mr. Pleydell, (another low bow,) I dared not have hoped for your assistance to poor country gentlemen at this period of the session.'

Pleydell took snuff, and eyed him with a glance equally shrewd and sarcastic—'I'll teach him,' he said aside to Mannering, 'the value of the old admonition, *Ne accesseris in consilium antequam voceris.*'

'But perhaps I intrude, gentlemen?' said Glossin, who could not fail to observe the coldness of his reception.—'Is this an open meeting?'

'For my part,' said Mr. Pleydell, 'so far from considering your attendance as an intrusion, Mr. Glossin, I was never so pleased in my life to meet with you; especially as I think we should, at any rate, have had occasion to request the favour of your company in the course of the day.'

'Well, then, gentlemen,' said Glossin, drawing his chair to the table, and beginning to bustle about among the papers, 'where are we?—how far have we got? where are the declarations?'

'Clerk, give me all these papers,' said Mr. Pleydell;—'I have an odd way of arranging my documents, Mr. Glossin; another person touching them puts me out—but I shall have occasion for your assistance by and by.'

Glossin, thus reduced to inactivity, stole one glance at Dirk Hatteraick, but could read nothing in his dark scowl save malignity and hatred to all around. 'But, gentlemen,' said Glossin, 'is it quite right to keep this poor man so heavily ironed, when he is taken up merely for examination?'

This was hoisting a kind of friendly signal to

the prisoner. 'He has escaped once before,' said Mac-Morlan drily, and Glossin was silenced.

Bertram was now introduced, and, to Glossin's confusion, was greeted in the most friendly manner by all present, even by Sir Robert Hazlewood himself. He told his recollections of his infancy with that candour and caution of expression which afforded the best warrant for his good faith. 'This seems to be rather a civil than a criminal question,' said Glossin, rising; 'and as you cannot be ignorant, gentlemen, of the effect which this young person's pretended parentage may have on my patrimonial interest, I would rather beg leave to retire.'

'No, my good sir,' said Mr. Pleydell, 'we can by no means spare you. But why do you call this young man's claims pretended?—I don't mean to fish for your defences against them, if you have any, but——'

'Mr. Pleydell,' replied Glossin, 'I am always disposed to act above-board, and I think I can explain the matter at once. — This young fellow, whom I take to be a natural son of the late Ellangowan, has gone about the country for some weeks under different names, caballing with a wretched old madwoman, who, I understand, was shot in a late scuffle, and with other tinkers, gipsies, and persons of that description, and a great brute farmer from Liddesdale, stirring up the tenants against their landlords, which, as Sir Robert Hazlewood of Hazlewood knows——'

'Not to interrupt you, Mr. Glossin,' said Pleydell, 'I ask who you say this young man is?'

'Why, I say,' replied Glossin, 'and I believe that gentleman (looking at Hatteraick) knows, that the young man is a natural son of the late Ellangowan, by a girl called Janet Lightoheel, who was afterwards married to Hewit the shipwright, that lived in the neighbourhood of Annan. His name is Godfrey Bertram Hewit, by which name he was entered on board the Royal Caroline excise yacht.'

'Ay?' said Pleydell, 'that is a very likely story!— but, not to pause upon some difference of eyes, complexion, and so forth—be pleased to step forward, sir.'——A young seafaring man came forward.—— 'Here,' proceeded the counsellor, 'is the real Simon Pure—here's Godfrey Bertram Hewit, arrived last night from Antigua *via* Liverpool, mate of a West Indian, and in a fair way of doing well in the world, although he came somewhat irregularly into it.'

While some conversation passed between the other justices and this young man, Pleydell lifted from among the papers on the table Hatteraick's old pocket-book. A peculiar glance of the smuggler's eye induced the shrewd lawyer to think there was something here of interest. He therefore continued the examination of the papers, laying the book on the table, but instantly perceived that the prisoner's interest in the research had cooled.—It must be in the book still, whatever it is, thought Pleydell; and again applied himself to the pocket-book, until he discovered, on a narrow scrutiny, a slit between the pasteboard and leather, out of which he drew three small slips of paper. Pleydell now, turning to Glossin, requested the favour that he would tell them if he had assisted at the search for the body of Kennedy, and the child of his patron, on the day when they disappeared.

'I did not—that is—I did,' answered the conscience-struck Glossin.

'It is remarkable though,' said the advocate, 'that, connected as you were with the Ellangowan family, I don't recollect your being examined, or even appearing before me, while that investigation was proceeding?'

'I was called to London,' answered Glossin, 'on most important business, the morning after that sad affair.'

'Clerk,' said Pleydell, 'minute down that reply.— I presume the business, Mr. Glossin, was to negotiate these three bills, drawn by you on Messrs. Vanbeest and Vanbruggen, and accepted by one Dirk Hatteraick in their name on the very day of the murder. I congratulate you on their being regularly retired, as I perceive they have been. I think the chances were against it.' Glossin's countenance fell. 'This piece of real evidence,' continued Mr. Pleydell, 'makes good the account given of your conduct on this occasion by a man called Gabriel Faa, whom we have now in custody, and who witnessed the whole transaction between you and that worthy prisoner—Have you any explanation to give?'

'Mr. Pleydell,' said Glossin, with great composure, 'I presume, if you were my counsel, you would not advise me to answer upon the spur of the moment to a charge, which the basest of mankind seem ready to establish by perjury.'

'My advice,' said the counsellor, 'would be regulated by my opinion of your innocence or guilt. In your case, I believe you take the wisest course; but you are aware you must stand committed?'

'Committed? for what, sir?' replied Glossin. 'Upon a charge of murder?'

'No; only as art and part of kidnapping the child.'

'That is a bailable offence.'

'Pardon me,' said Pleydell, 'it is *plagium*, and *plagium* is felony.'

'Forgive me, Mr. Pleydell; there is only one case upon record, Torrence and Waldie. They were, you remember, resurrection-women, who had promised to procure a child's body for some young surgeons. Being upon honour to their employers, rather than disappoint the evening lecture of the students, they stole a live child, murdered it, and sold the body for three shillings and sixpence. They were hanged, but for the murder, not for the *plagium*.* Your civil law has carried you a little too far.'

'Well, sir; but, in the meantime, Mr. MacMorlan must commit you to the county jail, in case this young man repeats the same story.—Officers, remove Mr. Glossin and Hatteraick, and guard them in different apartments.'

---

* This is, in its circumstances and issue, actually a case tried and reported.

Gabriel, the gipsy, was then introduced, and gave a distinct account of his deserting from Captain Pritchard's vessel and joining the smugglers in the action, detailed how Dirk Hatteraick set fire to his ship when he found her disabled, and under cover of the smoke escaped with his crew, and as much goods as they could save, into the cavern, where they proposed to lie till night-fall. Hatteraick himself, his mate Vanbeest Brown, and three others, of whom the declarant was one, went into the adjacent woods to communicate with some of their friends in the neighbourhood. They fell in with Kennedy unexpectedly, and Hatteraick and Brown, aware that he was the occasion of their disasters, resolved to murder him. He stated, that he had seen them lay violent hands on the officer, and drag him through the woods, but had not partaken in the assault, nor witnessed its termination. That he returned to the cavern by a different route, where he again met Hatteraick and his accomplices; and the captain was in the act of giving an account how he and Brown had pushed a huge crag over, as Kennedy lay groaning on the beach, when Glossin suddenly appeared among them. To the whole transaction by which Hatteraick purchased his secrecy he was witness. Respecting young Bertram, he could give a distinct account till he went to India, after which he had lost sight of him until he unexpectedly met with him in Liddesdale. Gabriel Faa farther stated, that he instantly sent notice to his aunt, Meg Merrilies, as well as to Hatteraick, who he knew was then upon the coast; but that he had incurred his aunt's displeasure upon the latter account. He concluded, that his aunt had immediately declared that she would do all that lay in her power to help young Ellangowan to his right, even if it should be by informing against Dirk Hatteraick; and that many of her people assisted her besides himself, from a belief that she was gifted with supernatural inspirations. With the same purpose, he understood, his aunt had given to Bertram the treasure of the tribe, of which she had the custody. Three or four gipsies, by the express command of Meg Merrilies, mingled in the crowd when the Custom - House was attacked, for the purpose of liberating Bertram, which he had himself effected. He said, that in obeying Meg's dictates they did not pretend to estimate their propriety or rationality, the respect in which she was held by her tribe precluding all such subjects of speculation. Upon farther interrogation, the witness added, that his aunt had always said that Harry Bertram carried that round his neck which would ascertain his birth. It was a spell, she said, that an Oxford scholar had made for him, and she possessed the smugglers with an opinion, that to deprive him of it would occasion the loss of the vessel.

Bertram here produced a small velvet bag, which he said he had worn round his neck from his earliest infancy, and which he had preserved, first from superstitious reverence, and, latterly, from the hope that it might serve one day to aid in the discovery of his birth. The bag, being opened, was found to contain a blue silk case, from which was drawn a scheme of nativity. Upon inspecting this paper, Colonel Mannering instantly admitted it was his own composition; and afforded the strongest and most satisfactory evidence, that the possessor of it must necessarily be the young heir of Ellangowan, by avowing his having first appeared in that country in the character of an astrologer.

'And now,' said Pleydell, 'make out warrants of commitment for Hatteraick and Glossin until liberated in due course of law. Yet,' he said, 'I am sorry for Glossin.'

'Now, I think,' said Mannering, 'he's incomparably the least deserving of pity of the two. The other's a bold fellow, though as hard as flint.'

'Very natural, Colonel,' said the advocate, 'that you should be interested in the ruffian, and I in the knave—that's all professional taste—but I can tell you Glossin would have been a pretty lawyer, had he not had such a turn for the roguish part of the profession.'

'Scandal would say,' observed Mannering, 'he might not be the worse lawyer for that.'

'Scandal would tell a lie, then,' replied Pleydell, 'as she usually does. Law's like laudanum; it's much more easy to use it as a quack does, than to learn to apply it like a physician.'

CHAPTER LVII

Unfit to live or die—O marble heart !
After him, fellows, drag him to the block.
MEASURE FOR MEASURE.

THE jail at the county town of the shire of ——
was one of those old-fashioned dungeons which
disgraced Scotland until of late years. When the
prisoners and their guard arrived there, Hatteraick,
whose violence and strength were well known,
was secured in what was called the condemned
ward. This was a large apartment near the top
of the prison. A round bar of iron, about the
thickness of a man's arm above the elbow, crossed
the apartment horizontally at the height of about
six inches from the floor; and its extremities were
strongly built into the wall at either end.* Hatteraick's ankles were secured within shackles, which
were connected by a chain at the distance of about
four feet, with a large iron ring, which travelled
upon the bar we have described. Thus a prisoner
might shuffle along the length of the bar from one

---

* This mode of securing prisoners was universally practised in Scotland after condemnation. When a man received sentence of death,
he was put upon *the Gad,* as it was called, that is, secured to the bar
of iron in the manner mentioned in the text. The practice subsisted
in Edinburgh till the old jail was taken down some years since, and
perhaps may be still in use.

side of the room to another, but could not retreat farther from it in any other direction than the brief length of the chain admitted. When his feet had been thus secured, the keeper removed his hand-cuffs, and left his person at liberty in other respects. A pallet-bed was placed close to the bar of iron, so that the shackled prisoner might lie down at pleasure, still fastened to the iron-bar in the manner described.

Hatteraick had not been long in this place of confinement, before Glossin arrived at the same prison-house. In respect to his comparative rank and education, he was not ironed, but placed in a decent apartment, under the inspection of Mac-Guffog, who, since the destruction of the Bridewell of Portanferry by the mob, had acted here as an under-turnkey. When Glossin was enclosed within this room, and had solitude and leisure to calculate all the chances against him and in his favour, he could not prevail upon himself to consider the game as desperate.

'The estate is lost,' he said: 'that must go; and, between Pleydell and Mac-Morlan, they'll cut down my claim on it to a trifle. My character—but if I get off with life and liberty, I'll win money yet, and varnish that over again. I knew not the gauger's job until the rascal had done the deed, and though I had some advantage by the contra-band, that is no felony. But the kidnapping of the boy—there they touch me closer. Let me see:—This Bertram was a child at the time—his evidence must be imperfect—the other fellow is a deserter, a gipsy, and an outlaw—Meg Merrilies, d—n her, is dead. These infernal bills! Hatteraick brought them with him, I suppose, to have the means of threatening me, or extorting money from me. I must endeavour to see the rascal;—must get him to stand steady; must persuade him to put some other colour upon the business.'

His mind teeming with schemes of future deceit to cover former villainy, he spent the time in arranging and combining them until the hour of supper. Mac-Guffog attended as turnkey on this occasion. He was, as we know, the old and special acquaintance of the prisoner who was now under his charge. After giving the turnkey a glass of brandy, and sounding him with one or two cajoling speeches, Glossin made it his request that he would help him to an interview with Dirk Hatteraick. 'Impossible! utterly impossible! it's contrary to the express orders of Mr. Mac-Morlan, and the captain (as the head jailor of a county jail is called in Scotland) would never forgie me.'

'But why should he know of it?' said Glossin, slipping a couple of guineas into Mac-Guffog's hand.

The turnkey weighed the gold, and looked sharp at Glossin. 'Ay, ay, Mr. Glossin, ye ken the ways o' this place.—Lookee, at lock-up hour, I'll return and bring ye up stairs to him—But ye must stay a' night in his cell, for I am under needcessity to carry the keys to the captain for the night, and I cannot let you out again until morning—then I'll visit the wards half an hour earlier than usual, and ye may get out, and be snug in your ain berth when the captain gangs his rounds.'

When the hour of ten had pealed from the neighbouring steeple, Mac-Guffog came prepared with a small dark lantern. He said softly to Glossin, 'Slip your shoes off, and follow me.' When Glossin was out of the door, Mac-Guffog, as if in the execution of his ordinary duty, and speaking to a prisoner within, called aloud, 'Good-night to you, sir,' and locked the door, clattering the bolts with much ostentatious noise. He then guided Glossin up a steep and narrow stair, at the top of which was the door of the condemned ward; he unbarred and unlocked it, and, giving Glossin the lantern, made a sign to him to enter, and locked the door behind him with the same affected accuracy.

In the large dark cell into which he was thus introduced, Glossin's feeble light for some time enabled him to discover nothing. At length he could dimly distinguish the pallet-bed stretched on the floor beside the great iron bar which traversed the room, and on that pallet reposed the figure of a man. Glossin approached him. 'Dirk Hatteraick!'

'Donner and hagel! it is his voice,' said the prisoner, sitting up, and clashing his fetters as he rose, 'then my dream is true!—Begone, and leave me to myself—it will be your best.'

'What! my good friend,' said Glossin, 'will you allow the prospect of a few weeks' confinement to depress your spirit?'

'Yes,' answered the ruffian sullenly — 'when I am only to be released by a halter!—Let me alone

—go about your business, and turn the lamp from my face!'

'Psha! my dear Dirk, don't be afraid,' said Glossin —'I have a glorious plan to make all right.'

'To the bottomless pit with your plans!' replied his accomplice; 'you have planned me out of ship, cargo, and life; and I dreamt this moment that Meg Merrilies dragged you here by the hair, and gave me the long clasped knife she used to wear— —you don't know what she said. Sturm wetter! it will be your wisdom not to tempt me!'

'But, Hatteraick, my good friend, do but rise and speak to me,' said Glossin.

'I will not!' answered the savage, doggedly— 'you have caused all the mischief; you would not let Meg keep the boy; she would have returned him after he had forgot all.'

'Why, Hatteraick, you are turned driveller!'

'Wetter! will you deny that all that cursed attempt at Portanferry, which lost both sloop and crew, was your device for your own job?'

'But the goods, you know——'

'Curse the goods!' said the smuggler, 'we could have got plenty more; but, der deyvil! to lose the ship and the fine fellows, and my own life, for a cursed coward villain, that always works his own mischief with other people's hands! Speak to me no more—I'm dangerous.'

'But, Dirk — but, Hatteraick, hear me only a few words.'

'Hagel! nein.'

'Only one sentence.'

' Tausand curses—nein ! '

' At least get up, for an obstinate Dutch brute ! ' said Glossin, losing his temper, and pushing Hatteraick with his foot.

' Donner and blitzen ! ' said Hatteraick, springing up and grappling with him ; ' you *will* have it then ? '

Glossin struggled and resisted ; but, owing to his surprise at the fury of the assault, so ineffectually, that he fell under Hatteraick, the back part of his neck coming full upon the iron bar with stunning violence. The death-grapple continued. The room immediately below the condemned ward, being that of Glossin, was, of course, empty ; but the inmates of the second apartment beneath felt the shock of Glossin's heavy fall, and heard a noise as of struggling and of groans. But all sounds of horror were too congenial to this place to excite much curiosity or interest.

In the morning, faithful to his promise, Mac-Guffog came—' Mr. Glossin,' said he, in a whispering voice.

' Call louder,' answered Dirk Hatteraick.

' Mr. Glossin, for God's sake come away ! '

' He'll hardly do that without help,' said Hatteraick.

' What are you chattering there for, Mac-Guffog ? ' called out the captain from below.

' Come away, for God's sake, Mr. Glossin ! ' repeated the turnkey.

At this moment the jailor made his appearance with a light. Great was his surprise, and even horror, to observe Glossin's body lying doubled across the iron bar, in a posture that excluded all idea of his being alive. Hatteraick was quietly stretched upon his pallet within a yard of his victim. On lifting Glossin, it was found he had been dead for some hours. His body bore uncommon marks of violence. The spine where it joins the skull had received severe injury by his first fall. There were distinct marks of strangulation about the throat, which corresponded with the blackened state of his face. The head was turned backward over the shoulder, as if the neck had been wrung round with desperate violence. So that it would seem that his inveterate antagonist had fixed a fatal gripe upon the wretch's throat, and never quitted it while life lasted. The lantern, crushed and broken to pieces, lay beneath the body.

Mac-Morlan was in the town, and came instantly to examine the corpse. 'What brought Glossin here?' he said to Hatteraick.

'The devil!' answered the ruffian.

'And what did you do to him?'

'Sent him to hell before me!' replied the miscreant.

'Wretch,' said Mac-Morlan, 'you have crowned a life spent without a single virtue, with the murder of your own miserable accomplice!'

'Virtue?' exclaimed the prisoner; 'donner! I was always faithful to my ship-owners — always accounted for cargo to the last stiver. Hark ye! let me have pen and ink, and I'll write an account of the whole to our house; and leave me alone a couple of hours, will ye—and let them take away that piece of carrion, donner wetter!'

Mac-Morlan deemed it the best way to humour the savage; he was furnished with writing materials and left alone. When they again opened the door, it was found that this determined villain had anticipated justice. He had adjusted a cord taken from the truckle-bed, and attached it to a bone, the relic of his yesterday's dinner, which he had contrived to drive into a crevice between two stones in the wall at a height as great as he could reach, standing upon the bar. Having fastened the noose, he had the resolution to drop his body as if to fall on his knees, and to retain that posture until resolution was no longer necessary. The letter he had written to his owners, though chiefly upon the business of their trade, contained many allusions to the younker of Ellangowan, as he called him, and afforded absolute confirmation of all Meg Merrilies and her nephew had told.

To dismiss the catastrophe of these two wretched men, I shall only add, that Mac-Guffog was turned out of office, notwithstanding his declaration, (which he offered to attest by oath,) that he had locked Glossin safely in his own room upon the night preceding his being found dead in Dirk Hatteraick's cell. His story, however, found faith with the worthy Mr. Skreigh, and other lovers of the marvellous, who still hold that the Enemy of Mankind brought these two wretches together upon that night, by supernatural interference, that they might fill up the cup of their guilt and receive its meed, by murder and suicide.

CHAPTER LVIII

To sum the whole—the close of all.

DEAN SWIFT.

As Glossin died without heirs, and without payment of the price, the estate of Ellangowan was again thrown upon the hands of Mr. Godfrey Bertram's creditors, the right of most of whom was however defeasible, in case Henry Bertram should establish his character of heir of entail. This young gentleman put his affairs into the hands of Mr. Pleydell and Mr. Mac-Morlan, with one single proviso, that though he himself should be obliged again to go to India, every debt, justly and honourably due by his father, should be made good to the claimant. Mannering, who heard this declaration, grasped him kindly by the hand, and from that moment might be dated a thorough understanding between them.

The hoards of Miss Margaret Bertram, and the liberal assistance of the Colonel, easily enabled the heir to make provision for payment of the just creditors of his father, while the ingenuity and research of his law friends detected, especially in the accounts of Glossin, so many overcharges as greatly diminished the total amount. In these circumstances the creditors did not hesitate to recognise Bertram's right, and to surrender to him the house and property of his ancestors. All the party repaired from Woodbourne to take possession, amid the shouts of the tenantry and the neighbourhood; and so eager was Colonel Mannering to superintend certain improvements which he had recommended to Bertram, that he removed with his family from Woodbourne to Ellangowan, although at present containing much less and much inferior accommodation.

The poor Dominie's brain was almost turned with joy on returning to his old habitation. He posted up-stairs, taking three steps at once, to a little shabby attic, his cell and dormitory in former days, and which the possession of his much superior apartment at Woodbourne had never banished from his memory. Here one sad thought suddenly struck the honest man — the books! — no three rooms in Ellangowan were capable to contain them. While this qualifying reflection was passing through his mind, he was suddenly summoned by Mannering to assist in calculating some proportions relating to a large and splendid house, which was to be built on the site of the New Place of Ellangowan, in a style corresponding to the magnificence of the ruins in its vicinity. Among the various rooms in the plan, the Dominie observed, that one of the largest was entitled THE LIBRARY; and close beside was a snug well-proportioned chamber, entitled, Mr. SAMPSON'S APARTMENT—'Prodigious, prodigious, pro-di-gi-ous!' shouted the enraptured Dominie.

Mr. Pleydell had left the party for some time; but he returned, according to promise, during the Christmas recess of the courts. He drove up to Ellangowan when all the family were abroad but the Colonel, who was busy with plans of buildings and pleasure-grounds, in which he was well skilled, and took great delight.

'Ah ha!' said the counsellor, 'so here you are! Where are the ladies? where is the fair Julia?'—

'Walking out with young Hazlewood, Bertram, and Captain Delaserre, a friend of his, who is with us just now. They are gone to plan out a cottage at Derncleugh. Well, have you carried through your law business?'

'With a wet finger,' answered the lawyer; 'got our youngster's special service retoured into Chancery. We had him served heir before the macers.'

'Macers? who are they?'

'Why, it is a kind of judicial Saturnalia. You must know, that one of the requisites to be a macer, or officer in attendance upon our supreme court, is, that they shall be men of no knowledge.'

'Very well!'

'Now, our Scottish legislature, for the joke's sake I suppose, have constituted these men of no knowledge into a peculiar court for trying questions of relationship and descent, such as this business of Bertram, which often involve the most nice and complicated questions of evidence.'

'The devil they have? I should think that rather inconvenient,' said Mannering.

' O, we have a practical remedy for the theoretical absurdity. One or two of the judges act upon such occasions as prompters and assessors to their own door-keepers. But you know what Cujacius says, " *Multa sunt in moribus dissentanea, multa sine ratione.*" * However, this Saturnalian court has done our business; and a glorious batch of claret we had afterwards at Walker's. Mac-Morlan will stare when he sees the bill.'

' Never fear,' said the Colonel, ' we'll face the shock and entertain the county at my friend Mrs. Mac-Candlish's to boot.'

' And choose Jock Jabos for your master of horse ? ' replied the lawyer.

' Perhaps I may.'

' And where is Dandie, the redoubted Lord of Liddesdale ? ' demanded the advocate.

' Returned to his mountains; but he has promised Julia to make a descent in summer, with the good-wife, as he calls her, and I don't know how many children.'

' O, the curly-headed varlets ! I must come to play at Blind Harry and Hy Spy with them.—But what is all this ? ' added Pleydell, taking up the plans;—' tower in the centre to be an imitation of the Eagle Tower at Caernarvon—*corps de logis*— the devil !—wings—wings ? why, the house will take the estate of Ellangowan on its back, and fly away with it !'

---

* The singular inconsistency hinted at is now, in a great degree, removed.

'Why then, we must ballast it with a few bags of Sicca rupees,' replied the Colonel.

'Aha! sits the wind there? Then I suppose the young dog carries off my mistress Julia?'

'Even so, counsellor.'

'These rascals, the *post-nati*, get the better of us of the old school at every turn,' said Mr. Pleydell. 'But she must convey and make over her interest in me to Lucy.'

'To tell you the truth, I am afraid your flank will be turned there too,' replied the Colonel.

'Indeed?'

'Here has been Sir Robert Hazlewood,' said Mannering, 'upon a visit to Bertram, thinking, and deeming, and opining——'

'O Lord! pray spare me the worthy Baronet's triads!'

'Well, sir,' continued Mannering; 'to make short, he conceived that as the property of Singleside lay like a wedge between two farms of his, and was four or five miles separated from Ellangowan, something like a sale, or exchange, or arrangement might take place, to the mutual convenience of both parties.'

'Well, and Bertram——'

'Why, Bertram replied, that he considered the original settlement of Mrs. Margaret Bertram as the arrangement most proper in the circumstances of the family, and that therefore the estate of Singleside was the property of his sister.'

'The rascal!' said Pleydell, wiping his spectacles, 'he'll steal my heart as well as my mistress—*Et puis?*'

'And then, Sir Robert retired after many gracious speeches; but last week he again took the field in force, with his coach and six horses, his laced scarlet waistcoat, and best bob-wig—all very grand, as the good-boy books say.'

'Ay! and what was his overture?'

'Why, he talked with great form of an attachment on the part of Charles Hazlewood to Miss Bertram.'

'Ay, ay; he respected the little god Cupid when he saw him perched on the Dun of Singleside. And is poor Lucy to keep house with that old fool and his wife, who is just the knight himself in petticoats?'

'No—we parried that. Singleside-house is to be repaired for the young people, and to be called hereafter Mount Hazlewood.'

'And do you yourself, Colonel, propose to continue at Woodbourne?'

'Only till we carry these plans into effect. See, here's the plan of my Bungalow, with all convenience for being separate and sulky when I please.'

'And, being situated, as I see, next door to the old castle, you may repair Donagild's tower for the nocturnal contemplation of the celestial bodies? Bravo, Colonel!'

'No, no, my dear counsellor! Here ends THE ASTROLOGER.'

NOTES

CHAPTER XXXIX

Note F, p. 128.—TAPPIT HEN

THE Tappit Hen contained three quarts of claret—

> Weel she loed a Hawick gill,
> And leugh to see a Tappit Hen.

I have seen one of these formidable stoups at Provost Haswell's, at Jedburgh, in the days of yore. It was a pewter measure, the claret being in ancient days served from the tap, and had the figure of a hen upon the lid. In later times, the name was given to a glass bottle of the same dimensions. These are rare apparitions among the degenerate topers of modern days.

Note G, p. 128.—CONVIVIAL HABITS OF THE SCOTTISH BAR

The account given by Mr. Pleydell, of his sitting down in the midst of a revel to draw an appeal case, was taken from a story told me by an aged gentleman, of the elder President Dundas of Arniston, (father of the younger President, and of Lord Melville). It had been thought very desirable, while that distinguished lawyer was King's counsel, that his assistance should be obtained in drawing an appeal case, which, as occasion for such writings then rarely occurred, was held to be matter of great nicety. The Solicitor employed for the appellant, attended by my informant acting as his clerk, went to the Lord Advocate's chambers in the Fishmarket Close, as I think. It was Saturday at noon, the Court was just dismissed, the Lord Advocate had changed his dress and booted himself, and his servant and horses were at the foot of the close to carry him to Arniston. It was scarcely possible to get him to listen to a word respecting business. The wily agent, however, on pretence of asking one or two questions, which would not detain him half an hour, drew his Lordship, who was no less an eminent bon vivant than a lawyer of unequalled talent, to take a whet at a celebrated tavern, when the learned counsel became gradually involved in a spirited discussion of the law points of the case. At length it occurred to him, that he might as well ride to Arniston in the cool of the evening. The horses were directed to be put in the stable, but not to be unsaddled. Dinner was ordered, the law was laid aside for a time, and the bottle circulated very freely. At nine o'clock at night, after he had been honouring Bacchus for so many hours, the Lord Advocate ordered his horses to be unsaddled,—paper, pen, and ink were brought—he began to dictate the appeal case—and continued at his task till four o'clock the next morning. By next day's post, the solicitor sent the case to London, a chef-d'œuvre of its kind; and in which, my informant assured me, it was not necessary on revisal to correct five words. I am not, therefore, conscious of having overstepped accuracy in describing the manner in which Scottish lawyers of the old time occasionally united the worship of Bacchus with that of Themis. My informant was Alexander Keith, Esq., grandfather to my friend, the present Sir Alexander Keith of Ravelstone, and apprentice at the time to the writer who conducted the cause.

CHAPTER XLIX

Note H, p. 252.—Lord Monboddo

The Burnet, whose taste for the evening meal of the ancients is quoted by Mr. Pleydell, was the celebrated metaphysician and excellent man, Lord Monboddo, whose *cœnæ* will not be soon forgotten by those who have shared his classic hospitality. As a Scottish Judge, he took the designation of his family estate. His philosophy, as is well known, was of a fanciful and somewhat fantastic character; but his learning was deep, and he was possessed of a singular power of eloquence, which reminded the hearer of the *os rotundum* of the Grove or Academe. Enthusiastically partial to classical habits, his entertainments were always given in the evening, when there was a circulation of excellent Bordeaux, in flasks garlanded with roses, which were also strewed on the table after the manner of Horace. The best society, whether in respect of rank or literary distinction, was always to be found in St. John's Street, Canongate. The conversation of the excellent old man, his high, gentleman-like, chivalrous spirit, the learning and wit with which he defended his fanciful paradoxes, the kind and liberal spirit of his hospitality, must render those *noctes cœnæque* dear to all who, like the author, (though then young,) had the honour of sitting at his board.

NOTES

Note I, p. 255.—Lawyers' Sleepless Nights

It is probably true, as observed by Counsellor Pleydell, that a lawyer's anxiety about his case, supposing him to have been some time in practice, will seldom disturb his rest or digestion. Clients will, however, sometimes fondly entertain a different opinion. I was told by an excellent judge, now no more, of a country gentleman, who, addressing his leading counsel, my informer, then an advocate in great practice, on the morning of the day on which the case was to be pleaded, said, with singular bonhomie, 'Weel, my lord, (the counsel was Lord Advocate,) the awful day is come at last. I have nae been able to sleep a wink for thinking of it—nor, I daresay, your Lordship either.'

ADDITIONAL NOTE TO GUY MANNERING

Galwegian Localities and Personages which have been supposed to be alluded to in the Novel

An old English proverb says, that more know Tom Fool than Tom Fool knows; and the influence of the adage seems to extend to works composed under the influence of an idle or foolish planet. Many corresponding circumstances are detected by readers, of which the author did not suspect the existence. He must, however, regard it as a great compliment, that in detailing incidents purely imaginary, he has been so fortunate in approximating reality, as to remind his readers of actual occurrences. It is therefore with pleasure he notices some pieces of local history and tradition, which have been supposed to coincide with the fictitious persons, incidents, and scenery of Guy Mannering.

The prototype of Dirk Hatteraick is considered as having been a Dutch skipper called Yawkins. This man was well known on the coast of Galloway and Dumfries-shire, as sole proprietor and master of a *Buckkar*, or smuggling lugger, called the Black Prince. Being distinguished by his nautical skill and intrepidity, his vessel was frequently freighted, and his own services employed, by French, Dutch, Manx, and Scottish smuggling companies.

A person well known by the name of Buckkar-tea, from having

been a noted smuggler of that article, and also by that of Bogle-Bush, the place of his residence, assured my kind informant, Mr. Train, that he had frequently seen upwards of two hundred Lingtow-men assemble at one time, and go off into the interior of the country, fully laden with contraband goods.

In those halcyon days of the free trade, the fixed price for carrying a box of tea, or bale of tobacco, from the coast of Galloway to Edinburgh, was fifteen shillings, and a man with two horses carried four such packages. The trade was entirely destroyed by Mr. Pitt's celebrated commutation law, which, by reducing the duties upon excisable articles, enabled the lawful dealer to compete with the smuggler. The statute was called in Galloway and Dumfries-shire, by those who had thriven upon the contraband trade, 'the burning and starving act.'

Sure of such active assistance on shore, Yawkins demeaned himself so boldly, that his mere name was a terror to the officers of the revenue. He availed himself of the fears which his presence inspired on one particular night, when, happening to be ashore with a considerable quantity of goods in his sole custody, a strong party of excisemen came down on him. Far from shunning the attack, Yawkins sprung forward, shouting, 'Come on, my lads; Yawkins is before you.' The revenue officers were intimidated, and relinquished their prize, though defended only by the courage and address of a single man. On his proper element, Yawkins was equally successful. On one occasion, he was landing his cargo at the Manxman's lake, near Kirkcudbright, when two revenue cutters (the Pigmy and the Dwarf) hove in sight at once on different tacks, the one coming round by the Isles of Fleet, the other between the point of Rueberry and the Muckle Ron. The dauntless free-trader instantly weighed anchor, and bore down right between the luggers, so close that he tossed his hat on the deck of the one, and his wig on that of the other, hoisted a cask to his maintop, to show his occupation, and bore away under an extraordinary pressure of canvas, without receiving injury. To account for these and other hair-breadth escapes, popular superstition alleged that Yawkins insured his celebrated Buckkar by compounding with the devil for one-tenth of his crew every voyage. How they arranged the separation of the stock and tithes, is left to our conjecture. The Buckkar was perhaps called the Black Prince in honour of the formidable insurer.

The Black Prince used to discharge her cargo at Luce, Balcarry, and elsewhere on the coast; but her owner's favourite landing-places were at the entrance of the Dee and the Cree, near the old Castle of Rueberry, about six miles below Kirkcudbright.

NOTES

There is a cave of large dimensions in the vicinity of Rueberry, which, from its being frequently used by Yawkins, and his supposed connexion with the smugglers on the shore, is now called Dirk Hatteraick's cave. Strangers who visit this place, the scenery of which is highly romantic, are also shown, under the name of the Gauger's Loup, a tremendous precipice, being the same, it is asserted, from which Kennedy was precipitated.

Meg Merrilies is in Galloway considered as having had her origin in the traditions concerning the celebrated Flora Marshal, one of the royal consorts of Willie Marshal, more commonly called the *Caird* of Barullion, King of the Gipsies of the Western Lowlands. That potentate was himself deserving of notice, from the following peculiarities. He was born in the parish of Kirkmichael, about the year 1671 ; and as he died at Kirkcudbright, 23d November, 1792, he must then have been in the one hundred and twentieth year of his age. It cannot be said that this unusually long lease of existence was noted by any peculiar excellence of conduct or habits of life. Willie had been pressed or enlisted in the army seven times; and had deserted as often ; besides three times running away from the naval service. He had been seventeen times lawfully married ; and besides such a reasonably large share of matrimonial comforts, was, after his hundredth year, the avowed father of four children, by less legitimate affections. He subsisted in his extreme old age by a pension from the present Earl of Selkirk's grandfather. Will Marshal is buried in Kirkcudbright Church, where his monument is still shown, decorated with a scutcheon suitably blazoned with two tups' horns and two *cutty* spoons.

In his youth he occasionally took an evening walk on the highway, with the purpose of assisting travellers by relieving them of the weight of their purses. On one occasion, the Caird of Barullion robbed the Laird of Bargally, at a place between Carsphairn and Dalmellington. His purpose was not achieved without a severe struggle, in which the Gipsy lost his bonnet, and was obliged to escape, leaving it on the road. A respectable farmer happened to be the next passenger, and seeing the bonnet, alighted, took it up, and rather imprudently put it on his own head. At this instant, Bargally came up with some assistants, and recognising the bonnet, charged the farmer of Bantoberick with having robbed him, and took him into custody. There being some likeness between the parties, Bargally persisted in his charge, and though the respectability of the farmer's character was proved or admitted, his trial before the Circuit Court came on accordingly. The fatal bonnet lay on the table of the court ; Bargally swore that it was the identical article worn by

371

the man who robbed him; and he and others likewise deponed
that they had found the accused on the spot where the crime was
committed, with the bonnet on his head. The case looked
gloomily for the prisoner, and the opinion of the judge seemed
unfavourable. But there was a person in court who knew well
both who did, and who did not, commit the crime. This was the
Caird of Barullion, who, thrusting himself up to the bar, near the
place where Bargally was standing, suddenly seized on the bonnet,
put it on his head, and looking the Laird full in the face, asked
him, with a voice which attracted the attention of the Court and
crowded audience—'Look at me, sir, and tell me, by the oath
you have sworn—Am not *I* the man who robbed you between
Carsphairn and Dalmellington?' Bargally replied, in great astonishment, 'By Heaven! you are the very man.'—'You see what
sort of memory this gentleman has,' said the volunteer pleader:
'he swears to the bonnet, whatever features are under it. If you
yourself, my Lord, will put it on your head, he will be willing to
swear that your Lordship was the party who robbed him between
Carsphairn and Dalmellington.' The tenant of Bantoberick was
unanimously acquitted, and thus Willie Marshal ingeniously contrived to save an innocent man from danger, without incurring
any himself, since Bargally's evidence must have seemed to every
one too fluctuating to be relied upon.

While the King of the gipsies was thus laudably occupied, his
royal consort, Flora, contrived, it is said, to steal the hood from
the Judge's gown; for which offence, combined with her pre-
sumptive guilt as a gipsy, she was banished to New England,
whence she never returned.

Now, I cannot grant that the idea of Meg Merrilies was, in the
first concoction of the character, derived from Flora Marshal,
seeing I have already said she was identified with Jean Gordon,
and as I have not the Laird of Bargally's apology for charging the
same fact on two several individuals. Yet I am quite content
that Meg should be considered as a representative of her sect and
class in general—Flora, as well as others.

The other instances in which my Gallovidian readers have
obliged me, by assigning to

> Airy nothing
> A local habitation and a name,

shall also be sanctioned so far as the Author may be entitled to
do so. I think the facetious Joe Miller records a case pretty
much in point; where the keeper of a Museum, while showing,
as he said, the very sword with which Balaam was about to kill
his ass, was interrupted by one of the visitors, who reminded him

NOTES

that Balaam was not possessed of a sword, but only wished for one. 'True, sir,' replied the ready-wited Cicerone; 'but this is the very sword he wished for.' The Author, in application of this story, has only to add, that though ignorant of the coincidence between the fictions of the tale and some real circumstances, he is contented to believe he must unconsciously have thought or dreamed of the last, while engaged in the composition of Guy Mannering.

GLOSSARY

a', *all*; at a, *at all*.
abune, *above*.
ae, *one*.
aff, *off*.
afterhend, *afterwards*, 187.
ahint, *behind*, 131.
aiblins, *perhaps*, 84, 88.
ain, *own*.
alane, *alone*.
an, *if*.
ance, *once*.
ane, *one*.
anent, *concerning*, 28.
Antiburghers, *a sect of presbyterian dissenters who conscientiously refused to take the oath required from burgesses; (the 'auld-lichts' of Mr. J. M. Barrie's novels)*, 24.
arena, *are not*.
atweel, *well*.
auld, *old*.
awa, *away*.
aweel, *well*.
ay, *yes*, 31.
ay, aye, *always*, 24, 78.

bairn, *child*.
baith, *both*.
ballant, *ballad*.
banes, *bones*.
barkers, *pistols*, 36.
barrow-tram, *the shaft of a wheelbarrow: by met. applied to a raw-boned, ungainly person*, 215.

bauld, *bold*.
bedral, *beadle, sacristan*, 337.
belang, *belong*.
bell the cat, *very nearly equivalent to the phrase 'to take the bull by the horns,'* 79.
berlins, *galleys*, 146.
bide, *endure*, 130; bides, *resides*, 203.
bide off, *keep off*, 215.
big, biggit, *build, built*, 312, 229.
binna, *may not be*, 311.
birling, *carousing*, 129.
bit, *place, spot*, 144; bit, *diminutive*, 25, 117.
blearing your ee, *blinding by flattery*, 131.
blude, *blood*.
bonspiel, *curling tournament*, 30.
bountith, *see fee*.
bourtree-bush, *elder-bush*, 315.
bowl, *handle (of a stoup of liquor)*, 203.
bowster, *bolster*.
brag, *boast, defy*, 88.
braw, *fine, brilliant*, 229.
brock, *badger*, 111.
broom, *warrant*, 34.
buck of the second head, *second-rate dandy*, 115.
buirdly, *stout, stalwart*, 312.
by, *beyond*, 26; *beside, compared to*, 89; by common, *more than common*, 187.

ca', *call*; ca'd, *called.*

cadie, *street porter*, 95.

caird, *tinker, gipsy,* 371.

callant, *youth,* 114.

ca't, *call it.*

cam, *came.*

camstane, *chalk-whiting,* 78.

camsteary, *obstinate and unruly,* 278.

canna, *cannot.*

canny, *gentle, cautious.*

caption, *judicial order for apprehension for non-payment of a debt or non-fulfilment of an obligation,* 25.

care o' me, have a, *mark my words,* 247.

carl, *fellow, churl.*

carle, waf, *waif, insignificant churl,* 131.

cast up to me, *threw in my teeth,* 129.

cauld, *cold.*

caulkers, *the projection of a horse-shoe sharpened for frost,* 120.

caution, *surety,* 73.

chappit, *struck,* 77.

cheerer, *glass of spirits with hot water and sugar,* 198.

chield, *fellow,* 34, 278.

chuckie, *pebble, stone,* 87.

chuckies, *fowls,* 198.

claes, *clothes,* 118.

clashes, *gossip,* 30, 137.

clatter, *confused talk,* 249.

clean aff thegither, *at daggers drawn,* 130.

clod, *throw with violence,* 214.

close, *alley, narrow passage of a street,* 80.

cock, *(in curling) the mark aimed at,* 29.

coft, *bought,* 31.

colly-shangie, *uproarious quarrel,* 187.

compliment, *gratuity,* 26.

concurrents, *confederates,* 34.

couldna, *could not.*

coup, *upset,* 247.

Court of Session, *the supreme court of Scotland,* 119; *see also* Inner-house *and* Outer-house.

cracks, *gossip, conversation,* 129, 269.

craig, *rock,* 130.

crappit-heads, *puddings made in the heads of haddocks,* 26.

craws, *crows,* 199.

crooks, *windings of a river,* 155.

crown o' ta causeway, *middle of the street,* 79.

cry in, *call in,* 27.

cutlugged, *crop-eared,* 87.

cutty spoon, *short horn-spoon,* 217 371.

daft, *crazy,* 222.

darbies, *handcuffs,* 35.

daur, *dare.*

deacon, *elected chairman of trade guild,* 27.

defeat, *fatigued,* 26.

deil, deevil, *devil.*

deuke, *duke.*

didna, *did not,* 26.

ding, *beat, upset,* 119.

dinna, *do not.*

disna, *does not.* 79.

dominie, *pedagogue,* 69.

donnert, *stupid,* 187.

doo, *dove,* 78.

dooms, *minced oath equivalent to 'damned,'* 32.

douce, *sedate, sober.*

dow, didna, *did not do,* i.e. *could not endure,* 132.

dowie, *doleful, sad,* 188.

dram, *glass of spirits,* 204.

draps, *drops.*

GLOSSARY

dreed, the weird's, *the destiny is fulfilled*, 214.

drew up, *became familiar, cohabited*, 90

dry-handed, *unarmed*, 35.

dust, *uproar*, 41; election-dust, *election contest*, 88.

ee, *eye*; een, *eyes*.

eilding, *fuel*, 199.

eneugh, *enough*.

fa', *fall*.

fand, *found*.

fash, *trouble, annoyance*, 117, 191 277.

fashious, *troublesome*, 278; *fastidious*, 191.

feckless, *pithless, feeble*, 31.

fee and bountith, *wages and perquisites*, 132.

fee, in, *in full legal possession*, 69.

feifteen, the, *the fifteen judges of the Court of Session, the supreme court of Scotland*, 41, 119

fiar, *one who has the reversion of property*, 99.

fient a haet, *devil a bit*, 311.

fiking, *fidgeting*, 191.

flesh and fell, *muscle and skin*, 278.

flisking, *bouncing, skipping*, 197.

forgat, *forgot*.

forgien, *forgiven*.

fou, fu', *full, tipsy*.

frae, *from*.

freendless-like, *apparently without a friend*, 24.

friar's chicken, *chicken broth with eggs dropped in it*, 26.

fule-body, *fool*, 214.

gad, the, *see* note p. 352.

gae, *gave*.

gaes, *goes*; gaed, *went, gone*.

gang, *go*.

gar, *make*; garred, *made, compelled*, 238 271.

garnish, *furniture*, 188.

gate, *direction*, 202; gate, *way*, 29, 79, 109.

gathered the fernseed, *rendered herself invisible*, 202.

gauger, *exciseman*, 25.

gaun, *going*.

gear, *possessions*.

gentles, *gentlefolk*, 191.

gey, *very, considerable*.

ghaists, *ghosts*.

gie, *give*; gied, *gave*; gien, *given*.

giff-gaff, *tit-for-tat*, 136.

gliff, *short time*, 188.

glim, *light, lanthorn*, 50.

gotten, *got*, 103

gowan, *daisy*, 35.

gowk, *cuckoo*; hunt the gowk, *fool's errand*, 200.

'greed, *agreed*.

greet, *weep*, 109.

griego, *short cloak*, 35.

gudeman, *master of the house*.

gudewife, *mistress of the house*.

gude, *good*; gudes, *goods*, 103.

guide, *direct*, 222.

guisarding, *masquerading as Christmas mummers*, 84.

hae, *have*; haena, *have not*.

haet, *see* fient.

haill, *whole*; haill water, *entire water-side*, 119.

hanger, *cutlass*, 31.

Hansel Monanday, *the first Monday of the Year when gratuities are given; resembling the English Boxing Day*, 26.

GLOSSARY

mark, = 1s. 1⅓d. *of English money.*
maun, *must* ; maunna, *must not.*
mind, put in, *cause to remember,* 114.
minded, *paid heed to,* 331
Monanday, Hansel, *see* Hansel.
morn, the, *to-morrow,* 78.
mortification, *settlement in mort-*
main, 113.
muckle-coat, *great coat,* 34.

na, *no.*
nae, *no.*
naebody, *nobody.*
naething, *nothing.*
nane, *none.*
nappery, *household-linen,* 191.
needcessity, *necessity,* 354.
neibors, *neighbours.*
ne'er-do-weel, *ne'er-do-well, wastrel,*
130.
niffering, *bargaining,* 35.
niffy-naffy, *finical and fastidious,*
191.
no, *not, do not.*

o't, *of it.*
ony, *any.*
or, *before.*
ordinary, for, *as a rule,* 26.
ou, *oh,* 26.
oursells, *ourselves.*
outcast, *quarrel,* 199.
Outer-house, *the lower court, or*
original side, of the Court of
Session, presided over by a single
judge from whom an appeal lies to
the ' Inner-house,' 29.
ower, *over, too.*

peel, *border watch-tower,* 87.
peenging, *whining,* 130.
pickle, *few, small quantity,* 200.
pike, *pick, dig,* 136.

pit, putten, *put.*
pockmanky, *portmanteau,* 203.
pocks, *bags,* 136.
poppling, *bubbling, rippling,* 312.
poschay, *postchaise,* 31.
powny, *pony,* 118.
prigged, *entreated,* 329.
prin, *pin,* 78.
puir, *poor.*

rade, *rode.*
randy, *riotous, disorderly,* 330.
rape, thack and, *see* thack.
redding, *putting to rights,* 306.
reek, *smoke,* 244. reeking, *steaming,*
42.
rigs, *ridges,* 103.
rinning, *running* ; rins, *runs.*
ripeing, *searching,* 201.
roughies, *withered boughs,* 318.
rouses, *carousals,* 51

sackless, *innocent,* 24.
sae, *so.*
sair, *sore,* 90.
sall, *shall.*
sap, *dunderhead,* 242.
sark, *shirt,* 27 ; sark-fu', *shirtful,*
205.
satisfied the kirk, *performed the*
penance and paid the ecclesiastical
penalties for a breach of the seventh
commandment, 90.
saugh, *willow,* 312.
saul, *soul, mettle,* 217.
saulies, *mutes,* 103.
saut, *salt,* 108.
schelm, schellum, *worthless fellow,*
54.
screed, *bout,* 205.
shand, *base coin,* 32
shealing, *shelter, hut,* 312.
shears, *divides,* 87.

379

GUY MANNERING

sheriff-substitute, *resident county magistrate*.

sherra, *sheriff*, 197.

shoon, *shoes*, 26.

shouther, *shoulder*.

sic, *such*; sic like, *such like, similar*, 79.

siller, *money*, 119.

silver-cooper, *kidnapper*, 59.

simple body, *plebeian*, 79.

skeel, *skill*, 79.

skits, *tricks*, 25.

slashers, *cutlasses*, 35.

slounging, *slouching*, 35.

Soulis' mistake. *By tradition King Robert Bruce, wearied with constant complaints of the tyranny of Lord Soulis, exclaimed petulantly, 'O boil him if you want to, but let me hear no more of him': the unintended sentence was carried out literally*, 89.

spaeings, *prophecies*, 204.

spaw-well, *magic well*, 130.

speir, *ask*, 35.

spleuchan, *tobacco pouch (here used as a purse)*, 277

splores, *frolics, riots*, 278.

spring, *tune*, 87.

start, *inform*, 60.

steek, *stitch*, 72; *shut, lock*, 198.

stibbler, *a term applied in ridicule to a probationer*, i.e. *candidate for a clerical benefice*, 214.

stickit, *stuck*.

stiver, *small Dutch copper coin*.

stockit, *stocked*, 82.

strae, *straw*.

streek, *lay out a corpse*, 202, 203.

strippit, *stripped*.

sture, *grim*, 131.

suld, *should*.

sune, *soon*.

swore by the salmon, *the great and inviolable gipsy oath*, 61.

syne, *since*.

tailzie, *entail*, 276.

tak, *take*; ta'en, *taken*.

tappit-hen, *see p.* 367.

tat, *that*, 79.

teind, *tithe*, 120.

tell'd, *told*, 79.

thack and rape, *thatch and rope*, 264.

thae, *those*.

thegither, *together*, 88.

thir, *these*.

threep, *declare, persist*, 311; *superstition*, 203.

tike, *dog, cur*, 330.

till, *to*; till't, *to it*.

tod, *fox*, 316.

tongue of the trump, *wire of Jew's harp*; *see note p.* 20.

Tron, *a church of that name in Edinburgh*, 77.

tuilzie, *skirmish*, 25.

tup, *ram*, 79.

twa, *two*.

twasome, *two*, 327.

umquhile, *late*, 329.

uncanny, *unlucky, dangerous*, 311.

unco, *strange, extraordinary, very*.

uphaud, *uphold*.

wad, *would*; wadna, *would not*.

waf carle, *waif, insignificant churl*, 131.

wale, *choice*, 332.

wa's, *wall's*, 312.

wame, *belly*, 187.

warlock, *wizard, witch*, 244.

waur, *worse*.

way, *line of business*.

weans, *children*, 201.

GLOSSARY

wear the jacket, *ride as jockey,* 115.

weel put on, *well dressed,* 269.

weepers, *white cuffs on the sleeves worn at funerals,* 103.

weird, *destiny,* 214, 253.

weized, *drove,* 31.

well to pass, *in comfortable circumstances,* 101.

werena, *were not.*

whaten, *what.*

whiles, *sometimes.*

whilk, *which,* 24.

whisht, *hush.*

whistled, *given information,* 35. See also p. 278.

wife, *woman,* 26.

win, *get,* 206.

winna, *will not.*

word o' mouth, *verbally,* 86

worriecow, *hobgoblin,* 214.

wuss, *wish,* 145.

wyte, *blame,* 205.

yoke thegither, *fight,* 88.

This book was designed by
William B. Taylor
for Edito-Service S.A., Geneva

Printed in Switzerland